AMERICAN FICTION

VOLUME 15

AMERICAN
FICTION

VOLUME 15

The Best Unpublished Stories
by New and Emerging Writers

Bruce Pratt, Editor
Steve Almond, Finalist Judge

n RIVERS
e PRESS
w MSUM

© 2016 by New Rivers Press
First Edition
Library of Congress Control Number: 2015953392
ISBN: 978-0-89823-346-9
eISBN: 978-0-89823-347-6

Cover design by Bikash Rai

The publication of *American Fiction Volume 15* is made possible by the
generous support of Minnesota State University Moorhead, The McKnight
Foundation, the Dawson Family Endowment, and other generous contributors
to New Rivers Press.

For copyright permission, please contact Frederick T. Courtright at
570-839-7477 or permdude@eclipse.net.

New Rivers Press is a nonprofit literary press associated with
Minnesota State University Moorhead.

Alan Davis, Director and Senior Editor
Nayt Rundquist, Managing Editor
Kevin Carollo, MVP Poetry Coordinator
Bayard Godsave, MVP Prose Coordinator
Thom Tammaro, Poetry Editor
Thomas Anstadt, Co-Art Director
Trista Conzemius, Co-Art Director
Wayne Gudmundson, Consultant
Suzzanne Kelley, Consultant

Publishing Interns:
Laura Grimm, Anna Landsverk, Desiree Miller, Mikaila Norman

American Fiction book team:
Brittany Butler, Kris Campbell, Oleana Herron, Jesse Wierzchowski

 Printed in the USA on acid-free, archival-grade paper.

American Fiction Volume 15 is distributed nationally by
Small Press Distribution.

New Rivers Press
c/o MSUM
1104 7th Avenue South
Moorhead, MN 56563
www.newriverspress.com

CONTENTS

EDITOR'S NOTE

Eddington, Maine, October 20, 2015

Autumn's last blaze lies splashed along the ridge across from my house—revealed for the first time in two decades by the clear cutting of several acres of a neighbor's forest. While I miss the alders and maples, oaks and birches, spruces and poplars that once blocked this view, I revel in the opportunity to drink in the riot of color rising from our narrow gore to the top of Black Cap Mountain on these cool, cobalt-blue, mid October days. Last evening as I stared across the stumps and scrubby new growth where the trees once stood, it occurred to me that editing an anthology and practicing sustainable forestry have much in common.

Great short fiction gains traction by revealing character, and excising that which is not elemental to the story, as a way, if you will, of opening up the *view*. The literary equivalent of a masterful painting, a well-crafted short story is eloquent but uncluttered, precise but concise, and employs imagery and detail with scrupulous care. The more engaged the reader is in the narrative the more he or she *sees*.

I search the submissions for fully realized stories that spring from richly imagined characters, are sustained by the skillful use of language, and never read like segments of, or sketches for, longer works, thus my selection of the finalists is not a clear-cut, but a slow, considered, highly selective harvest.

I don't use screeners, or have assistant editors, because I believe I have a responsibility to give each author's work the due consideration I would want the editor of another journal or anthology to give to a submission of mine, and am haunted by the reality that my selections are unavoidably influenced by my prejudices and preferences. I also know that I likely rejected stories that will find a home in distinguished journals and collections.

We were honored and excited to have Steve Almond, award-winning author of short fiction, memoir, non-fiction, and opinion as this year's judge, and deeply appreciate the diligence and thoughtfulness he brought to the process. His introductory notes point out how daunting a task it was for him to choose the contest winners from the stories selected for this issue and we thank him for his excellent work.

The previous edition of *American Fiction* won the Gold Medal for short fiction from the Midwest Independent Publishers Association— the first anthology to be accorded this award. I have no way of knowing if this year's volume will be so honored, but can assure you that these stories are every bit as deserving of such praise, and that the selection process was an arduous, though enjoyable, task.

A final word of thanks is due to the authors of the more than six hundred stories entered in this year's contest. I read once that short stories *published* in literary journals in this country have been, on average, rejected more than twenty times, thus every submission is an act of courage and optimism. We wish all those writers success and wish that we had room for more of the other fine pieces we received.

—Bruce Pratt

INTRODUCTION: I AM LOOKING TO BE KIDNAPPED

Let me say it as plainly as I can: short stories are the reason I became a writer. Novels, memoirs, journalism, poems—all lovely and essential. But for me the short story has always been home. This dates back to my time as a reporter in El Paso, Texas, and the afternoon I was assigned to write a feature story about the writer Rick DeMarinis.

I hadn't bothered to read any of Rick's work because I was 22 years old and didn't realize that literature might have anything to do with me. I was busy reviewing heavy metal concerts and trying to fool women into sleeping with me.

But just as a matter of due diligence, I dropped by the library on the way to the interview and picked up a collection of DeMarinis stories and began to read one called "Insulation." It was about a guy who lived in fear of being struck by lightning. I read that story straight through, without once thinking about anything other than this guy and his terror. Then I read it again, this time more slowly. It was as if I'd been kidnapped by another man's imagination, and by his gentle understanding of the fears that drive our lives.

Within a few months I'd devoured every story DeMarinis had ever written. I moved on to Lorrie Moore, Jennifer Egan, John DuFresne, Grace Paley, Tony Earley, Barry Hannah, Denis Johnson, Larry Brown. I read their stories in a fever.

You know what happens next. Writers are nothing more than jealous readers. That's how it always works.

So I began writing my own dreck, pale imitations of these masters mostly. That's fine. It's part of the process. I wrote and wrote and wrote and every now and again, when I wasn't trying so hard to impress the reader, an actual story emerged from the wreckage of my ego.

By "actual story" I mean a streak of language capable of taking me away from myself and into the world of some other poor soul.

The joy of the short story for me has always resided in the urgency and intensity of the form. This is the reason, I've always felt, that stories are a harder sell than novels. Because with a story you can't zone out. You have to meet its intensity with your full attention. When done right, it's a flat-out kidnap, every time.

And that's why it was such an honor and a pleasure—but also a sublime burden—to have to select the winners of this contest. I might have chosen any one of the 21 stories I received as the final judge. To be perfectly honest, I had trouble even narrowing the pack down to ten, let alone five, let alone three.

I want to offer specific words of praise to the winning stories, but only after stressing the obvious: the stories I selected were not "objectively better" than the ones I didn't choose. They simply appealed to my own sensibility.

I also want to cite two stories, in particular, that I deeply admired but that didn't make my top three, those being "India, 1899," which was a startling evocation of the imperial mindset as well as a tragedy of the first order, and "Brazil," which documented with astonishing beauty the isolation of the immigrant experience.

As for the top three, I'm under orders to rank them, but I can assure you that I loved them all, because for me they all performed that same sacred literary function: they made me feel more alive for having been read.

"Bikes of the Danube" was an utterly original story, full of inventive language and driven along by a fantastic plot. It's a story about desire amid deprivation and about friendship and loyalty and the sad truth that we cannot save everyone who deserves to be saved.

I'd never read anything quite like "San Man" either. The tender and ruthless language of the narrator consistently surprised me, and forced me to see the world in new and more vivid ways. It's a short story about the objects and lives that get discarded in our midst, and the men—like our narrator—who have to bear witness to this loss. There's a shocking twist at the end, but one that never feels manipulative. On the contrary, it's clear that the narrator will never recover from what he's seen—in much the same way as the narrator of Frank O'Connor's classic "Guests of the Nation."

As for the winning story, "The Naked Mole Rat Experiment," I can only say that it's a searingly sad story, and that I felt absolutely staggered by the loss that Deano, our eight-year-old heroine, has to absorb.

I felt completely immersed in her world. I adored the specificity of her world. But what captured me ultimately was the unembarrassed portrayal of loss here, the way in which Deano struggles to save her father from dying, struggles with the guilt of his passing, then struggles to keep him alive through memory.

"That whole afternoon Mum and I sat in the warmth of the sun and told stories about Da," the author writes, at the end, "as if by talking about him we could bring him back, if not all of him then just parts, the parts we remembered, and missed, and wanted so much to hold onto."

This might as well be the description of what a great short story does, and why I continue to return to my favorites over and over.

What a gift to be asked to read 21 stories of such deep human intent. Any of them might have won this prize. And as far as I'm concerned, all of them did.

—Steve Almond

HAND-PICKED

THE NAKED MOLE RAT
EXPERIMENT

NICOLE IDAR

1. *State Your Problem.*
   Identify the question that your experiment will attempt
   to answer. Asking "how" or "why" is often a fruitful way
   to begin.
   —*The Scientific Method: A Pedantic Approach*

"Tell me, how an eight-year-old girl *suppose* to act when her father
got cancer, ha?"

That's what Mom said to the cops when they came to our house
to take back the naked mole rat I stole from the National Zoo. Mom
told the cops about Da being sick. Then she explained my experiment and called me a "little scientist." The cops called her "ma'am,"
but I could tell that they thought Mom's a weird Asian lady who
doesn't speak English properly. I gave Mugi back to them so they
wouldn't arrest me for stealing federal property.

Mugi's the naked mole rat I stole. I knew his name because he
told me what it was. Animals talk to me, I can't explain it. Auntie
Jiffy—she's my South African Auntie, she's always saying "I'll see
you in a jiffy" when she means "I'll see you soon"—she thought I
read the *Charlotte's Web* book she gave me for Christmas too many
times. When I first told her that I could hear animals talking, she
said "Oh *shame!*" She didn't mean I should be ashamed; that was
her way of saying "Aw, that's sweet." Then she said, "You want to
be like that girl from *Charlotte's Web*, don't you, so you can talk to
animals too?" I didn't care what my Auntie said. I *can* talk to animals—any kind of animal.

Except for the crab in my father's throat.

"*Cancer* is Latin for crab," Mom told me. At first I tried to cast out

Da's crab the way Auntie Jiffy said Jesus cast demons out of Legion. When Da was napping, I stood by his bed and yelled, "Come out of the man, thou unclean crab!" He woke with a start, all mad, and said: "Deano! What's the shouting for?"

My name's Marie, actually, after Marie Curie. Mom says she's a scientist who figured out how to use radiation to kill cancer. Radiation's something Da knows a lot about; before he got sick, he was an oncologist—that's the kind of doctor who treats cancer with a special light humans can't see. At school I'm Marie, but at home I'm Deano, because when I was little I used to sing along whenever Da played Dean Martin songs in the car, and that got Da started calling me Deano. Later, I later found out that it's Dean Martin's real first name, except he spelled it "Dino." The nickname's stuck, and now I can't do anything about it.

"Sorry, Da," I said, though I wouldn't have been sorry if the crab had left my Da alone. After that, I went searching for another crab to talk to, just to see if I could. I got my chance when Mom and I were at Jade Pagoda, a Chinese supermarket in northern Virginia. While Mom stopped by the Chinese medicine counter I went up to the bubbling tanks at the back, squashed my nose against the glass, and said to a green crab, "Hey, Uncle Crab, are you okay in there?"

The crab scuttled forward, all excited, and said I was a kind girl to ask. Then he told me to tell the supermarket staff that he didn't like having those blue elastic bands wrapped around his claws. Which is how I know crabs *do* talk.

Not Da's crab, though. I wish I could've talked to it, gotten it to stop making Da's body shrink. Mom had to buy Da new pants because he lost his round Christmas-pudding belly. He lost his hair, too. He never used to wear baseball hats B.C. (before cancer). Afterwards, he wouldn't leave the house without one. When he took his hat off, the little bit of red-gold hair he had left looked like it had been spun into yellow straw.

"Da's got cancer of the esophagus," Mom told me. This was after she and Da got back from the doctor. Da had been having problems swallowing.

I didn't know what an esophagus was, so Mom explained. I kept picturing a crab squeezing Da's esophagus shut with its claws. Soon, getting that crab out was all I could think about any more.

*   *   *

2. *Make Careful Observations.*
   It is essential that you observe your object of study closely and keep a record of what you see. Careful observations are the foundation of scientific discovery.
   —*The Scientific Method: A Pedantic Approach*

My best friend Kerrie says I'm kind of a science nerd; a science nerd who talks to animals, that's me. I blame Da for the nerd gene. For my last birthday, he got me a book called *The Scientific Method: A Pedantic Approach* that Mom said is "Eh, too advance" for a kid who's only eight. Da and I tried out lots of the experiments they suggest in the book, but that was B.C.; after Da got sick, we switched to other activities.

"More *Life on Earth,* Da?" I grabbed the remote and settled on the couch beside him.

It was a Saturday evening in early fall, in Washington, the District of Columbia, the DisCo, Da likes to say whenever anyone asks where we live. Mom was upstairs taking a long bath—her usual weekend thing. Da and I were watching nature documentaries—our new weekend thing. Da loved any show about wildlife. He was born in England and grew up in Jo'burg, and he went on lots of game drives when he was little. He left South Africa when he was a "young scrapper" (Da's words) to go to medical school in England. Mom's from Malaysia; she met Da in London when she was studying to be a nurse and he was studying to be a doctor. Da brought Mom to D.C., where I was born, and where we live now. Auntie Jiffy, Da's older sister, lives just down the road, which Mom says is "*Ai-yo,* too close."

"This is the episode with the mole rats in it." Da wagged a finger at the TV screen. "We had mole rats in South Africa."

"Is a mole rat half mole and half rat?"

"Not exactly. It's a rodent that lives underground, like a mole. There's a naked mole rat colony right here at the National Zoo. Maybe we'll go see them some time."

I liked it when Da talked about things we'd do when he got well. While he was watching *Life on Earth,* I walked over to the kitchen and peered into the freezer.

"Da!" I yelled. "What kind of ice cream today?"

Da had to eat every few hours, but he'd forget if I didn't remind him.

"Mr. Snowman!" Da yelled back, because he knew I liked making it for him.

I scraped vanilla bean from the carton, piling three scoops one on top of the other, snowman-style, adding chocolate buttons for eyes, and an orange candy corn for a nose. Then I wrote down what Da was eating in a notebook Mom used to keep track of Da's meals. When I asked why we had to record everything Da ate, Mom said cancer patients have to count calories just like dieters, but for the opposite reason: to make sure they don't lose too much weight. Mom's a nurse; she knows these things.

"Last time I always tell your father: must lose weight! Cannot be so heavy, no good for you! Now all I say is: *eat, eat, eat,*" Mom said, shaking her head.

When I got back to the living room, I handed Da his snowman. He took it without looking at it, and when he was done eating he didn't lick the spoon like I did. Right after the bit on *Life on Earth* about mole rats, Da fell asleep.

I turned the TV off, covered Da with a blanket Mom kept by the couch, and observed him for a bit, to see if he was sleeping okay. In my journal, I wrote the time Da started his nap. Mom didn't ask me to do that—it was my idea, I tried to keep a record of how often Da napped each day, and for how long, because I thought that if he rested more maybe he'd get stronger. After making a few more notes, I wandered out into the yard. Evenings, there's a cardinal called Lyle who swings by the birdfeeder for sunflower seeds, and if I'm around he likes to say hi. That day, he asked me why he hadn't seen me in a while. I told him I'd been busy looking after Da.

"It's good that you're helping," Lyle said.

"But all I do is watch TV with Da and bring him snacks."

"Nothing wrong with that. You're helping in small ways."

"I don't want to help in small ways. I want to help in a big way. I want to make Da better," I said. "I just don't know what to do."

Later that night, I hung around outside the kitchen and eavesdropped on Mom and Da when they thought I was upstairs doing my homework. I heard Mom say something about a tumor, that Da was having surgery to get it out.

"At least the tumor still small. Is a good sign," Mom said.

"The question is, what's Dr. Singam going to find when he cuts me open?" Da said.

"Eh, please! Don't talk like that, John."

"I know exactly what can go wrong, that's the trouble—I know too much," Da said.

I stole upstairs to my room after that, and instead of doing homework, I curled up on my window seat. The deck lights were on outside, so I could see the leaves scattered across the pinewood floor. There was a time when Da used to sweep the deck every day.

I asked Da once why leaves fall, and he told me that when it gets cold, trees grow these cells along their leaf stems that nudge the leaves farther and farther away from their branches, until they drop off. The leaves have to die once these cells sta~

We were in the yard, and after Da went back to raki~ up a yellow leaf and held it up to the light. The lea~ could see my hand through it, but I couldn't see~ me about. The wind took the leaf right out of n~ as it whirled away, higher and higher, unti~ my reach.

*   *

3. *Identify Possible Independent Variables.*
   Recall that your experiment will measure the effect of
   one factor, the independent variable, on another factor,
   the dependent variable. Your observations may lead you
   to several independent variables of interest, but
   eventually, you will need to focus on one.
   —*The Scientific Method: A Pedantic Approach*

At the Brookland Animal Rescue Center where Auntie Jiffy volunteers, I got to talking with Brewster. He's a super smart German Shepherd who lives with Miss Zee, the manager. Miss Zee says I'm responsible for my age, so she lets me take Brewster for walks by myself. While Brewster and I circled round the rescue center, I told him about the biopsies Mom said Da's been having as if I understood what any of it meant. Then I slumped onto a bench, tired out. Brewster put his chin on my knee and told me his good news: he'd just qualified as a therapy dog.

"A therapy dog—what's that?" I asked.

Brewster told me that sick people feel better just being around him. I asked Miss Zee why, and she said that when patients are with Brewster, their bodies release a chemical, oxytocin, which helps them heal faster. As Auntie Jiffy was driving me home, I asked her if she could bring Brewster over to visit Da.

"You'll have to ask your mother, little *puku*," she said in the same clipped accent Da's got.

After Auntie Jiffy dropped me off, she and Mom got in a fight because Da hadn't been wearing the Saint Peregrine medal a priest at Auntie Jiffy's church blessed specially for him. Mom didn't invite Auntie Jiffy in, so they stood and argued at the front door. made more noise than the howler monkeys Da and I saw on Earth.

o proud to admit he shouldn't have turned his back on these years. You need to tell him not to be so proud," She told me once that Da's mom and da, Grandma Henry, were observant Catholics like she was, but Da never showed any interest. They died before I was born, so I never got to meet them.

"So, if John goes to church, God's going to heal him, is it?" Mom's shorter and smaller than Auntie Jiffy, but she made up for it by having a louder voice.

I couldn't stand seeing them fight. I pushed between them, put my finger to my lips, and shouted, "SHUSH!" They both stared at me as if they'd forgotten I was there. Auntie Jiffy turned, got in her car, and pulled away without waving her hand out the window.

Later, when Mom was in the kitchen making bread pudding, Da's favorite dessert, I asked her about her quarrel with Auntie Jiffy.

"She shouldn't wind me up like that," Mom said, straightening her glasses with a nudge of her wrist. And then, because she's always telling me it takes two people to argue, she added, "I also shouldn't have been rude to her. Actually, she can be very kind."

I climbed up onto a barstool and watched Mom slice bread into triangles. "Mom, is God going to make Da better?"

Mom made a soft snorting noise.

"Is not about God, Deano. Is about medicine. Dr. Singam is a good surgeon. After he takes out Da's tumor, is easier for Da to eat; right now, is very hard for him to swallow because his throat is all closed up."

"It's that stupid crab," I muttered.

"What crab?" Mom was confused at first. "Oh, you mean the tumor?"

Mom told me that tumor cells look like tiny crabs; they grow these long thin fingers around a hard shell, so maybe that's why Hippocrates thought to call tumors "crabs."

"I know Da's crab isn't real," I said. "It won't answer me when I talk to it."

Mom wiped her hands on a towel and came over to give me a cuddle. She knew talking to animals was the one thing I'm good at.

*   *   *

4. *Note: Expect Setbacks.*
   Conventional approaches to the scientific method often
   neglect to mention this obvious yet fundamental point.
   Before you begin the work of conducting experiments,
   remember that in science, as in life, there will be setbacks.
   Always be prepared to overcome them.

   —*The Scientific Method: A Pedantic Approach*

A few days after Da's surgery, Mom drove us to the hospital to
pick him up. Usually she had plenty of questions about school,
or what Kerrie was up to lately. That day, she was quiet. When
I tried to show her the card I made for Da—a fat brown mole
rat standing in front of the National Zoo holding up a sign that
said, "Now That You're Better, Come Visit Me!" Mom just said:
"That's nice, Deano."

When we got to the hospital, I ran to Da's room to give him his
card and a big hug. He was so thin I could feel his bones through
the sleeves of his shirt. An aide in purple scrubs wheeled Da to the
hospital entrance, and a few minutes later, Mom pulled up. She left
the engine running while she hurried out to help Da into the back
seat so he could lie down if he felt like it.

"Don't fuss," Da said, brushing past Mom and getting into the car
on his own. Mom stood there as Da shut the door on her. She caught
me watching and turned her face away as she walked around the car
to the driver's side.

"Can we go to the zoo to see the mole rats like you promised, Da?"
I asked, buckling myself into the front seat.

"Let's see how I feel, Deano," Da said.

I could see Mom watching Da in the rearview mirror. She gripped
the steering wheel as if she were afraid it might come off.

After we got home, Da said he was tired and had to take a nap. I
went up to my room and read until I didn't feel like it anymore, then
searched all over the house for Mom. I found her in the garage, just
sitting in the car. I slipped in beside her and hauled the door closed.
Mom turned her head to look at me.

"Da's not doing so well, Deano."

My heart was beating fast, like hummingbird wings. "You said Da's surgery was going to get rid of his tumor!"

Mom stared at her hands. "Da's got more tumors than we thought. Dr. Singam didn't know how many. Not until the surgery."

I ran a finger along the edge of the car seat. "What's going to happen to Da?"

"We try radiation. And this drug Dr. Singam recommended."

"What kind of drug?" I asked, as if I might have heard of it.

"Is call JH 482, an experimental drug. Maybe Da might be a bit cranky from now on, but he's not angry with you; is the medicine making him tired. Okay?"

I leaned my head back against the car seat. "Mom, remember Brewster from the rescue center?"

"Ya?"

"Brewster's a therapy dog, he helps sick people get better. Can he visit Da?"

"I don't think is a good idea, Deano."

"Miss Zee says that when patients spend time with Brewster they feel good. It's because of a chemical called oxytocin."

"Deano . . ."

Though her voice was gentle, I could tell she was going to say no. "Auntie Jiffy's right. You won't let other people try to help Da!" I yelled.

I could see tears in Mom's eyes, but I was so mad at her I didn't care. It was so quiet I could hear that low hum I always noticed when I was alone in the car and the doors were closed and the windows rolled up. I pushed the car door open and jumped out, ran up to my room, and threw myself onto my bed, burying my face in a pillow. I wanted to slam my door, but Da was napping and I didn't want to wake him. If I could, I'd have slammed every door in the house.

*   *   *

5. *Formulate Your Hypothesis.*
Let your observations guide you toward a hypothesis,
i.e. a statement predicting how the independent variable
might affect the dependent variable. Note that your
hypothesis should be testable, meaning it is possible
to design an experiment to verify its claim.
                                    —*The Scientific Method: A Pedantic Approach*

While I was watching TV by myself one evening, a documentary
called *Miraculous Tails* came on. It was about animals who can
sense disasters before they happen, sniff out diseases people don't
know they have—that kind of thing. I was about to change the channel when the voiceover said: "A miraculous animal that scientists
think might hold the key to curing cancer is a bizarre subterranean
rodent known as the blind mole rat."

I grabbed the remote and turned the volume all the way up as the
TV camera zoomed in on a familiar furry face.

"This is *spalax ehrenbergi*, the Eastern Mediterranean mole rat.
Scientists have been studying mole rats like these for fifty years, and
have yet to find a single case of cancer. In fact, mole rat cells aren't
just resistant to cancer—it appears that they're able to *kill* cancer
cells . . ."

"Mom!" I yelled. "Come quick!"

The voiceover went on: "Both the *spalax* and its relative, the
naked mole rat, are cancer-resistant *miracles*. They may well pos-
sess the secret to curing cancer once and for all!"

While the credits rolled, I raced into the kitchen. Mom was standing at the stove, stirring soup in a saucepan. The soup smelled like
the kind Mom's mom, Po Po, would make for us whenever we went
to visit her in Malaysia. Po Po would toss ginseng and red dates and
black fungus into a big pot with a whole chicken and pretty soon her
house would smell of herbal soup. Mom had never made one of Po
Po's soups for dinner before. She knew Da didn't like the bitter taste.

"Mom, scientists think mole rats can cure cancer!"

She just stared into the soup, her glasses steaming up. At last she said, "Deano, is not so easy to cure cancer. Nobody knows how. We have to do more experiments."

I was starting to feel mad at her again, and I didn't want to be. *Mom didn't see* Miraculous Tails, I told myself. *She doesn't understand.* As if she could sense me fuming, she moved closer and gave me a kiss on the head.

"Go wake your Da. Tell him is time to eat."

I stomped upstairs, imagining that my footsteps were making the house shake. It didn't matter how much noise I made—Da had to get up anyway.

"What's for dinner, Deano?" Da asked, after I knocked on the door and poked my head into the bedroom he and Mom shared.

"Nothing good," I said, sulking.

At the dinner table, Mom tried to get Da to drink the herbal soup. "The herbalist at Jade Pagoda said it help his cancer patients. You try and see? Maybe it can ease the side effects from that drug you take."

Da frowned. "So your herbalist did a double-blind experiment?"

Mom pressed her lips together. "How you know herbs don't work if you don't try even one time?"

Da tossed his spoon aside. "I'm going for a walk."

"No way you're walking around in the dark by yourself. I come with you."

Da pushed his chair back, making a loud screeching noise. "Mei," he said to Mom. "I don't want you to come. Now *leave me alone*."

Mom watched Da limp across the room, her lower lip trembling. We both watched as he stormed out the front door and slammed it behind him. To distract her, I stood over the steaming pot of soup and spooned a big ladleful into my bowl. After blowing on the soup a few times, I drank it all down.

"It doesn't taste so bad, Mom," I told her, but she was gazing at Da's empty chair as if she had to keep watch over it until Da came back. After a couple of minutes, we heard Da's key in the front lock. He must have been too tired to walk very far.

"You feel like eating, John?" Mom called to Da, but he ignored her and went straight upstairs.

The next day, while Mom and Da were at the hospital for Da's checkup, Auntie Jiffy sat me down and told me that I had to bring Da 'round to God.

"When you go to Heaven, don't you want to see your father there?"

I asked Auntie Jiffy what Heaven was like.

"It's like South Africa, darling."

She described how the wavering grass made a soft rushing noise when the wind blew. How even in winter there were leaves on all the trees, and the air felt warm. How the stars seemed to move across the night sky like herds of wildebeast.

When Mom and Da got home, I told them I didn't want Da to be left out of Heaven. Mom was furious with Auntie Jiffy. I hid at the top of the stairs and listened to them fight. Then Da chimed in. He hardly ever shouts, but that time he yelled.

"Could the two of you stop bloody talking and give a dying man some peace?"

I clamped my hands over my ears and ran to my room. When Mom came to tuck me in for the night, her eyes were swollen; she'd been crying again.

"Is it true what Da said about dying?"

"Is the drugs, Deano. He doesn't mean it."

But I didn't believe her. Da wasn't getting any better—nothing he'd tried so far had worked. Surgery, radiation, the experimental drug, none of it had helped. Mom wanted Da to drink Chinese herbal soup, and Auntie Jiffy wanted Da to pray, but he wasn't going to do what either of them wanted, and I knew it. It was up to me, now, to help Da. I had to try.

Long after I was supposed to be asleep, I was still looking up stuff about naked mole rats and cancer on the computer in my room. I couldn't wait for a bunch of scientists to finish their experiments—I had to come up with my own. In my journal I wrote THE NAKED MOLE RAT EXPERIMENT and underlined it. Then, I wrote MATERIALS NEEDED and listed:

Naked mole rat (live)

Sneakers

Backpack
Disguise?

Luckily, I knew exactly where I could *find* a naked mole rat. The only problem was how to *steal* one. I checked the National Zoo website and found out where the naked mole rats lived: in the Small Mammal House, and on the map I pulled up online, it looked like kind of a hike getting there from the main entrance, but at least it wasn't right next to the Zoo Police Station, either. I spent the rest of the night working out escape routes and stuff like that, and by the time Mom came in to wake me for school, I had a plan all figured out.

*   *   *

6. *Test Your Hypothesis With A Controlled Experiment.*
In a controlled experiment, you will test how ONE independent variable affects the dependent variable. Before you start, be sure to make a note of the set-up for your experiment, the procedure you plan to follow, and the results you expect to see.
– *The Scientific Method: A Pedantic Approach*

The next few Saturdays, while Da rested at home and Mom stayed with him, I asked Auntie Jiffy to drive me to Kerrie's place. Kerrie lives right by the National Zoo. While Kerrie's mom thought we were at Tia's down the block, and Tia's mom thought we were at Kerrie's, the three of us trooped over to the zoo to scope out the naked mole rats and rehearse the steps in my plan.

Once we'd rehearsed so many times we felt as if we could do it blindfolded, it was time to put the plan into motion.

The Saturday Kerrie and Tia were going to help me steal a naked mole rat, we arrived at the zoo at one-thirty as planned. Kerrie and Tia took their assigned places in the Small Mammal House while I loitered by the naked mole rat enclosure. I peered through the glass and watched a little pink mole rat nose its way along a clear plastic tube. Its hairless body was wrinkled all over, as though it had been soaking in the bath for too long. Every few minutes, I checked my watch. It was getting closer to 2 p.m.: almost time to Meet A Small Mammal, like the zoo website said. Another couple of minutes went by. Then, behind me, I heard a little voice cry, "Let me out! Let me out!"

I spun around to see a naked mole rat trapped inside a clear plastic box. A blond man in a National Zoo shirt and khakis was holding the box up and motioning toward me.

"Can you guess what this animal is?" the blond man asked, bending toward me. He seemed surprised when I knew the answer. The photo ID clipped to his belt loop told me his name was Ed. I told Ed that I was writing a school report on naked mole rats, and smiled my best smile.

"Could you take a picture of me holding the mole rat?" I said. "I could hold the box—you don't have to take the mole rat out or anything. It'll just take a second. Please?"

Ed let me take the plastic box with the mole rat in it. I handed him an old digital camera that no longer worked and backed away one step at a time, looking behind me and pretending to search for a place to stand. I raised one hand to signal Kerrie, and she hit PLAY on the recorded sound of a blaring fire alarm she'd saved on her phone. While the families around us covered their ears, I stuffed the mole rat box in my backpack and bolted for the exit. Kerrie and Tia stayed behind to distract the zookeepers and give me a head start. I knew which way to run—I'd planned it all out. On a busy Saturday afternoon, it wasn't so hard to melt into the crowds. I ran all the way to Kerrie's house and spotted Auntie Jiffy's car waiting outside. I'd asked her to pick me up at two-twenty, and she was there, right on time.

"Deano, why are you panting?" she asked, as I jumped into the car. "Where'd you come from? Why weren't you in Kerrie's house?"

"Kerrie's mom took us to the zoo. There was a wasp—it chased me. I think it's outside my window—oh Auntie Jiffy, please drive!"

Maybe because she knew that I'm allergic to wasps, Auntie Jiffy stepped on the gas. At first I kept turning around and checking the back window, to see if maybe the Zoo cops were after us, and finally Auntie Jiffy noticed and said, "That wasp can't still be following you, darling." So I told her that there wasn't just one wasp, a bunch of them were on our tail, and I swear she sped up a little.

Back home, I ran straight to my room to check on the mole rat I'd stolen. Mugi—he told me his name first thing—seemed impressed that I'd managed to steal him away. He wasn't as naked as I thought; there were little white hairs all over his body, fine as cat whiskers. From snout to tail, he was almost as long as my 2B pencil.

"You speak English, huh?" I said. "Aren't you from Kenya?"

"Kenyans speak English. It's a Commonwealth country. Besides, my colony's from the Philadelphia Zoo, so I've lived in America all my life. Now that I've answered your question, can you tell me why I'm here?"

I told Mugi that Da was sick and needed mole rat cells to kill his tumors. "I don't know if it'll work, it's an experiment. Please, Mugi, you've got to help my Da. I'll take you back to the Zoo after this, I swear."

Mugi thought for a moment. "What's the experiment?"

I explained it to him. I wanted to do a dry run while Da was napping, but an hour before dinner, Da said he had stomach pains, and Mom had to drive him to the hospital. Auntie Jiffy came over to watch me, and at the dinner table she tried to get me to eat some of Mom's Malaysian-style mac and cheese, which was just the regular kind with curry powder in it. I sat there and glared at my bowl. In the middle of dinner, Mom called, and after Auntie Jiffy hung up she said she was going to drive me to the hospital to see Da.

"I need to wash up," I said. I ran upstairs to grab Mugi's box and a pack of Q-Tips. Then I stuffed everything in my backpack and dashed down the stairs.

"What's wrong with Da?" I asked Auntie Jiffy in the car.

"Your Mom says he's unconscious, Deano. I'm going to get us to the hospital as fast as I can."

Even with the heater in Auntie Jiffy's car blasting hot air in our faces, I couldn't get warm. I sat on my hands until they felt numb. By the time we got to the hospital Da was already in the ICU.

"Da had a heart attack," Mom told us, her face pale.

Auntie Jiffy grabbed Mom and me with a quick sweep of her arm, pulling us into a hug. I tried to stay calm.

"Can I see Da?" I asked.

"You can't go into his room, he's resting. But you can stand outside," Mom said.

"It's all right. You take her, I'll wait here," Auntie Jiffy said.

Mom led the way to Da's room. When we got there, I peered in. Da was lying in a narrow cot. His eyes were closed; he was sleeping. A plastic mask covered his mouth. It scared me to see him so still.

"I just want to stay here and watch Da," I said.

"I'll give you a few minutes, Deano."

After she left, I went right into Da's room and hovered by his bed. I snatched a Q-Tip from my backpack and swabbed Mugi through the breathing holes in his box. Then I leaned over Da and rubbed the Q-Tip all over his throat. "Please, God," I whispered.

At first, nothing happened. I was about to try again with another Q-Tip when I saw Da's eyes flutter open.

"Da!" I yelled. "It's me, Deano!"

Da tugged at his mask. He stared past me as if he couldn't see me at all.

"Mom! Da's waking up, come see!"

Two nurses came running into Da's room. Da kept struggling to get out of bed. He ripped the tube from his arm, and there was a mad scramble as the nurses struggled to hold him down.

"Stop it! You're hurting him!" I shouted.

An aide grabbed my backpack and forced me out of Da's room. Mom was waiting for me outside. She watched the nurses get to work with her hands clasped together, her lips bluish beneath the fluorescent light. I ran to her and she reached for me and held me tight.

"Mom! Tell them to stop hurting Da!"

"They're trying to help him, Deano . . ."

"He's seizing!" one of the nurses shouted.

"DA!" I yelled.

I wanted to go to him, but Mom held me back. When the doctor came to give Mom and Auntie Jiffy and me the news we didn't want to hear, I bawled so loudly Auntie Jiffy had to take me outside to the parking lot. I clung to her, sobbing, while she whispered "Oh my angel" over and over in my ear.

*   *   *

7. Draw Your Conclusions.

In the final step, examine your findings and determine if you should accept, reject, or refine your hypothesis. Do these six steps suggest that the science of discovery is rigid and formulaic? In practice, it isn't. But science is a voyage into the unknown, and when we find ourselves facing great uncertainty, it is understandable that we should seek to rely on a guiding method, a practice that offers what might feel like the comfort and familiarity of a centuries-old ritual . . .

—The Scientific Method: A Pedantic Approach

"Da would be happy to see this yard looking so nice, ha?" Mom said one afternoon, many months later.

It was a warm spring day, and Mom was kneeling in a flowerbed, weeding. Da used to help her; now I was her assistant. While she was busy pulling up dandelions, a squirrel leapt from a tree branch onto the roof, landing with a light thud. We watched as it scampered toward the new birdfeeder hanging outside the kitchen window.

"The man at the gardening center told me this feeder guaranteed squirrel proof," Mom informed me.

Mom and I watched as the squirrel wedged its feet between the roof tiles and swung over the edge, dangling upside down like a trapeze artist so it could reach the lid of the feeder. Two seconds later, it lifted the lid with one paw and reached in for some birdseed, just like that.

"Shoo!" Mom shouted, getting up and clapping her hands to scare the squirrel away. It made a low growling noise I'd never heard a squirrel make before. I got in front of Mom and shook a warning finger at it.

"Stop that! Don't you dare threaten my Mom!"

The squirrel stared at me with its polished black eyes. Finally, it did a backflip onto the roof and ran off.

"Long time I haven't seen you talking to animals." Mom slid her arm around my shoulder.

"Yeah, well, I don't. Not anymore." I burrowed the toe of my sneaker in the grass. There was a question I'd been thinking about for a long time, and now, finally, I felt I could ask it.

"Mom," I said. "Did I . . . did I kill Da?"

She blinked many times in confusion. "Why you say that?"

"Because right after my mole rat experiment, Da died."

"Is not your fault—what happened to Da."

"But I rubbed those mole rat cells on his throat . . . did I make him sicker?"

"Deano, Da had a seizure." She looked right into my eyes. "You didn't do anything wrong. I understand why you feel bad, because I feel so bad. Every day I ask myself, why I didn't notice Da was sick sooner? Why I never made him get treatment early? Why we wait so long to try that JH 482? So many things I feel bad about."

"No, Mom, you didn't do anything wrong either."

She reached up to take off her glasses and wiped her eyes on a little hand towel she kept in the pocket of her purple batik housedress. When she put her glasses back on, her eyes were still misty.

"You know how come I never get mad even after I found out you stole that mole rat from the zoo, Deano?"

"No, how come?"

"Because . . ." Her voice caught in her throat. "I also would do anything to save your Da."

I flung my arms around her legs and hid my face in the skirt of her housedress. She let me cling to her until I stopped sniffling.

"Mom?" I leaned back and looked up at her. "Do you think Da

will forgive me for not saving him?"

"Is not Da who has to forgive, Deano." She knelt in front of me. "You must forgive yourself."

"How do I do that?"

Mom was quiet for a time. "Maybe when you remember something about Da, you let yourself feel happy."

I told her I would try.

Later, after we were done weeding, Mom and I walked over to the flowering magnolia tree at the far end of the yard and sat on the slats of the white oak bench. Both the seat and the grass beneath were covered in white petals that smelled like the inside of a honey jar. I didn't tell her that, for a long time, I hadn't been able to think about Da without wanting to cry. It was as if those last terrible moments in the hospital swept away every happy memory in my head. But while I was sitting on the bench with Mom, I remembered something. This was where Da and I sat the Sunday before his surgery.

Da wore the blue scarf Auntie Jiffy knitted for him looped around his neck. His cheeks and nose were pink from the cold. I slipped my hand into the pocket of his jacket and he took my fingers in his. His big hands were always so warm. I told Mom that and she told me a story.

"The first time Da took me out was wintertime. He took me walking by the river. I forgot my gloves; my hands were so cold. Da never need to wear gloves at all, he didn't have any, so he grab my right hand and warm it up, then after a while he go to the other side and grab my left hand and warm it up. He walk like that all the way home."

I tilted my head toward her shoulder. "What else do you remember, Mom?"

"Later I tell you." Her smile was wistful. "I want to hear about the science experiments you and Da used to do . . . *ai-yo*, for hours I didn't know what you're both up to . . ."

I told her about the radio-controlled UFO Da and I built once, and how we kept flying it past Auntie Jiffy's house, only she never noticed. Mom laughed and said Auntie Jiffy could be very "blur,"

which was Mom-speak for "unobservant." That whole afternoon
Mom and I sat in the warmth of the sun and told stories about Da,
as if by talking about him we could bring him back, if not all of him
then just parts, the parts we remembered, and missed, and wanted
so much to hold onto.

SAN MAN

ANNABELLE LARSEN

First time out, the end of my shift, a piece of sun was up. Because I was a rookie, I was on the nightshift partnered with Lou, who couldn't hear right, cause of shell-shock. We covered Brooklyn and Queens. So cold, your balls froze.

"Next time we're taking turns—twenty minutes driving the hopper to get warm, then twenty liftin' cans," Lou said.

I scraped a piece of dried tomato skin off my boot on the curb. Something always stuck, no matter what.

Right after Korea, guys needed work. I never saw any action, just shipped from Camp Lejeune to Twenty-nine Palms and back again. Before I knew it, the war was over. All us sad sacks had clamored for union benefits and good pay—Teamsters' Local 631. The New York Department of Sanitation gave us the once-over—it was a lottery system. The way they billed it, you'd think it was a tit job, but that was bunk. I prepared by moonlighting at Delahanty's in Manhattan: a ragtag gym filled with wannabe-boxers and tough guys. During the day, I worked at a deli slapping sandwiches together. Guys at the gym gave me funny looks on account of my wiry build. I never lifted weights in my life, but being newly married, I needed a steady gig; so I couldn't fail. Thousands of guys took the test. They started with the physical part, lifting eighty-pound weights in reps of a hundred on the right and left, a hundred sit-ups with sixty-pound weights on the chest, and a broad jump—that sort of stuff. Then you have to pass the written; they threw in a bunch of common sense questions about the city. I got a high score, but I still had to wait to get picked from the lotto. I waited six months before my number was up and they called me in. I was lucky, half the guys on my street in Astoria were still doing odd jobs, trying to make it. The other half, like me, caught the ring.

Second night out, a woman came from behind the truck and said, "Do you take human garbage?" She jumped on the back of the hopper and just sat there in the muck. We didn't know what to do, so we made a call to the boss. We weren't allowed to touch her while she was in the hopper; she could've turned around and said we put her there. After a while, some of the neighbors heard the ruckus, came out and got her; we couldn't move the truck with her in there. I was squatting, wiping off her housecoat the best I could with an old mopeen we had curled up on the dashboard of the truck, but she still smelled like fish. The smell was like the place my ma was sent.

I was a kid when my dad sent her away; she was young, had some kind of cancer. She was in a hospital on Roosevelt Island, called Welfare Island back then. My godmother took me there only once to visit. They had a lunatic asylum, a prison, and for poor people who weren't going to last, a hospital. Outside was landscaped nice with pine trees and flowers. But the buildings were made of dark stone, the brick lighthouse was thin and crumbling. From the walkway, I saw where they kept the sick children. Some were wheeled out onto the patio for fresh air. I was sure I was gonna be put in there with them—all the drooling kids who couldn't hold their heads up. I could make out through the big glass windows pictures painted on the walls of little winking boys in blue sailor suits and kids holding hands. I guess they were meant to be like companions to watch over the dying; a trick on the kids to get them into thinking this was a fun time. All these people put away on a little island, I figured so nobody would see them.

When we walked into the building where my ma was, I saw a sign above the corridor archway that read something like: THIS IS YOUR LAST STOP. I looked up at the sign, sucking in my breath. My godmother knew it was my ma's last days, so she wanted to make sure I saw her, but the nurse said I had to be eighteen to go in. I was ten, but looked younger. My godmother lied and said I was of age. The nurse gave me a stick of Doublemint gum. Ma was sleeping in a metal-framed bed with rollers on the bottom. The beds were lined along the length of a corridor as far as I could see, all the patients faced the window; the sunlight came in there nice. The space in between the beds could barely fit a body. From across the river, I could see Manhattan and Queens. All the time she was in the hospital, I could've been looking out the window from our apartment in Astoria, waving, and maybe she'd have seen me.

By the time the neighbors coaxed the woman away from the hopper and back home to have a cup of tea, it was early morning. I was standing still, enjoying a tiny square of weak sun. All those sick people and my ma, lined up like sardines. The smell of fish and onions was still in the air and on my gloves. I patted my union badge. I always had an emotional feeling to light; I guess 'cause of working in the dark. It was sort of a relief; the sun reminded me of Ma.

Part of the job was hauling the garbage up to the Bronx, to the transfer stations. The stations were in Negro-town, where no one complained, or if they did, nobody cared. We spilled the stuff we collected into concrete pits and then it was compacted into cubes; you couldn't even recognize it was trash any more. When we opened the mouth of the truck and those fumes were released, all the night crawlers would get that sweet stench and you never knew what was gonna come outta that hopper. The rats ran up one arm and down the other—that fast—like you were a human highway. And then the fat roaches swarmed in. Guys looked like they were doing a jig trying to shake 'em off.

After a few months on the job, I learned another site for dumping was at Fresh Kills on Staten Island. All the garbage from Manhattan used to be dumped there. I would go on extra trips to watch the scavengers. Regrets creep up on you at funny times. I shoulda been a trumpet player. When I was a teenager, I took lessons and my teacher would say, "Ya gotta good lip, kid." I would've been far away from this place, touring with Louis Prima and Keely Smith. In my satin tux, watching Keely rub her nose. *I should stay away, but what can I do . . . ?* At Lejeune, they played for us; me and a bunch of the guys pushed so hard against glass doors we busted them just to get up front. The happiest time in my life swingin' with those songs. I could hear the trumpets underneath the sound of the trucks and the gulls at the dump. It was a chance to get away from my wife yakkin' on the phone. San men learned from the scavengers, taking switchblades to abandoned couches, ripping the backs, turning them inside out to find coins.

With a pageboy hairdo like Keely, Madge had a voice of silver coins. We hired her as a maid for a time in the summer. My mother-in-law lived downstairs and always kept an eye out 'cause she didn't trust anyone. Another yakker. "She needs too much," she'd say, "People like that are always lookin' for a handout. They depend on the government for handouts and are always on the church's soup kitchen line."

Madge lived in our neighborhood, but her dad never made it back from Korea. A young girl, only fifteen. She was what you might call "slow." It was just her and her ma and some little rat of a dog.

Round and round I go . . . Scavengers at Fresh Kills searched for the recoverable stuff: copper, brass, old shoes, discarded envelopes, furniture, anything you could make a dime on. I did some gleaning of my own. Why not? It was a wasteland. Seagulls kamikazed from the sky, stray dogs fucked, rats galloped, and the ghosts thrived on all the forgotten-ness. My trumpet would have gone good there; I could have serenaded the scenery, played a low C. That would have been hoping for a different outcome. The ashes from the incinerators filled the horizon with black-and-blue smoke. A meadow full of ash that grew like hills and upward slopes; I imagined the ashes forming small buildings and trains, taking us all away some day. Made your skin itchy, your eyes teary from the stench. You could barely see the san men milling around because of the vapors; the bodies looked scrappy in the dusty air. I don't know if it's true, but an article in the newspaper had said there were only two man-made structures visible from space: The Great Wall of China and Fresh Kills.

During the summer, my wife got sick; some sort of appendicitis thing. She was in the hospital a week. My wife's mother was particular about how things looked and hired Madge to do some cleaning around the house while she was away. I never took much notice of

Madge before she came to work for us. I guess because she was sort of hidden away, or we ignored people like her who went to the soup line. My mother-in-law got Madge to work on the cheap. One morning I was tossing a drink down before I hit the sack, and she came in with colored buckets and mops dangling from both her arms and hands, looked like a butterfly. I thought she had the wrong house, but she clucked her tongue, her red lips in a slanted smile.

"The missus hired me," she said.

I told her I was going to sleep.

"How can you sleep in the day?"

"The only way I know how—take a drink and bury myself under the blankets."

"In this heat? Tape up some aluminum foil on your windows; that'll block out the light."

Yeah. My wife and her mom wouldn't be happy with that.

Madge was only around till my wife got back. When she came home, right away she started in on the complaining: the house was a mess, she couldn't find anything, things were in the wrong places, and what was her mother thinking hiring a good-for-nothin' girl who only dirtied the place up? Yakking on the phone, she told the same story to all her girlfriends: how horrible Madge was and how Madge's mother was a good-for-nothin'. I was so beat from the job, I went straight to bed.

One night in the neighborhood, at the end of the summer, Madge's ma saw our hopper pass by, calls out to me and gives me a box. I thought she was giving me some kind of present for letting Madge work, so I just waved her off, telling her it was okay. "No, no, please. I have to give you this," she said.

I open it up; their dead Chihuahua is inside.

She asked what I was gonna do with it.

I told her we'd go to the incinerator and have it cremated.

We just threw it in with the rest of the garbage. The next morning, Madge saw us come around the corner; she was waiting there. She wanted the dog back so she could say goodbye. I had to tell her it was already gone. She made a whimpering sound when she walked away. She turned to look back at me, like she wanted to tell me somethin', but then I guess she changed her mind. I didn't see her much after that; she was the kind they hid away anyway.

The animals I found, dead and alive, were mostly cats. Making a run in Brooklyn, I was about to toss a can when I thought I heard some muffled mews, and sure enough, it was a bunch of orange kittens all curled up in a pillowcase. Some people threw in loose garbage, like fish heads, with the cats. They were left over the week-end, so by the time we got to them, they were covered in maggots. Once you catch a whiff, you never forget the smell of a maggot. The smell of flowers left to rot in a vase of stagnant water, only worse. When an animal is left for a longer period, the thing just crumples in your hands like dust. I never knew that before about death; that you can feel it in your hands crumbling.

Eight or nine months went by, we were in a downpour; rain makes the cans heavier than they already are. Near dawn, we were on our last stop around my neighborhood and Lou tips a can to dump the water. Some of the trash comes spilling, and I picked up paper bags, bottles, empty packs of Clorets, Playtex gloves, chased after a Ban Roll-On deodorant—when I see what looks like one of my wife's dresses. I remembered 'cause I bought the dress for her on our honeymoon in Puerto Rico. The honeymoon was hard won. We had to grovel so her parents would pay on account I wasn't making spit before the Union. She had to have it. Thought it looked tropical or some shit, said it was a Puerto Rican love song of a dress because of the pictures of the sand, the blue sea, and the beaches with palm trees. Fit all her curves just right, a nice hourglass shape. When she wore it, she said, she would always think of us and remember. I didn't know what it was doing in the trash, all soggy and dirty, but rounded, puffed up like it was filled with something. I touched it with the tip of a Coke bottle and whatever was inside was thick—didn't move. When I pushed again, a tiny bluish hand fell out— looked like wax. A newborn, with a slip tied around the throat.

I said, "Hey, hey, hey!"

Lou went back in the hopper and just sat there.

Fingers were shakin'; still wet, they kept slipping out the holes of the pay phone on the corner when I dialed the police. They came by and interviewed us, took pictures, and carried the dead baby away. I never said anything about the dress. An incident report was written up at the job, and I took some sick time.

Days later, the Daily News printed the story:

> Sanitation workers found a dead newborn in the trash in Queens yesterday morning. "They noticed something lying underneath some spilled trash that looked like a body," said Kenneth Quinn, a Sanitation Department spokesman. The workers called the police. The truck was parked in front of a dilapidated two story house when the baby was found. The infant's body, which was unclothed, was taken to a nearby medical examiner's office for an autopsy. "Why didn't they give the baby to a church?" asked John Grant, who owns a business across the street.

Then a week later, a picture of the girl who confessed. I couldn't stop staring at the picture of the girl. She said she liked the way I smelled—Madge, with her pageboy hair. Head down, a cop had her by the arm, pulling her into the precinct. My wife never noticed her dress was gone or, if she did, she never said anything. I was surprised by that; I thought the dress held some special meaning for her. But she was always on the lookout for somethin' new, some new thing. A refrigerator instead of the icebox, the Magic Chef range had to have a fluorescent back panel, a new car—all that stuff was important. I never mentioned how I saw the palm trees lumped up in the rain—the little fingernails. I showed her the picture of Madge in the paper.

"I don't remember her," she said.

"Sure you do, I said, she worked for us cleanin'."

"No. Don't remember."

BIKES OF DANUBE

ANDREW STANCEK
for Anne

The bike my mother gave me for my thirteenth birthday was red, shiny, and much too big. I'd spent over six months dreaming of it ever since I first saw it in the front window of Bratislava's largest sporting goods store. I wanted it more than anything I'd ever wanted. But it was—no doubt about it—much too big.

The argument I presented to my mother, night after night, was that I only had a few months left in the ZDS Elementary School, and since I was practically an adult in high school, I needed an adult bike; the bike I'd been riding ever since I was ten was a disgrace. It was a kid's bike—too small. I could not possibly be seen on it anymore. My mother knew that over the past year I'd witnessed screams and tears, vases and figurines thrown in anger. After my father moved out at Christmas, she was exhausted and guilty about having put her only son through such misery. The bike was her offering on the altar of peace, but she drove a hard bargain just the same: my report card at the end of the year would contain no grade other than Excellent, I would not only receive my red Pioneer scarf but make a serious effort to be selected as Pioneer Chief for my school, and most importantly, I'd stop spending all my time with Igor, my best friend whom my mother considered a bad influence. The first two parts of the deal I accepted with no hesitation, but giving up my friend was, of course, unthinkable. I agreed, knowing that I promised only that I would not spend *all* my time with him.

The Sunday of the birthday celebration with my family, after the midday wienerschnitzel, roast potatoes, and red cabbage, the cake with sparklers, and grandfather's teary speech welcoming me into manhood, I took the new bike out for a trial ride. Even with the seat and handlebars at their lowest setting, I could not ride it sitting: the frame was too large. I crashed it three times while Mother, my grandparents, and my aunt Taia watched and counseled me to wait until I grew into it. I only allowed my frustrated tears to burst out once they grew tired of watching me and offering advice. But I was not giving up. I would not wait. My knees and elbows could get scraped but my spirit would persevere. The bike was not scratched and I'd master it. Some of my classmates had growth spurts practically overnight, and while waiting for mine, I'd keep riding until I was skilled enough to begin training to race professionally. That was how Smolik started, I was sure.

My elbows and knees were covered with iodine when I went to sleep that night. My mother had laughed, saying I'd lost enough blood to need a transfusion. But I drifted off with visions of first place ribbons at the end of bike races. It was 4:37 a.m. on my bedside clock when I woke, hearing pebbles thrown against my window and a voice yelling, "Tomas! Tomas, wake up!" I tried to jump up and run but was jabbed by needles of pain in my elbow and back, so instead, I limped to the window. The shape was unmistakably my best friend. "Yes, yes, you're not dreaming, it's me," he called, his voice hushed. "Let me in. I need to wash up."

I swallowed all my questions. Why on earth was he at my house? In the middle of the night? Needing to wash up? What trouble chased him here? For a second I thought of the promise to my mother, but I stumbled out the door of our flat and down the stairs to the front door. His clothes were torn, his face and arms were covered with blood, his eye was swollen and starting to darken and a gash just above was bleeding. He put a finger to his lips, motioned us both upstairs. "Later," he whispered. "Let's get inside. Help me."

His shirt was ripped right down the middle, hanging down; his pants only stayed up because of a belt; he was filthy and wincing. Can't wake Mother, I thought, as I ran water in the tub for him to wash up and clean his wounds. If Mother hadn't woken yet, she may not. The blood would wash off and stop on its own, he said. I rummaged through my dresser, brought out my largest shirt and pants, several sizes too small for him but better than his rags. I was burning up with mystery. He'd clearly been beaten, probably by a gang.

Beatings were not unusual in the Podhradie area where he lived with his mother, but Igor and his mom had nothing worth stealing—often not even enough for bread by the end of each month. Something prompted an attack. Why did he come to me?

When he came out scrubbed, the shirt sleeves reached partway up his arms, the pants partway up his calf, but his eyes burned and the blood was washed off. "Leave a note for your mother," he whispered. "I'll tell you on the way to school." I occasionally went to school before Mother woke up. Her purse was on the kitchen table and I "borrowed" twenty-five crowns so we could eat. It was only an hour before my alarm clock normally rang.

The streets were already bustling with noises of street cleaners and delivery vans. My stomach growled, but I was more interested in his mysteries.

"What's going on, Igor? Who beat the crap out of you?"

"My mother . . . took off. She hasn't been paying the rent for months and when I got home Friday, I found a note on the kitchen table with two hundred crowns. She said I was old enough to manage. I know I will be. Like she did after the war when it was really hard. But the scum around our place must have watched when she scrammed, and figured she left me money. So last night about eight of them jumped me, told me that all I have is theirs and I'd better not show my face there again. Good thing I had most of the money inside the shoe I was wearing."

Street kids, gangs, gypsies—all were commonplace. Two hundred crowns would keep him fed for three weeks, maybe a month. He could try an orphanage, but the street would probably be easier. Street people managed. He was resourceful enough.

Smells of coffee, pastries, and minestrone soup came wafting out of an all-night cafe. School was impossible to face on an empty stomach. Workers coming off a night shift, bleary-eyed, sat at one counter, mugs of beer and shot glasses of rum in front. A kerchiefed housewife—a net bag with carrots and turnips peeking out—slurped her tea. Igor asked for a bowl of tripe soup with two extra slices of bread; I settled for coffee and a poppy seed bun. I suddenly remembered my new bike. Igor had said my mother could not withstand my onslaught and her guilt, and I began to tell him all about it. He listened, but his eyes fluttered to a close, and he put his head down on the counter.

Fifteen minutes later, we trudged along Red Army Street towards the Manderlak and the sporting goods store which had earlier displayed my shiny red bike, now chained up inside our flat. As we approached we noticed a crowd. The rumor had been flying around for months, but we never believed we'd experience something this momentous.

Until a few days ago the window had displayed three adult bikes, two kids' ones and a tricycle. Today the throng was staring at a single object: centered in front of a black curtain was a bike, on the surface quite ordinary, race-scratched and race-scuffed, draped with a pair of black cycling tights. Behind, a sign in enormous gold letters: *Jan Smolik, PBW Winner, 1964* and a huge poster of the famous victory hand-pump.

Igor elbowed himself to the glass. The rabid bike racing community had been buzzing that the legendary bike was on its way to Bratislava. We were now actually watching a shop assistant put last touches on the display. Smolik's bike. Smolik's race tights.

In terms of the number of followers soccer was the country's most popular sport, but, in terms of passion, bicycle racing had the most obsessed crowd, and Igor and I ranked at the top. We knew the stories of racers, international and local, the inside scoop on the stages of the big races, argued about the merits of Anquetil, of Louison Bobet, of Charly Gaul. But the most important race in our universe was Tour Prague-Berlin-Warsaw, and the greatest star in the pantheon of racers was Smolik, the Czechoslovak who won it a year ago, in 1964, after he turned professional at fifteen.

Over the next half hour the crowd thinned and went about their business: work, school, everyday lives. Igor and I remained, transfixed. Neither of us mentioned school—face-to-face with Smolik's bike and Smolik's tights, our school's inevitable punishments were forgotten. The church clock gonged ten when a burly policeman sidled next to us, admired the display, measured us with the lawgiver eye. "So, *ulicnici,* school does not appeal to you today? Only Smolik?" Igor's leg twitched and I thought of running. If I ran one way and Igor the other, the policeman would probably catch neither. But where could we run? When we played hooky before, we wandered by the Danube, but today's attraction was right here.

"Let me walk with you a bit, check if, perhaps, classes are held even on National Smolik Day." He chuckled at his wit as we sauntered along Red Army Street. Already I felt my palms stinging from the smacks our teacher was sure to administer. "Who's your teacher?" the policeman asked.

"Comrade Houskova, know her well—excellent teacher." He nodded as we approached the cast iron gates of ZDS School, where we were in the highest grade: ninth. "She knows her duty. She'll make your life miserable."

Igor saw my chin quiver. "Smolik," he mouthed. "Think Smolik." His bearing was that of a proud cadet as he arranged his face into a grin, brushed the uncombed hair off his scratched forehead, itched his broken nose, tucked my borrowed shirt that was too small for him into his pants. He knew Comrade Houskova would make another attempt to beat him into tears—her project ever since the first day of school.

"Smolik," I mouthed the incantation and my spine straightened. I set my hand into a Smolik victory pump fist. "Smolik, victory."

Our classroom door opened a crack after the policeman's rap and we heard Comrade Houskova's soprano leading the class in the folk song "*Tancuj, Tancuj, Vykrucaj.*" Zuzka Kahanova, a mousy classmate, stared wide-eyed at the uniform, then us. "Comrade teacher," she cried, "it's the police!"

Houskova sang out, "At-ten-tion!" Twenty-eight thirteen-year-olds jumped up and stood ramrod by their desks in the prescribed manner. The policeman tipped his broad-shielded hat. "At ease, youngsters. Sit." Nobody moved. Houskova bustled to the door and called, "Sit." Only then our classmates folded back into their desks, commanded by the supreme authority. She glanced at Igor's grin and my set teeth and then turned to our companion.

"Work be honored, Comrade Spytal. How are these two wasting your time?" Her words were sharp but the tone was not her classroom staccato. I saw she knew this man. Her green eyes sparkled and her body seemed to soften.

He licked his lips, pleased. "Sometimes duty can be pleasant, Comrade, isn't it so?"

She colored and waved her hand, "You two, get to work. I'll deal with you soon enough." Igor marched, but I glanced back before I reached my desk. I suddenly realized Houskova was younger than my mother, perhaps even than my aunt Taia. Had I smelled a whiff of perfume on her? Seconds later she was back but her attention was elsewhere and did not notice the rubber band shot by Janko Mraz.

At recess, Houskova called us to her desk, centered under the portraits of President Novotny and Comrade Brezhnev, to mete out our appropriate punishment. I promised that my mother would meet her and then Igor was treated to an eagle glare. "I have only seen your mother once, the very first day. I think it's your father I'd like to meet. I have no contact information. Where is he?"

"No father, Comrade," Igor said. She grumbled as she scribbled in her book. "Your mother, then. Tomorrow—first thing. Dismissed."

At the end of the day, I turned to Igor, "What do you mean you have no father? My *Oci* does not live with us, but I have one. The gypsy hooligans have fathers. Even Zelena, in my old neighborhood, whose mother rolls drunk in the streets—she has a father."

"I don't," he said. "My mom always says there's no such person. Then she pours herself a *borovicka* and threatens to get the belt. So I stopped asking." I dropped it. Racing, racers, and the history of racing were so much more interesting than fathers.

Over the next days, we often stared at the bike in the store window. We roamed the streets of Bratislava, ran along the banks of the Danube, watched the barges, went down to the stone steps of the fishermen, threw rocks into the river. Our classmates kicked a soccer ball on the Dunajska playing field while their mothers perched on surrounding balconies and screeched. I regularly helped myself to a few crowns from my mother's change purse and treated him to a hot meal from the railway station cafeteria. At the charity outlet, we got him clothes. Money was another subject we didn't need to discuss.

One morning, Comrade Houskova cleared her throat in preparation for a lecture. "Think of the heroic deeds of Slovak partisans who fought the Nazis in the Tatra Mountains in 1944. In the gloom of war, governed by collaborationist Nazi puppets, the young resisters hid in mountain caves and performed anti-Nazi acts of sabotage at night. Imagine the courage," her voice grew husky. "Think of the miners who sacrifice light to gift us with coal. Think of the field workers whose blisters help them exceed the Five-Year Plan. The past is filled with great men. But even in the present, greatness is possible. How will you make your mark?"

One by one our classmates provided approved answers: mailman, store clerk, bus conductor. Comrade Houskova narrowed her eyes and shook her head when I announced I'd be a poet but did not comment.

Igor, without hesitation, said, "I will become Smolik."

Houskova screeched, "What kind of nonsense is *that*? How can you be so backward?" The girls tittered but the boys didn't laugh. In Houskova's view, most of us were stupid, not worthy of her class. But Igor was singled out as backward. He had no father and a mother who missed parent-teacher meetings. His clothes were shabbiest, his hair longest, and he smelled. But his greatest offense was not cringing like everyone else when she passed and broke rulers smashing them against our palms.

The heroism lecture was a preamble to the highlight of our schooling so far: a first step on the road to Party membership. Ever since we were six, we'd heard that the greatest accomplishment to strive for was to join our older brothers and sisters as Young Pioneers and march in parades with red scarves around our necks. After suitable preparation, we'd be allowed to wear the uniform all day during the monthly Young Pioneers Day. "No one in my class," Houskova said, "has ever been denied the honor." Throughout April, we drilled for the written test on the principles of the Party.

But Igor stopped coming to school. I was the only one who knew he had no home and no money. I'd asked my mother if he could stay with us for a few days, without mentioning why. My mother turned me down flat.

"You are of different sorts, Tomas," she said. "I know you've been friends and you both like this crazy biking, God only knows why, but it would be good for you to make new friends, boys who have ambition, who are studious, who will do something with their lives. Igor, well . . . Perhaps even girls, Tomas. Are there no nice girls in your class who could be friends?"

Swallowing tears, I slammed the door and took out my bike. When I returned, she did not refer to our conversation or my tantrum but I knew moving him in was out of the question. When I tried to explain he just waved his hand. "Of course you can't. I wouldn't want that. My mother was right. I can manage." I asked about his sleeping and he shrugged. "Don't worry about it. The less you know, the better. I'm tough."

The drilling at school continued, but Igor missed it all. Every few days, I'd find him waiting around the corner from the school as I was on my way home. The wind was wintry, the ground frozen, too cold for *gulicky*. We wandered by the grey, goose-bumpy Danube. Igor turned to me as we stared at soaring gulls. "What would it be like, to be a gull?"

I frequently dreamt of flying. But I also saw their scrawny forms and had seen dead ones on the bank. "Hungry," I said.

He frowned. "Yeah, but . . . think of the freedom, going anywhere you please."

"Pretty hard to grow wings, though," I said. "A bicycle would be easier. Like Smolik."

He seemed on the verge of saying something, thought better of it. "Yeah, you're right. Wanna go have a look at the bike?" In the display, the Smolik bike shone; the upraised victory fist was held high. "Do you think I could race on it?" He stretched out, flexed his muscles.

"Pedal it, maybe, but race?"

He wiped a runny nose with his fist. The window began to reflect the headlights of passing cars. An ambulance screeched by, horn blaring. Even if no one was home yet, I could not postpone the jog past the broken streetlights. I shivered, and my stomach growled.

"Igor," I said, "did you want to come for supper?"

He shook his head. "Nah. You go on home. I'll stay a while."

I did not insist. If I brought him home, Mother would rage.

The next day, I took the usual pilgrimage on my own. A group twice as large as the usual Smolik acolytes milled around the display, yelling.

"How could they do that?" someone screamed.

"Swine!"

Where the window used to be, a sheet of plywood, no glass. On it, already tattered, a small sign. *Administrative Reconstruction.* I wiggled to the glassed side: no bike, no tights, a few shards of broken glass, a dark reddish stain. I felt faint.

"Does anyone know what happened?" I turned to the nearest boy.

"They say someone broke the window with a brick and stole them. Bloody liars! Some creep in administration probably sold them."

I sat on the curb, head between my knees. Igor wouldn't be that crazy, that bold, would he?

When I opened our front door, yelling about the calamity, my mother peered over her glasses, red pen still on a set of papers. "Why would anyone want a used racing bike? The shop sold it to a Westerner with too much money and they're covering up."

That night I stared at the ceiling, wide awake, hearing the squeals of trolley buses, ambulances, and police cars, burning up and drinking one glass of water after another, driving my mother to yell, "Just stop it, stop it right now and go to sleep."

The next day when I got home from school, my mother handed me a copy of Rude Pravo, turned to page three, her red pen outline around a story headlined *Crime in Cycling.* Hooliganism continues unabated, the story told us, with stores along main streets suffering smashed windows, and even national sports treasures being stolen. Tougher jail sentences would no doubt deter criminality.

"How is your own bike riding?" Mother asked. "You never leave the bike unattended, right? Maybe these hoodlums would value a new bike higher than some relic." It wasn't worth explaining; she'd never understand. The sports daily had the robbery on the front page, with a quote from an official hinting darkly at Western conspiracies and international smuggling gangs. I felt sick but was relieved that a gang must be responsible.

A week passed with no news of the bike and no sign of Igor. During recesses, I tried to talk racing with Milos Rebry but he knew no good stories. Peto Smrek asked where Igor was, and I could only shrug. After school I wandered by the Danube, one day even played defense in a pick-up soccer game. Then one morning, as I arrived early, the policeman I knew stood with Igor next to Houskova's desk. My friend had welts on his face; a torn shirt-sleeve gaped. I sat close enough to Houskova's desk to hear their mutterings.

The policeman hissed under Houskova's glare. "One of your charges, Comrade Houskova, living on the streets? A black mark on your record, isn't it? Can you afford another?"

"How dare you try to throw your weight around here? Unlike some others, I know my duty." Her vibrant soprano reverberated in alto depths. But I stared at Igor. Was he connected to the Smolik bike disappearance?

Once the fat uniform left, Houskova yelled, "Off into the corner! No mollycoddling for you!"

She stared at each student in turn before her oration. "You've been born at the dawn of a new age. You had no need to fight against oppression by landowners, factory owners, and other bloodsuckers. You stand on the shoulders of giants. You are therefore expected to behave in exemplary ways." At day's end, I waited outside while from the classroom I heard Houskova's rumble. "Reform school is all that's left for you. Your mother has to come tomorrow." Igor's silence dragged before I heard, "Dismissed."

When he trotted out I joined him along Podhradska Street. A few streets later he said, "You can keep your trap shut?"

Then, out of the side of his mouth, "I have them. I did it. It's too big but I can control it. If I stand on the pedals I can. He won on it and it's mine. I only take it out at night, right by the Danube, on the narrow path for the fishermen, the wobbly ground. No one can take it from me there. If I train all spring and summer, if all I do is train and train, in September I'll go to the Racing Club and show them how good I am, and they'll take me. I'll race. I'll be free." The gull circling above laughed. It soared above the Danube, swooped down for a fish but came up beak empty.

"Can I ride it, too?"

"You're not tall enough. I won't allow it to get wrecked."

"So now what? What are you going to do?"

"Ride it. Ride it every day. And then ride it some more."

"You have a place to sleep? You eat?"

He shrugged. "I don't care about any of that. As long as I can ride it."

We slowed entering the depths of Podhradie, the broken-down area under Bratislava's medieval castle, where the homeless, the drunks, and the gypsies lived in boarded up holes, in hovels made of plywood, in wrecks of condemned houses, where people were reputed to have gone in, never to be seen again. Igor grunted at a bottle-waving derelict with four mangy dogs. No street lights of course, the cobblestones uprooted, heaps of refuse, reek of rot. I followed Igor as he swished through winding paths, squeezed through piles of rubble, past growls. After a sharp turn, he lifted up a jagged, rusty fence and we jumped down. We were in the dusky gloom of a cellar, the air smelling of rotting potatoes, beets, turnips. I squinted but only saw blankets, rags, netting.

"So, where . . . ?"

He snorted. "You think I'd leave them out in the open, so any *trulo* could find them? Some of these *chujos* will slit your throat for a drink. Anything they can steal, pawn, sell." A toddler screamed nearby; a board *rat-at-atted* in the wind. His breathing in the cramped space was raspy; he strode to a corner, moved a pile of boxes revealing a trapdoor outline. "Whoever used to live here needed a place to store valuables," he whispered and lifted. In a space just large enough, the red surface gleamed and Igor caressed it.

"Can I touch?" My voice came out hoarse. "Let's take it out."

I reached for the handlebars, expecting to be singed. Even behind the store display window it had cast a spell, but now I tingled. It was un-ridable, I saw. Yet he'd been riding it, so maybe I would, too.

"Some of the way to the Danube, along the steep path, I ride it— but mostly I walk. By the river, I'll show you my training area." He threw a leg over and wobbled standing on the pedals. He hopped off to run along a neck-breaking path around rusty bins. Riding again, he took sharp turns without braking, then stopped till I caught up. "I walk it in this rocky part."

"Let me?" I asked. He nodded and I guided it until we arrived at the Danube promenade.

"Dangerous here," he said. "Busybodies, no-goods of all kinds. One time a policeman whistled and yelled for me to stop. Once we get down to the river, it's only old geezers and their fish."

He took the bike. Dusk already, area deserted, the path narrow and straight, I could see all the way to the Park of Culture and Enlightenment. He rode off. I ran next to the cold Danube; Igor slowed at half-hidden stone steps, swished along the narrow path bordering the river, all the way to the protruding pier, where the wealthy moored their boats. He pedaled into the distance, finally returned squealing to a stop, breathless. His teeth glistened in a tri-umphant smile.

"Going pretty fast, no?" he said. "I've had crashes, but never hurt it, not even once. My elbows and knees, yeah, but not the bike."

"Can I try a little?"

He held it while I put a foot on one pedal and threw my leg over. It was much too big. My behind was touching the crossbar; I'd never be able to sit and touch the pedals. "Igor . . . just like with my bike, I can pedal standing up. I don't have to sit."

"If you feel yourself falling, protect it," he said and let go.

I put my weight on one side, then the other. I was riding it! After a few meters I jumped off and he ran up, gripped it. Someone was ambling down the path.

"Igor!"

"He's okay. He fishes here. He's seen me." The old man took out a fishing pole and sat on a stone perch without showing the least interest in kids and a bike.

I became aware of the darkness. Even if my mom had been late, she must be home by now. "Igor, I . . ."

"I know. You have to go."

"Will you come to school tomorrow?"

"Nah. What's the point? Houskova will make sure I don't get the scarf. In the fall, I'll get into the Racing Club. I know I will."

"How will I . . ."

"Where I live now, it's too dangerous for you. Come here after school and you might see me."

I wanted to train, too. But I still had a mother, a home, even a father.

Igor mounted the bike again. "See you. . ." I watched his back get smaller until he disappeared.

I ran all the way, not stopping to wipe snot off my face. At home, my mother harangued only a little before we ate and she sent me to bed.

The Pioneer test drills took up our school days, with Houskova's ruler bruising many knuckles. My mother would not allow me to go to the Danube. On Thursday, we all wrote and passed. Friday morning, we wore white shirts; the boys' hair gleamed with pomade; the girls reeked of forget-me-not perfume. At ten, we marched to the gym, filled with a congregation of expectant parents. The First Secretary of the local MNV expounded on the great honor being bestowed upon us, warning us to be ever-vigilant as Houskova beamed. The creaky amplifiers burst out with the Internationale. One by one, twenty-nine of us crossed the stage, and the Secretary handed each new Pioneer his red scarf. Parents cheered and wept. When my turn came, I felt a stab, as I accepted the scarf, thinking of Igor, perhaps at this very moment riding along the Danube.

We paraded with our red scarves, had pictures taken together, individually, and with our parents. Neither my mom nor I mentioned my absent father. Although lunch was liver dumpling soup and *sauerbraten*, my favorites, I could not swallow, and soon my mom dismissed me. Still in white shirt and red scarf, I ran to the Danube, past families taking newly-minted Pioneers to restaurants, towards the Park of Culture and Enlightenment. No sign of him. The Danube seemed sinister, the wind cold, the gulls' cawing and swooping forlorn. My fingers picked at the stitching of the red scarf, then switched to rubbing the wet spots on my white shirt.

I sat and waited. The church clock high above gonged six times, and my mother was sure to be expecting me. Suddenly noises came from the church direction: yells, whistles, the whine of a police car and another whine from the opposite direction, the commotion getting ever closer. Then the screams were at the stone staircase. "Don't let him get away!" More sirens.

I saw Igor balancing the bike down a path at Smolik-speed. He grinned and whizzed by. Someone screamed, "Cornered. No way out. We've got the thieving hoodlum!" I ran to follow, heard the tromping of military boots. Another group of khaki uniforms closed in from the other side. I screamed, "Look out! Up ahead!" but he did not seem to hear or care. He approached the long pier, the last barrier between himself and the onslaught, turned onto it, nothing but the river ahead, but did not slow. A few meters before the edge, he looked back, face twisted in ecstasy. His legs continued the strokes; he took his hands off the handlebars. He gave the huge Smolik victory hand-pump and tore into the ribbon at the end of his race. The bike flew in the air for a few meters as his hands continued to pump. Then half the wheels were under water, then they were gone, only his head and upstretched arms visible . . . then nothing. I collapsed on the pier, surrounded by both sets of pursuers. We all stared where we had last seen him. The river flowed past; someone yelled for a boat, for an ambulance, for the water rescue team.

I kept the promise I gave my mother. The report card at the end of the year had no grade other than Excellent. I put my name forward for Pioneer Chief but was relieved not to be chosen. That toughest part of the promise, not to spend all my time with Igor, well, I kept

that part, too. Even though I'll soon be tall enough to ride my shining red bike, I lost my passion for bikes of all sorts. I walk along the
Danube alone and watch the soaring of the gulls.

STRANGERS

CODE OF THE WEST

SAHAR MUSTAFAH

Three days after Letti Vega disappeared, her body was found in an excavated lot. Her bottom half was naked and bruised. A construction crew had drained a large hole of rainwater and discovered her face-down. Her feet were steeped to her ankles in the wet clay, and her long brown hair was tangled like reeds around her shoulders.

Two Watford City detectives showed up at the trailer park. They were leaning against a shiny black Tahoe near the entrance to the park, smoking cigarettes, and flicking the ashes away from their shoes. They waited for Riyad Nasrrawi.

Riyad shivered as soon as he stepped out of the trailer. The brisk morning air penetrated his sweatshirt. The start of September had been cold and wet.

"Did you have any interactions with Ms. Vega outside the restaurant?" the first detective—shorter and pudgier than Riyad, with brown hair thinned across the crown—asked.

"No," Riyad answered. He wasn't sure what to do with his hands as he stood there for the interrogation. He finally stuck them in the pouch of his sweatshirt and rubbed his key medallion with his thumb inside the fold.

"Do you know anyone who would want to harm her?"

Henry Elbert's face flashed across his mind. "No," Riyad said again.

"How long you been working out here?"

"You mean in Watford?" Riyad glanced behind him where other men were emerging from their trailers. A few wore the baseball caps with *JT Flooring* stitched in orange. He hoped he wouldn't be late for work and have to explain why to the site superintendent.

"In North Dakota, sir," the detective clarified.

Riyad knew to the exact hour how long he'd been there. "Uh, a year and a half, I think. I was in Fargo before here."

"Where'd you say you're from, sir?" This came from the second detective. He was also shorter than Riyad, but he had the build of a boxer—broad shoulders and a chest that narrowed to a tight waist. His neck was wide and comical underneath his shirt and tie. Both detectives were wearing jeans and boots.

"Near Chicago," Riyad told him.

"That's where you lived, sir," the first detective said. "What's your nationality?"

"I'm an American citizen," he told them.

The men looked at each other. He knew what they were really asking, but he wouldn't make it easy for them. The first one continued to press him: "Are your parents originally from this country, sir?"

Riyad shook his head. "They're Palestinian."

The second one began to write in a small notebook he pulled from a back pocket of his jeans. "Did you say from Pakistan?"

"No. From Palestine." Riyad wondered if they knew where that was.

"Are you Muslim?" the first one asked. He pronounced it as *mooz-lum.*

"Yes," Riyad said, though he hadn't ever been a practicing one. He fasted only a few days during Ramadan and that was only for show, to keep his mother from nagging him about haram. He didn't drink or eat pork, but he didn't pray five times a day, either. Still, he wanted to ask the detectives how this line of questioning was relevant to the murder of Letti Vega, and if they knew the first mosque in the United States had been established in Ross, a town less than a hundred miles northwest of Watford City. But he knew it was better to keep his mouth shut and cooperate.

When a follow-up question didn't come, Riyad took it as his cue to move between them and walk over to his car. His beat-up Oldsmobile was covered in a layer of red dirt from the construction site where he worked—not the same site of the body. His Illinois plates were splattered, but still visible.

Five of the Mexicans from another crew had already taken off. Riyad believed they'd had nothing to do with Letti Vega's murder.

Still, they didn't need Immigration sniffing around. The Watford City police didn't hassle the project managers over the sudden departure of half their crew; they, too, were confident the Mexicans weren't responsible. They'd been working for Dane & Holtz, Inc. much longer than Riyad, and everyone knew they'd be back as soon as the dust settled. Despite his innocence, his paranoia heightened like the perked-up ears of a skittish cat. For a moment he thought of taking off too, but there wasn't anyone waiting for him in Illinois. No one was keeping him in North Dakota either, but he stayed.

He filled up at a gas station on Main Street. The sky was a grey blanket with wrinkles of dark clouds. Inside the food mart, he poured coffee in a Styrofoam cup and carefully placed the lid over it while other customers moved past him, trying not to touch him—so it seemed to Riyad. The cashier didn't reply to his greeting, only offering a jerk of his chin.

Above rolls of lottery tickets, a small mounted TV flashed images of Letti Vega. Every news station showed the same two photographs: Letti Vega as a high school senior, her cap slightly tilted, yellow tassel dangling; and Letti Vega in a green dress with white polka dots, standing beside an old brown-skinned woman—her grandmother, maybe. Riyad had only ever seen her in a denim shirt and tan pants, the uniform all the waitresses wore at Briggs, a restaurant off Highway 85 where she'd been working.

Riyad paid for his gas and coffee and pushed open the door, feeling a dozen pairs of eyes boring into his back. A drizzle came down and coated his thick hair. He climbed back in his car and wiped his head with some clean napkins he kept stashed in the glove compartment.

He drove past Briggs, slowing down to view the bustle of news reporters. The restaurant had a log cabin façade, its sides paved in red brick. A group of news reporters stood in the parking lot with clear plastic raincoats over their suits and dresses, holding umbrellas with one hand and microphones in the other. He caught glimpses of vans with station signs from as far as Billings and New Town.

He pulled onto the construction site of Phase 2 of Autumn Creek, an apartment compound. His crew did the flooring for a hundred units. Rental buildings sprung up like concrete weeds in Watford City, another boom town. Riyad had worked in Dickinson and Fargo for the last year, on motels and senior living complexes. He wasn't sure where he'd go next once the construction ended. He'd been steadily pushing northwest, the country seemingly stretching out forever. Maybe Williston would turn up something for a few months. He figured Montana wouldn't be too friendly.

"Heard cops been askin' you questions," a voice behind him said. It was Tim O'Halloran, a veteran crewman from Minnesota who'd begun ribbing Riyad the moment he arrived on the site last spring.

"Mind your own business," Riyad said over his shoulder.

O'Halloran sidled up close to him. He smelled like soap and sawdust. "You the killer, Ali Baba? Ha?" He gave a mean snort. The other men laughed.

"What the fuck you talking about, man?" Riyad snapped.

O'Halloran stopped walking. "Ah, what's he need with one chick?" he jeered. "They get a hundred virgins in heaven if they blow up a building."

Riyad turned around. "Fuck you, man!" He took a few steps towards O'Halloran. The other man was twice his size and weight, but Riyad had to make a move or it would be open season on him for the rest of the job.

"Knock it off!" the site super yelled from yards away, waving his clipboard in the air. "We got work to do. Gather 'round." The men huddled in a semi-circle while the super ran down the weekly quota of tasks.

Henry Elbert stood beside Riyad. He had an interminable cough and was looking paler than usual. His eyes were red-rimmed. Henry, Riyad, and another man, Nick Osman, shared a trailer, keeping their monthly expenses down while they finished the job. There'd been a fourth roommate, a guy from Jamestown—home of the World's Largest Buffalo—but he left three days after he'd arrived, muttering about missing his girlfriend and dog.

As the super rattled off notes from his clipboard, Henry fell into a fit of coughing.

"Fuck, man," Tim O'Halloran complained. "You tryin' to get the rest of us sick? Go see a fuckin' doctor, why doncha?"

Henry skulked a few feet backwards, flicking his reddish-blond hair, still damp from a shower. Most of the men showered before they went to sleep, but Henry took two: one in the morning and one immediately after work. He pressed his fist against his colorless lips and his body shuddered for the rest of the meeting. Riyad felt sorry for the guy. Henry Elbert was someone the other men disliked as much as they did him, "an Ay-rab come to the Wild West."

"Alright, that's it. Now get to work," the super ordered the crew, waving his clipboard in the air again.

Inside the third floor, Riyad fastened his knee guards and stooped to the cement floor.

With his trowel, he applied the adhesive for each laminate panel in a circular motion. The repetition made him feel steady and calm, the tension from his confrontation with Tim O'Halloran seeping out of his muscles. He was glad to be working indoors. He remembered the crews in Fargo last winter who'd suffered subzero temperatures finishing a roof or putting up siding to meet their quota for the month.

He pulled off his sweatshirt, revealing the bright orange company shirt JT Flooring had given each employee. Rain poured the whole day, coating the new unit windows and blurring the outside.

*   *   *

Riyad hadn't been back to Briggs since the body was pulled from the hole. It was a saloon-style restaurant where the regular crews ate steak-burgers and drank beer for lunch and dinner. Riyad ate there once a week, sometimes alone and sometimes with Henry Elbert, and Jesús Padilla—a Mexican he'd met back in Fargo—who had given Riyad a lead on the job in Watford City.

They'd eaten at Briggs just two days before a Missing Person report was filed for Letti Vega. "I'm going to Florida," Henry had said over his fried chicken dinner. "Fuck the cold and dust. I'm going to get one of those wiener wagons by the beach. I'll be fucking made. I just need to save some more cash. Then I can blow this shithole." He cleared his throat, making a low guttural sound like an animal. An elderly couple seated nearby had turned and grimaced at him.

Jesús was undocumented and didn't contribute much to the conversation of Florida and wiener wagons. His brown eyes roamed over Henry's face, then past him and Riyad to the men whooping at the bar. Riyad couldn't read Jesús's face, but there was a glint of contempt in his eyes.

The three of them avoided sitting at the bar with men like Tim O'Halloran and his buddies who turned even more territorial, their elbows hanging off the polished counter, each of them loudly vying for the attractive bartender's attention. One time the restaurant manager had to be called to settle down O'Halloran's crew when one of them tried to climb over the bar.

Riyad preferred a booth when it was only him and Henry. Jesús occasionally returned to the trailer park with the other Mexicans who were smart about their paychecks and packed their own lunches. Back in Fargo, when Riyad had asked him about kids, Jesús had raised three fingers and proudly grinned. Riyad wondered if it was easy to forget about them and legal papers and a wife when you were chomping down on a steak-burger. Maybe that's why Jesús spent time with him and Henry. Everyone had something—or someone—to forget, even if it was just for a little while.

Briggs was open seven days a week. The interior was dimly lit with heavy lacquered wooden tables and high-backed booths. Heads of bison, deer, and brown-and-white speckled cows were mounted along the perimeter of the dining hall. Hanging above the hostess podium was a framed document called "Code of the West" in old-fashioned Western typeface. The walls were lined with WANTED posters of real Briggs criminals, including the Dalton Brothers, a trio of bank and train robbers, and a woman named Belle Starr: a celebrated horse thief.

Riyad saw the same three or four waitresses every time he dined there. They huddled close to each other to gossip at the refreshment station, touching each other's shoulders, reaching over one another for a coffee mug or a bunch of plastic drinking straws.

Letti Vega usually served them during her shift, and if the hostess started to lead them away to another part of the restaurant, Henry would ask her to seat them in Letti's area, without mentioning her by name.

She wasn't like the other waitresses. She smiled politely and said hello, then immediately took down their order. She spoke Spanish to Jesús when he had a question about an item. She never asked "How's it going, boys?" or "You almost finished Phase 2?" the way Emma Sue or Casey—the white waitresses—asked the construction men. Their faces were tanned year round and their pants were snug around their asses, not loose-fitting like Letti's. Her body was slender with small breasts and a short torso. They lingered at the tables where architects and PMs looked over blue prints, and they laughed long and heartily at the masculine quips.

Letti wore a light-pink polish on her short-clipped nails. The first time she'd served them, Riyad noticed something of a tattoo creeping out of the hem of her sleeve. It might have been a flower petal or the edge of a butterfly wing. When she was waiting for an order to come up, she smeared lip balm across her mouth and checked her cellphone.

The other men didn't seem to notice her. Except for Henry. He never said more than "please," "thank you," and "what's the soup today?" but it was obvious to Riyad that he was enamored with Letti, though she appeared to be less aware of him as she was of the other men who bellowed and knocked drinks on their tables. She performed her duties like she was inside a protective bubble. Others instinctively remained at bay, leaving her undisturbed.

Even Henry had left her alone, though Riyad could see words forming on his lips, anticipation shining in his eyes. When she brought their order, Henry only looked down at his food and nodded.

*   *   *

After work, Riyad ate at Taco John's, then drove south on Highway 85, gladder than usual for his Oldsmobile. Most of the crewmen didn't own transportation. He knew a few who had hitched all the way from Michigan or Iowa for work. The men had formed carpools, but if anyone asked, he obliged them with a ride in the morning or dropped them off at the nearest bar after a long day. He never accepted offers for a free beer in return.

He drove past the oil fields where pump-jacks dipped into the ground like rocking horses.

There was something painfully lonely to Riyad about the constant dipping—this quiet, uninterrupted motion reminding him that it didn't matter where he was in the county or state—life was unbroken. You had to put up with what you were dealt. Crews full of Mexican and white men showed up every day. Apartment buildings went up where desolate land had been.

There'd be someone else to replace him in his trailer cot as soon as he was gone.

He pulled off near the Maah Daah Hey trail and watched the sun set. The first time he drove west from Fargo, the badlands took him by surprise, jagged buttes suddenly swelling around him and stratified valleys waking him from the torpor of a hundred miles of flat terrain. The highway was like a concrete serpent slinking through the hills of Watford City. The crew from Fargo suggested he stop at Theodore Roosevelt National Park to see the buffalo.

"You can only go six miles in," the park ranger had informed him. She was a middle-aged white woman with a round, pleasant face. "Erosion. You'll see the roadblocks." She had a map ready to hand him. "That will be twenty dollars, sir."

Riyad fished in his wallet. He'd cashed his last check from the Fargo job and all he had was a few hundred-dollar bills. "Can you break this?" He extended one out of his car window.

The ranger shook her head. "Can't help you with that." She gave him a map anyways and said, "You'll get us next time, sir. Enjoy."

It had been early May and the buffalo were molting, their fur hanging in patches from their flanks, looking less majestic than

Riyad had imagined. He pulled off the path and watched a pair graz-ing several yards away. They chewed the new grass and snorted indifferently.

It was fall now, and the buffalos would be coated in fur again. A steady rain came down and Riyad turned off the wipers. A thin sheet covered his windshield. Next month was October and Phase 2 would be finished. He was glad Letti Vega's body hadn't been dumped on his site. Then he felt awful. A young girl was dead and all he could think about was completing a job so he could move on.

He took out his cellphone and listened to Marwa's message again. It was nearly two years ago and he still hadn't erased it.

"I'll wait another year, if you want. I deserve more, but I'll wait for you."

She had not intended to be unkind. It was a fact. Arabiyat like Marwa were accustomed to a certain lifestyle that he couldn't provide.

He imagined her holding her cellphone with one hand and rub-bing the tip of her middle finger over the nail of her pointer finger like she did when she was thinking hard about something. The day before he left, they parked on the lakefront in Chicago outside the Adler Planetarium, where the view of the city skyline was the best. Marwa had looked at him, but Riyad sensed she wasn't really seeing him. He wanted to reach over and kiss her eyelids shut and press his lips against her thick lashes. Instead he had gently squeezed her arm, pulling her out of a reverie of their life together.

When he was twelve years old, his father died of a blood clot in a prison in central Illinois. He'd been sentenced to five years for illegally cashing food stamps at his grocery store. His uncle and cousin were also convicted. Riyad never drove a BMW or Range Rover like the other boys from school. He started working at four-teen, riding his bicycle to a gas station five miles from the cramped condo he rented with his older sister and his mother in Orland Hills.

Marwa lived on a two-acre lot with her family. It was a sprawling all-brick house with a circular driveway and a four-car garage. She drove a white Escalade with tinted windows from the dealership her father owned. So many things kept Marwa out of his league, but she was drawn to him for some reason. Maybe it was the quiet way he moved among the other puffed-up guys, or maybe it was his inability to treat her badly, which most of the *arabiyat* would take as love.

"What will you do now?" she'd asked him. They watched people jogging and walking along Lake Michigan. In the distance, the movement of the gigantic Ferris wheel was imperceptible.

Marwa was graduating from UIC while he'd been working for a family-owned flooring business. That had given him enough experience for North Dakota.

He'd never been farther than Wisconsin, but he owned a car and he had a say over where he could go. His mother and sister had cried when he told them he was leaving. Their farewell felt more like an acknowledgement of failure than a herald of opportunity.

Riyad started the wipers, the horizon visible again in the thinning light.

He drove back to the trailer camp and parked his car next to a black Camaro that belonged to his roommate Nick. He unlocked the door of his trailer and climbed in. Nick was watching TV and thumbing through an auto magazine. He gave Riyad a look and shook his head in the direction of Henry's curled up body.

Sweat and farts permeated the trailer. Riyad pushed out a small window over the kitchen sink then squatted down next to Henry. "You okay, man?"

Henry cleared his throat, the low guttural sound muffled by his pillow. "Leave me alone."

Riyad stood and looked over at Nick who shook his head again. "Fine. I'm gonna wash up."

Before turning in, he sat on his cot and watched the nightly news with Nick. There was a twelve-inch TV screen fitted into a shelf at the opposite end of the trailer. New details on the murder revealed a young man who Letti Vega apparently had been seeing. He was taped huddled under an umbrella, exiting the Watford City police station with a white man in a suit—his lawyer, no doubt. As reporters followed him to a waiting car, he kept his head down, his long brown hair obscuring his face.

A blonde news anchor stated, "Friends of Vega say they had no idea she had been involved with Johnny Lopez, a twenty-three-year-old janitor at Good Christian Academy in nearby Charbonneau. Tonight, authorities say he is not being charged, only questioned. We'll have more on that case as further information becomes available. Now let's go to Tom Haverson to see what's in store for weather for the Great Plains. Tom . . ."

Riyad watched Henry's cocooned body. It made no perceptible movement during this latest revelation.

"Good night," Riyad told Nick. He pulled the kitchen window shut.

"Night." Nick flicked off the TV and a light switch over his cot.

Wind hissed near the trailer door, the cold air penetrating the seams. Riyad turned over on his side and faced the wall. He was still awake when he heard a small whimper, but Riyad didn't sit up to check what it was. Instead, he pulled his blanket over his shoulders and soon he was asleep.

The next morning, Henry Elbert was gone. The detectives showed up again, this time talking to Nick and letting Riyad through without a word.

*   *   *

"These gueros are wasted, man," Jesús warned Riyad when he pulled onto the site. A light rain was falling and the orange construction flags flapped hard in the wind.

Riyad looked over at the management trailer. "Is the super here yet?"

Jesús shook his head under his jacket hood. "Don't know."

"Come on," Riyad said, his shoulders tightening. "Just ignore them." He nudged Jesús in the arm.

They walked toward the apartment building, away from Tim O'Halloran and a small crowd that had assembled around him. He was swaying on his heels, a bottle of Jim Bean in his hand. One of his buddies was trying to release it from his drunken grip. When O'Halloran caught sight of Riyad, he charged.

"It was you! You dirty sand-nigger!" Tim O'Halloran shouted, pushing Riyad in the chest. He stumbled backwards, tripping over a pallet of flooring panels.

"Fuck you!" Riyad shouted, pain tearing through his back. Jesús helped him to his feet and kept a hold of his arm, pulling him away.

"You terrorist fucker!" O'Halloran tried to push through the barricade of men holding him back. "Get the hell off me!" He teetered for a moment, then steadied himself.

The super jumped out of a construction trailer. "You'd better calm down." He stood in front of O'Halloran with his hands up. "You quiet down or I'll call the cops."

"Call the fuckin' cops! You're lettin' a killer go!" O'Halloran yelled at him.

"Get him out of here before I have him locked up," the super instructed the men. "Let him sleep it off. And you tell him if he shows up with alcohol on the site again, he's fired."

O'Halloran suddenly turned limp at this threat and permitted the men to half-carry him to a pickup truck. They drove off the site, a swirling dust of gravel in their wake.

The super walked over to Riyad. "You alright, son?"

The throbbing in his lower back had dulled, but a sharp pain shot through his legs when he took a step forward.

"You need to go to the hospital?"

Riyad shook his head. "I'll be fine," he said. Jesús helped him to a pile of mortar bags covered in tarp. He sat down in a sharp wince of pain.

"Take the morning off and see how you feel," the super instructed him.

By noontime, Riyad could barely stand in his trailer, let alone sit up on his cot. "Fuck," he muttered.

He called the super who drove him to McKenzie County Hospital where they gave him some painkillers and a cold compress and assured him it was nothing more than a mild sprained back—no permanent damage.

"Do you want to press charges?" the super asked him on the drive back to the trailer camp. His tone suggested he hoped there would be no more bad press on the construction site.

Riyad gazed out the window at the oil fields. Despite the rain, small fires blazed from gas flares. They looked like torches, strange beacons of something he could not name.

"No. I don't know," Riyad said. He was humiliated and in the worst pain he'd ever felt. "I'll think about it."

In the end, he decided not to press charges. He knew it wouldn't make friends of the other men, but he certainly couldn't afford any more enemies. When he returned to work several days later, no one acknowledged the gesture, but they left him alone.

Soon he was able to drive himself to work and the first chance he got he headed down Highway 85 at the end of his shift. Thunderstorms had gradually moved east, leaving the valleys looking electrified in the grey-blue dusk. He would miss this part of the country once Phase 2 was complete.

He pulled off the highway and turned off the ignition. He reclined the seat. A dull pain throbbed in his lower back, but it wasn't unbearable. His eyelids felt suddenly heavy, and he closed them and rested his head against the cool glass of the driver's side window. At first, he didn't fight the images of Marwa and Letti Vega and Henry Elbert as they floated across his mind.

Then something stabbed at his heart and he opened his eyes. Maybe Henry realized even a wiener wagon was too big and Letti Vega was the final straw. One more thing he couldn't have.

Riyad felt nauseous. He quickly turned the ignition to open his window. He breathed in the badland air. His head cleared again and he steadied his gaze on the sun's descent. It cast long and wide shadows in the valley and over the browning steppe.

Maybe there was still a chance to leave. He couldn't go back to Illinois—the land was too flat. Not Florida, either. Too humid. Maybe California—a town near the ocean. A new calm washed over him. The sun had finally set leaving a brushstroke of pink and orange across the horizon. After a few more comatose minutes, he pulled back on the highway.

The trailer park was quiet. Most of the men were out drinking or asleep. Riyad parked his car between two pickup trucks and climbed out. He looked at his trailer, wondering how far Henry had gotten.

The first blow to the back of his head brought an explosion of white-hot light beneath his eyelids. The second one brought darkness.

Tim O'Halloran lowered the lead pipe and nudged the slumped body with the tip of his boot. "Should've stayed where he come from."

It was barely a whisper, but the two other men heard him and nodded, though neither of them had ever really known where that place was.

DESPERADO

ROBERT MCGUILL

The old woman leans across the typewriter, looking through the window at a sight she's seen a million times before. Except this time it's different. Why? Because most of the down-and-outers who pass this way only pull off the road to check a map or catch a few winks under the cottonwoods. But this one, this roughneck boy in the battered white pickup, he's been sitting there in that hot cab under the ferocious July sun for twenty minutes. Engine idling. Jawing to himself.

She sips tea from the mug that's gone cold at her elbow. It's not exactly highbrow entertainment, snooping on a man as he disintegrates in public, but out here where folks spend their Saturday nights bobbing for apples and beating their spouses with empty whisky bottles, it's nothing to sneeze at either. She watches a bit longer, then turns from the window, and puts her rheumy gray eyes to the typewriter, pecking out another line.

She probably ought to be suspicious, an old woman like her, living out here in the middle of the prairie with no one for miles to hear her cry out if she gets hurt, or come to her aid if some sudden misfortune were to descend upon her. But she isn't. Suspicious, that is. She's lived here her whole life and seen everything there is to see of human behavior, good, bad, and otherwise. So a scrawny young roughneck loitering in her parking lot, talking to thin air, hardly warrants a yawn much less something as grievous as a raised eyebrow. She's seventy-two-years-old, for Christ's sake, and everything she's ever believed sacred or held dear was stolen from her or stomped to bits by her father long, long ago.

She smiles, lips curling with the bitterness of half-realized revenge. Her daddy, Tom Ellis, would have boiled over if he saw her here, frittering away the day at the keyboard when she should've been setting tables. Or hustling orders. *There's your goddamned reason the place is suckin' wind*, he'd have shouted, stabbing at the air with his finger. *You've been sittin' on your dead ass all day, shirkin' the chores!*

Yeah, old Daddy would have blown his top, for sure, seeing her like this, hunched over the typewriter, *tap, tap, tap*. He'd have kicked and bitched like a mule, demanding she quit "pretending" she was a goddamned writer and get back to the goddamned honest work of looking after his café. That, or taste the back of his hand. But he was dead, Daddy was—stone dead some forty years now—and the café, rest its tired old soul, wasn't far behind. Condemned, as it had been, to slow starvation the year the Wyoming DOT built the interstate down in Rawlins that siphoned off all the tourists.

She reaches the end of the line and spanks the carriage return, glancing out the window for another quick look-see. The boy's still talking to himself, muttering up a storm, and looking every inch the lost sheep she's certain he must be. Oh, how the prairie could bring a man to Jesus! She shakes her head. She's known many a preacher who'd have loved to meet up with a young colt like the roughneck boy. Fella who'd already been green broke by the destitute ways of the prairie.

She chuckles, though not unkindly, as she watches him carry on, making strange gestures the shapes of which grow or shrink depending on whether he's agreeing or disagreeing with the other, more private self he's talking to. *Poor boy*, she thinks. *Poor, poor boy.*

The highway out front was once the main route to Yellowstone. The central spur in the old Atlantic–Yellowstone–Pacific. It was the only passable road that went from one end of Wyoming to the other, and anybody with an automobile and a mind to take in the geysers and paint pots had no choice but to traverse it.

The road was marked with big yellow stones in those early days, the initials AYP crudely stenciled on their granite faces. But whatever the massive rocks added to that desolate landscape, it was her daddy's café—this sad little dump of a restaurant—that supplied the true local color to outsiders from the east. The Bright Spot was, unlike the ghost it had become, a bustling stopover for tourists, tour busses and fancy motorcars. A cash cow in a country better suited to ornery, slat-ribbed steers.

But it was I-80 that had done the café in. The year the big four-lane freeway was opened to travelers, the Bright Spot's once overflowing till went as dry as a flatland creek, and the tourists the old woman's business depended on drifted south along with all the money.

She wishes now she'd never been on the television talk show. Until she'd run off to New York, she'd been so used to the nothing Daddy had left her, so conditioned to believing the gate to the outside world had been closed and locked, she'd stopped bothering to rattle the latch. Made peace with her miserable little life. The café's sad slide into oblivion. Then along came J. S. Stockton with his article in *The Wall Street Journal*—the one he scribbled down after spending an hour with her at the lunch counter last summer, believing he understood what it was to spend your life living alone on the prairie—and everything changed. Fast. First for the better, then for the worse.

Within a week of the story's coming out, she was contacted by a studio producer who told her he'd read the piece with great delight, and wished to make her a guest on his program.

"Why?" she asked, pressing the phone to her good ear.

"Because we've never had anyone like you before," he said. "You live alone on the range. You write romance stories. It's straight out of the movies, Betty, and I won't let you say no."

Two weeks later, she stepped out of a cab onto the streets of the city and found herself in a whole different world. Only it didn't take the skyline to impress her. One invigorating draught of the stinking metropolitan air and she was there. A believer. New York was everything Daddy had warned her it was—and more—and as she breathed it in, she cursed him for everything he'd done to keep it from her.

She looks down at the half-filled sheet of paper. Words stumbling over themselves. She hasn't strung together two good sentences in more than six months, and her imagination feels as cold and dead as winter. She lays her fingers on the keys, but gives up without a fight. Sighs and wanders over to the kettle on the stove.

Daddy would have disapproved of her running off to New York. He'd have shouted at the top of his lungs, calling her vain and irresponsible. Stupid, letting business slip away like that, as if you could tap paying customers from a spigot whenever you wanted.

You ain't nothin' special, little darlin', she could hear him bellow. *You just think you are! You thought they'd care about your silly little stories, dint you? But you were wrong. You were only there so's they could sell soap. That, and have a little fun takin' you down a peg. Makin' fun of the little ol' country bumpkin who just fell off the turnip truck.*

She fixes her tea and shuffles back to the desk. Looks out the window and sees the roughneck boy has finally shut off the engine.

She'd been working on a story the afternoon J. S. Stockton dropped in. He was on his way home from Jackson Hole where he'd been researching a lifestyle piece about the rich and famous. He'd driven up to the store in his rented Pontiac, hoping to fill up on gas, but after being greeted by three retired pumps—rusted, listing every which way on a concrete slab that was itself broken and crumbling—he decided to wander inside, and see if he couldn't scare up a bite of food instead.

"That the real deal?" he'd asked, poking his head in the door, hooking his thumb at the arch of flaking red paint in the window. *WORLD FAMOUS SAGEBRUSH HAM.*

The old woman had glanced up from the keyboard, and rested her arm on the chair back. "Wouldn't say it if it wasn't true."

Stockton paused a moment as if deciding whether or not to stay.

"Mind?" she said with a nod. "You're letting the flies in."

He smiled apologetically and stepped inside, the wooden door clattering shut behind him. He was tall, thin, and gangly, with legs just long enough to keep him one step ahead of trouble. Funny looking if you stared at him too long.

He glanced here and there, lifted his eyes to the menu board on the wall behind the counter, and adjusted his thick black glasses. It took him a good half minute before he ran his finger under the lip of his mustache and decided to order. "All right," he said, "I'm in." He turned to her with a pleasant face. "Can't pass up a sandwich with a name like that, can I?"

Stockton took a seat at the counter and made himself comfortable, and she could guess by the way he carried himself that he was a man who'd been everywhere. Everything about him looked relaxed, even-paced, and easy.

She fixed him a sandwich and poured them both a tall glass of lemonade, listening as he told her the story of his trip west. She was impressed by the way he spoke. By the way his narrative seemed to follow the strict outline he kept in his head. He said the "new" Jackson Hole reeked of money and celebrity. Even the air smelled rich. "You can't swing a dead cat out there," he told her, "without hitting a movie star or a big name sports figure or a television celebrity."

The ceiling fan beat back the afternoon heat—*whup, whup, whup*—and the radio chattered in the background.

"All the old ranches are gone. Bought up, carved up, turned into condos," he said. "The town's as swanky as Aspen—maybe more so, I don't know. Anyway, you wouldn't believe it if you saw it."

He had a soft voice, J. S. Stockton did, and a long chin that rightly or wrongly lent an air of scholarship to his face. When he spoke, the corners of his mouth hooked upward, losing themselves beneath the bristles of his mustache, and his narrow green eyes twinkled as if he were carrying a private joke in his back pocket.

After a while, he sat up, dusting his hands. "Okay," he said, "moment of truth, young lady." He set his half-eaten sandwich on the plate and gave a conspiratorial grin. "Is there any sagebrush in this 'world famous' sagebrush ham? Or is that just something you tell the greenhorns?"

"Sagebrush?" The old woman looked at him, forthright and unembarrassed. "God, no. Not a twig,"

Stockton seemed surprised. Disappointed, even. "Really? None at all?"

She shook her head, smiling.

"Why the name, then?"

"Why?" A mean, stuttering little laugh trembled across her lips. "Because Daddy wanted it that way, that's why. Whatever Daddy wanted, Daddy got. There wasn't anything ever started or finished here at the Bright Spot without Daddy's say-so. Including the names of things."

"Well it's a damned good bite," Stockton said, raising the sandwich to his eye and giving it an admiring nod. "I can't recall eating a sandwich this good. Ever."

The roughneck boy, he's climbed down out of the cab and popped the pickup's hood. When it yawns open, he hauls up and stands on the bumper, bending over the engine. Jiggling wires as if he's looking for a faulty connection. Is he dangerous, she wonders? Something to worry about? Or does he just look that way, poised over the open gears there, like a rodeo circuit rider fixing to mount a bull? She can't decide. She figures it's probably a bit of both, the richer of each extreme depending on the nature of the narrative you place him in.

He hops down and straightens himself in one smooth motion, frowning, looking some-kind-of-broken-hearted-sad in his faded jeans and worn-out pearl-button shirt. A loser's loser. Your dyed-in-the-wool down and outer, if she's ever laid eyes on one. She follows the movement of his hand as his fingers find their way into the breast pocket of his shirt and come back with a mangled cigarette, watching as he smoothes the thing between his thumb and forefinger. Lights it with a stick match scraped across the sole of his boot.

"Secret?"

"Yeah," Stockton pressed. "If it's not sagebrush, what is it? Some special kind of ham? There's something different about it, I know that. I just can't put my finger on what it is."

The old woman pointed an unpainted fingernail at a pendant dangling from the cash register. A salesman's sample. Tiny plastic doodad, shaped like a ham, hanging from a keychain. On its side, imprinted in little gold letters were the words, "Swift's Premium."

"It's store bought?" Stockton shook his head, smiling at having been fooled.

"Over in Casper."

He turned his eyes back to the sandwich, pursing his lips as if perhaps he didn't believe her.

"In the old days, they came out of Omaha," the old woman said. "Shipped here in big wooden reefers on the Union Pacific. We'd pick them up at the train station platform, and Daddy would bring them home and simmer them out back in big kettles on a kerosene stove."

"That's it?" Stockton said. "That's the secret?"

The old woman shrugged as if to say, what do you want? Daddy's only real secret, she told him—and for the record, they were talking *hams* here—was to slice the meat thin after the ham had cooled in the icebox. That, and wrap up the cuts in wax paper before setting them out on a graniteware platter.

Stockton took off his glasses and cleaned them with his shirttail, asking her how it was she could be so cavalier, giving away family secrets.

The old woman snorted, nodding at the window, prairie stretching from one end of the horizon to the other. "Not sure it makes much difference, anymore. Do you?"

Her eyes follow the roughneck boy's hands as he takes another drag on the cigarette and blows smoke at the sky. He's leaning on the fender now, roguish, boot jacked against the front tire, Tom Mix style, and she has to hand it to him, whatever he's doing, he's got a fine way of going about it.

Old Daddy, he doled out lies the way a felon passes bad checks. Made up stories left and right to keep her from running off with a fella like the roughneck here. He lied and bullied and filled her with the guilt of an entire congregation to keep her down where she was, in fearful ignorance of the world outside. He'd put his arm around her shoulder and smile, just like the Devil himself, and tell her the

only true salvation lay in the virtue of loyalty—the blessed simplic-
ity of family—and because she was young, she'd believed him.

Stockton dawdled over his lemonade, telling her it was his first
time in Wyoming. Until now, he'd only been west of Chicago
once—to Colorado, to cover the Stock Show in Denver. He confessed that, while the state had a stark beauty to it, the prospect of
living on the prairie would have tested his sanity. He didn't know
how she could live alone out here, in a place so cruel and empty.
So desolate.

She'd offered him more lemonade, and he'd pushed his glass
forward along the counter. She told him she was a writer herself—
penning short stories some twenty-odd years now—and that there
were days when the typewriter had been her only sanctuary. Her
one steady friend. Without it, she admitted with faraway eyes, she'd
have been tempted to slit her own throat.

Stockton did not laugh as she'd expected he might when she'd
offered up this confession. Rather, he straightened himself on his
stool, and with a respectful nod asked where she'd been published.
She reeled off two or three magazines. Rags she was certain he'd
never heard of. But he pretended to be impressed all the same.
Romances, you say? He pursed his lips. *Is that right?* He'd have
never guessed, he said, because, no offense, but this didn't seem the
kind of soil from which love stories sprang.

She'd gone to the desk, rummaged, and returned with a magazine, which she presented to Stockton. He thumbed it with interest,
inquiring in a professional tone after the inspiration for her characters, and she told him some of what he wanted to know, but not
all. Daddy, who had ruined her life with his ham-handed doings—
and who had always been the richest source of her material—went
uncredited. She knew it was a petty bit of revenge to omit his name
from the mix, but on the outside chance the old SOB could hear her
talking this far from hell, she didn't want to give him any cause for
feeling flattered.

"You're all that's left, then?" Stockton said.

"Just me. The last of the Mohicans."

"No husband?"

She shook her head.

"No kids?"

She looked at him, the light fading from her face. "No."

The roughneck boy takes one last puff on his cigarette before dropping the butt in the gravel and crushing it under his boot heel. When he's done, he walks back to the front bumper, grabs the yawning metal hood by its lip, and slams it shut.

Stockton drank his lemonade and told her he'd spent the Fourth of July in Town Square Park in Jackson, listening to chamber music and waiting for the evening's fireworks display. He said he'd bought himself a picnic lunch and a bottle of white wine, and staked out a nice place under the trees where the Tetons loomed as a backdrop to the night's festivities.

"Were they good? The fireworks?"

"Yes, of course. Just what you'd expect," he told her. "They were spectacular." He raised his chin. "What about you? What does the only person in a one-horse town do to celebrate Independence Day?"

The old woman shuffled over to the pastry case to fetch him a slice of peach pie. She stopped, knife in hand, and turned with a dismayed smile, telling him she'd spent the Fourth of July observing an old family ritual.

"Which was?"

She put the pie on a thick white plate and set it on the counter in front of him. "Burning the flags."

Stockton cocked his head and squinted.

"I burnt the old flags," she said, handing him a fork. "It's what we did every Fourth of July." She told him they used to stand on the side of the highway at dusk—she and her folks—watching the flames from the burning flags tear sad and ragged in the wind while Daddy blew taps on a military bugle.

"Daddy was postmaster," she explained.

"I see."

"It was his job to dispose of the flags in a dignified manner. So we saved them for the Fourth. It seemed like the natural thing to do."

Stockton raised his glass of lemonade and sipped.

"Daddy was the first postmaster of Hiland," the old woman said. "Then my mother. Then me." She picked up a fork, stealing a bite of his pie. "The job doesn't pay much of anything, but the government makes sure you're flush with flags." She gave her head a sideways jog, chewing as she talked. "I've got a whole box sitting in the back room. Every last one waiting its turn to be strung up and crucified by a hard Wyoming wind."

Stockton pointed with his fork. "Why am I not hearing any nostalgia in your voice?"

"Should you?"

"I don't know. Should I?"

She looked at him without blinking.

"The way you talk," he said, "your family sounds like a Norman Rockwell painting. Hell, the three of you out there on the highway? Standing in the starlight with your hands over your hearts? It gives me goose bumps just thinking about it."

The old woman turned her head, curiously. Pinching her shoulders, she stole another bite of his pie. She didn't say it to Stockton, but while he was out there in Jackson Hole, snacking on a baked croissant and waiting for fireworks, she was here in hell, standing on the shoulder of a ghost-town highway, as alone as a ghost herself, carrying out a backward tradition authored by a man whose sole vision in life was to see her in chains.

"Mr. Stockton," she'd said, "I suppose I've never thought of Independence Day the way most folks do."

Daddy, he'd insisted on knowing this store of his—this café and gas station he'd built from nothing—would not pass back into nothing when he was gone. But that sort of immortality could only be found in a son. A male heir who could not only fill his shoes, but fulfill his private laws of primogeniture. So, to ensure the Bright Spot would live on forever, cared for by a hand-chosen (and therefore trustworthy) successor, he solicited the Lord with solemn promises, and undertook a feverish campaign of nightly sex against the old woman's mother.

It took months, but come winter the following year, Heaven rewarded his patience.

"I've got me an heir!" he was said to have shouted the day the old woman was born. "I finally got me an heir!"

The old woman's mother had told her that Daddy had kicked up his heels and done a jig around the parlor when he received the news. But later, when the midwife led him into the bedroom to show him the fruit of his loins, he'd looked down in horror and shrieked, "My God! This child's been borned without a peacemaker!"

It was said it took Daddy two days in the company of a gallon jug to wash the taste of betrayal from his mouth, and that even the terrible, head-splitting hangover that followed had not been enough to sober him.

"Look," he told the old woman's mother, "this ain't the first time I've been double-crossed, and I expect it won't be the last, neither. But, goddamnit, Etta, I'm playin' me the hand I was dealt. I see no point withholdin' the pleasures of manhood from this child simply because she's a girl. That said, I aim to teach her everything I know—from huntin' and fishin' to fixin' cars and playin' baseball. Hell," he'd added, hooking his thumbs in the straps of his overalls. "If it'll do her any good, I'll teach her fistfightin', too!"

These were all promises Daddy kept. He was diligent in seeing she grew up in dungarees and brogans, that she wore her curly black hair cropped like a boy's, and that she learned to curse, shoot, and cheat at cards as well as the next man. It was a desperate dream her father had, but in the end, the old woman didn't disappoint. She became the son he'd always wanted.

She leans forward over the typewriter, blinking, rubbing her eyes. The roughneck boy, he's strolling toward the restaurant now, hat punched low on his head, and when she sees the bundled denim jacket under his arm, she raises her chin, high and curious, and a thin furrow of wrinkles crawls across her brow.

Pushing back from the desk she puts on her shopkeeper's face. When the screen door opens, groaning on its rusty hinges, and the boy's sorrowful-looking boots announce themselves on the wooden floor, she smiles and offers him a spritely good morning.

"Morning," he says back.

"Saw you sitting out there." She gestures at the window. "Was wondering if you if you were going to come in."

The boy looks at her strangely. As if he's comparing what he sees before him to a snapshot he's carried too long in his wallet.

"Truck alright?" she asks. "You were fiddling with those engine wires something fierce."

He raises his eyes to the overhead fan, blades chugging in lazy circles, then lowers them to the floor where slow-turning shadows wheel across the planks. "Truck's fine."

Bailing wire holds the boy's boots together, and his pearl-button shirt appears to cling to his back by the miracle of prayer alone. The old woman considers his raggedy ass and stops to wince at the condition of his eyes. A roadmap of capillaries stretches from one end of his corneas to the other.

Daddy would have hated this boy, she thinks. He'd have seen the glint in his roughneck eyes and known right off he was the sort who whisked bored young girls off their feet. Filled their heads with lies and enticed them into lonesome marriages that ended in heartbreak. Daddy would have served him a slice of pie, yes—laughing and jawing the whole time—but he'd have hated the boy. Even as he shook him down for his last nickel.

The roughneck swings his leg over a chrome stool at the counter and lays his bundled jacket on the Formica, taking note of the pies in the pastry case, the soda pop in the refrigerator, bottles arranged like a pretty glass rainbow.

"You got coffee?"

"I can make some."

"You ain't got any just sitting around? In the pot?"

A black-and-white photograph of Daddy—square-jawed, neck pinched in a high-collar shirt—hangs on the back wall from a single nail. He's staring at her with a pair of dark, accusatory eyes. There should always be coffee on the burner. She knows that.

"You in a hurry?"

"Might be."

"Well, it won't take but a minute. Settle in, and let me brew you some, fresh."

The roughneck taps the counter with his grease-stained fingers and draws the bundled jacket closer to his elbow. "All right," he says with a sigh, sliding his keys across the Formica. "If it ain't too much trouble."

His voice sounds tired, heavy with the freight of road dust and nicotine and too much sun, and the longer she studies him the sorrier she feels. He's got the look of a weary old dog, fresh out of tricks, new and otherwise. A man beaten down in a tug of shirt-sleeves between good and evil. Angel on one shoulder, devil on the other.

"Come far?" she asks, scooping coffee into the paper filter.

"Far?" He glances her way and nods. "Yeah. Far enough, I guess. Got a long road ahead, anyway." He points a lazy finger at the menu board as she sets the coffee to brew. "What's good up there?"

She leans sideways, scouring the list of dishes. "I like the pie," she says. "It's fresh."

"Peach?"

"Peach and apple both."

He taps his fingers, considering the choices, and takes a long unhurried glance out the window.

"They're both good," the old woman says, thinking she might just cut him a two-for-one deal. "I'll fix you one of each. You can eat a slice here, and take the other with you for later."

The coffeemaker gurgles, and she turns to check the brew. When she winds back around, she's staring at a blue steel .38 Colt revolver.

"I ain't gonna hurt you," the roughneck boy says right off, as if meaning to set ground rules they can both work with. "I just want your money."

The old woman stands there, frozen.

"Where's the safe?"

She looks up from the gun. "Safe?"

"I seen you on TV," he says. "On that afternoon talk show. One with the old guy with the white hair. You're the writer lady." He grins, nervously, and makes a clicking noise with his tongue. "You look a little different. But you're her all right."

She stares at him, saying nothing.

He chuckles, and tells her, "Now, come on. Where is it? Where you got the money hid? I know it's here. Where famous goes, rich follows, ain't that so? Show me the safe."

It's silly what she's thinking, and if she told anybody they'd probably say she ought to be fitted for a straightjacket. But the old woman's mind has gotten itself tangled in the words *famous writer lady*, and because the roughneck boy recognizes her—because he remembered seeing her on TV—she can't help it. She finds herself wanting to like him. Even help him if she can.

"Safe's over there," she says, pointing to the US postal station against the back wall. "But you don't want to go fooling with that thing."

The boy's eyes follow the end of her stubby finger. The postal station is nothing but a four-foot-wide polished oak facade with a barred teller's window, the words *US Mail* stenciled on the marquis. "Why not?"

She blushes, too embarrassed to say. One look inside the safe and he'll see she's as without money as she is talent.

"Because it belongs to the federal government," she tells him, using the only version of the truth she's willing to part with. "It's property of the US Postal Department."

"So?"

"So you'll be committing a federal offense."

The roughneck boy lets out a good hearty laugh when he hears this. "The hell." His eyes take a quick turn around the room, and he gets up on his tiptoes and cranes his neck in the direction of the window. "Well," he says, "just go on and open it, anyway. If it takes 'em as long to hunt me down as it does for 'em to deliver my mail, I expect I'll be long gone."

"You're looking at a felony," she says, trying to be helpful, adding, "I'm not trying to discourage you. I just want you to know the score."

"Open it."

She tells him all right, suit yourself, you've been warned, and shuffles to the safe where she creaks to one knee and begins working the combination. "I'm a federal employee," she says. "They'll make a big deal of you pointing a gun at me."

The roughneck boy taps her head, lightly with the pistol barrel. "Just shut up, and do what I say."

Reluctantly, she does what he tells her, and when the safe clicks open, she swings back the metal door and reveals a solitary canvas sack, mostly empty, cinched at the neck with a braided drawstring. She holds the sack up, and he motions, with a jerk of his head, and tells her to put it on the counter.

"Now go back and close up the strongbox," he orders her, stealing another glance at the window.

She does.

The roughneck boy undoes the drawstring on the sack and gives the bag a little shake. Peers inside, blinks twice, and sighs. "Hardly worth the time, was it?" He smiles. "Just like that interview you give that guy on TV. A big fat joke."

The old woman stops what she's doing and looks up at him as if he's committed some bitter sacrilege. Broken some sacred trust between them, and when the safe door swings shut behind her small, determined hand, the goodwill she'd felt is locked away inside it.

The roughneck wags the pistol lazily in the direction of the cash register at the front of the store. "What do we got in the till, huh? Let's have that, too. Gotta be something in this joint worth stealin'."

She rises slowly to her feet and smoothes her apron.

"Quick now," he says, pushing the barrel of his pistol against her back. "Real quick."

He marches her to the cash register where he orders her to empty the tray's contents onto the glass countertop. Nice neat piles, no monkey business. Start with the coins, he tells her, but when loose change begins to prove cumbersome, he abandons the idea and says just stick with the paper.

The old woman lays out the whole miserable sum—thirty-two dollars—and the boy sneers at the meager take while wasting no time snatching up the loose bills and stuffing them into his pocket.

"Mighty sorry about the inconvenience," he says when he's finished. "But I reckon I need it more than you. Little as it is."

The old woman's eyes follow his hand as he pushes the revolver into the waistband of his jeans.

"You musta been young once," he says with a less-than-penitent smile. "I reckon you remember what it was like being broke."

He backs up to the lunch counter, yanks his denim jacket free, and does a hurried quickstep to the front door. Exiting, he turns briefly and touches the brim of his hat. The screen door clatters shut behind him and silence reclaims the restaurant.

The old woman stands there, staring, looking at the nothing she's been left with—*again*. Yet when the sound of the truck door opening and closing reaches her ears, a vindictive little smile turns up the corners of her mouth. Moving to the window, she watches the boy pat his shirt pockets and turn down the sun visor, scouring the cab for the thing he'll never find.

He rifles the door pockets and console. Runs his fingers along the floorboard, his expression darkening with each pass of the hand. Then, in a moment of angry recognition it hits him, what she's done, the thieving, underhanded old crow, and his eyes narrow and fly back to the restaurant where they meet hers, gloating, in the dusty glass of the window pane.

The old woman counts three seconds between the time the boy realizes he's been double-crossed, and the moment he hops down out of the cab and sprints back to the restaurant.

The rickety wooden door bangs open and suddenly he's standing there, staring at her, fuming. "Where are they?" he huffs, his breath coming in short hard bursts. "Where'd you put the keys?"

She points to the postmaster's station. "They're in the safe."

He blows out a relieved sigh. Catches his breath, and draws the pistol from his waistband, waving it at her. "Go *get* 'em."

The old woman stays where she is.

"You hear me?" the roughneck boy shouts. "I said go get 'em!"

She shakes her head no, and he raises the pistol and sets his teeth and snarls like a dog. But she still doesn't budge.

"Shoshone's thirty miles west," she says defiantly. "Powder River's thirty miles east. North and south, there's nothing but open range. You've got nowhere to run, Slim."

"Get me the keys."

"I won't, no."

He curls his finger around the trigger, but the old woman only scoffs at him. She won't be bullied, she says. Her daddy schooled her in the ways of willow switches and belt buckles and worse, and if the boy hasn't already noticed, she's seventy-two-years-old and long past a fear of dying.

The roughneck, he takes a menacing step. But it's all bluff, and the old woman knows it. "When I was nineteen," she says, "my daddy broke my jaw. I went behind his back and took a job with the public schools down in Georgia, and he beat me for it. My bag was packed. I had a train ticket on a Pullman, and I was as good as gone. But I had to give it up. Know why? Because you can't teach school with your mouth wired shut."

She raises her chin, inviting him to strike her. Daring him. "You can do to me what you like, but you're never getting those keys."

The roughneck boy's eyes scurry around the room as if he might find what he's looking for hiding in some dark corner of the café. He aims the pistol at her, retracts it, aims it again. His hands go twitchy, and he glances at the front window.

"I'll make you a deal," the old woman says.

"What?"

"I'll make you a deal."

"Deal? What kinda deal?"

"I'll trade you the keys for the pistol."

The roughneck boy, his shoulders tremble and he breaks into a near-hysterical laugh. "You crazy old bat!" He raises his arm as if this time he does mean to strike her. "Who do you think you're talking to, anyway? Do I look like a fool? Get me the damned keys before you get hurt."

She reminds him again he has nowhere to run. He can trust her on this, she says, because if there had been any way to escape this god-awful place, she'd have found it years ago. This was hell, she told him. The City of Dis. Once put here, you were here for good.

The roughneck boy, he just looks at her.

"Give me the gun," she says.

"Go piss up a rope."

She shakes her head as if she sympathizes with his dilemma. "It's the only thing that's going to get you out of here," she says. "I'll lock it in the safe, and give you the keys in return. We'll call it even."

The boy's eyes do a scared little dance while pinpricks of sweat break across his forehead. Outside, away in the long tall distance, a tanker engine rumbles, and when he hears it the expression on his face goes hard and desperate.

"It's the only way," the old woman says.

The roughneck boy gathers himself and, sneering, puts up one last front. Store-bought bravado. "Hell it is," he says with a sweep of the arm. "I can walk out of here right now if I want to. I still got a thumb, ain't I? I can hitch a ride right out of the state."

"From who?" she says. "Look at you. You'd be out there for a week, waiting for someone to stop." She takes him by the shirtsleeve. "The gun's nothing," she says in a small voice. "The money's nothing. Don't let your pride send to you to that terrible hole of a prison in Rawlins. It's the keys you want."

The roughneck boy, he yanks free at this and takes a step back. His eyes fleeing to the door.

"If you leave the pickup here," she warns, "they'll trace the registration. They'll know who you are inside an hour. They'll take you for a boy who hurts old women, and when they do, they'll be looking to give back in kind."

The rumbling of the approaching tanker shakes the air, rattling the window panes.

"The keys," the old woman pleads. "It's the only way."

An air horn peels and the boy wheels to see the lumbering rig fly past the window, dragging its shadow down the road behind it. When he turns back, the old woman is standing before him with her hand out, palm turned upward.

"It'll be all right," she says. "I promise."

The boy looks deep into her old woman's eyes, then snares one last fleeting glance at the window at the front of the store. He slaps the pistol against her palm. Laughing. "Here," he says indignantly, "Take the son of a bitch. I don't care."

They stand in silence, each staring into the other's eyes. Daddy, he watched from the picture frame on the wall. The old woman could feel him, grinning. Proud of his work. Proud of the thing he'd created. Proud to be vindicated of the aspersions cast upon his character. Yes, yes, he'd broken her goddamned jaw. But look! Couldn't she see? Without a beating or two—without him teaching her the vagrant ways of the world—she'd have squandered her whole life, living in books. Or surrendered herself to a worthless husband, or both, and never lived to see this, the moment of her triumph.

She lowers her eyes and turns the pistol in her hand, thumbing open the breech, studying the load. Muscle-memory looks after the rest. With a quick roll of her wrist—just like Daddy had taught her in her tomboy youth—the cylinder snaps shut with a deep, rich, satisfying click.

She points the pistol at the boy. "Turn out your pockets."

"What?"

"Turn out your pockets."

"Why?"

"Because I said so."

The roughneck stammers, working up a chest full of righteous bluster. But before he can manage a single word, she fires a shot across his shoulder.

The photograph on the back wall explodes in the deafening blast, glass face shattering, frame splintering into a sad pile on the floor. Daddy? He's left staring at the tin ceiling, a hole parting the hair on his head.

She looks at the boy with lightless eyes. He's in a heap, five feet in front of her, groveling, arms tangled around his frightened head. He'd dropped to the floor so hard and fast when the gun went off, he'd knocked his own hat to the ground. Sent it rolling under the table where it sits upturned on its crown.

A wisp of smoke curls upward from the pistol barrel, rising toward the tin ceiling. But the old woman doesn't pay it any mind. She's staring at the cowering boy, studying him as if he were a lizard that had just scurried in off the prairie.

"Fetch your lid," she says soberly, pointing the .38 at his hat. "I like you better with it on."

He quickly does as he's told, jamming the hat on his head and letting his hands fall instantly to his sides.

"There," she says. "That's better."

She tells him again to empty his pockets, and this time he does, no arguing, producing a three dollar pocket watch and, along with the greenbacks from the till, forty-seven cents in change.

The old woman palms the watch, bringing it close to her pale, cataract-ridden eyes. Stares at it, closely, as if the image behind the crystal bears witness to some grim reckoning.

"Time does funny things to people," she says, turning the piece in her palm. "Wicked things." She returns the watch to the table and raises her head. "How old are you?"

The roughneck's eyes are tracking the bore of the weaving pistol barrel.

"Well?" She thumbs back the hammer.

"Twenty . . . four."

She nods, eyes going strangely distant. "I remember twenty-four." She looks past his shoulder to the old Royal typewriter sitting on the desk. "I was a wild one, just like you. Daddy tried to beat it out of me, but he didn't have any luck."

The room is deathly quiet.

She speaks from the distance of vaporous memory.

"Old Daddy, he ran this place like a despot," she says. "I swore I'd never be like him. But look, here I am! Setting policy with a six-gun."

Her bottom lip begins to quiver, but she wrestles it into submission. Raises the pistol and aims it at the blister of shattered plaster on the wall. The place where the black-and-white photo of Daddy used to hang. She aims, thumbs back the hammer, un-thumbs it, and lets go a dreadful sigh.

"You promised me the keys."

She passes the roughneck boy a quick look, a cauterizing stare.

"We got us a deal," he says. "Remember?"

She says nothing, backing her way to the front door with the Colt trained on his chest. She shuts the door and sets the deadbolt.

"My eyes aren't so good anymore," she says, blinking. "But even so, I can usually see trouble a mile off." She scratches the side of her head with the pistol barrel, points it again, and says, "So how come I never saw it with you, I wonder?"

The roughneck boy, he looks at her like she's a crazy woman.

She lowers the gun and shakes it at him. "Was it those eyes made me look the other way?" Reaching behind her back, she turns the paper sign in the window so it reads CLOSED. "That smile?" She wags the gun. "You're a good-looking fella. You know that?"

The roughneck's eyes take off on a wild chase around the room as if searching for a place to hide.

The old woman circles him, slowly, raising and lowering the .38. "I spent the better part of my life waiting for a nice-looking boy like you to walk through my door. But now—now when it finally happens—it's not because you want to sweep me off my feet, but because you want to *rob* me."

She pulls out a chair. Sits and rests the butt of the pistol on the tabletop. It occurs to her she's been robbed by one man or another most of her life. Hell, she'd even robbed from herself back in the day when Daddy had convinced her she was boy.

"You know what I'd do if a character like you showed up in one of my stories?" she says.

The roughneck stares at the loaded pistol.

"Well, how about this?" she says, voice drifting. A thoughtful look weighing on her brow. "I wouldn't throw you out. No, I wouldn't. I'd hang on to you, see if I couldn't work you in one way or another."

The roughneck, his hands begin to tremble now, and he shoves them in his pockets and makes another plea for the keys. "Come on," he says, whining like a little boy that's been cheated out of a dime on a rigged bet. "You promised."

A cold look comes to her eyes. "Maybe I lied."

When the roughneck throws back his head and moans, the old woman just chuckles. "No," she says. "You're too damned interesting to crumple up and toss in the trash. What I'd do if you were to show up in one of my stories is, I'd trim you back some. Rearrange a few of those rough ends and give you a different style. One that would take you places."

The roughneck boy is still glancing around the room as if he's looking for someone or some*thing* to save him. But all that's there is the old woman, and the shot-up photograph lying in a heap on the floor.

She rises slowly from the table. "Move."

"Where to?"

"There." She points the gun at the arched doorway leading to the main living quarters.

"I want them keys," the boy frowns, taking a few hesitant steps. "You promised me my keys back."

"You'll get them."

"When?"

"When I'm good and ready."

She raises the pistol, and the young roughneck walks until he finds himself at a dead end in the back bedroom. There, he throws up his hands. "What's this? Huh? This supposed to be some kind of joke?"

The old woman centers the pistol on his chest and tells him to keep going.

"Goin'? Goin' where? There ain't nowhere left to go!"

"Go to the other side of the room."

He stalls, watching her. His raised hands begin to sag. "I want them keys, lady."

"I told you. You'll get them."

"When?"

"We're taking the scenic route," she says. "Get over there by the window. I want to see you in the light."

The room's small, cluttered with pictures of the old woman's family, every one of whom has locked eyes on her and the roughneck boy, staring at them with an odd mixture of suspicion and pity.

A small, quilted bed with a hand-carved headboard takes up most of the room. Next to it is an antique nightstand on which rests a lamp with a beaded shade. Beneath the shade rests a cluster of picture frames. Frames that hold the faces of ghosts.

"You have a girl?"

"What?"

"A girl," the old woman says. "A sweetheart."

The young roughneck shrugs. "I did . . . once."

"Did you love her?"

He looks at the old woman as if she's lost her mind. "What the hell is it to you?"

"What's her name?"

He stares.

"What's her *name*?"

She thumbs back the hammer.

"Braelyn."

The old woman's eyes relax their grip on him, and her head lists to one side, lips curling into a curious smile. She forms the girl's name out of the empty air, saying it twice under her breath. When she turns back to the roughneck, she says, "Why don't you close your eyes. Close them real tight and think about Braelyn."

"What for?"

She frowns. "So you can walk out of here with the same number of parts you walked in with."

He watches as she takes a seat on the edge of the bed.

She bites her bottom lip and smiles, hoping Daddy's seeing this. Hoping he's spinning like a top in his grave up there on the hill out back, the selfish old sonofabitch.

The roughneck boy puts out a hand as if to protest some un-named grievance, but the old woman stops him. Cold. "Another move," she says, resting her palm on the gun's hammer, "and I'll start subtracting."

The boy's body goes rigid, and he raises his hands higher in the air.

"Remember, Slim," she says, "If I decide to pull this trigger, the only thing anybody's ever going to ask, is, *How come you shot his pecker off first, Betty?*" An unexpected thought takes hold of the old woman when she says this, and her lips gloss over with a tempting smile. "Why, they'd probably invite me back on that TV show if I were to go and do something notorious like that," she says. "Don't you think? I suspect shooting you would make me doubly-famous. A regular desperado."

The young roughneck nods, making a reassuring gesture. "Go easy, lady. Real easy. I'm right here, doing just like you say."

"Are you thinking about your girl, Braelyn?"

"Yeah. Yes."

He's closed his eyes, but only half way, and the old woman knows he's bird-dogging her every move. But no matter. He can watch all he wants. She's got the drop on him, and they both know he isn't going anywhere. Not real soon, anyway.

"Can I have my keys? Please?"

The old woman reclines on one elbow, waves the .38 in a loose circle. "Not just yet. First," she says, beaming a dreamy, faraway smile, "imagine this here is your gal Braelyn's bedroom, and there's music playing in the parlor."

She nudges off one open-toed shoe and lets it fall to the floor with a *clop*. The other follows a breath later. "Pretend she's just lit a candle and put it on the nightstand." She sets to humming a creaky, old-time melody. "Pretend it's your first time together, and your heart's breaking to tell her something. Something big and powerful and important. What are you going to say?"

"What?"

"What are you going to tell her?"

The roughneck boy, he struggles, mightily, to produce an answer, but ends up throwing out his hands and begging. "This is stupid. You're the one what's making all this up. Why don't you tell me what I'm supposed to say?"

The old woman's eyes flash with rage. She clenches her teeth, and her tiny finger tightens around the trigger. "You'd best play along with me, Sugarfoot. I'm not in the mood to be trifled with."

The roughneck boy holds up his hands and tells her, *all right, all right, take it easy. Don't get your feathers ruffled.* He says he was only joking, and he thinks for a long miserable moment, and says, "I was gonna tell her—"

"Not *that* way!" The old woman clicks the hammer to a full cock and squares the black bore of the barrel on his crotch. "Say it like this," she instructs him with a vicious tinge of glee. "Say, 'honey . . . honey, I'm on fire for you.'"

The roughneck, he's sweating hard now, and though it's a hot summer day he's begun to tremble as if he's got himself a fever.

"Say it," she says.

He repeats the words, slowly and with great caution.

The old woman smiles. "I bet you'd look fine without that shirt on," she tells him, her voice all raspy and breaking. "Why don't you dance for me. Dance for me real nice and we'll see about those keys."

LET THIS CUP PASS FROM ME

CHARLES KOWALSKI

A crusader for truth and justice. Whenever people called me that, I never knew whether they meant it sarcastically, but I always tasted the rusty residue of irony on my tongue. Truth and justice? If I ever met the one, I would have to run away before it could tell me how often I've betrayed the other: how many murderers are free because of me, how many crimes have been committed by repeat offenders who would have been safely off the streets if I hadn't done my job so well.

What, then, was my crusade for? For the right of every human being, innocent or guilty, to life. My given name is George, and with every convict I saved from the gurney, I saw myself striking a blow against the bloated, bloodthirsty dragon called the Texas Department of Criminal Justice. Letting the great state of Texas know that it is not greater than God.

And so, as much as the arraignment of Michelle Rourke shocked the nation, I think I can safely say that no one was more astonished than I was.

*   *   *

Michelle Rourke walked into a Dallas police station one afternoon and confessed to the murder of her husband, Connor, the genial owner of the popular Shamrock and Bluebonnet pub, and a renowned teacher of Irish dance until a fall from a ladder left him quadriplegic. For the two years since then, she had been an exemplary caregiver—right up until the day she killed him.

According to the police report, she was completely calm, even cheerful, as she recounted serving him a tall glass of orange juice laced with vodka and tranquilizers, and then, once she was sure he was out cold, covering his head with a plastic bag for good measure.

She handed them the keys to her house, and they found exactly what she said they would: his body in bed, still warm, and the glass on the kitchen counter, unwashed, with her prints all over it and traces of the fatal cocktail at the bottom.

And when she finished giving her statement, said the officer who took it, she laughed. Long and hard, as if she were watching the funniest movie ever made.

*   *   *

When I first saw her at the Dallas County Jail, she smiled and greeted me as graciously as if she were welcoming me into her living room for tea. An occasional tremor in her hands was the only sign I saw that she was feeling at all nervous; her face was completely relaxed.

"Mrs. Rourke, I'm George Dismas. The court appointed me as your attorney."

"Thank you for coming, Mr. Dismas. I told them I didn't need a lawyer, but I suppose things will go more smoothly if we observe all the formalities. Due process and all that."

I tried to hide my dismay. She was one of those. An advocate for so-called "death with dignity," all set to go to prison and tout herself as a martyr for her cause. I put those people in the same category as the abortionists and executionists. As if there were any "dignity" in mortals arrogating the power that rightfully belonged to God alone. As if there were anything in that but shame.

If it was a prison term she wanted, the judgmental part of me would have been happy to oblige and let them slap her with a nice long one. But in my line of work, *Do not judge and you will not be judged, do not condemn and you will not be condemned,* was not an abstract philosophy; it was a practical necessity.

"Mrs. Rourke, if your husband asked you to help him end his life, we could try to have the charge reduced to aiding suicide. That's a state jail felony, six months to two years, and maybe a fine of up to . . ."

She cut me off with a vehement shake of her head. "Mr. Dismas, if you knew what kind of background my husband came from, you wouldn't suggest such a thing. Every man in his family could be a candidate for Pope, and every woman could probably persuade the College of Cardinals to make an exception and consider her too. If any of them even let the thought of suicide cross their minds, they'd have their confessors on speed-dial within a minute. No, let me be very clear: This was me. All me."

"Why, then?"

"Simply because I couldn't stand the thought of being cooped up in that house changing bedpans for the rest of his natural days. So I took out a life insurance policy for him, and when the paperwork came through, I put him out of my misery. That counts as murder in the hope of remuneration, doesn't it?"

The phrase stopped me short. It came straight from the Texas Penal Code, and it made the difference between murder and capital murder.

"Well," I said after a pause, "that usually means murder for hire, or taking out a contract on someone . . ."

"There was a woman last year, wasn't there?" she interrupted. "Suzanne something, executed for killing her husband for an insurance payout. There's your precedent."

Her words hit me like a bucket of ice. I wondered whether any defense attorney in the history of the profession had ever had to deal with a client like this one. And if not, then why did I, out of all the lawyers in the world, have to be the first?

"Mrs. Rourke, do you . . . do you *want* to be executed?"

She smiled and nodded. "Yes, please. And I rely on you, as my attorney, to make sure that happens."

"Why, in Heaven's name?"

She burst out laughing.

She turned her face away and put up a hand to hide it. It took a full minute for her laughter to subside enough for her to take a few deep breaths, only to launch into another fit. After several attempts, she finally regained enough composure to speak again.

"It's not your duty to know why, is it, Mr. Dismas? It's your duty to—how does it go?—zealously represent me. And if I don't get the death sentence, I might just file a Sixth Amendment appeal for ineffective assistance of counsel."

*   *   *

I sat in my office later that evening, trying to divine what was going on inside Michelle Rourke's mind. My gaze drifted to the wall, where a framed verse from Ezekiel hung: *As surely as I live, declares the Sovereign Lord, I take no pleasure in the death of the wicked, but rather that they turn from their ways and live.*

The life-insurance policy smelled like a red herring. A guaranteed-issue policy, the only kind she would likely have been able to get for her quadriplegic husband, would pay only a fraction of its promised benefits if he died within the first few years. If financial gain really was her motive, why not wait until she could claim the full amount? And what use would she have for the money anyway, if she planned to put herself on death row right afterwards?

In any event, the next step was clear: arrange a competency hearing and have her declared legally insane. If she wanted to be executed, then she was obviously irrational, and therefore should not be executed.

Her laughter, I thought, must hold a clue. The officer who took her statement had seemed to regard it as the gloat of a triumphant villain, but to my eyes, she looked more like a schoolgirl trying valiantly but vainly to suppress a fit of the giggles. Surely it was a sign of some kind of psychological disorder.

It took only a few clicks of the mouse to find what I was looking for. *Pseudobulbar affect (PBA) refers to sudden, uncontrollable fits of laughing or crying, far out of proportion to the patient's actual emotional state, and sometimes even contrary to it.*

I scrolled down to look for causes. As soon as I read the list, an electric current ran through my scalp.

Michelle Rourke was perfectly sane. It was the world around her that had gone mad.

*   *   *

When I visited her on the eve of her arraignment, she greeted me as cheerfully as before. "Good afternoon, Mr. Dismas. Have you found a way to expedite my execution?"

I took a seat and faced her squarely. "Mrs. Rourke, how long have you known about your condition?"

Her coy smile slipped, and a guarded edge crept into her voice. "What condition do you mean?"

"You tell me. Is it a brain tumor? Or MS?"

Her shoulders slumped in the defeated manner of a suspect cornered in an interrogation.

"After the accident," she said, "my husband completely lost the will to live. Dancing was the only thing that ever mattered to him; being trapped in an immobile body was worse than a hundred deaths for him. Never a day went by without him talking about how he just wanted to go to sleep and never wake up. I kept hoping that he would eventually come to terms with it, and tried to give him a reason to want to go on living. But after hearing the same thing every day for a year, I finally asked him, 'Do you really mean that? Because if you do, we could always go to Oregon . . .'

"That was the first time, since the accident, that I heard anything remotely like a laugh out of him. 'I can't even get up to take a shite; how the hell were you planning to get me to Oregon? And besides, can you imagine what it would do to my parents if they heard that their son chose to end his life? That his body couldn't be buried in consecrated ground, and his soul couldn't go to heaven? No, there's nothing for it but to stay the course, damn it all to hell.'

"So I soldiered on, giving him the best care I could. But starting around last month, I began to find myself tripping over carpets, and dropping things when I tried to cook. Connor and I together had won the Irish Dance World Championships the year before his accident, Mr. Dismas. *Clumsy* is the last word anyone would use to describe me. But it started happening more and more often, so I finally went and saw a doctor."

She straightened up and cleared her throat, as though preparing for a dramatic recitation. "Amyotrophic lateral sclerosis. I can pronounce it perfectly; aren't you impressed? But of course, that didn't make it any easier to say to Connor. The closest I came was one day when we saw something on the news about it, and I asked him: 'What would you do if I came down with a degenerative disease like that?' He said: 'Don't be saying such a thing. Don't even be thinking it.' But I kept pressing him until he answered: 'Then I really and truly would ask you to slip a Mickey Finn into my milkshake. The Church be damned.'"

My heart went out to her, and I struggled to keep it from showing in my face as pity. But whatever appeared there instead must have looked like judgment, for she slammed her hand on the table and demanded: "What would you rather I'd done, Mr. Dismas? What would the State of Texas rather I'd done? What would the Holy Roman Catholic and Apostolic Church rather I'd done? Force him to go on watching from his bed as the body of his wife and caregiver slowly shut down? He was afraid that if he chose to die, his family would think he was in hell. I was more afraid that if he chose to live, I would *know* he was."

Once she had caught her breath, I asked the question that had been nagging at me the whole time. "Why did you go to the police?"

"You know something, Mr. Dismas? In Texas, there's one kind of injection that a doctor can't prescribe, but a judge can."

"A lethal one."

"Exactly. Try to buy or sell it, and you go to jail, but if you're already *in* jail, you can get it for free."

"But if all you wanted was to die, why drag the courts into it? Why gamble on their finding you guilty of capital murder, and then wait, maybe for years, for the sentence to be carried out? Wouldn't it have been easier just to mix enough of that cocktail for two?" *Easier for you and me both*, I added silently.

"Oh, yes. Clink our glasses, and slip away peacefully together? Of course, it was tempting—much more attractive than wasting away in prison while the governor and Lou Gehrig ran their slow-motion race for the privilege of killing me. But if Connor and I were found together with the same drugs in our blood, everyone would have thought it was a done deal between us. That would have defeated the whole purpose. There couldn't be the slightest suspicion that he was in on it."

"You couldn't have left a note?"

"Too risky. What if his family somehow didn't get it, or didn't believe it? They needed to see solid proof, on TV and in the papers, that our infallible courts had declared me a murderess and Connor an innocent victim. And if they want to console themselves by imagining me sizzling in hell, that's fine. The important thing is that in their eyes, Connor is now a martyr. He's assured a place in heaven."

There is no greater love than this, Our Lord had said, *than to lay down your life for those you love.* But even then, He must have realized that dying would be the easy part. It was the long walk to Calvary—the condemnation, the beatings and taunts, the fleeing backs of your most trusted friends—that would make the cross at the end come almost as a relief.

"Well, Mr. Dismas," she concluded, "you've heard my confession. Now, here's my last request." She leaned in and spoke in a confidential voice. "It goes without saying that everything I've just told you is under attorney-client privilege. As far as the world outside this room is concerned, I cold-bloodedly murdered the man who loved and trusted me more than anyone. I have forfeited my right to life. When they stick that needle into my vein, they will be doing the world a big favor. Whatever it takes to convince the judge of that, you say it. Understand?"

"Mrs. Rourke . . ."

"Mr. Dismas, this shouldn't be hard for you. This is *Texas*, for God's sake. More executions every year than the next five bloodiest states *combined*. If someone actually *wants* to join the party, surely there must be some way to get her an invitation."

*   *   *

I went home by way of church. At that hour, it was open but empty except for a few old ladies in black who seemed to be permanent fixtures. I walked down the aisle, genuflected, and took a place in the front pew. From where I knelt, I had a perfect view of the enormous crucifix hanging behind the altar.

The deeply etched lines in the brow, the mouth open in a grimace of agony, and the eyes turned to Heaven in a final plea made it clear which Gospel had inspired the sculptor. This was none of Luke's magnanimous Jesus, who scarcely seemed to feel the nails in his palms as he forgave his executioners, comforted the criminals crucified alongside him, and serenely commended his spirit into his Father's hands. It was not even the simple resignation of John's "It is finished." This was the raw, unvarnished, painfully human Jesus of Matthew and Mark, captured at the moment when the last breath left his body in an anguished cry of "My God, my God, why have you forsaken me?"

"Why?" I heard my own voice echo that one word of His, loading the monosyllable with a multitude of questions. "Why did it have to come to this? Why did this have to happen to You? And why, in Your name, does this have to be happening to me?"

The motionless lips spoke silently in reply.

What would you have done, George, if you had been there with Me? Handed Me a two-and-a-half-by-three-inch papyrus? "George Dismas, Esq., criminal defense attorney, specialist in crucifixion cases"? Do you suppose you could have persuaded Pontius Pilate to let Me walk away from this cross?

*   *   *

"State versus Michelle Rourke."

Michelle's steps faltered as they led her into the courtroom. The guards had to take a tight grip on her arms to steady her until they handed her off to me, in a mockery of a father giving his daughter away on her wedding day: *Congratulations, she's your problem now.*

"Mrs. Rourke," the judge intoned, "the grand jury has returned an indictment stating that, on or about the seventeenth of March, the crime of murder, in violation of section 19.02 of the Penal Code, a felony of the first degree, was committed by Michelle Rourke, who did knowingly, willfully, and unlawfully, with malice aforethought, cause the death of another human being, Connor Rourke. Is Mrs. Rourke prepared to enter a plea at this time?"

Michelle spoke before I could. "Guilty, Your Honor."

Her voice broke on the last syllable. Her lips trembled, and she blinked as her eyes filled with tears. She sat down, lay her head on the table, and launched into an uncontrollable fit of sobbing.

For a minute that felt like an eternity, her sobs drowned out even the sound of the judge's gavel as he vainly pounded it and called for order. Even I, who knew they could simply be another manifestation of her nervous disorder, felt them tearing at my heart.

When she finally recovered herself, the judge went on in a subdued voice. "The court accepts Mrs. Rourke's plea of guilty. We can proceed directly to sentencing. Does the State have any recommendation?"

The assistant district attorney took off his glasses and blinked several times. He had probably never seen anyone plead guilty at an arraignment, much less to a murder charge, and Michelle's tears had evidently touched a spot in his heart as well.

"Your Honor," he said, "considering that Mrs. Rourke voluntarily turned herself in and clearly feels remorse for her crime, the State believes that clemency is in order. We would be satisfied with something in the neighborhood of twenty to thirty years."

"Mr. Dismas?"

I glanced at Michelle. Her eyes met mine, and projected the same desperate plea I had seen from dozens of other clients, all terrified of facing the same fate that she was of being spared.

I took a deep breath, and traced a surreptitious cross on my tie.

"Your Honor," I said, "my client has confessed to premeditated murder in the hope of remuneration. I recommend that, under section 19.03 of the Penal Code, the charge against her be amended to capital murder."

Shocked murmurs broke out around the courtroom, and the judge pounded his gavel again, but the sounds touched my ears only faintly, as if from a great distance. All my attention was fixed on Michelle, as she leaned over and whispered:

"Thank you, Mr. Dismas. Thank you."

*   *   *

The judge granted the prosecutor's request for what they both thought was mercy. Michelle Rourke was sentenced to twenty years. She was out on parole in five, possibly because some prison official had read the vitriolic comments roiling about her on the Internet: "I have to spend every cent of my paycheck on medical bills, while my tax dollars go to provide free health care for that psycho bitch? Maybe when I finally go broke, I should kill someone too!"

By the time she was released, her arms and legs were practically useless. They had to push her out the prison gate in a wheelchair. She needed constant care, but unsurprisingly, no one came forward to provide it.

So I did. I spent as much time with her as I could every day and hired caregivers for the rest. After all, it wasn't as though I lacked for free time. Once I became known nationwide as the defense attorney who tried to send his own client to the gurney, you can imagine what happened to my legal career.

One evening, I sat by her side, spooning clear soup into her mouth. Her sense of taste was unimpaired, and she always seemed to be savoring every mouthful, even of plain chicken broth, as if she were in a Michelin-starred restaurant. She was acutely aware that the day would come soon when she could no longer swallow and would need a tube for nourishment. And not long after that, for oxygen.

"George," she said, "I have a favor to ask."

"Sure."

As soon as the word was out of my mouth, I was afraid she would ask me to mix her the same cocktail she had served her husband. But instead she said: "No machines. They wouldn't use needles and tubes to kill me; don't let them use them to keep me alive. Let nature take its course. Can you and your God handle that?"

I nodded.

She looked away, to a place beyond my field of vision. "Do you believe God judges us when we die?" I hesitated long enough that she answered herself. "Of course you do. You couldn't have spent a career defending murderers if you didn't believe in some level of justice beyond the human kind." She looked back at me. "Too bad you can't come with me. If what you believe is true, I'm *really* going to need a good defense attorney."

"You'll have the best," I said. "He knows very well how trying to save someone you love can land you on the wrong side of the law. And He also happens to be the Son of the Judge."

"Nepotism? So that's how it works in heaven, is it?" She still retained enough control over her facial muscles for a wry smile. "I'm not too worried, really. After all, any God who could put me through worse in the next life than I've already been through in this one would have to be one sick son of a bitch."

*　　*　　*

One night, some time later, I dreamed of flying over hills and forests so deeply green that I knew I had to be in Ireland. I flew through the gate of a castle and came to a gentle landing in the grand hall, where a couple was dancing to the music of fiddles and pipes as hundreds watched and clapped along. One of the dancers was Michelle. The other I had never met in person, but I knew his face from the numerous photographs around her house.

Here, gravity seemed not to be so much a law as, at most, a judicial precedent. The same lightness that allowed me to fly allowed her to leap so high that her kicks almost touched the rafters. When her partner's feet beat a rhythm on the floor, they moved so fast that I could scarcely tell how many he had. When the music came to an end, the couple took a bow to thunderous applause and cheers, and Michelle caught my eye and winked.

The next morning, when I went to her house and let myself in, I found what I expected. Her body lay vacant in bed. Her soul had gone dancing.

TRANSLATION

CHARLOTTE SCHENKEN

It was hot. The useless July air stuck to me like plastic wrap, and the moisture that seeped from inside me dribbled down to all the secret places of my body. Sweat between my breasts, between my legs. I hated it. And the nausea. I thought the nausea was supposed to go away, but it really didn't.

After the school let me go, I walked every day. I ended up some places I'd never imagined, would never have gone to, but it didn't matter. One afternoon, I wandered into a farmers' market that looked like an old Norman Rockwell painting—junky cars and trucks lined up on the tarmac, stuff spilling from the back ends of them. Cucumbers, corn, tomatoes. Summer stuff. Ripeness tainted the air, making it almost too potent to breathe.

I walked up and down the rows, waving my hands in front of my face, moving the air, moving the flies, moving the heat. So hot. I needed some water to ease my gluey mouth, but parking lots don't have fountains, so I kept going. People chattered, exclaiming in happy voices. "Look at those strawberries!" they said. "Those tomatoes!" Planning the night's dinner. Enjoying themselves.

I passed a splaylegged card table that looked ready to collapse under the weight of a pyramid of cantaloupes. Made me smile because my mind could see it going down, launching a fusillade of cannonballs, their roundness protecting their slimy juices and seeds and their pink flesh while they bombarded the unsuspecting shoppers.

I purchased one and carried it to a bench that baked in the sun. An old woman was there, fanning herself. Room for me to sit, so I did. I put the fruit on my lap, reached into my purse for my knife. I stabbed through the rind, then pulled the blade away from the fruit and scrolled the tip of it against the curve of my stomach. I remember the satisfaction as I drew it through the fabric of my shirt, then through my skin into my actual flesh.

I spent a while watching the blood ooze. There wasn't a lot, but enough. I let my fingers play with it and then wiped them across my shirt, marking a big X on my belly. The woman next to me asked, her voice a little shaky, "Do you need help, dear?" I waved her off.

At home, I washed the shirt and mended it. I found a bandage for the cut on my stomach. I reproached myself for the whole thing, but a part of me had felt free and good so the other part wasn't really sorry. It seemed as though there was a disagreement between two parts of me. Between the person I'd always been, the one I'd known forever, and this other one.

*   *   *

There's a beginning to all this. And an end, I guess, but I don't know it yet.

It began on that first school day after Christmas vacation which was, predictably, out of control. My students were wild. So wired-up from the time off and all the chocolate Santas and new toys and who knows what other five-year-old excesses that they could hardly sit still, let alone concentrate on the differences between "cat" and "mat." They'd forgotten everything they knew about standing in line and raising their hands and had clearly been practicing bedlam throughout the whole vacation. Crazy. Seemed more like herding birds than teaching school. I was glad when the last bell rang.

The evening started out calmly enough. Ordinary. Soup and crackers for supper, and the news. Washing up and straightening up. All the while, I was thinking about my bed with its ironed pillowcases, and that maybe there might be a good movie on television.

I filled the cat's bowl and put the trash out. Decided to skip the television and the newspaper both. In my haste to get into bed, I cut my prayers a little short, relatively sure that the Lord would forgive me. I managed to finish my rosary before I gave in, putting the beads and my glasses in their spots on the table, and dropping, like a stone, into sleep.

Later on, I was aware that I'd heard the sound of glass breaking, but it had fit so neatly into my dream that I ignored it. It was a wonderful dream, involving champagne in tall flutes and handsome tuxedoed men, and me, enjoying the unfamiliar role of being both charming and charmed. I could feel the silk of my beautiful dress, red and seductively sweet as it kissed my legs. I danced, loving the admiring glances that poured over and into me. Imagine a 1950s movie. Audrey Hepburn, maybe, and Carey Grant. Definitely not me, but, equally definitely, a great pleasure. I slept and dreamed happily until I felt his hands on me.

Once, in one of my self-defense classes, we had to practice screaming. The tough-looking police sergeant we had for a teacher must have thought it funny to see a bunch of middle-aged women punching the air, mouths stretched wide, polite little noises coming from them, but he managed to keep his face straight and his attention on his duty, urging outrage and anger until each one of us was able to produce a healthy yell. In class, I was the best, really got into it, reached deep into my chest to find the noise and then let it burst from my lungs. It had been fun. Now inside my head, I heard my own wild voice, but I couldn't open up my throat and set it free. Classic bad dream screams. I couldn't make any sound at all except a sort of whimper, weak and insufficient and serving only to aggravate him.

All the while I was making these noises, he was at me. Violent things. Hitting me when I tried to get away, biting me, tying me to the bed so that I couldn't fight. Couldn't run. He stroked my face, and his hands and his skin and his foul breath were all over me and I couldn't do a thing about it. Couldn't stop his awful eyes from looking at me or his hands from tearing at my nightshirt. The sweet, waxy stink of his ski mask made my stomach twist.

I couldn't bear any of it, let alone all. "Be a bird," I said to myself, but when I rose to fly, my glance dropped down and I beheld his heaving back and my own wet face, and then I fell to earth again. After a while, I stopped fighting. Inside my head, I took myself to church, to my favorite pew, and listened to the music and felt calm.

Strange. Two Elizabeths. One being bitten and raped, the other tranquilly worshipping God. The air that poured in through the broken window was so cold that I felt almost grateful for the warmth of his body when he touched me.

*   *   *

The people at the hospital were solicitous and kind. There were so many of them—police and EMTs, and sex crime nurses—that I was amazed. A whole group of people dedicated to one single type of crime that I'd never thought much about before. They all patted me gently but not familiarly. Part of their training, I guess.

I told them over and over again that I was fine, good, not hurt, not traumatized, hadn't seen my assailant, had no idea who he could have been. I was adamant about my religion's prohibitions against the treatments that they offered me, their pills and scrapings and such.

When they finished with me and set me free to go clean myself, I showered until my body couldn't take it any longer. I made myself as dry as I could with their thin towel, then pulled on the scrub suit they'd given me. I thought, *It's over.*

There were nurses again, and then discharge papers. Instructions about follow-up appointments. Farewells in upbeat voices. Awful. I couldn't wait to get out, but I had to hold myself together or I knew they wouldn't let me leave. I didn't realize until I got home how it would feel to be back in my apartment. I never thought.

"No," I said when they offered hotels, companions, and other comforts. "No." I denied the existence of my family, wanting nothing so much as to be alone, but when I got to my door, my hand shook so badly that I couldn't open the lock. I heard this moaning, then realized it came from me. I changed it to a hum. Took a deep breath. Got the door opened and looked around. It wasn't too bad until I got to my bedroom, which had been cleaned up but still, even though someone had boarded up the broken window and taken the sheets away, seemed as torn and violated as it had been when they freed me from it.

I slept on the sofa with the door to the bedroom locked and my desk pushed against it to make sure it stayed closed.

*   *   *

Awakening the next morning, I dealt first with the new day—bathroom, teeth, prayers—and then with the old one. I pushed it aside, resolved that I would not spend the rest of my life dwelling on one man's crime. "He has to live with what he has done," I said out loud. "I don't." Later, I said to myself, "Do the things you've always done." I thought about that, trying to remember yesterday, then said, "Coffee, and so forth."

I made it to school. On that first day, sitting carefully on the bus's hard seat, I concocted a story about all the cuts and bruises. An uneven sidewalk, my clumsiness, a stone wall. I hummed as I practiced it in my mind. Long before the first bell, I stood, as I did each morning, at the door to my classroom. Still humming, but at least I was there. There was no need for anyone ever to know what had happened.

Time went on, and I worked at getting back to being myself. It helped that it was winter. January is one of my favorite times at school, because of its coziness. When recess ended, the children swarmed back into the classroom, cheeks blooming, giggles spilling over. They had a special kind of sweetness in winter. I loved them then, unbearably.

We relearned the cat and mat things, and the standing in line. I read to them, stories that entranced them. They sat in a drugged and dreamlike state for as long as my voice went on. As for me, my plan was working. I re-found myself, and everything was almost the way it had been until the day that, along with the vomit I cleaned from the rim of the toilet bowl, I had to clear my mind of the unknowing. "A child," I said to the cold tiles. I dragged a cloth across my face and rinsed my mouth. Went back to that day's work.

I ate saltines in the mornings to steady myself for my students, and went home at night needing only soup and sleep, so tired that I occasionally forgot to pray. There were voices in my head: "Do not abandon yourself to despair" bickered endlessly with "My God, my God, why hast Thou forsaken me?" Sometimes, for all their divine topics, their interchanges sounded like my kindergarteners' squabbles. They distracted me when I should have been paying attention to something else, but, other than that, I was okay. I could do whatever I had to do.

*   *   *

But, when I thought about it, I wasn't completely sure that I could do a baby. I didn't want to be a mother, never had. I just wanted to teach, to show normal little kids how to be good grownups. I didn't want to take them home with me at night or clean up after them or do any of that stuff. My plan was to let somebody else have them and then let me borrow them, teach them about arithmetic and spelling and kindness. I loved my work. I loved those children, but I didn't want to have my own and I certainly didn't want any part of this one, the one inside me, the one my rapist had shoved into me.

Then my mind lightened: maybe I'd lose it? That thought cheered me for days. It allowed me to hope that God-in-his-Mercy would come to my rescue without my actually having to do anything. Because I couldn't stand the thought of looking up the clinic's number, of calling for an appointment, of turning the doorknob. Of sitting in the waiting room and all that. Of bearing the sin instead of the child. I opted to put my future in the hands of God. He, unfortunately for me, chose inaction and I stayed pregnant.

One Sunday, after Mass, I stopped Father Kelly and made an appointment to talk, but then I cancelled it. After that, I went online for information, and found horrible stories of ex-mothers—or non-mothers?—carrying unbearable guilt instead of the child. No one mentioned the life that the woman might otherwise have had. No one mentioned how tending the baby would be like nurturing the memories of the man, diapering those memories, feeding them at your breast.

While I was struggling with this, the window of time for termination drifted by. In a way, that made me happy: the decision part was over.

The voices stayed with me, but they backed away from their homilies and spoke about ordinary things, like grocery lists and lesson plans.

*   *   *

The police and the rape counselor had long since stopped calling. Except for work and the conversations in my head, I was pretty much alone. Memories of the old me—the middle-aged woman who was content with her good, small life—shrank with time, and the emptiness left behind began to fill with the fluttering of something I didn't recognize. It frightened me, but not a lot. It made me nervous and snappy and sharp-tempered but there were times when it also felt right.

Out in the world, the growing thing stayed quiet, as if to keep our secret low. When we were alone, I let it out. I stormed around my apartment. I broke things. Cut myself and let the blood go, left it wherever it dripped. I ignored the cat until her litter box grew so foul that she wouldn't use it. My garbage overflowed. Sometimes, I could see the mess, smell the sourness of the sheets and towels, and sometimes I felt the shame but it didn't bother me enough to do the things that needed to be done. I heard myself humming endlessly while I picked at my nails and gnawed on the flesh of my fingers. I knew how bad things were, but I didn't care.

In the mornings, after my rages, I could usually go back to being myself. Could rebecome Elizabeth. It took some work. In the beginning, the alarm would drag me into a consciousness that was sticky with halfremembered dreams. I'd stumble, still pajamaed, to the pile of clothes in the corner. Pick up something to wear, and leave. Later, I got better at it. I'd wake, make my bed, wipe the counters, empty out the dregs of last night's wine, and move on.

I remember those mornings as being like fire drills: orderly and silent. I made sure that there was food and water for the cat. I gathered up my things—lesson plan, lunch, a book to hold so I could look busy—and left, careful to lock the door behind myself.

*   *   *

More time went by and I found that I no longer liked my work. I could barely be civil to those children and simply put up with their unending energy. "Good morning," I would say. They'd giggle or look at me seriously as they replied and then ran off to engage in the bad behavior of the day: pinching each other or poking at the gerbil or whatever. They swirled around the room, squealing, until, worn out with happiness, they dropped into their places in the reading circle. They made me want to scream.

Anthony, skinny and whiney, kept grabbing at me. "You okay, Miz Reilly? You okay?" The others didn't say much, but they watched me. I remember humming a lot. The children liked it, and hummed along with me. After a while, the classroom sounded like a little beehive, but Father James's office was too far away for him to hear it. Nothing wrong with humming, anyway.

"Miz Reilly, Miz Reilly," they shouted.

*   *   *

When I could no longer avoid telling my mother of my situation, I arranged to meet her at a scruffy little diner that I liked. Not so much for the food—it was slippery with grease—but the owner was a sweet man who never failed to call me darling or dearie or something silly, and always asked about my students. He was so nice that I forgave him for the coffee, a lukewarm, translucent liquid, which nowadays made my stomach turn. I could even overlook the table being sticky, but I think it bothered my mother.

"Now what," said Mama, after we'd finished with the pleasantries and I'd broken the news about the pregnancy, "are *you* going to do with a baby?" It was a strange comment. Unexpected. Not how I wanted this to start, but I should have known.

Her eyes stabbed at me. Mine evaded the contact and, instead, watched the milky slime-trail of the spoon I was pushing around on the table.

She went on, "You do hate the little ones, Lizzie. You know that. Even when you were a girl . . ."

"Ma—" I wanted to ask what her comment had to do with my situation but then realized that, in her eyes, it was connected. That I was still an unhelpful child who needed to be reminded of her failings.

She sighed, raising her hand to push a blonded tendril from her forehead, then shifted in her seat. She looked as though she were entertaining a bothersome idea and said, in the verbal equivalent of a pointing finger, "You, of all people. Having a baby."

She doesn't even know the bad part, I thought to myself. *So why isn't she happy?* I laid my hand over my mouth, pressed it hard. Locked my words inside. Thought about how stupid I was to have forgotten.

"No one gets pregnant by accident nowadays, Lizzie. Least of all you, with your methodical little mind." When she raised her coffee cup, some of the liquid sloshed over the cup's brim and splattered onto the table top and my sleeve. The humming started in my head but I was able to mute it. I was strong, remembering from before just how little use it was to argue with her.

"Have you finished yet, Mama? Your coffee?"

She sat up straighter in her chair. "Don't try to evade me, Liz. You haven't told me anything, not even who he is." A softening. "Tell me," she said, "What's he like?" Then, "Is he going to marry you? Honestly, I didn't even suspect that there was someone in your life." Then, accusingly again, "Why didn't you tell me? For heaven's sake, Elizabeth, I'm your *mother.*" The expression on her face grew slightly sullen. "You always have to keep everything a secret, don't you?"

"I can't talk about it, Mama," I said. "I made a mistake." I didn't define the mistake, didn't say that my error had been my stupid hope in her. To myself I whispered, *I can do this.* And then, aloud, "I'm sorry, Mama."

Things changed then. The daughter, with all her sweet obedience, flew away, and my own fierceness emerged, making the cups rattle dangerously as I carried them back to the counter. I steadied myself, caged the creature until a better time.

When I went back to the table for my purse, my mother was fixing her makeup. She put the lipstick down. "Elizabeth . . ." she said.

"Sorry, Mother." I could hear my own voice. Sharp. Angry. A little piercing. The voice of a hawk or a falcon, not some sweet singing bird. Inside my head, I finally said, *You bitch.*

*   *   *

By July, by the time of my walk to the farmer's market, real sleep had become a precious gem for me. The fetus thumped relentlessly at my ribs, and my nights were full of terrible dreams. Images of my assailant flitted through them, snarling or laughing, raising his hands to me, angrily or—strangely—gently. Sometimes he had a beard and piercing eyes and wore Jesus clothes. Others, he was just dirty and mean-looking. The baby was never in my dreams. I guess because it hadn't started yet, when he got me.

Over the weeks, the wispy pictures and bits of sound began to assemble themselves into an image that had a certain familiarity to it. Maybe I was seeing my assailant, maybe not. It didn't matter because now that I could imagine him, I had the idea of watching for him. Part of me said, "Just looking for him," but the other part really wanted to find him. And maybe pay him back a little.

*   *   *

So I began to enjoy myself again. I'd tried work and the children and church, but it was actually hunting, sharp-eyed, for that one particular man that gave pleasure back to me. I treated the whole thing like a well-loved job: showed up every day, stayed focused, my heart fluttering with excitement. And anger. I loved my anger. How had I lived so long without it?

The work of searching wasn't easy because there were so many details to check. I had to discard this one for his dark skin, that one for the kindness in the eyes. None of them fit exactly, but I kept looking, knowing I'd find him. The thing in my belly, hidden beneath my shapeless clothes, proved he existed.

I didn't have a plan beyond the chase but there wasn't really a need for one. I'd know what to do when I found him. Think of how a falcon finds his prey. Does he accept the first small rodent that he sees? But when he finds the right one, he knows what to do.

*   *   *

After a while, all that hunting began to make me feel edgy. One night, I slipped a knife into my purse. A cheese knife was all it was. Not big, but very sharp, and long enough. "Just in case," I said to myself. The next night was better than all the ones that had preceded it.

Whenever I was outside, I was alert. Watchful. At home, the windows and doors in my apartment were locked, checked, and re-checked, and my new alarm system was always on. Still, the knife gave me a better sort of protection. It was in my hand. It comforted me. I reached for it whenever someone spoke to me or looked in my direction.

At school, I had been late so many times that the principal called me in for a conference. I dragged my body to his office.

Father James sat behind his desk, "Talk to me," he said, in his kindest voice. "Tell me why you've changed so." His fingers tapped the official-looking papers on his desk. "You have a wonderful record. Unflawed. But in the past few months, you have become habitually tardy."

He shifted in his chair. There was the tiniest creak from his plastic collar and I thought that it must pinch at him constantly, remind him of the strictures of our faith just as my too-tight waistband reminded me. "What has happened, Elizabeth?" he asked. "There are complaints from the parents of your students and from your fellow teachers about your rages. Rages!" His cheeks reddened. "You are a kindergarten teacher. Rages are not acceptable." He stopped, inhaled, looked down at his hands, and then unfisted them. Inhaled again. "Tell me, Elizabeth, what is wrong? Let us work together to fix it for you," he said.

He waited for an answer. There really wasn't one that I could give. Or that I was willing to. It was too complicated.

Finally, he broke the silence. "Is there anything I can do to help you through what's troubling you?"

I shook my head. His sympathy tempted me, but I resisted. "I'll pray for you," he said.

*   *   *

The third time he summoned me, I knew what was coming, and wasn't sure whether I was glad or sad. If I felt anything by then, I didn't know what it was. Numb, I guess. I folded my hands in my lap and waited.

His message turned out to be short and to the point. "Summer vacation starts soon enough. Why don't you take the rest of the term off? We'll find a substitute, and then you and I will talk when it's closer to the new school year."

"Thank you, Father." I could hear my own cold voice. I smiled and rose, feeling strangely freed, like a falcon that has been unleashed and sent out to hunt.

*   *   *

While I was searching, I discovered the pleasures of counting: tallying the number of times I chewed my food, measuring my steps as I walked, marking the beat of the music that I heard either in my head or on the streets. I recited poetry, pounding it out in a hard and stringent rhythm. I said, "I should have been a pair of ragged claws . . ." I said, "Mary had a little lamb." I chanted whatever came to mind, for the most part not noticing the wide berth that others on the street left around me. Not caring when I did notice because the counting kept my mind soothed and occupied. The hypnotic thump of the words relaxed me and it kept me from coiling myself too soon for the strike. It prevented my spending the hate and power before the proper time. The humming helped as well.

Now that I had the knife—in my purse or in my hand all day, beneath my pillow each night—I was distressed at my inability to find the man. My hunts got longer. I trembled a lot. Fear? Anger? Glee?

One night, my counting was interrupted by a revelation: I could practice. Have a sort of dress rehearsal. See how he, whoever he was, liked being captured and immobilized and powerless.

I set what my mother had called my methodical little mind to work on that project. I decided that, for my practice target, I needed some kind of disposable person rather than, say, one in a suit on his way to a meeting. It had to be a person who was not likely to rush off to the police, should things work out that way. Someone who would not be missed if he failed to show up somewhere. And a passable stand-in for my rapist.

That kind of person wouldn't fit into conventional neighborhoods, so my regular walks needed to go into seedier places, ones where those people might naturally be. My plan, previously unfocused, was getting bigger, growing a shape. I began to have a feeling for what I was doing. I'd find him and scare him and hurt him just a little.

My streets grew drearier. Full of thrift shops and Salvation Army outlets and bars. Empty apartment buildings, their windows boarded up with plywood. Bars with dark neon signs. Vacant lots, abandoned cars, and bars. I passed a lot of men, not one of whom looked right. Up one street and down another but I couldn't commit to one.

I'd begun to despair of ever finding a suitable substitute, let alone the real man, when, suddenly, there he was. Not perfect, but close enough, good enough to practice on. He identified himself by his awful eyes. I remembered those eyes. The smell of him was right. He spoke but, overwhelmed by the moment and by the serendipity of it all, I was unable to process what he said. I nodded. "Yes," I saw him. I knew him. To myself, I said, "This is the one." Maybe it was, maybe not.

He mistakenly took my nod of recognition as one of assent, and almost immediately, had me in the alley, thrown up against the wall, his hands snatching at me, and then he was tearing at his own clothes, pulling at himself with one hand and groping at me with the other. I don't think he noticed the baby.

The brick wall was an unexpected chill against my back, but the knife was in my hand. I'd thought that there would be more time, but good habits pay off and it was there when I needed it. Truthfully, my intention had been only to mark him, to practice with the knife against flesh, but he seemed so foul that I forgot myself. I should have been happy after I drew the blade across his arm, lightly, but it wasn't enough. I cut at him, stabbed at him, penetrated him, forced the blade into him. Plunged. I was carried away by it all, couldn't stop. He grabbed himself wherever I'd stabbed last, but I cut so quickly, so joyously, that he couldn't keep pace with me.

I loved seeing his face, which spoke clearly of his shock at the violence being mine and not his. I loved his speechlessness. He didn't make a sound, seeming to have lost that ability. I remembered that feeling, the impotence, and was hating the memory of it and enjoying his helplessness when, all at once, he came back into himself.

"Bitch," he shouted. "Fucking bitch." He pushed me away from him and then down to the gritty pavement. He kicked me, again and again, chanting all the while, "Bitch, bitch, fucking bitch," his words marking the rhythm of it all. I twisted and tried to cut at him, but my grip on the knife slipped and it spun off into the dimness, the clatter of its disappearance lasting long after I'd lost sight of it.

The kicking continued: head, flank, head, shoulder, everywhere. Belly-belly-belly. Oh, God.

When it was over, when he'd stopped and was gone, I uncurled. Stood. Could walk despite the cramping. Went home. Locked the door, washed myself, and went to bed. Slept.

I was awakened by contractions. At least, I suppose they were contractions. I had no one to ask, and no one to hear, or to know if I used the wrong word. I thought of calling 911 but didn't. Too reminiscent of that other night.

I muffled my cries with my quilt, and used the brass spindles of the bed to hold against the flexing of my muscles. The labor seemed to go on forever, to swallow me up, to erase me. I couldn't think at all. My brain wouldn't work but my body wouldn't stop. I kept saying to it, "No, wait," but it wouldn't.

I really wanted someone to say something kind to me or to hold my hand, but there was no one there and no one came, so I did it all alone. Like an animal.

Eventually, when I had thrust the child from my body and it lay between my legs, still attached and part of me, but separate now, and dead, I threw my face to the sky and howled.

BRAZIL

ROSANNA STAFFA

Au wa wakaré no hajimé
Meeting is only the beginning of separation
(Buddhist Proverb)

She sat looking outside, smoking. Every evening, at 7:45, a thin man with a backpack walked by, staring straight ahead to the horizon. He had stubble. His skin was pale. He shuffled like someone who worked hard in exchange for nothing. Buses going fast lifted strands of his light hair. The man did not see her. He never changed his pace. On he went.

She opened a map of Minneapolis and marked with a pencil all the places where the man might disappear at night. She passed her fingers through her hair while thinking: here, here or here. In the flickering glow from the television, alone with the map, she grew to like the night. Her light was the last to go off in the building.

The husband came home late, when she was already asleep. He was an architect; after work, he treated customers to dinner and drinks at The Red Stag on 1st Avenue or The Libertine in Calhoun Square. They rarely made love, mostly on Saturday mornings. She knew he wanted to when he became playful.

Sometimes sleep was necessary; she took pills. Her sister sent them from home in Brazil—they were strong. She tried to dream her old kitchen, the window, the way the light fell on her mother's hands when she sat sewing. She tried to dream the smell of lemons and oranges on the countertop.

They had met in São Paulo five years earlier. It was a hot summer; the sky was white. She was drinking from a fountain. She undid her hair, shook it loose, and put her head under the stream. He looked at her while she did, leaning against the wall of a café, his hands in his pockets. She turned and held his gaze. He told her that she looked like a *vìtima de afogamento*, a drowning victim. She laughed, a child's gurgle.

They made love in a hotel room. Sad songs on the radio, a blue chair by the bed. He knelt and unlaced her sandals, intent like a dressmaker.

"You want to?" he stopped and asked. "Yes?"

She took the barrettes off her hair; it was thick and long, gathered on top, tendrils brushed her neck.

"Yes," she said, her lips forming the word in English for the first time.

Her mother said to the American man that he could marry her child. She was a widow with two daughters and no money; she had a history of silences and violent moods. The one advice she gave was not to keep a bird in the house, it would bring death. All her life she forbid her daughters to sing at the table, lest they would marry a drunk, but the one who left for America liked the taste of wine on a man's tongue, she liked the honey of fado in her throat at a table where there was nothing to eat but bread.

It was a small wedding. When the taxi to the airport took off, the mother called out her name. In the rearview mirror she saw her get smaller and smaller, a tiny doll with mouth opening and closing.

"It's okay," the husband said, "it's okay."

In Minneapolis, she thought of her mother's hair getting white far from her, in Brazil. Soon, her mother would need glasses to read, a cane to walk; the mother who had never taken a lover or downed a drink would be too old for everything.

It was summer. This time the husband came home early, with his sleeves rolled up, tie loosened. He had crazy eyes.

"You sit in the dark?" he asked. He took a sip from her glass. "Drinking Barbera?" He knew the name of wines and restaurants. He knew how to touch her body and where. He asked questions like a child, knowing the answer. "You let your hair down?" He invented himself every night with different clients like a hooker. He did not know you could do it just for yourself, alone in a room with no light.

He moved around in the dark touching everything with the stealth of a burglar. Her cigarettes, pen, keys. He examined a notepad, bringing it close to his eyes. Everything seemed to stir up a silent rage.

She sat in the dark in the evening—that was all. Here was her glass of wine, a loaf of bread and the knife to cut it; a chair was by the window. A thin man walked by at 7:45.

"You eat bread for dinner?" the husband asked.

There was a strangeness to everything now that he was there. She put her hair back up. He watched, unsmiling. A pungent waft reached her nostrils; she had not showered.

"I can switch the light on," she said. The husband rustled closer.

"No," he said, "no light."

He pulled a chair to the table. His hands went to his face, his mouth.

"I want to talk," he said. He jiggled change in his pocket. "I might be fired. I lost a big client."

He had said this once before, years back. That time they walked and walked, following nothing. They were devoured by streets with no lights near Webber Park. They found fields of dandelions twitching in the dark. Music was playing somewhere, blurred by the wind. They followed the sound and found a bar, an airless box with Christmas lights still on. He kissed her shoulder, her chin. The drinks filled them with the most unforgiving lust. She told him he had been her only love. He knew it was not true, but that night it was. He did not lose his job.

"I could be fired," he repeated now.

The day she left São Paulo, her sister told her that everything returns.

Around their apartment building in Minneapolis, there were only patches of mini malls, burnt grass, nowhere to go.

"No," she said. "You won't be fired."

"I could. Everything might change."

"Things don't ever change," she said. She always woke up from the same dream, the same desire. "It does not matter what happens. It's never too much to take."

"What do you mean?"

"We are like dogs. We get kicked, get up, and go back for more."
He went to the refrigerator and got himself a beer.
"How are you?" he asked.
"Okay," she said, pronouncing it with a double k.
"Like what, okay?"
"I'm fine," she said. He came to her, pushed a strand of hair off her face; brushed his lips by her ear.
"You are leaving me," he said.
"No," she said.
"You are missing home?"
"No," she said.

It was the answer she always gave; there was nothing to miss. In São Paulo, she had shared a bed with her mother and sister. When she was old enough, she went to clean houses with them. The job made her cruel. She stole money from the older clients to buy cigarettes and a bottle of aguardiente for a boy with eyes color de chocolate. In the Ibirapuera Park, he lifted her skirt and took her against an Araucaria tree, telling her what he wanted to do to her while he did it. He was very beautiful and always sad. She wanted him again and again.

"In your sleep you speak Portuguese," the husband said.
"That will stop," she said.

She worked on her English daily; she made lists of new words. She scrubbed the house, rearranged the furniture. She starched his shirts so stiff they hung in the closet like ghosts. Dreams were something she could not alter. They were lighter than smoke; they did as they wished.

The husband picked up a cigarette, played with it. There were his boots in a corner, there was his jacket hanging from a peg. There was no sign of anyone else in the house except for the chair at the window.
"You sit here?" he said. "And do what?"
"I look outside."
The husband went to look out the window. There was nothing.
"A man goes by," she said.
"What man?"

"A man with a backpack, at 7:45." There had been only one evening he showed up late, just when she thought that he would not come.

"He walks by and that's it?" The husband locked eyes with her, as if his attention could change her story.

"That's it," she said.

"You wait and a man walks by?" He had a short laugh, like a bark. "You two talk?"

"I see him walk every evening, that's all," she said.

In São Paulo, she waited for the boy with eyes color of chocolate by a fountain and sometimes he came. Then he did not. O fin, the end. She still waited. One afternoon, the American man came. His eyes were sparkling gray; he was lithe like a girl. He watched her put her face under the stream. She held her breath and counted. Her sister told her that by 180 if you don't breathe you die. She barely made it to 37. The fountain was flowing right now in São Paulo, tiny cotingas birds and paserines were drinking from it.

"Describe this man," the husband said.

"He has a backpack." She remembered the man a bit different every night, just before he appeared. A few times he staggered; cars passed too close. "He is just a man with a job. He walks to it and back."

She did not want to speak of the man; it made him into someone else. She thought of all the things that were gone from her: her mother's brush, barely the size of a palm, the stack of bus tickets held by a pink rubber band, half an inch high at the most.

"A job, yeah." The husband's energy had a buzz, like a swarm of insects. "You only see him in the evening?"

"Yes." She sometimes listened at night, thinking the man was somewhere in the city making a noise she could not hear.

"What job could he possibly have?"

"He must be a clerk in a small grocery store," she said. A small fish, so tiny no one would even detect him moving in the aquarium of his life, and much less catch him. She imagined the man sweeping floors, piling boxes of sauce, rearranging fruit; a fugitive from some terrible life.

"There are no small grocery stores here; you are thinking Brazil."

"Pode ser, maybe." She laughed.

"I wonder how far he walks," he said.

"I think he lives close." She wanted the man to have a home nearby and someone waiting for him, but he did not seem to walk towards a desire.

The husband kept glancing out the window. "How long ago did he go by?"

"A few minutes. Why?" she asked.

He grabbed the car keys.

"Don't," she said. "You'll scare him."

"So he'll run off. Let him run. It's no big deal. What are you afraid of? Maybe, who knows, I'll even offer him a ride."

"It's a bad idea," she said.

"You wait here," he said. He was leaving. "I'll be right back."

"I will come with you," she said.

He drove the car out of the garage, pressed his foot on the accelerator and it took off with a screech. The city seemed barely there in the dark, streetlights suspended above empty sidewalks. She anticipated seeing the man in the distance at any moment. Perhaps he wanted a car to stop, a man in a shirt and tie to tell him that everything would be fine.

"It's all so quiet," she said. The harsh neon lights from fast food joints saturated the car. Empty streets spread out in front of them. Four minutes. Seven. Deserted still. In Brazil, night was like day; families strolled, friends met, kissing once on both cheeks.

"Maybe he is fine as he is," she said.

A light drizzle started.

"What kind of man wants to walk in the rain?" The husband laughed.

"Maybe it's still all right," she said.

"It's night." He turned to look at her, hard like a cop. "He worked all day. He is walking in the rain." He went back to staring ahead; she saw his savage concentration. "He can't have covered much ground on foot." One night, she had driven all over like this, gravel crunching, no lights, looking for the boy who tasted of cigarettes and aguardiente.

"He's gone," she said. She heard her accent; the words came out a bit like singing.

"No, here he is," the husband said. In the distance, the thin man with a backpack was walking. "I got him. Here we go."

The man disappeared in the shadows of trees and trucks, then popped up again like a burst of music. It seemed he was playing a game with them in the car. The acid light from a store that sold CDs and video games washed over him. He took a sharp left on 66th Street. It was a precise turn, a soldier's maneuver.

"Did you see that?" the husband said. There was the maze of the ER parking lot leading to Fairview Hospital to the left. It was dimly lit.

"He's going to the ER," she said. A sudden illness, a wound, an unspeakable tiredness. A doctor in a tiny room with no windows would tell him the future.

"No, he's walking on," the husband said. The Southdale Mall was further down to the right, with a jigsaw of multi-level buildings and parking structures. It would be easy to lose track of him there.

"The mall is closed now, he must know that," he said. "Why go there?"

She had returned to the fountain in São Paulo even when she knew she would find only sparrows. A one-armed woman who sold roses there read her palm: love, money; she moved her hand like a wing: a voyage.

If the man with the backpack kept going on 66th Street, he could disappear in the deserted lots of Jerry's Garage, a Best Buy and Blockbuster gone out of business.

"Perhaps he is homeless, he sleeps there," she said. She squinted to detect some kind of hermit's nest, a rustling. But on the man went.

"He's flying," said the husband.

The man went to the Southdale Mall. The parking lot was empty, the stores closed. There was nothing but wind; nowhere to go. He started crossing the parking lot.

"Fine. We keep going too," the husband said.

"He is getting picked up here," she said. Someone cared for the man, would take him home. She strained to see it: a car waiting, the man with the backpack approaching the passenger's side. But the man was walking on.

"That's not it," the husband said.

The man slowed down, looked around. He paused, seemingly for no reason. There was something unsettling about him when he wasn't moving.

The husband stopped the car. They watched the man go through the Southdale Mall parking lot. There was a sound of flapping tarp somewhere. Theirs was the only car. The strangeness of it all made her laugh.

"Look, what the hell is he doing?" the husband said.

The man was walking straight ahead toward Macy's. The store was closed, the lights dimmed. The counters were barely visible beyond the thick glass doors, the floors shiny as from an oil spill; it looked like the interior of a crashed boat.

"It's terrible," she said.

The man turned his head and she saw his face. There was a frozenness to it. He was old. He had the angular features of the last man she had taken care of in São Paulo, who spent the day dozing off in a wheelchair, his eyelids fluttering. She would read to him. The house was filled with bookcases floor to ceiling. He did not want her to clean, just read. One time he peeled an orange for her, he opened the slices like petals. He told her of the walks he took when she wasn't there: museum, parks. She never said: no, it's not possible. She washed him delicately, with a sponge.

"Whoa, he's old," the husband said. He chuckled.

"It's enough," she said. "Let's go home."

"No, wait," he said. His voice was scratchy. "Aren't you curious?"

The man with the backpack drifted away from the Macy's doors, then stood, shifting his weight. He had puppet legs, wobbly.

"Really, no," she said.

Sometimes the old man in Brazil rose to his feet to reach a book, tried to move a step and fell. She had not said it was foolish or raised her voice. She thought it was like in the stories she read to him: a somewhat heroic act. The old man staggered and fell more and more, and she would help him back up. For a time they struggled together ferociously, with this one single intent.

"Jesus," the husband said, "I just want to give him a hand." He lowered the driver's window. "Sir! Excuse me," he called out.

The man with the backpack whipped around.

"Sir!" The husband waved. The man seemed frozen in a kind of dance pose. "Sir! It's raining, I'll give you a ride home."

"Don't scare him." She said. "Maybe he is not well. He has a condition. Something."

"Ok, I'm getting out of the car." The husband stepped out, slammed the door shut.

"Leave him alone," she said.

The man was standing just a short distance away; his arms were long, his face thin. He remained silent, fists clenched, mouth slightly open. She got out of the car.

"Look here, it's just a gesture," the husband said. He had the tentative tone of someone convincing himself. She wanted to say that this was a mistake, they should go, but she was confronted by a glimmer of hope in the man's eyes, mixed with confusion.

"Don't worry. It's okay, sir," she said to him. "Really okay."

"Now my wife is getting wet too," the husband said. His tone was harsh. The man mouthed something, his body twitching; he moved a step back.

"Wait, wait. Don't worry, sir," she said. Her voice was blurry and soft, like tipsy. They would give the man a hand when he expected nothing.

"Listen . . . I'm sick and tired of standing in the rain here," the husband said. This seemed to frighten the man. He moved backwards, stumbled, and caught himself. "Come on. You walk by our house on Townes Road in the evening."

The man jerked back and turned to go, his arms flailing. His feet slipped on the wet cement; he tripped and fell. He crouched like a supplicant, moaning. The husband edged towards him.

"For heaven's sake, let me help you. Let's not make a big deal out of this."

"Don't touch him," she said.

"I'm not going to touch him," the husband said. The man rose to his knees. He scrambled to his feet; emitted a cry like a bird.

"Are you okay, sir?" she said. "We are leaving. We don't mean to upset you."

The man took off, cutting across the parking lot.

"Sir! We are going," she cried out. "Please don't worry. We are leaving."

The man turned his head back for a moment; he had a brutal expression, tight. He raised a fist. His face was drenched by tears, rain, or both.

One afternoon the old man in Brazil had surprised her with her hands in the drawer with his cash. She pleaded innocence, still clutching the money to buy cigarettes and aguardiente for the boy who did not come to the fountain anymore.

"Good," the old man said. "Now I know who you are." His mouth was trembling. He watched her cry. He said that he did not want to see her again.

At home, she pushed her mother and sister away. She broke plates, glasses, wanting them to beat her with their fists like a donkey. When they did, she did not raise her hands in defense.

The man with the backpack was running off, his shoes splashing.

"I'm sorry," she cried out, "We scared you. It won't happen again. You can still walk by the house." She started after the man. She kept telling him that everything would be again as it was before.

She heard the husband calling her, then his hurried steps; she did not turn, did not slow down. The husband's voice trailed off in the distance. He was gone, had given up or returned to the car. There was only the sound of her breathing and the man walking. She kept going. The man with the backpack was very fast. His clothes wet, he was gleaming on and off like a lure. He picked up speed; she tried to keep up but started losing ground. The man took a turn on Xerxes Avenue, where the dark was dense, the roads a labyrinth. He disappeared. She walked on seeing nothing. She did not recognize the streets. She stopped. The old man in Brazil wanted an ancient poem read to him over and over. He mouthed the words with her: From here to nowhere. And back again.

There were lights in the distance. In a mini mall on York Street, a small coffee shop selling pastries was still open. It had a French name; it was empty. She had no purse, no money. Her clothes stuck to her body, drenched in rain and sweat. During a family stroll, as a child she had hid in the Ibirapuera Park and fantasized being left behind. She told herself that she would never see her home again: the bread, the hard bed, the roaches. Her shoes were full of pebbles, and after a while she heard nothing but wind in the trees. Later she lied to her mother, told her that she had not been afraid, had not cried. The mother despised weakness. To the mother, even her hair was too soft.

She sat at a small table by the door of the coffee shop and cupped her face in her hands. A tall waitress came; she was quite old. She stood, staring at her from behind thick glasses.

"You can use my phone if you want to," the waitress said.

"I'm okay, thank you," she said.

The waitress brought her coffee without being asked.

"You are lost?" she asked.

She nodded a yes.

"I can give you directions," the waitress said, "if you tell me where you live."

She sipped the coffee; it was very strong, the way she made it at home.

"You want me to go?" she asked.

"You can stay as long as you like. You can stay till someone comes and gets you," the waitress said. There was a clumsy kindness in her voice. "It will be fine again tomorrow."

One morning, the old man in Brazil had tried to come to greet her when she walked in, and fell. He remained trapped on the floor, wedged in the small space between a bookcase and the counter. When she tried to pull him up she slipped down too. They both lay on the floor. On her back, catching her breath, she looked at the books of poetry she had read to him over the weeks. She went to the bookcase first thing each day, wanting more. The poets all sang of lovers not interested in them, haunting, magnificent. A Roman poet envied the sparrow his woman adored; he watched while she let it play on her finger. The floor was getting cold, brushed by a gust of wind from the balcony. She tried to get up but the body of the old man was an impediment. He was clutching her hard, like a man drowning. They remained on the floor for a while, in silence. It was quiet. His head rolled to her chest and rested there; she instinctively moved closer.

"Everything ends," the waitress said, "but I'm sure it was good while it lasted. That's what matters, really, that it was beautiful."

She took one more sip of coffee; cradled the warm cup in her hands.

"Yes, it was good," she said. "It was beautiful."

LOVERS

A SOFT PLACE TO REST

MELISSA SCHOLES YOUNG

Leonard told Travis, who hadn't asked, that he liked the silky ones best, but he'd settle for nylon too. "Just don't give me no farm girl ones, ya know? Big and cottony don't do it," Leonard said carrying all the weight of his one sided conversation.

Travis nodded and jangled his car keys in his pocket. He leaned up against the bar, waiting to pick up take-out: three breaded and fried pork tenderloins as big as your head on sesame buns with dill pickle spears on the side. One for Travis, one for Jenny, and one for her good-for-nothing boy, Ronnie, who Travis thought was old enough to get a job and buy his own damn tenderloins. Jenny would tell him to be nice, "or else," so he was, mostly. Picking up dinner at Scoville's showed he was trying and listening, even though she said he never did.

Leonard drank Bud from a can and poked at a bowl of stale bar peanuts in search of Chex Mix bits. Every few minutes, he coughed, then took a long drag on his Camel and swatted the smoke from the air as if he wasn't the one putting it there.

Leonard drained his beer; the dew from the glass glistened in his scraggly grey ZZ Top beard. He yawned like a happy dog, showing off his few teeth—yellow and crooked—which made him look older than his fifty years. He wore a navy blue ball cap, which was frayed at the edges, with a faded Harley skull printed on the front. "They got to be clean, too, if you know what I mean," Leonard whispered, shrugging his bushy eyebrows.

Travis watched the Cardinals on the screen above the bar. Molina recovered two foul balls from Wainwright.

"None of them stained ones," Leonard continued.

Travis didn't want to encourage him, but he just couldn't resist. "What do you do with them? The panties, I mean. Once you get 'em?" he asked, shaking out his reddish-brown rattail. The bartender, a heavyset woman with a shelf of a bosom, came around the corner and told him it would be a few minutes; the grease wasn't hot enough yet. He accepted a beer on the house in exchange for the wait.

"Really? You want to know? Most people just want to know how I get the panties in the first place." Leonard narrowed his eyes and grinned, tempting him.

Travis looked up at the ball game again. It was a Friday night. He was bone-tired from a double shift at the cement plant. He just wanted to go home, see Jenny, and feed his dogs.

"Well, I'll tell you," Leonard answered. "You won't believe me, though. You'll have to see it for yourself."

Travis took the bait. "See what?"

"I make quilts," Leonard said. "Quilts outta panties. Real pretty ones. I teach guys like you to make 'em too. Soft and silky quilts. Quilts like your grandma made but with panties, so it's all soft where you lay your head."

"Don't you have a pillow?"

"Don't need a pillow. Not when I can lay my head on a blanket of panties. Can't think of a better place to sleep on the whole god damn earth." He slid a card across the bar to Travis. "You'll call. They all do." Then Leonard laughed so hard he gave himself a righteous coughing fit.

Travis parked his Ford as close to the trailer door as possible so the food wouldn't get soaked when he carried in through the rain. Jenny's S-10 was there but Ronnie's Camaro, which Jenny had begged Travis to pay the insurance on last month, wasn't. *Maybe he ain't here,* Travis thought, relieved.

"Food!" Ronnie shouted from the couch when Travis came through the door, wafts of fried grease—acrid and animal—preceding him. Travis' favorite mutt, Huck, wagged his tail so hard it whipped Travis' legs. Then the dog sat obediently on his haunches and released a hopeful drool.

"Get the door," Travis told Ronnie. "Closing it's the least you could do."

Jenny came around the corner from the bathroom. "Oh, boys. Be nice," she said. "Let's set the table. Ronnie, move your stuff."

"But I was studying there," Ronnie said, rifling through the plastic food bags and pulling out a pickle. He shoved it into his mouth whole. Pus-filled red pimples lined his weak jaw as he chewed. He wiped away pickle juice with the back of his hand, then rubbed it absently through his blond crew cut. He'd turned sixteen a few months before, and Travis reminded him every chance he could that with a car and a license came responsibility. He needed to get a job, and quick, so he'd be around the house a lot less.

"You ain't studying on a Friday night, and I know it. Move, boy," Travis shoved the books to the floor with one sweep of his arm. "There. Now there's room. Have a seat, Jenny." He held out his hand to help her step over Ronnie's mess and slide into the booth at the back of the kitchen. It was barely big enough for the two of them. Travis remembered the first time she'd stayed over, before she mentioned the kid, and they'd sat together naked in the booth, sharing a blanket and eating scrambled eggs and bacon right off the skillet. Jenny'd fed Huck from her fingers. Now she shooed him away if he begged at the table. A lot had changed in six months.

"I'm sitting on the couch anyway," Ronnie said. "I'm watching my show."

"Turn it off. Your mom said it's time to eat."

"Come on, Ronnie-boy. Travis brought food. Let's sit and eat. I want to hear about what happened to the car." Ronnie sat back down on the couch and opened the Styrofoam lid on his lap. He shoved a bite of breaded fried loin into his mouth and shrugged his shoulders.

"The car?" Travis asked. "The one I just paid a $278 insurance bill on?"

"Oh, he'll pay you back, won't you, son?" Jenny patted Travis' hand. "He will. Let's just eat."

"He don't even have a job. How's he gonna pay for anything? I want to know what happened to your goddamn car, boy." Travis slammed his open palm on the Formica table. "Answer me," he said through gritted teeth. "Now!"

Jenny looked at her hands in her lap, then out the window at the rain. Ronnie chewed and kept his eyes on the TV Huck retreated to a corner and tried to make himself a smaller dog. Travis stared at Ronnie, waiting.

"Sandwiches smell good," Jenny said, turning back to the bags. She pulled out the two remaining containers and put one in front of Travis. "Hope they put in slaw."

Travis stood up from the table, crossed the four feet to the couch, and grabbed the sandwich out of Ronnie's hand. "I said, 'tell me what happened to the car.'"

"I ain't got to tell you nothin'," Ronnie answered. He leaned back into the couch cushions and pulled out a Camel he'd swiped from Travis. Then he patted the side of the couch, calling Huck to him.

"We don't smoke in this house," Travis said, grabbing the dog by the collar and holding him at his side. He looked at the sandwich in his hand and waited for Ronnie to ask for it back. Then he dropped it at Huck's feet and let him go.

Ronnie put the cigarette between his lips, pulled his lighter out of his pocket, lit the end, and took a draw. "Then I guess we're leaving this house," he said. He grabbed his mom's car keys and headed out the door.

Jenny watched him go, then packed up her sandwich slowly. "I've told you a hundred times not to pick this battle. You just can't leave it alone, can you?" Ronnie beeped the car horn twice.

"What, me? This ain't my fault—you know that. Listen, Jenny." Travis stood in front of the door.

"I'm done listening. You know what your problem is?" Jenny said, sliding on black sunglasses and plastic gold sandals. Travis didn't answer. He knew she'd tell him either way. "Your problem," she repeated, looking at him with her chin in the air, "is you think you got everything all figured out. There's only one way and it's Travis's way. You put people in these little boxes and expect folks to stay there. Anything don't fit your small view—like a kid you didn't plan on—gets cut. Things are always one way."

"Just listen, honey."

"Move. I told you not to make me choose, because you ain't gonna like the choice." She reached under his arm for the door handle. "Move." He stepped aside. She let the door slam behind her; the shredded mesh screen billowed out in response. Travis remembered again that he needed to replace it. The grandfather clock in the corner, the one Jenny had bought on sale at Kmart for his thirty-ninth birthday, chimed seven times.

Travis watched through the broken screen as her truck drove away. Ronnie flew him the bird through the cab window. Back in the house, Travis turned the TV to the ball game. Cardinals were losing six-four. *Figures*, he thought. He turned it off and sat down to eat his cold sandwich while Huck licked the floor for scraps.

The next weekend, Travis found Jenny's panties in his laundry. They were stuck to the back of one of his black t-shirts. He'd spent his days mostly drunk between shifts or shooting squirrels in his front yard and letting the dogs gnaw on the carcasses. Jenny wouldn't return his calls. Ronnie sent him a text with one word in caps: ASSHOLE. Travis hoped Jenny would come back with or without her useless son. He couldn't sleep without her.

But he had her panties—a lacy baby blue pair, size nine. It was the only thing she left behind, which surprised him most; she'd already packed the night she left. She must have been waiting until after dinner to tell him. He folded the panties up carefully into a little package and tucked them in the back pocket of his jeans, where he found Leonard's business card.

Out loud, Travis muttered to his dogs: "What the hell." Then he called Leonard to see if he could come over and have a look at the quilt made out of panties.

It was a risk. Jenny always said he was scared of risks, but he had forty-eight hours until his next shift and not a single thing to do.

The path leading up to the house was filled with long-stemmed metal flowers. They stood almost three feet tall. Intricate leaves climbed up thick, stubby stalks. There were tulips with tight shiny cups, daisies with open-faced golden smiles, and one giant sun-flower, its center painted black, its face dripping wilted silver petals.

"I'm a welder," Leonard called through the screen door. He watched Travis study the metal garden. "That's what I do for a livin' anyway, but I like to think I'm an artist of sorts. When I ain't quilting, I make flowers. Sometimes butterflies, too, but I keep them in the back. Neighbors already think I'm a little weird, know what I mean?"

"Kind of cool," Travis admitted, shifting his weight from side to side on the sidewalk. He stroked the blue silk in his pocket and thought of the warm, moist spot between Jenny's legs.

"Well, you look like shit," Leonard said, holding open the screen door to Travis.

The house was nicer than Travis expected; a brick two-story with white trim. The front yard had been recently mowed. A Harley parked outside was the only hint that a man like Leonard lived inside.

"Friends call me Shovelhead, for my engine. You can call me whatever you want, just as long as you call." Leonard slapped Travis on the back. "Come on in. I know you want to see it. Everybody does." Leonard wore a Stones t-shirt that was probably white once but was now faded to a cream color and yellowed at the armpits. The house smelled of cigarette laced with air-freshener. A machine mounted above the door squirted a chemical spray over Travis' head. Leonard inhaled deeply. "Ah. The ocean breeze," he said. "Don't get much better than that, does it?" The men walked together into the kitchen, and Leonard gestured toward one of the chairs at the table. "Want something to drink?"

"Like what?" Travis asked. His eyes searched the clean counters and came to rest on a lime-green dishtowel embroidered with the phrase: *I only quilt on days that end in Y.*

"I just made some iced tea. Want that? It's got lemon in it. Sweet, too." Leonard opened the fridge door. Rows of bread, sandwich-meat, and apples were lined up. Half-empty but tidy. A plastic pitcher of tea was sweating on the shelf next to a gallon of skim milk.

"Iced tea? Sounds good. Thanks." Travis drummed his fingers on the table as he waited. Then he shoved his hand into his pocket and fished out the panties. He folded them and waited. Leonard brought two tall glasses of tea to the table and scrunched up his face, studying the panties sitting between them.

"Can I smell them?" Leonard asked. He locked eyes with Travis and slowly reached toward the panties. "Sometimes the panties tell me what kind of quilt they'd like to become."

Travis stared at Leonard's hovering fingers. "Nah, I don't think so." Travis shook his head. Just for a second, Leonard creeped him out, and Travis thought this was all a mistake.

"I'm just messing with you, anyway. I ain't gonna smell your old lady's underwear. But you can tell a lot through smell. I made a quilt with this old timer once and I swear the room smelled like cinnamon every time we put in a stitch. That guy missed his mama something fierce."

"She ain't my old lady anymore," Travis said, draining his tea. He wiped his mouth with the back of his hand.

Leonard fished out a napkin from the lazy susan and slid it across the table to him. "Is that right? Well, I could have guessed that. Let me show you my fabric room."

Travis followed Leonard down the hallway and through a guest room door on the left. Two shelves of folded fabric, arranged neatly by patterns and color-hues, lined the walls opposite a large work table covered with well-worn cutting mats.

"These are my tools," Leonard said, waving his hands over a line of rotary cutters, scissors, and seam rippers. "A man needs his tools."

"How come you got two sewing machines?" Travis nodded toward the pair of Singers in opposite corners.

"Makes the work go faster. Men can be impatient, you know. And one of those was my Mama's. She taught me to sew. Maybe she wanted a girl, but she got me."

"And now you teach men to quilt?"

"Well, I'll teach anybody, but it seems to be my calling to work with guys. It just happened, I guess. Started out as a probation thing at the old folks' home for a little ol' DUI. Found out I kind of liked teachin' what I already knowed."

"Did the panty thing just happen too?" Travis inspected a red plaid quilt hanging from a rack. In the center of each block was a lacy black g-string attached with satin bows.

"I like challenging fabrics. Silk and satin and lace can be tough on a machine. I'll show you how, though. How about you pick out some prints you like and we'll start with a block? I'll show you a couple of patterns. I recommend the Ohio Star for beginners. She's real pretty but simple enough."

"What am I looking for?" Travis asked, shuffling his hands through the stacks of fabrics.

"Anything that catches your eye, really. You've got a blue in the panties so you could pick some more blue and a contrasting color, like yellow."

"Ain't yellow a female color? You know. It's kind of girlie."

Leonard leaned back in one of the chairs at his work table and stretched his arms behind his head so that his wiry black pit hair was fully exposed. "How about we don't worry about something like that right now, okay?"

Travis chose a navy paisley and a yellow-checked fabric. He laid the panties on top of the fabric and liked what he saw. Leonard tossed over a black polka-dot one.

"What if they don't fit together? You know, what if the colors don't match?" Travis asked.

"The thing about quilting is sometimes you just have to make it fit. Even if the pieces don't seem to go together—you can turn a square sideways or upside down, expand the border, or look at it from a different angle. Sometimes you change your plan."

"You ever just give up on one? Find one that just won't work?" Travis folded the black polka dot so that it bordered the blue and yellow prints. The patterns he thought were too busy faded against the dotted contrast. He placed the panties delicately on a creamy white and noticed how they became the feature of the block because of the bold black border.

"Nope. Never. It'll turn out. Quilts always do. Sometimes it's just not how you thought they would, but that's the art in it, see? Let's get to work. There's too much talking and not enough quilting. Now, hand over those panties."

An hour later, Travis finished his first block, and Leonard assured him that the next one would go faster. He sent him home with a bag of fabric to cut more strips, a rotary cutter, and a mat. Travis placed the block carefully on the passenger seat and drove straight home to show Huck, who sniffed it and wagged his tail appreciatively. Then Travis tucked the block under this pillow and pulled out the shopping list Leonard had written:

Panties (whites, blues, pink)
Queen bed sheet for backing (white, blue, or yellow)
Black thread

There was a quilting store down on Broadway across from Bones's Tavern; he was pretty sure he peed on their doorstep once at 2 a.m., but he wouldn't be caught dead in a store like that. It would have to be Wal-Mart, even though Leonard complained about the quality of their materials. He was almost out of dog food anyway, so it was time to make a run into town for supplies. Before he went, he scoured the house to see if by chance Jenny left anything else behind. He found a faded white bra hanging on the back of the bathroom door, but he remembered she called it her "sleeping bra" because it was falling apart and torn. It was not quilt-worthy. He checked underneath the mattress where he stashed condoms, but all he found were empty wrappers. Her nightstand was cleaned out just like the bottom two drawers of the dresser. Travis sighed, loaded Huck in the back of his truck, and left for town with the other dogs barking him down the driveway.

The Wal-Mart parking lot was more crowded than Travis liked for his mission. He parked far away from the entrance so no one could scratch his door and locked Huck in the cab. Inside, he loaded a huge bag of Alpo in his cart thinking he'd stash the other stuff beneath it and maybe use the self-checkout line. He steered the cart toward Housewares and read the labels on sheets. He chose the one that looked fanciest and had the highest thread count, whatever that meant. A group of ladies in the next aisle over were talking about patterns and making clothes for their grandbabies, so he moved in their direction.

"They just don't make clothes like that no more," a tired voice declared. "Gotta make your own if you want 'em to last."

"Uh huh," her companion agreed. "Shelby bought these clothes over at the JCPenny in Quincy, and I swear they fell apart after one washing."

"Ain't that the truth?"

"'Scuse me, ladies," Travis interrupted, "can either of you point me in the direction of black thread?"

"What for?" one of them asked, putting her hands on her hips.

"Um. My wife asked me to pick some up," he lied.

"No. I mean what she gonna use it for? It'll matter."

"Oh. She's making a quilt."

"Okay," the lady said. She guided her cart down the aisle. "You'll want bobbin threads."

"Might need variegated too."

"Uh huh."

Travis spent the next half hour learning about cotton, polyester, and quilting threads. He decided to pick up his own rotary blade and the ladies recommended a seam ripper, too.

"How come?" Travis asked, examining the sharp tool that seemed to undo what he's was trying to do.

"Oh, you'll make mistakes, honey," one of the ladies assured him, patting his arm, "especially a first timer like you."

"It's for my wife," Travis said.

"Uh huh." The ladies waved good-bye and watched as he rolled away.

Back home, Travis cleared the kitchen table and unpacked his supplies. He heated up two cans of pork and beans and spooned some into Huck's bowl on top of the Alpo. After eating, he ironed his fabric and began cutting the assigned strips. He liked the repetition and the methodical task. He liked keeping his hands busy. The sound of the blade against the fabric was certain and decisive, just like Jenny said he'd never be. He let his mind wander to the panties.

He missed her soft whimpers and the heat of her back when they spooned in bed, before Ronnie ruined everything.

After he cut the material strips for his squares, he called Leonard and left a voicemail about his progress. *I done those strips you wanted me to. Guess I need to sew them now. I got the other stuff too. Except the panties. But I'll work on that. Give me a call back. Thanks. It's Travis, by the way. Okay.*

He checked the ball game, but the Cardinals were losing again. He flipped through the channels and stopped on the Eleanor Burns show. He remembered Jenny watching it once while she finished off his last Klondike bar. On the screen, the quilting lady wore a cheery red cardigan, and her mousy brown bangs bobbed in her face when she cut her material. "It's best to wash each of the fabrics first to check for shrinkage," she explained. Travis didn't know that. He wondered if it was too late. The corners of her eyes wrinkled under her wire-rimmed glasses and wide grin. She assured him that even he could make a quilt in a day. With the right help from Eleanor, it was that easy. *A day?* He didn't need something *that* easy. He needed something that lasted. Eleanor's quilt looked so sturdy, not like those cheap Wal-Mart throws with the threads hanging loose before you even left the checkout. She introduced her new scallops, vines, and waves template and the demonstration was too much for Travis's skill level. His mind wandered and he started thinking about what kind of panties Eleanor Burns wore. They're probably cotton. High-waisters, for sure. Or maybe that grandmother exterior hides a sex kitten? What does underwear say about a woman, anyway? Jenny seemed to have underwear for every occasion. If it was Fruit-of-the-Loom, he knew she needed her space. Cramps, probably. Lace and bows were invitations. Frisky, probably. He always thought underwear was a means to an end, something in the way of his real goal. When he first met Jenny, she only wore black or red panties. Her legs were always shaved. Once she started staying over more and moved Ronnie in, all that stopped. Everything she'd liked about Travis—his corny jokes, his devotion to Huck, his optimism about the Cardinals—annoyed her. She picked at him constantly if Ronnie was around and ignored him mostly when he wasn't. A woman like Eleanor wouldn't do that. He watched her toss scraps over her shoulder like confetti and giggle at her own naughtiness. Travis turned up the volume and began sewing his strips into blocks.

Leonard called the next day and invited Travis for lunch. He served tomato soup and grilled cheese sandwiches. "You quilt. You cook," Travis said, biting into his third wedge of buttered, gooey bread, "I just may marry you."

"Nah," Leonard answered, untying his apron and folding it back into a kitchen drawer. "I like the ladies. And their panties. I'll bet you're a boxers kind of guy. Not my thing."

Travis shifted in his seat, imagining how embarrassed he'd be if Leonard saw the skid marks on his tighty whities. Jenny always said she could bleach them, but he said he didn't care, which wasn't true at all.

"I'll wash, you dry, okay?" Leonard tossed a dishtowel at Travis. "Then we'll quilt." Travis joined him, hip to hip, at the kitchen sink.

Travis's full belly and good mood lasted until the third time his machine ate both the thread and his carefully cut quilting strips. "Goddamn machine!" he yelled, knocking over his chair and dropping the material to the floor. Leonard picked it up and smoothed the wrinkles with his calloused palms. "It don't like me at all," Travis whined. "No one does."

"Settle down," Leonard told him. "It ain't personal. It just takes a lot of patience to get it right. Every time it eats your thread or gobbles up a strip, you just start again. See? That's how." He rethreaded Travis' machine and bit the thread with his teeth. Then Leonard handed Travis the seam ripper. "Take it out. Start again."

"Starting over takes too long."

"Sometimes it's the only way." Leonard clucked his tongue and turned back to the square he just finished.

"Why the hell do you do this anyway?" Travis looked around the room at the mess: the discarded fabric scraps littering the floor, the threads stuck to every surface, the piles of half-done projects saved for another day.

Leonard sighed. He pulled off the reading glasses he needed to see the eyes of the needles and let them hang from a chain around his neck. Another pair of glasses perched on top of his head. "Come on," he said, "I'll show you." He led Travis back down the hall to his own bedroom. He opened the door to a tidy, sunshine-filled room and nodded toward the throne-like bed covered in an emerald green quilt made entirely of panties. Dozens of panties. Every panty style ever invented. A panty heaven.

Travis shook his head. "I ain't . . ."

"Oh, shut up and get in," Leonard said. Then he nudged Travis under the quilt, pulled it up to his chin, and tucked him in. "There, now. That's why. Like I said, everyone needs a soft place to rest. You just lay there awhile. And next time, because there will be a next time, bring more panties."

A week later, Travis stitched the final block with a black thong he stole from the YMCA's lost and found. Leonard contributed two cotton briefs with bows he swiped at the Laundromat and attached the polka dot border. Travis stood drinking a cold beer and watched as Leonard put the backing on with an embroidery machine he stored in the garage next to his bike. After the final stitch, they gathered around the quilt and admired their work. Leonard nodded toward a particularly challenging block that they had to redo three times and Travis just smiled. Then Leonard wrapped the quilt around Travis' shoulders like a cape and patted him hard on the back. They made promises to meet next week at Scoville's for celebratory tenderloins and Travis drove away with the quilt folded into a silk bag on his passenger seat. Halfway home, he turned his truck around and drove to the apartment complex on the edge of town where he heard Jenny was renting. He spotted her truck in the parking lot and dialed her number. Jenny picked up on the first ring.

"Travis, is that you?"

"It's me. I'm outside. Can you come out?"

"Why? What d'you want?"

"I just want to show you something. Come see. Please? Then I'll leave. Promise."

"Ronnie ain't here. You want to come up?"

Travis thought about it. He did want to come up. But he didn't want to like this. "Nah. You come down. I want you to see this."

A few minutes later Jenny slid into the cab beside him. She shoved the quilt out of the way to make room. Travis watched her and waited. "What?" she finally said, and pulled out a cigarette.

"I made it," he began. "I made this quilt. For you." It was a lie. Travis didn't really want Jenny to take his quilt, but he wanted her to want to. He watched her cigarette burn, worried about the smoke and ash.

"You what? Why's it got . . . what are those? Are those mine?" Jenny grabbed at the quilt—her long fingernail catching a cotton crotch—Travis hugged the material to protect it. Jenny put her hand on the doorknob, blew smoke toward him, and waited to see if he'd stop her. He didn't want to play her game anymore. He'd made a mistake with Jenny, but he wasn't going to live it. He kept his grip firm on the fabric but rolled down the window for fresh air. "You didn't make shit," she spat.

"I did too. I made the whole goddamn thing." Travis pulled the quilt into his lap. Its fluffiness piled up and covered the steering wheel.

Then a car horn beeped. Ronnie fishtailed into the parking lot, spraying a cloud of dust and rock.

Jenny smiled, then erupted into a fit of giggles. She laughed at Travis, at this thing that mattered to him.

"Get out."

"You don't have to ask me twice!" Jenny yelled and slammed the door shut behind her.

"You don't deserve it!" Travis screamed, his voice muffled by panties.

At home, Travis wrapped himself and Huck in the quilt together and cuddled up on the couch. Huck busied himself licking and appreciating each panty block. Travis flipped through the channels until he found Eleanor, who promised him it would be okay. "You'll make mistakes," she said, "but you can always fix 'em. They don't call me 'the Stripper' for nothing."

THE FLIGHT OF
HERMAN ENGELMANN

JILL KALZ

It wasn't a place for women. Not that we went out of our way to discourage them from coming out, understand. But it was easier when it was men only. Simple. Uncomplicated. Comfortable. When a woman showed up on the flying field, it was like turning everyone's transmitter to the same channel—and waiting for all hell to break loose.

I used to farm a stretch just outside Essig, in Milford Township, and for the last six years before I turned it over to my nephew, I kept up a strip of grass right down the center of it. Sixty feet wide, 500 feet long. A runway for my buddies. The WingDings—that's what we called ourselves; a bunch of crazy nuts and their radio-controlled airplanes. Oh, a couple younger guys from New Ulm and Sleepy Eye drove out once in a while and flew helicopters and all sorts of odd contraptions—one joker even built a flying pancake, pats of foam-core butter on top and all—but most of us flew warbirds: Corsairs, P-39s, Zeros, Spitfires. Like we always said, "Bigger flies better."

I loved to fly, especially my Sukhoi. As soon as I finished work for the day, damn if I wasn't heading out to the flying field with my girl, fueling her up, and dancing her into the sky. I had routines that changed with the weather. Blue skies lit a fire under my ass, and I looped and swooped that plane to the snap of Herb Alpert and the Tijuana Brass. We didn't have a sound system out there or anything, just a makeshift lean-to we could sit under for some shade when we weren't flying. But I heard the trumpets clear in my head as soon as the wheels left the ground. Same as I heard Louis Armstrong on those partly cloudy days, the ones with little wind and the high cirrus clouds, when I'd turn on the smoke and arc and dip and fly through my own white rings. She flew so effortlessly. Made a guy forget his body had weight, that he wasn't sitting up there beneath that canopy.

But just like a woman, the Sukhoi had a mind of her own and did what she pleased, no matter how I sweet-talked her. Had a few minor bumps over the years—crunched the landing gear once when she caught a bad crosswind coming across the corn, busted more than a few props, all repairable stuff—but I lost her altogether right after Doc's hip problems took a turn for the worse. One minute, she was winking at me in the light of a September evening, and the next, she was gone.

Doc Johnson and I had grown up just down the road from each other. We'd gone to twelve years of Catholic school together, farmed neighboring fields for more than forty years, and we were both members of the WingDings. But that's where our similarities ended.

Doc was a crotchety son-of-a-bitch. Tight, too. Always tracking things to the penny. Whenever it came time to split the tab over at Smiley's after a day of flying, he'd get out his pen and start figuring on a napkin, trying to divide some cheese-bread, a couple pizzas, and a few pitchers of beer five ways, though he didn't have any cheese-bread, he'd tell us, on account of his high cholesterol, so he didn't think he should have to pay anything toward that, and he'd had only one glass of beer all night, making his share for the pitchers proportionately less. The bill at Smiley's never amounted to much over $40 anyhow, so eventually, after watching Doc carrying the ones and rounding up to the nearest cent for a good five minutes, one of us (usually me) would figure the hell with it and just pay the whole thing. And you know, he never once offered to cough up the tip. How he ever conned Lila into marrying him, I truly will never know. Couldn't have been his looks. Man was uglier than a mudfish. Never knew what she saw in him that the rest of us didn't.

I was the bachelor farmer of Milford Township, which meant I got invited to plenty of folks' holiday gatherings and had other guys' wives bringing me helpings of beef roast, fried chicken, and stuffed pork chops during planting and harvest seasons. Not a bad deal. Jerry's wife, Joan, was always good for a few batches of homemade kraut in the fall. Edwin's wife, Dot, kept my cellar stocked with jars of plum and apple jelly, pickles, beets, squash, and pumpkin. Frank's wife, Phyllis, as round as she was tall, could be counted on for pans of bars and a couple rhubarb or caramel apple pies. And Doc's wife, Lila? She'd stop over with some cleaning supplies once a month and whip my place into shape. We'd tell each other jokes and talk a bit about the local news—who'd died or gotten ticketed for speeding, the drop in corn and soybean bushels, how the New Ulm boys were bound to choke at State again this year . . . that type of thing. The house always looked, smelled, and felt better after she'd been there.

"Jesus, Herm," she said once, scrubbing the burner pans in a sink full of suds. "All I'm asking you to do is maintain. Just once, couldn't you make potatoes without letting them boil over?"

I was sitting at the kitchen table, flanked by newspapers, airplane magazines, and a set of paints, working on my latest treat from the hobby store: a new pilot for my Corsair. Not all my planes had pilots—some didn't have enough clearance beneath the canopy, even though a pilot isn't much more than a set of shoulders and a head, and some just looked better without them—but I thought the Corsair deserved one.

I shook my head and said, "I ain't got time to sit and watch water boil, woman. I got a farm to run here, you know."

"Oh, but you've got time to sit at that table for an hour, trying to get just the right shade of red on your little doll's lips there."

"That's different."

"Yeah, that's different, alright."

"And she's a *pilot*, not a *doll*," I said. "Geez, Lila, I'm disappointed in you. Get the terminology right, would ya? Haven't Doc and I taught you anything over the years?"

"How can she be a pilot with no arms and no legs?"

"She's a handicapped pilot. There are handicapped pilots, you know. This one, well, she steers by . . . wiggling her torso."

"Are you sure she doesn't steer by wiggling her *boobs*? That's quite a set she's got."

"Really?" I said, turning my new pilot in my hands and fingering the hard plastic bumps. "I hadn't even noticed she *had* boobs. Huh."

"Ach," Lila said, slapping my shoulder with a wet yellow glove, "*you're* a boob."

The screw in Doc's left hip started worming its way back out in November 2005, the day before Thanksgiving, and the screw in the right hip did the same in December, on Christmas Eve, while Doc was helping unload presents from the back of his son's truck. The pain of two loose hips dropped him to the snow like a heavyweight punch. They were ten-year hips, the doctors had told him back in '93. Doc, of course, being Doc, got his money's worth and managed to sneak in a couple extra years. But time was up now, so the family hauled him into the emergency room, where he was poked, doped, pricked, x-rayed, and then wheeled back out to the truck with an appointment card for surgery and a less-than-happy "Happy Holidays" from a nurse who'd pulled an unlucky shift.

A month later, when they opened him up, the son-of-a-bitch was all soured inside, full of infection. Doctors claimed they'd never seen so much pus. They took out the left hip but kept the right one in. It wasn't as far gone yet as the left, and I suppose they figured the man needed *some* way to move around, at least a little bit. They certainly couldn't put the new hips in with all that infection, so they scraped and scrubbed everything clean as they could, sewed him shut, and soon after started him on forty-five days of antibiotics. Pills *and* shots.

Fool should've gone into a nursing home where he would've had trained people taking care of him—that's what the doctors said, too. But nursing homes cost money, see. So instead, Lila got some quick lessons from the hospital staff on how to change dressings, how to handle a syringe, how to roll her husband so she could change the bed sheets, how to move his legs so the muscles didn't get all spongy. She also learned where to support him so he could get out of bed and across the hall to use the toilet, how to keep his pain in check, and how to monitor everything that went into Doc's body and everything that came out. Doc's two boys loaded their dad flat on his back into the older son's truck, drove him home to the farm, and laid him on the bed. And on that double bed, staring at the ceiling, is where Doc Johnson stayed for the next forty-five days.

Lila stopped over at my place the second week of February, cleaning supplies in tow. I hadn't seen her since before Christmas, before Doc's hospital adventures began, and I was beginning to wonder if she'd just stop coming by. After all, taking care of Doc was a full-time job when he had two *healthy* hips. I couldn't imagine the work it took when the guy had one missing and another with popped hardware. And really, in the dead of winter, when I wasn't out in the field and all I had to do was build and fix airplanes on my kitchen table, I should've been able to keep my own house clean. But I was glad she came by. I'd missed her.

"Word over at Smiley's is you and Doc won the lottery," I said, "and you've been holed up, filling cream cans and plotting where to bury them once the ground thaws."

"Actually," Lila said, unwrapping her scarf and shaking off the snow in the doorway, "we haven't even been home. We've got body doubles living over there at the house. Doc and I have been partying down in the Bahamas since Christmas." She rolled up the sleeves of her turtleneck, exposing forearms white as the snow she'd just shaken off. "See my tan?" she said with a wink.

She walked right over to the kitchen sink and started filling it with hot water. Bubbles puffed out of the soap bottle and floated to the ceiling like tiny pink pearls.

"How's Doc doing?" I asked, getting back to the wing I was sanding.

"Fine," she said. "He pretty much just lies there. Does a lot of crossword puzzles, holding the magazines up over his head. Has to use a pencil, though, because, you know, pens won't write upside down."

"Need those NASA pens, like the ones the astronauts use."

Lila pulled out the stovetop burners and looked at the crusty drip pans. She scowled at me and dropped the pans into the sudsy water. Then she opened the oven, pulled out all the racks, and coated the inside with white foam. "I'm just going to let that sit for a while," she said. "I don't know what kind of explosion you had in there."

"Oh, that would've been the lasagna," I said. "Made myself a treat for New Year's. Garlic toast and everything." I picked up a finer gauge sheet of paper and continued sanding. "Used the wrong pan, though—too small—and that tomato sauce and cheese just bubbled out all over the place. Boy, what a mess."

"I see that," Lila said. She picked up her tote of cleaning supplies and walked behind my chair. "I'm going to make a quick pass through the bathroom. Any explosions in *there* I should be made aware of?"

"No, I try to keep that pretty clean."

"Good."

"Say," I said, raising my voice once Lila left the room, "you going to the WingDings' party over at Carl's Saturday night?"

"Doc's not supposed to go out while he's on his meds," she yelled back. "So, no."

"Well, *you* can still come. Have a beer, talk with the wives. Food's always good, and you have to eat anyhow, right? I'm sure they'd put together a to-go box for the patient."

I heard her spray more white foam—a different white foam—all over the shower doors and tub. I heard her lift up the toilet seat and squirt bowl cleaner around the rim. Then came the frantic squeaking as she scrubbed the water spots and flecks of toothpaste from the mirror. She ran water, wet a sponge, and wiped it across the tile, the shiny chrome fixtures, and the shower doors she'd sprayed—the soap scum already lifted and carried on the bubbles' backs. I heard the stiff bowl brush, the flush, and the gurgle. I heard the mop slap the crackly linoleum. But I didn't hear Lila say anything.

I stopped sanding and, with my voice raised again, said, "So, what do you think about Saturday, then?"

After a long pause, Lila flipped off the bathroom light, walked back into the kitchen, put on her yellow rubber gloves, and said, "I'll think about it."

Nothing beats broasted chicken, baked potatoes with sour cream, and bottles of Schell's on a cold February night. Carl set us up in the back half of the dining area, even pulled out the paper placemats with the red poinsettias in the corners, seeing as how it was supposed to be our club's Christmas party. Before the meal, my buddy Dean showed some of the video he shot last summer: footage of the WingDings out at the flying field, some from his trips to AirVenture and the air races out in Reno. 'Course I'd forgotten to bring along the screen like I said I was going to, so we tried projecting right onto the wall. But Carl's is covered in wood paneling—that real dark-brown stuff—so that made it tough. Then Dean taped a bunch of placemats together. Worked pretty good, though every once in a while someone's plane nosedived into a poinsettia, just like a hungry bee.

No one mentioned Doc and Lila until we started passing around the dinner rolls.

"It's gotta be bad over there," Joan said quietly. "But you know Lila. She won't say nothing."

Dot clucked her tongue. "Woman's going to work herself into an early grave, that one is," she said. "I tell you, I wouldn't do it. Waiting on that man hand and foot. She's a prisoner in her own home. Can't even leave him long enough to get her hair done, for Christ's sake."

"Come on, Dot," Edwin said slyly, bumping her shoulder. "You saying you wouldn't play nurse if I was laid up like that?"

"If you were as ornery as Doc, hell no." Dot coated her roll with a thick layer of butter. "Have you ever heard that man say one kind word about her? Ever? And it's not like they don't have the money to pay for home health care. Oh, they have it. Doc just won't part with it, is all."

"When's he go see the doctor again?" Jerry asked.

"March 10th," I said.

"And what happens then?"

"From what Lila told me, if his blood work looks okay, they'll schedule him for surgery down in Rochester."

Dot shook her head. "I'll bet Ed's left nut this is not going to end well."

Edwin set down his knife and fork and leaned back in his chair. "C'mon, now," he said. "Why you gotta bring my sack into this?"

"Pfft," Dot said. "It's not like you need that old thing anymore anyway."

A few days after the party, the weather turned nasty—nastier than we'd seen in years. A foot and a half of fresh snow, followed by highs in the teens—below zero. The entire state was a neglected freezer, every building frosted over like an old TV dinner. Like everyone else, I stayed in; I made a double batch of chili, fiddled with the engine I'd been building, and watched plenty of *Andy Griffith* reruns. And I watched the calendar, too, hoping March would roar in with good news for us all.

"What's this?" Lila asked, taking the rose from my hand.

"They had a deal at the Holiday station this morning," I said. "Buy a dozen donuts, get a free rose. Some sort of St. Patrick's Day special."

"Well. Thank you. Don't often see neon green roses . . . edged in silver glitter. Do I get a donut, too?"

"A what? Oh—I ate them all."

"Herman Engelmann, you ate a dozen donuts for breakfast?"

"No, I gave a few to the gal behind the counter—real nice gal—and then I ran into Edwin and gave him a few for him and the wife, so no, I didn't eat them *all*. No. Geez. What do you think?"

Lila snipped a bit off the stem and stuck the flower in a tall water glass. "Well, good," she said. "You eat twelve donuts and you'll be bound up for a week."

I sat back down at the kitchen table and started paging through my latest issue of *Sport Aviation*. "I'm just happy Doc's finally going to get that surgery," I said. "June'll be here before you know it, so . . . Been a tough haul for you. For Doc."

Lila set the makeshift vase on the counter, pulled out a chair, and sat at the table with me. That was my first clue that something wasn't quite right. She never did that—never sat down when she came over.

The clock ticked. The fridge hummed. The pages of my magazine crackled as I flipped them, ads for landing gear, flight schools, and camshafts buzzing for attention. Lila folded her hands on the table, carefully stroked and kneaded each dry, reddened joint.

After a few minutes, I leaned back and switched on my portable radio. "KNUJ's even getting all Irish today," I said. The radio popped and spit before a pair of concertinas bounced their way into the room. "Heard it in the truck this morning. I don't know. Do we really need a 'Danny Boy' *polka*? Sometimes those fools over in New Ulm just don't know when to leave well enough alone."

Lila cleared her throat and resettled herself in her chair. "Say," she began, still focused on her fingers, "remember a few weeks back, when we had all that snow and then the god-awful cold?" She didn't wait for me to answer. "Well, I mean, who doesn't remember that? Of course you remember that. Everyone remembers that. It just happened." She looked long out the window, then at the flower on the counter. "I tell ya," she continued, "I felt really stuck inside. Inside the house, I mean. And then when I went outside, with those five-foot drifts alongside the garage, cripes, I felt—I felt stuck there, too. Stuck. Couldn't move. Couldn't breathe. There was nowhere to go *in*side, and nowhere to go *out*side. Just—well, there was just nowhere to go."

The words hung in the air a bit, then settled on our shoulders.

And just like that, the space between Lila and me shifted. So quick, so slight, no one sitting with us would've noticed. Like a twitched finger on a stick and the resulting tick of the ailerons that takes a plane off center and rolls her left. I'd known Lila more than forty years, but at that moment, I didn't know what to say.

Thankfully the radio announcer spoke up for me. He read the

station ID and told us that even though the local temperature was twenty-five, with the wind chill it felt more like one.

This is the beauty of Minnesota; less than two months later, the corn was in, and I was out at the flying field in jeans and a T-shirt, putting up flight after flight till the sun told me to stop playing, go home, and make supper. Lila had come out to the field a few times since the start of spring to watch me and the other guys fly. I brought along the trainer, thinking she might like to learn how to fly herself. I offered a number of times, but she always shook her head. I told her if she was afraid of losing a finger flicking the prop, I'd show her how to use my chicken stick. No shame in it. I still used it once in a while. She waved her hand at me, urging me to shut up and take off so she could sit back and enjoy a good show. We didn't talk much about Doc. In fact, she rarely mentioned his name at all.

Since St. Patrick's Day, Lila was stopping over at the house at least twice a week—barely giving me time to get the place dirty between visits. I found myself bypassing the rug by the back door just to leave muddy boot prints on the linoleum; making my frozen pizzas without a pan so the cheese would ooze through the racks and cement itself to the oven floor; and brushing my teeth wide-mouthed for the biggest spatter pattern on the medicine cabinet mirror.

I knew why I was doing it; I didn't want Lila to feel like she was wasting her time. I had to give her something to clean, and I liked having her over. Like I said before, the place felt lighter and brighter after she'd been there; the air smelled fresher because of the soaps and disinfectants and the perfume she wore.

But I'll be honest now; it was more than that. My messes gave me excuses. Of course Lila has to come over, I told myself. I'm a schluppy bachelor farmer who can't keep his pots from boiling over, or the lime from choking the holes in his showerhead. She's doing me a service, helping out an old friend, making sure I don't become buried in my own filth and trigger a batch of rumors throughout the township. She's *not* coming over to escape her life at home—I assured myself—to get away from Doc and his demands. She's *not* coming over because she feels anything more for you, you tired old fool, than friendship. It's the messes and her need to clean them up that brings her by. I make my many messes to give her something to do, to give her reason to come talk smart and keep me on my toes. I do *not* make them so I can pretend we're together, pretend she's chosen me and I've chosen her, pretend the rest of my days will start and end with her. Because that would be wrong. *That* would be *wrong*. And thoughts like that could only hurt a man.

I had to hear myself say it out loud, so one morning after she'd finished vacuuming, I said, "Say, Lila. Does Doc know how often you come over here?"

"Why?"

"Well," I stammered, "I just don't want to cause any trouble or get in the middle of anything. Know what I mean?"

"Doc always knows where I am," Lila said, winding up the vacuum cord. "I tell him when I'm coming over. There's no sneaking going on, if that's what you're worried about." She tucked the vacuum inside the hall closet. "You and I are just friends, Herm."

"No, I know," I said. "Sometimes I just wonder if Doc—"

"And besides, with the surgery coming up next month, I'll be sticking closer to home, helping Doc recoup, and you'll have your house all to yourself again. No one to keep putting down the toilet seat."

"Probably better for me to sit anyway," I said. "Aim's been for shit lately."

Lila smiled. "Speaking as the woman who cleans your bathroom, I can vouch for that. Good thing you don't *fly* as off-target as you *pee*. They'd be finding pieces of balsawood all over the county."

That evening, I drove east to New Ulm. It was Made-Right Night at the Legion, and I hadn't been to one all year. I ordered three sandwiches with the works (ketchup, mustard, pickles, and raw onions), a bag of chips, and a Diet Pepsi. And I started talking to a woman at the bar nursing a rum and Coke—a widow from town named Shirley. I made her laugh, and she touched the back of my hand.

Before I knew what I was doing, I asked her to join me for dinner at the Kaiserhoff the next night. A date. My first date in more than twenty years.

None of us could believe it. But ten days after Doc's surgery, his sons were racing him back down to Rochester, fever boiling his blood and straining his every seam. The doctors opened him up, and in the cool of the O.R., infection hissed like a snake.

So out came the new left hip, the old right one, and with them any chance of Doc walking again. No matter what the doctors gave him, no matter how much or for how long, Doc stayed sour through and through. Guess that's just the way he was meant to be.

His boys started building the ramps as soon as he came back home. They said Doc didn't want any visitors, so I just watched from my kitchen window—the loads of plywood, the hospital bed delivery, Lila running to the store—until the corn got too high for me to see anything below the Johnsons' second floor.

I flew a lot that summer, took advantage of the hot, dry weather to test out a few new planes, catch up with the rest of the WingDings, keep my mind off Lila and the things I imagined going on in that house. Doc's boys said their dad sat on the front porch a lot in his wheelchair, watching our flights, but that when they asked if he wanted a ride to the field, he shook his head and grunted. He said no one wanted his crippled ass out there, said he didn't want people looking at him funny and feeling sorry for him.

I never brought Shirley out to the field. In fact, she came out to the farm just once. I always met her in New Ulm for our dates. She didn't seem very interested in flying and referred to me and the guys as "you boys and your silly toys." But that was okay. I liked having my own hobby with my own friends. I'd been alone for so long that it was tough for me to find a balance between time with Shirley and time without. She was a sweet gal, but I think we both knew we wouldn't last long.

"Hello, stranger," Lila said, standing on the step, smiling, holding

her tote of cleaning supplies with one hand and a pan of choco-
late-covered bars with the other. "Been a while, so God only knows
what you've done to the place. Thought I might need reinforcements:
fresh batch of Special K bars."

"Come in! Come in!" I said, holding the door. "But you know you're
not supposed to do labor on Labor Day. It's a law or something."

Lila set down the tote and pan on the kitchen table and did a quick
sweep of the room with her eyes. "Looks good!" she said. "I'm
impressed, Engelmann. Although I'm also a little hurt. Doesn't look
like you need me anymore."

"Well, I wasn't sure if you were coming back, so . . . it's true. I'm
trainable."

"I never doubted."

"How's Doc doing? I sure was sorry to hear the news. Just awful."

Lila sighed and started unpacking her tote. "The boys and their
families are over visiting, so he's not quite so owly today. But he's
angry. And bitter. The meds help with the pain, but he's getting more
and more depressed. I'm sure I'd feel the same way, knowing I was
never going to walk again."

I watched as she filled the sink with suds, her back to me. I hesitated a moment, then asked, "You thought at all about getting him
into a nursing home?"

Lila chuckled. "You know as well as I do he'd never leave the
farm. Plus, he's my husband, you know—bum steer that he is. For
better or worse."

"Well, sure," I said, "but that doesn't mean you have to give up
your life for his, does it? I mean, no one ever sees you anymore. I
never see you anymore. You never get out—"

"I get out plenty."

"Out, sure, to get groceries, to pick up Doc's drugs . . . but what
about coffee with the gals? Or going shopping? Just laughing and
having a good time?"

Lila rinsed a glass and carefully placed it on the drying rack.
"Listen, I've got a man at home who can't take a shit without me.
I've got two grown boys who don't know how to act around their

own father anymore. Me having a good time is the last thing on my list right now."

"I'm just saying—"

"I know what you're saying—"

"I'm just saying you have to get yourself some help. You're a tough bird, Lila, no doubt about that. But you can't do it all yourself. No one could."

Lila turned around to face me. Hard lines drew down the corners of her mouth, and her look took me in with a chill. "You know," she began quietly, "I envy you. I do. To be able to pick and choose the parts of life you like best. Avoid the work of it. Run away from the messy parts. You want to spend your days in the clouds, you can. Whatever Herm wants to do, Herm does. You aren't responsible for anyone except yourself. You don't even have a goddamn dog."

I looked down at the table and nodded. She was right. "It's just—I just wish things were different for you," I said. "That's all. I—hell, I don't know."

Lila shook her head and covered her eyes with her hand. "No, I'm sorry. I'm sorry." She exhaled. "I know you're trying to help. I think I'm just overtired. You got anything to drink?"

And that's when she noticed the photo on the fridge door.

"Who's this?" she asked.

"Oh, that's Shirley and me at the winery," I said. "Shirley owns a bookstore over in New Ulm. We've been sort of dating the past few months. I haven't had a chance to tell ya." Lila kept staring at the photo. "I don't know what possessed me to ask her out in the first place, 'cause, you know me, I don't do that. I *never* do that. Me going out on dates . . . Crazy. Crazy stuff. But I asked her and she said yes, so . . . Widowed. No kids. Nice gal. Smart, too. When I hug her, you know, it's just like I'm hugging you."

It was instantaneous. The moment the word "you" came out of my mouth, I regretted it, and regretted it bad, wanted to fly it right back down my throat. But I fumbled the controls. "What I mean is—"

Lila turned back to the sink and pulled out the plug.

I started again. "What I mean is, you're both basically the same size—short and small—and so when I—"

The drain gurgled. Lila rinsed the sink clean, draped the yellow gloves over the faucet to air-dry.

I couldn't level her out. "Lila, I don't want you to think I pretended . . . That's not what I—"

She continued to stand at the sink with her back to me, looking out the window at the corn now bled of its green, looking at the rooflines of her house and out-buildings rows and rows away.

"I can't come over any more, Herm," she said finally.

I slid back my chair and stood up. Lila walked to the table and wrapped her hand around the cleaning tote handle. I'm not sure how long we stood there, unable to breathe, the air between us turned thick and heavy as exhaust. It could've been a couple minutes. Maybe an hour. I honestly don't know.

I wanted to tell her I loved her. Should've told her I loved her. I should've stopped her at the door when she looked at me that last time, the smallest, tired smile trying to break. I should've held on tight when she said she'd choose me if she could, if things were different, if it wasn't already far too late. That's what I should've done.

But instead, I said nothing. Did nothing, except let her walk out the door and close it behind her.

I should've stayed inside after the last of the dust kicked up by her truck slipped into the corn. Should've drank myself into a long sleep so I'd have had time to catch my breath, fix the parts inside me that weren't working. I should've stayed as close to the ground as possible.

But instead, I grabbed my Sukhoi and headed out to the flying field. I put her up fast and snapped her, rolled her, pushed her inverted into countless spins. My hands shook. No wind. No sound except the buzz of the engine.

I watched her but didn't really see her until she winked, a flash of deep gold light off the canopy. Then she flew straight up, the red star on her tail soaring. I hadn't touched the elevator and frantically tried to correct, get her out of the climb. She hesitated, stalled, then turned nose-first toward the ground. Dead stick. I shook the radio and watched, helpless. "No, no, no, no," I cried as she dove into the corn and shattered.

It wasn't long after that I called up my nephew. Sold him the land. Moved here to New Ulm. I'd been meaning to get out of farming for a while anyway—body can't do what it used to, you know—and the stuff with Lila just sped things along. The WingDings took most of my planes off my hands. Not much room in the apartment. They wouldn't let me sell them all, though, said I couldn't get out of the club *that* easily. And they made sure I didn't wait too long to put up another flight after I lost the Sukhoi. Gotta get back on the horse, they said.

They talk about Doc once in a while at our meetings, and I might catch a little news about Lila, but not much. I think about her a lot, wonder what she's doing at different times of the day, what she thinks of me now.

Sometimes, on clear summer mornings, early, before the sky slips sure into pink, before the day's first freight train whistles through the valley, hugging the river, I'll walk to the end of the block, lick the tip of my index finger, and hold it up in the air to check wind direction. Old habit. And more often than not, she's blowing from the west.

GOING DOWN

STEVE FAYER

On a sweltering end-of-June afternoon, in the borough of Brooklyn, in the year 1950, Patsy Costello knelt to cut pale pink roses in her mother's garden on Martense Street. She held the thorned stems to the sun. She thought of Larry Doyle.

A block away, a trolley rolled and lurched up Church Avenue, its windows open wide, a boy clinging to the outside of the car. From his hold on the window bars, Beans McBehan surveyed the Avenue with one-eyed caution, then dropped to the tracks below, running with the trolley as it slowed. He, too, thought of Larry Doyle. It was Doyle who had taught him the art of the free ride.

The Brooklyn air was quiet on this summer Saturday. Irish and Italian shoeshine boys slow-pitched pennies against the subway entrance at the corner of Church and Nostrand Avenues, their cries muffled in the heat. The street tar under McBehan was soft and sucked at his shoes. He had traveled half the borough and had no place to go. Beans was convinced that only Larry Doyle could understand. Doyle would recognize a follower without a leader, a hustler without a hustle, a one-eyed natural who had fooled himself into thinking he could see in more than one dimension. And perhaps, the boy thought, the spirit of Larry Doyle in whatever heaven or hell it occupied had something to do on that day with sending ninety thousand men across the 38th parallel into South Korea. All to change Beans's life. To shift the course of world history as a favor for a friend.

Beans borrowed a pair of tinted glasses to disguise his glass eye, memorized part of the chart and peered through his fingers to chant the rest. A desperate Navy took him in, shipped him by bus to boot camp in Bainbridge, Maryland. Bainbridge was, in that oppressive autumn, so hot in the afternoon sun that recruits who locked their knees at attention soon fell dead away, so cold at night in the uninsulated wooden barracks that he and most of the recruits slept in full gear—turtleneck sweaters, chambray shirts, and dungarees. Scuttlebutt was, if you lost more than half-a-day in sickbay, you'd have to repeat the months of boot camp hell. When the barracks came down with the flu, when the recruits formed into ranks looking more dead than alive, when Beans fell asleep even as he walked his post with shouldered rifle, waking as he banged into the corner of the barracks at one end, and into the Dempster Dumpster at the other, neither he nor anyone else in his company reported sick.

It had not occurred to him that there would be WAVES. On the first marches of the day to and from the mess hall, the men followed the perfume of the WAVE companies. In the thick morning air, they could hear the songs of these pussy-stripers drifting back at them in wavering, off-key soprano: *"Oh the blouses in the Navy, they say they're mighty fine. But it would take Lana Turner to fill the front of mine. Oh the Navy, Oh, the Navee . . ."* Passing a WAVE column one early morning, his company formed a single file, risking a month of extra duty to grab at the girls. He could not believe his luck. The prettiest of the girls had grabbed back at him. After a few days of flirtation, she agreed to meet after lights out in back of his own barracks. She was a young sailor's dream, blonde, green-eyed with flecks of fire in the iris, and possessed of a country girl bawdiness, the laughter rising deep from within her belly, pushing her high bosom against the starched cotton of her uniform. Such a young woman would never have looked at him in his civilian life. She was a gift from on high, perhaps from as high—or as low—as Doyle's soul had risen. Inside the Dumpster, Beans had tried to get naked with her, but she couldn't hack it. Another night, they crawled under the barracks but the scattering of crushed cigarette packs and empty pints and used prophylactics had, again, put her off. He was still plotting sexual success, attempting to coordinate a twelve-hour liberty with her in Baltimore, and had, at the same time, just about mastered the manual of arms, smacking the turn-of-the-century

Springfield rifle with new authority, when during a captain's inspec-
tion the four-striper looked him straight in his glass eye, and asked
him what in hell he thought he was doing in this man's Navy. A few
days later, he was back in Brooklyn, mourning the unconsummated
relationship with the little blonde WAVE, Jewel was her name,
from Morganton, North Carolina. He could not forget that voice
smooth and thick with want, teasing words into southern syllables
he had never encountered before. Her skin, warming to his touch,
had smelled of Ivory Soap, the plain perfume conjuring far more
than its makers had intended. He sent her a desperate note. She
never answered.

The Navy sent him home wearing his dress blue uniform with
two Seaman Apprentice stripes on the left sleeve, stripes he would
not have officially earned until he graduated from boot camp. When
things got tough at home—the old man drinking even more, his
sisters all seeming to have come into their periods at once, com-
peting with each other and his mother—he went to an Army-Navy
surplus store, bought himself a "crow"—an eagle with one reversed
chevron framing electrical sparks—sewed it on the crease of the
left arm, halfway between elbow and shoulder, and became an
instant petty officer, a radioman third class. It was illegal as hell,
an imprisonable offense, impersonating a member of the US armed
forces, but he was in no mood for details. John Jarvis, a friend from
Holy Cross grammar school, was on the gate at the Brooklyn Navy
Yard over in Williamsburg. Jarvis forged a 24-hour liberty card for
him, requisitioned another "crow"—this one identifying him as a
member of an elite security unit and therefore immune to a lot of
questioning—and Beans moved into the Receiving Station. He got
himself issued a mattress cover and a blanket, ate three squares a
day on the mess deck, and spent a lot of time ironing his silk neck-
erchief—inserting a dime at the center, folding the silk carefully
around the coin, pressing flat each successive fold—spit shining
his dress shoes, and wandering in and out of the front gate, often
challenged but never stopped for long, as he bused back to the old
neighborhood for a look-see, or to catch a movie at the Flatbush, or

the Kenmore, or the Loew's Kings, or the old Granada Theater on
his own block.

He loved the Receiving Station—*shit paper, fart sacks,* all the
seagoing obscenity— and the smell of cooking grease, of lead paint,
of roll-your-own tobacco, of strong, stale coffee everywhere. Every
time he entered, his boy's heart accelerated at the criminal thrill
of taking the Navy, the entire nation, for free room and board. He
feared discovery, but what would they do with him? He was a civilian medically discharged, a one-eyed jack. They couldn't draft him
back into the Korean War. And if they threw him in the brig, well
fuck it. There would, again, be three meals a day.

Never been enough food at home; the old man was not loved on
the docks and had worked only sporadically. Beans and his sisters
had been reed-thin. But at the Receiving Station, he began to grow
fat—pork chops at least three times a week, sausage, frankfurters,
shrimp, all the potatoes you could eat, and on Sunday, steak with
eggs fried in the juice of the meat on the grill. He began to grow
out of the uniform, which was a danger, since he wasn't sure Jarvis
could manage a new set of dress blues for him. In any event, Jarvis
was shipping out. They were sending his ass to Korea attached to a
company of US Marines.

Beans shuddered at the thought of Jarvis forced to serve alongside the combat-crazy jarheads, and shuddered again at the thought
of his own coming exile from the Navy Yard. If Doyle were alive, if
he had not been run down by that Cadillac, he would have figured
something out.

Patsy Costello had not slept with another man since Doyle's
untimely death. She felt that Larry's death had been the final warning that the life she lived had made her a curse and a danger to men.
Her cousin, who had deflowered her at age sixteen—too young, too
young, she later complained—had died during the Second World
War, drowned in the merchant marine, or blown to pieces. She never
knew which. He had been collecting extra pay, she heard, working

the ammunition ships on the run to England. Her boss, Davidoff, the dentist on Beverley Road, who had been kind and sweet during the years of a long affair, Patsy sometimes accommodating him after hours in the dental chair, other times on the reception desk, now had a bad heart. His doctor blamed it on his diet—bread smeared with chicken fat, beef brisket, matzoh balls heavy as iron sinkers—but Patsy blamed it on herself. And then Larry—the true love of her young life, hero of the Catholic street world, smart and good-looking, a sweet-smelling boy, reeking of Old Spice even in his most private places—had suffered his brain concussion at the corner of Bedford and Church, playing the old diver's game, throwing himself in front of cars to scare and shake down the more prosperous motorists—all witnessed by Beans McBehan, his young accomplice. That fateful day, Larry's eyes did not flutter open. The cops had come, and an ambulance. Larry had died the next day, a priest and Larry's mother at his side.

Patsy Costello had, since then, lived a cloistered life.

On the day of Larry's death, Larry's best friend, the ill-fated Hubert McBehan, had lusted for her, had, in fact, chased her down Flatbush Avenue, bulging with need, and for that near-criminal pursuit later that same afternoon—she was convinced that she and providence had a role in it—he had lost an eye.

Patsy believed she knew the way the world worked. She had been educated in sin, after all, as a schoolgirl at Holy Cross. Sins venial, and sins mortal. And for all, there was required payment. She thought, sometimes, of becoming a nun, a bride of the overarching universe. There was something clean and final about a starched white wimple against a black habit.

They met where last they had seen each other, a few years before, on Flatbush Avenue, this time in front of the Woolworths where Beans, in his grammar school days, had done his share of shoplifting. It was during his last week at the Receiving Station, Jarvis's last week before shipping over.

Beans was looking good in his dress blues. They walked and talked, mostly of Larry Doyle. Patsy had been going to Larry's grave, carrying flowers from her mother's garden. Beans said he would like to go with her. Patsy could feel him studying her, measuring the swell of her breasts, the curve of her legs half hidden in a longer-than-fashionable dress. He breathed in audibly, hunting the scent of her.

"I don't know what Larry told you about me," she said.

"Larry told me nothing," Beans lied.

"I have made some mistakes," she said. "And loving Larry Doyle with all my heart was probably one of them."

There was a long and pregnant pause.

"Still, I treasure the memory of him," she said.

"And so do I." It was probably the first true thing Beans had said to her.

From Patsy Costello's bed on Martense Street, Hubert "Beans" McBehan could look across the backyards into the back window of his own apartment on Church Avenue, his mother a dim figure there, smoke curling from her cigarette.

Patsy's mother, Mrs. Costello, was off to Poughkeepsie to take care of an ailing sister. The house was quiet, the ticking of an old grandmother clock in the first floor hallway the only sound he could hear, save for the distant clang of a trolley car on Church Avenue, and sometimes a boat horn on the river.

Patsy was resolved that she was not going to undress for this boy, or to allow liberties. But there was a comfort in his male presence, a reminder of the Larry time, and when she put her head against Beans' chest, she inhaled the same Old Spice that had scented her Doyle romance.

Beans had an erection. She pretended to ignore it, as did he. Beans then did something that in all his previous encounters he had never done. He reached across Patsy, carefully keeping his hands away from breasts and other precincts she had forbidden, but then knelt down, lifted the hem of her dress, and, overcome, kissed her in the moist fold of her underpants.

He kissed her there again. Not one of her lovers—Larry Doyle, the dentist, the cousin long dead—had dared such a thing. Patsy felt herself crossing a line that, until that moment, she had not realized had been drawn. She put her hands out, intending to push this desperate boy away. But instead, she pressed his face down into the welter of her long dress and petticoat and underwear.

She wondered if he, too, would now be doomed. Whether such an act, outside the bounds of God's plan, would indeed be counted. The heat kindled all the spices of his aftershave. She could no longer help herself. Patsy felt herself slipping into territory unknown and fraught with peril. But she let herself slide, now curious about the sensations that an otherwise hostile and disinterested world was suddenly capable of delivering.

She made her confession at a church in downtown Brooklyn, one far removed from her own Holy Cross parish, to a priest unknown to her. Unwilling to endure a long lecture and even longer penance, she, after the "bless me father," introduced Beans into the catalogue of her sins as her husband, lying, she knew, at the risk of her immortal soul, as many women, she guessed, had done before. She had confessed time and again to fornication, with her cousin, now under the sea; with the dentist, now heart-damaged; with Doyle, now dead. She knew that drill. Father, I have sinned. But with this new development, she was afraid that there was no coming back, that even the Blessed Mother would disown her. In hesitant tones, she stepped carefully into the story, moving from slippery stone to stone in the river of her surrender. The priest, who had at first been bored, now seemed to come to attention.

Father coughed. "And did you then," he asked, "engage in the act of intercourse with your husband?"

Patsy did not answer.

Father bored in. "Did you achieve physical union?"

"Oh, no, father."

He coughed again. "Such kissing and intimate caressing are according to church law, lawful and good," he said.

Patsy was stunned.

The priest continued: "But the Holy Father in his address to new-lyweds has made it clear that moral law does not admit unbridled satisfaction of the sexual instinct merely for pleasure." He coughed again. "In the end, you must perform the marriage act in the manner that nature and God intend. You must cooperate with God in the creation of life."

Patsy's head was reeling. By not fucking Beans, it seemed, she had put her soul in jeopardy. Pacelli, the prelate of Rome, loomed above her, olive-skinned and solemn in gorgeous gown. The Holy Father, it seemed, had his Roman nose everywhere—including the most intimate reaches of her underwear.

It was not until she reached the clear sunshine in the open air of downtown Brooklyn that she reminded herself that Beans was not her husband. That there was no obligation to go all the way. But the idea intrigued her, that oral gratification should not be the end all and be all, that once slipping down that slope it was probably better on the long, sliding scale of sin to open oneself to come-what-may rather than announce this-far-and-no-more. Then, the sin would only be fornication, but fornication well intended.

She frowned. She knew she was rationalizing. She knew that her soul was in danger of a painful eternity.

In the Receiving Station, he had brushed his teeth until the gums bled, scrubbed the offending tongue, and rinsed with a bottle of foul-tasting mouthwash the color of ginger ale. His mouth caught fire. He feared some female microbe was already in possession of his body, multiplying wildly.

As soon as he closed his eyes, he saw again the rise of her pelvis, felt again the hunger in her. The two of them had been speechless. Patsy, her body limp, her eyes closed, unwilling to look at him. He had left, head down, aiming for a drugstore on Nostrand Avenue.

There were forces controlling his life, Beans was convinced, leading him into the abyss, and then scooping him out, pushing him into new experiences that he could not always understand. He believed

that Larry Doyle, sitting at God's right hand, was in his new incar-
nation a wise puppeteer, and that it was Doyle who had walked him
into Patsy Costello's bedroom and shoved his head in her lap.

*In chaste dreams, he was not attempting to persuade a thirteen-year-
old mahogany-colored girl under the shadow of the steel steps in a
Brooklyn schoolyard. She was not reproaching him in soft words
spoken in island British, not wetting herself in fear. And there was
no need. The idol of his life was still alive; no Cadillac had scarred
that handsome head.*

*In this troubled unreality, Larry Doyle fought off the outraged
black youths surrounding Beans McBehan. Larry broke that spear
of a stickball bat aimed for McBehan's head. Beans did not lose
his eye. He dreamed he would wake up whole. In his bunk. In the
Receiving Station.*

"Where you been keeping yourself?"

"Around," he said, not wanting to give his mother the satisfaction
of knowing how hard life was in exile from the apartment, and of
how illegally he had lived, violating federal law and the Uniform
Code of Military Justice.

He had not seen her for weeks and imagined she had grown even
older in that time, her red hair, the pride of her girlhood, gray and
carelessly pulled back from her face, her skin pale but freckled with
small, protective bursts of melanin, her once-full lips now thin, and
pressed together, unable to smile. She seemed to have grown thinner
beneath her housedress, her breasts unable to raise even a small swell,
perhaps retreated to another body where they were needed more.

As always, she smelled of bluing and starch, of Duz soap and
bleach. He looked at her washboard-reddened hands, remarked to
himself on the contrast with other females, the naughty, hungry fingers of the clean-scented Jewel, the soft, unwrinkled hands of Patsy
Costello, marred only by the smallest of calluses from her dental
hygienist work. His mind began to wander. What did Patsy Costello
smell of? Like grass, he thought. No, not grass. More like sun on hay.

His mother grabbed him by the shoulders, then to his surprise wrapped her arms around his ribs, and wept over him, mourning the lost opportunities, the lack of a center in her son's life, the scarring of his soul. A cascade of water sounded the alarm. Gurgle and pop. Stopper settling back into drain. From behind the opaque glass in the top half of the bathroom door, a masculine shadow loomed, coughing and spitting while the shadows of both hands rested against the inside of the glass. The boy wanted no confrontation with his father. He fled down the hallway stairs.

On Martense Street, he intercepted a young dental hygienist, dressed in starched whites, with freshly whitened oxfords, on her way down the front stairs of her home to a day of scaling and flossing, polishing and flirting with male patients as they lay with their heads cradled between her breasts.

Patsy worked the day with the knowledge that Beans was tucked away in her room on Martense Street. Remembering the touch of *his* lips and tongue as she worked between the lips, and around the tongues, of others. Hour after hour, she felt herself making him welcome, until the wetness was cold and uncomfortable on her thighs. As a small girl, she had imagined maleness, had peered curiously at the undersides of the equestrian statues that abounded in Flatbush, until at age sixteen her curiosity was half-satisfied by her cousin Brian, a merchant mariner also in his teens who had taken her virginity in a dark Church Avenue hallway, the feel of his endowments enormous, and somewhat painful, in the limbo of the unlighted vestibule. But she had not seen him, only felt him.

The seeing came later, with Larry Doyle, whose upright member haunted her still. It had a color of its own, different from the stark whiteness of Larry's otherwise plain Irish flesh. Truly different, as if painted by the devil to add to the temptation, the subtle blush and the various blood-pigments it contained ran together in her imagination still. She had held him within her, refusing to allow him to withdraw, wanting whatever he could procreate, his energy, his rascality, his handsomeness, the divine smell of him.

Her dentist lover was no Larry Doyle. Only a circumcised

curiosity, more exposed to the world than she had ever expected, and smaller, too, than expected, since the rumor among giggling parish females had been that Jews were the devil's own, over-endowed by their underworld creator. With what? Dr. Davidoff hardly qualified as anybody's demon. A little man, in every dimension. He had called the thing between her legs a *knish*. And his own piece of the affair, a *petzel*. Funny words given the enormity of the act which violated God's law. Davidoff had made a joke of it, but had flattered her with his terrible need.

"You are not doing it with him," Larry had cried just days before his death, incredulous that she would offer what he considered his. Larry disappeared from her life for months at a time, but still claimed full-time ownership. While his friend, Beans, the one-eyed survivor, the first in Patsy's history to go headfirst in pursuit of her affection, claimed nothing, except his own desperation. All this she thought as she cradled men's heads, and occasionally stared past their tobacco stained teeth to the bulge of their buttoned flies.

Meanwhile, Doyle's ghost as she had conjured it caromed from street corner to schoolyard to the most intimate recesses of Patsy Costello's body. He was condemned to the hell of her imagination. No fires, no physical torment. But in the pinball machine of the life after, Larry's outrage at her newest infidelity, this time with his best friend, sent his spirit ricocheting across Brooklyn. Or so Patsy thought as she plied the oral geography of her trade. Larry no longer imagined as a pink rose. But as a steel ball, out of control, dangerous in its hurtlings.

Years later, when Patsy miscarried her first and only child and stared at its miniature imitation of humanity—a girl certainly—in the toilet bowl, she blamed the loss on God and the avenging Larry Doyle, a punishment for past sins and present unfaithfulness. They did not flush the wee blue child. Instead, they buried it near Larry's own grave, an offering of sorts. Conceiving other children, she decided, would simply make her accessory to a whole series of small murders. So her body shut down, still open to her husband, H. Beans

McBehan, but not to his seed. She mourned the lost innocence of little Patricia, an infant named after herself, and prayed for the child's
unbaptized soul for the rest of her life. But would not give the world
or the priests the satisfaction of knowing it.

Early in life, Beans had come to that moment in which one turns
onto his future path—not the wet dream of orgiastic bliss but the
pragmatic reality. *If not now, when? If not this woman, who?* He did
not know if he had chosen this safe harbor or if it had chosen him,
did not know if he was simply following in Larry Doyle's pricksteps,
or if he had chosen her on his own, did not know if reaching out for
Patsy was in fact reaching out for Doyle. Did not know on the day of
Larry's death if he had been reaching out for Doyle in the person of a
mahogany-colored island girl in a Brooklyn schoolyard, a moment of
trespass that had cost him his eye, he, would-be seducer, surrounded
by the anger of the black street. But for half a century, he had been
loyal to his union with Patsy Costello, mother of his unborn child,
solace of his youth and middle age, and for most of those years had
driven a cab to support her. He concealed his handicap, bribing offi-
cials when necessary, making angry, one-eyed progress through the
five boroughs of the city of New York. More than one woman in his
cab had offered to take out the fare in trade and he had turned them
all down. Not that he had not been sorely tried.

Once, in the early 1960s, on a First Avenue sidewalk, he was
convinced he had seen the WAVE of his misbegotten naval career,
Jewel, in front of the Beekman Tower on the arm of a naval officer.
He had circled the block in a sweat of desire, and loss. And when
he returned Jewel was gone—the flash of her nylons, the lift of her
bosom in her tailored suit, the high gloss of her crimson lipstick, the
whiteness of her small, even teeth—once again lost. For an hour, he
idled the cab in front of the Beekman, waiting for the Jewel who
never reappeared. Beans was almost overcome by the Ivory Soap
scent of her skin, the molecules hovering there, so subtle, but so
persistent that they drifted back on him when driving in midtown
even in his later years when most of his senses were in serious
deterioration. But the union that had begun with his lips pressed

to Patsy's cotton pants had, in fact, endured. They had learned to tolerate the differences they could not understand, his silences, her chatter; his blindness to the details of their world, her obsession with them.

Patsy's breathing in their bed; her snore, which increased in volume from decade to decade; the tangle of her undergarments; even the sound of her on the hopper, that small feminine drizzle, consistent from day to day, year to year, had given some center to his life. But as the century ended, so did she. For Beans, her death at first offered immediate relief from constraints large and small, from the politeness and courtesy she had felt were civilization's due. But, after all the decades of marriage, the loss of Patsy hurt more than the sharpened broomstick that had taken his eye.

It was something he could confess only to a Larry Doyle. But he sometimes entertained the idea, on visits to the cemetery, that he was now wiser than Doyle, the all-wise, all-knowing, that having lived past the century to which they both belonged he had learned things that had been denied to Larry, whose soul and intelligence were twin prisoners, trapped in the days of their boyhood. These things he thought at the gates of the cemetery, the place where all the loves of his life were buried, save for Jewel. He pondered the gulf that separated mortal from immortal as he retreated behind a tree to relieve his cab-ruined kidneys, pissing on the unknown dead before paying his respects to a friend, the Larry Doyle whose restless spirit was believed to still wander the old neighborhood Beans had abandoned decades before.

In the reality of the new century, most of the Irish and Sicilians and Jews were gone, replaced by new immigrants from islands in the Caribbean, old businesses replaced by the new—storefront *iglesias*, cut-rate travel agencies, check cashing enterprises; the old Granada Theater building now intruding onto the sidewalk as a giant drug and variety store. But Beans imagined that the spirit of Larry Doyle still saw the world as it was, still harbored all the old hopes, still yearned for the days when a Cadillac was really a *Cadillac,* and an enterprising young man could make a few bucks if his timing were right, and if his accomplice could summon tears from what were then, in those days, two good eyes.

The first time Beans McBehan entered Patsy Costello, daughter of the dark Irish, with her black curls and troubled conscience, she said she didn't love him—but they both had loved Larry Doyle. And maybe, she said, that was enough.

Perhaps he should have taken offense. But life was never what you wanted it to be.

BEAN & LEAF

STEVEN OSTROWSKI

Sitting at his desk in the converted shed at the edge of the yard, Evan reads, again, the first stanza of a poem he's tentatively calling "The Old Men Go to Sudden Death."

Dawn. Needle-cold, eerie calm.
It's not fondness for each other
that brings four geezers to the pond;
they love that it's winter again.
Their bones crave ice—an urge
their brains have long locked in.
Most of what mattered about life
they've forgotten, though not
the mortal requirement to win.

An okay opening. Not there yet, but okay. It's the next three hundred lines that don't seem worth a shit. He's been working on the damn poem for more than a month, and it still doesn't arrive anywhere. No insight, no epiphany. Evan doesn't know what it's about anymore. Five weeks ago he felt nothing but hope for this one, now he regrets having committed so much time, so much of himself, to a piece of writing he damn well may have to abandon.

A sigh gusts up from his gut. It was the quiver of hesitation in her voice, the hint of a withholding: "Honey, I've got incredible news," she'd said early this afternoon on the phone, "about a research project I've been invited to participate in." Then, "But it's kind of complicated." She asked if he wanted to drive over to *The Bean & Leaf* in Old Norwood so they could discuss it face to face. Said she could be there at five-thirty but wants to be back at the facility by seven.

"You're going back to work tonight?"

"Well, because Caleb's willing to drive up from New Haven to fill me in on details face to face."

"Caleb?"

"Dr. Lutz. Caleb Lutz. He's the researcher who's asked me to work with him. He's from Yale."

"Do I know that name?"

After a moment's hesitation, Rebecca said, "I met him, briefly, four years ago when I was getting the doctorate. He guest lectured at one of our seminars. I mentioned it to you, but I'm sure you forgot. Anyway, honey, that's neither here nor there. He's a god in the field of neurophysiology. And he wants to do a project here at the facility. On balance and cognition for people with dementia. And he wants me to be part of it. It's totally flattering and an incredible opportunity."

"No, I'm sure it is."

Her voice grew animated: "We're going to work with some of my physical therapy patients, which is perfect because they're residents, so we can do thorough pre- and post-tests, observe them in their rooms and at meals, things like that." A minute later, she said she had to run, and to come to *The Bean & Leaf* if he wanted.

He should have kept working on the poem, or graded essays, but Evan googled Caleb Lutz. Born in London, Oxford trained, a dual American-British citizen. Teaching stints at Boston University and Colgate, now at Yale. A thousand publications, presentations, citations. A fucking TED talk with ten thousand views. A real neurophysiological god.

Evan began to remember details, as reported by Rebecca. After his lecture, Lutz had invited the five or six students in the seminar out for a drink, but it was so last minute that none of the others, nor the professor, was able to make it. So she and the god had a glass of wine together at a bar near campus and chatted about career opportunities in human physiology. Lutz opened her eyes to all kinds of possibilities, was how she'd put it. This was four years ago, but Evan recalls now—how had he forgotten this?—that when his wife walked into the bedroom very late that night, the expression on her face when she opened the bedroom door and found him sitting up, staring at her, betrayed something other than mere excitement about her future career opportunities. For the first time in their marriage, Evan wondered with gut-wrenching seriousness if Rebecca had just been unfaithful. But within a few days things were back to normal, and the fear faded, then disappeared.

Running his hand through his curls, Evan's fingers come away with an unruly clump of black and gray strands, which he flicks into the air. The insecurities have come flooding back, the ones he'd paid therapists a small fortune to banish from his psyche when he was a young man. Betrayal. Abandonment. A gut-deep feeling that he didn't quite measure up. Feelings that he'd thought were gone for good.

He breathes a few deep breaths, paces the cell-like shed. *Oh, Christ*, he tells himself, *relax. It's a fucking research project, not an excuse to have an affair. Don't catastrophize.*

When he's ready to focus on the poem again, he sits back down. Maybe the old men should be demented. Or just one of them. That could work. But what would a demented man look like on a frozen rural pond? It would surely show in his eyes. But would his muscle memory still function? Would dementia affect his ability to skate? Could he still stickhandle a puck, comprehend that the object of the game is to outscore the other guy? Rebecca will know.

Caleb fucking Lutz.

He stands again, paces, peers through the shed's one small window in the vague hope of a deer or coyote sighting. All he gets is a manic squirrel chase that ends somewhere high in an oak tree. He wants the poem to be about what happens, over time, to the kind of animal passion that's embedded in the brain of the lifelong athlete. About male competitiveness taken so far that there are psychic repercussions, repercussions to the soul. About grudge holding and the encroachment of death. And, if he can do it honestly, if it doesn't feel forced, about redemption. At least some small victory, some glimpse of insight, in the midst of inevitable loss. That first draft, written in a six hour fever of composition, had intensity and drive.

Now, after blunders of revision, the poem feels like it's dying of self-doubt. It's about as riveting as a tombstone.

"Fuck!" he shouts.

There are dozens of assisted-care facilities in this part of the state. Coincidence that he chose the one *she* works at? He flings a pencil into the ficus near the window.

*   *   *

A police car and a long strand of red plastic caution tape bar the way to Route 47—some sort of underground electrical emergency. Evan has to take the circuitous, hilly, back-road route from North Lyme to Old Norwood. The late summer air gleams and the trees and bushes radiate life. He wants to suck some essential thing out of this abundance, something that might balm the surface of his uneasy soul. Recently, at the urging of Michele Trakas, a colleague in the history department, he's joined the informal faculty meditation group she's organized, which turns out to simply be a focused concentration on breathing. Ever generous, cheerful, sixty-ish, never-married-but-still-looking Michele—God bless her soul—meets once a week with four or five people in an empty room in the student center. In a breathy voice she chants, "Let your thoughts and concerns float away. Focus on the breath. In . . . and out. In . . . and out." Not as easy as he would have thought. His mind, it turns out, is a 24-7 riot of concerns, memories, images. He wonders if the kids are okay at school. Frets about the fact that he and Rebecca haven't made love in two weeks. Doubts his abilities as a poet. Focus on the breath, Michele intones. Oh, right, the breath. After the session, when Evan and Michele walk to their cars together, she never fails to ask about how the kids are doing in college, but mostly she likes to know about Rebecca. How is she finding working full time again? Is it difficult, emotionally, for her to be in the presence of so many elderly, incapacitated people all day? Is it hard for him to adjust to her not being around as much? A little, he tells her, but she loves her work so much it's hard to begrudge her; she's been chomping at the bit for eighteen years to be a full-fledged, highly professional, academical-ly-oriented physical therapist. Now that she's got her doctorate and is working full time, and is director of physical therapy at Norwood Meadows, she's happier than he's ever seen her. How wonderful, Michele says, to be able to say *that*.

You're not supposed to meditate while driving, but Evan needs centering. He'll modify, and anyway there isn't a car in sight on this dappled country road. He breathes deeply and lets his eyes close for just an instant.

When they open, a white-tailed doe is bounding into the road out of a thick stand of pines. Dreamlike, it's six feet, then three, then a foot in front of him. Evan hits the brakes before he thinks to hit them but too late: the passenger side front end slams into the animal's rump, the sound like a sack of wet laundry dropped from a window. The doe slides and scrambles but doesn't fall. Trembling, stunned, she twists her head as if to have a good look at the bringer of her injury. But her soft, bulbous eyes don't judge him. *Kind sir,* they seem to say, *could this not have been avoided?* Blinking, the animal turns and, her body contorted by the hit, hobbles into the woods.

Evan pulls over to the first clearing he finds, shuts off the engine, and attempts to breathe himself back to calm. Calm won't come. He ought to get out and check for damage, but he doesn't care one way or the other about dents. He thinks, *is this a poem?* A husband hits a deer on the way to a meeting with his wife, a meeting in which she's going to tell him something that he knows in his gut will eventually end in disaster for their marriage.

Fuck that. Let someone else write that one. Better: one of the old hockey players hits and kills a deer on the way to the fiftieth annual two-on-two game at the pond. He plays, but he's so shaken up that the game is ruined for him.

*   *   *

A forlorn-looking man—could be thirty, could be forty—with long-ish, greasy black hair and wearing a cook's apron over his clothes

sprawls across the front steps of *The Bean & Leaf.* Evan has to climb
over his outstretched leg to get to the door. He locates Rebecca sitting at a small table in the center of the room, intently two-thumb
typing on her phone. How attractive and smart she looks with her
long, thick black hair brushed out like a cape, her form-fitting silvery
skirt, white button-down top with a thread-like silver necklace, and
white pumps. At the table to her right sit two priests, one elderly and
the other not much more than a boy. To her left, four swarthy men in
paint-splattered jeans and sweatshirts drink espressos and engage in
aggressive conversation in a foreign language. Evan wonders why
his wife, who is sensitive to sound, chose to sit so close to so much
commotion. The men must have come in after she did.

For almost twenty years now, when they meet somewhere, Evan
likes to say, "I don't know you, ma'am, but I'd marry you in a heartbeat if you'd have me." Rebecca's coy response is always, "You
never know."

When she looks up from her typing, he says, "Hey."

"Hi. Give me one minute." Her thumbs poke at the screen as her
sea-blue eyes assess the words. "It's just so important how I say this.
It's probably too long for a text."

"Who's it to?"

Small hesitation. "To Caleb."

"Ah."

"It's to save time when we meet later. Let me just read through it
one more time. I'll be right with you."

Evan glances at the younger of the two priests, a man whose face
is a broad orb of clear, pink skin. His wide brown eyes and boyishly
thick lips break into a mirthful smile. "Maybe difficult," he says
to his elderly counterpart, "but not impossible. With God, are not
all things possible? Let us trust and see what will happen." Evan
detects an Eastern European accent.

The old priest looks bemused.

Rebecca raises a give-me-one-more-second finger. Jesus, what
the hell can possibly be so urgent? The four men at the table to
the left argue on. In Portuguese. They're gruff, ruddy-skinned men;

their dark eyes betray hard-edged points of view. Only three of them actually argue. The fourth leers at Rebecca. He doesn't seem to care that Evan has appeared. Rebecca's probably a few years older than the guy, who looks to be in his early forties, but then, a beautiful woman is a beautiful woman.

Maybe one of the hockey players had an affair with one of his mates' wives. An ancient enmity that, even after a lifetime, feels raw for the cuckold. Evan will have to think more deeply about who these men are. The problem with the poem—one of them—is that the men are too generic right now. He remembers something Gina Lure, one of his undergrad mentors, a feisty woman with strong opinions, said when he was just starting to write: "If the poem is about a human being, give him a soul or it fails. Anybody who tells you otherwise is already dead." Somebody in the class asked her if employing the concept of the soul in a poem wasn't anachronistic and sentimental. Lure's response: "Only if the poet's a gutless, soul-less, intellectual weakling."

At last Rebecca lays her phone on the table and, as if she'd forgotten to breathe all the while she typed, exhales. Her eyes re-acclimate to her husband. "Sorry, honey. My head's spinning. In a good way, though. Thanks for driving over. How are you?"

"I'm okay. Anxious to hear more about your big news. At least I think I am."

As she reaches across the table to lay her hand on top of Evan's, Rebecca's glance dashes to and from the leering man.

"You are aware, then, that that guy has been staring holes through you. I hope he's willing to accept that you aren't available."

"Oh, stop."

In need of a prop, Evan says, "Give me one sec," and goes to the counter. The aproned barista, a husky black man with a teased-out afro, nods, and Evan orders a cup of fire ginseng tea.

"Be right up."

When it's ready, the steaming mug is so full that Evan has to tight-rope it back to the table. He halts to allow the elderly priest room to shuffle past him toward the men's room. Settling his drink carefully on the table, Evan's heart feels shaky under his ribs. "Okay. I'm ready if you are. Details."

Rebecca clears her throat. Eyes gleaming and fierce, as if she anticipates resistance, she says, "Yeah, so I've been asked to be a partner in this research project. It's an amazing opportunity for me to work with one of the leaders in the field on a project that could really help people, give them more mobility and freedom. This is what I've always dreamed of doing."

"And you'll be doing it with Caleb?"

"Well, yes." She speaks with control and patience. "People with dementia live with so much uncertainty, Evan. What's real and what's not real; what they can and can't do."

"I can relate."

"Oh, stop. You seem so . . . skeptical. Or something."

Evan's "Not skeptical at all" comes through a throat full of gravel. He sips his fire ginseng. "Look, I don't doubt for a second that it'll be good, important research. I know you'll do a great job. You always do. You've been a great mother; you were a great graduate student. And you've always been a great wife, too."

"Thank you."

"And Caleb is brilliant, right?"

Rebecca frowns. "Your tone is so . . ." Her shoulders drop. "I don't know. I'd hoped you be more excited for us."

Such a small word to cut so deep.

"I am. Or I will be. I just, I don't know, it's brand-new news, that's all. Do you know how long it will go on? The project?"

"It has to be finished by January. He's doing research overseas in the spring."

"Well, that's good."

"Good? Why?"

"Never mind. Will you publish your results? Present at conferences?"

"You know, we've been talking about doing this project for at least a year now and I never thought to ask him that."

"Wait, what? You've been talking with him for a *year*? I thought he called you last week about doing this."

"All I mean is, this isn't frivolous."

"But wait. Have you stayed in touch with him? You went out for a drink with him, what, four or five years ago? I thought that was the end of it. Have you stayed in touch with him since then?"

Rebecca touches the side of her nose. To the rim of her coffee mug, she says, "We've emailed each other once in a while. Not often. Evan, he's an important connection for me. What's the big deal?"

"I'm sure he's a very important connection." The various parts of his skull feel like they're coming unglued. He glances at the leering man, who's still at it. *Fuck you, buddy.* "Why didn't you tell me?"

"I don't know," Rebecca says. "Do you tell me everyone you have some kind of email correspondence with? That would be ridiculous."

"Tell me more about Caleb. You must have really impressed him over that drink, if he was inspired to keep in touch with you ever since."

"He considers it part of his calling to nurture people who really care about the field and who he considers promising."

"Magnanimous of him," Evan says. He doesn't intend for *every* utterance to sound like pure sarcasm. "Is he much older than you, Rebecca?"

"I don't know how old he is. I think he mentioned that he's probably not too far away from retiring."

"Oh?" Maybe the picture of him that Evan saw on one of the websites was taken a long time ago. Maybe he's less good-looking now. A safe old man. Maybe he can't get it up anymore.

Rebecca sips, then runs the tip of her tongue over her upper lip. "This is going to be important research, Evan. And I think Caleb and I will work well together. That's all there is to it."

Evan lifts his mug, thinks, *sounds like the way an affair begins.* If one hasn't already begun. "So, is he married? Kids? Grandkids? Great grandkids?"

"He has a daughter in grad school. And a son who's somewhere overseas, doing something or other. With an NGO, I think."

"So he's married?"

Rebecca glances at her fingernails. "Divorced."

The very word jabs him. "But he's an old man now, huh?"

"Old*er*. Good God, Evan. What *is* this interrogation?"

And suddenly he's a goddamn teenager again, sensing with chest-tightening desperation that a girlfriend is slipping out of his grasp, her heart moving toward some sexier, more exciting, *older* guy.

Breathe, dammit. This is not that.

Rebecca lifts and takes a peek at her phone, turns it over and lays it back down. "The thing is, this is going to be extremely time consuming."

"Okay."

"And of course I'm still going to be working full time. But, honey, I haven't been this excited for myself in a long, long time."

Because his flickering eyelids have a mind of their own, Evan has to press his fingers into them to calm them down. When the old priest slides back from the men's room, she and Evan watch him. The young priest stands, says, "Shall we carry on the mission then, Monsignor? So much work to be done." Gently, he hooks his arm under his elderly colleague's armpit and escorts him toward the door.

In a corner of the room, the barista has begun setting up a make-shift stage. He rolls a small amplifier into position, plugs it in, then carries in a microphone stand. He flicks a switch on the amp and speaks into the mic: "Testing, testing. Magical and mystical microphone, you are being severely tested."

"If someone's going to play music," Rebecca says, "I'm out of here. No way I can focus with somebody singing. Anyway, I've given you my news. You're obviously overjoyed for me."

"Don't be sarcastic, honey. I am happy for you. Don't go yet. Let me be honest with you about how I feel." Fingers of insecurity quiver in Evan's gut and the trick is not to let them squeeze into a fist. How honest can he be, though? Can he say, I'm afraid you're going to fall in love with this guy and leave me? Or, I'm afraid you've been deceiving me? So juvenile. "I'm a little on edge, is all," he says. "You're doing new things, with new people. It's thrown me off balance, I guess. No pun."

Rebecca listens, smiles, nods; sympathy softens her eyes. She's always responded best to frankness, has always been too driven to get things done to waste time beating around bushes. "It *is* an adjustment for you, isn't it? I have to realize that my changes affect you, too. I've been so caught up in my own life that I guess I haven't thought about how it's impacting yours. But, honey, you've got your teaching to do and your poetry to write and readings to give. Your men's league hockey and hanging out with the guys. You have a rich, exciting life."

Yes, separately our lives are certainly rich. "Speaking of which," he says, "I've been struggling to finish this long poem I've been working on forever. The one about the four old guys playing pond hockey? I'm sure I mentioned it to you."

"Oh, right. Yes."

He wonders if she actually does remember. She's all about the tangible, the practical, the physical. "I guess I want the damn poem to tell me what it wants to mean, you know? But it's being secretive and coy."

"Don't you often have to keep working through your poems before you're satisfied?"

"Of course. It's just that this one seems to deteriorate every time I come near it."

"Is it meant to be a little humorous? It sounds like it could be. I'm picturing *Grumpy Old Men* for some reason."

Evan chuckles. There isn't a shred of humor in the thing. *Jesus.* "No. It's dead serious. But I was going to ask you about dementia. About skating and balance and . . ."

Suddenly the intensity of the Portuguese argument escalates, and Evan and Rebecca fix on each other's eyes so as not to gawk. Evan breaks first, sees that despite the ruckus, the leering man is still leering. Except now he slides his black eyes off Rebecca and targets Evan. The healthy response, Evan knows, is to pretend that he doesn't notice, to smile at his wife and say something innocuous. But fuck that. He meets the man's glare with a scowl. He's prepared to have the crap beat out of him by the whole lot of them if it comes to that, but he'll damn sure go down swinging.

"*Evan*," Rebecca hisses.

"*Fuck* him. Do you feel naked enough?"

"*Ignore* him."

"Okay," he says, and keeps staring. "Should I ignore how fucking hot you are to be working with fucking Caleb, too?"

"*What*?"

"Nothing. Never mind."

Rebecca's high cheekbones flare. "Your paranoia is not attractive, Evan."

"I've got no cause for concern then?"

Her eyes blink rapidly and her lips tighten. "I'm not even going to . . ."

"Professor *Kamus*?" Evan holds his eyes on Rebecca. Finally, reluctantly, he turns. A young man with long, matted blond dreadlocks stands a few feet from their table.

"Yes?"

The young man's handsome, deeply tanned face breaks into a broad smile. "Neil Drummond. I was in your Intro to Poetry course at Northern a few years ago. Didn't have the dreads back then."

"Oh. Oh, yes. I remember now." He does. Earnest, interested, good attention span, sensitive, even somewhat facile with language; the kind of talented kid who someday might be courageous and masochistic enough to turn his pain into art. "Neil," Evan says, "this is my wife, Rebecca. Rebecca, Neil."

"Hi, Neil." Rebecca offers a composed smile.

Neil glances around the room. "My girlfriend Felicity was here, like, one second ago. Probably ducked into the bathroom. I really want her to meet you, Professor."

Evan's not in the mood for small talk with former students, even promising ones. He wants to talk about Caleb Lutz until it feels safe not to. "Was Felicity at Northern, too?"

"No. She went to Vermont."

"I like her name," Rebecca says.

Neil beams. "She's my soul mate, I swear. And I'd really like to introduce her to the professor who changed my life. Except she disappears sometimes."

"Women do that, don't they?" Evan immediately regrets saying this—it could be taken as sexist. Or as a passive-aggressive dig. Or as a prediction.

Three of the Portuguese men push back roughly from their chairs and stand up. Taking his sweet time, finally standing, the leering man fixes his gaze on Rebecca one more time, even raises a thick eyebrow. Evan exhales rage and cautions himself to do the right thing; he has no idea what that might be. Fingers gone to fists, he watches the motherfucker saunter out the door behind his comrades.

"I took a lot of courses at Northern," Neil is saying to Rebecca, "and, nothing personal, most of them flat-out sucked. But the poetry course I took with Professor Kamus—that was *cool*. I still remember a lot of the things he taught us. Indirection. Subtext. Reversals. The 'turn.' Funny thing is, I only took it because I needed a course in arts and sciences to fulfill some gen ed requirement. It was kind of a random selection. Not to sound Darwinian."

"Well, you were fit enough to survive the course," Evan says. "And you aren't the first person to find me through random selection."

"Yeah, but for me it was fate. I still write poems all the time. What was it you said: poetry is the great aphrodisiac? It's true, man." Neil grins. "But I guess you of all people know that."

"Did I say that?" Evan fakes a chuckle. "Anyway, what brings you to *The Bean & Leaf*, Neil? Beans or leaves?"

"Oh, I play here on Tuesday nights." When he says this, almost apologetically, Evan remembers him better. How the women in the class used to gawk at him, their lust undisguised, and how the kid had no clue. Whether it was modesty or obliviousness, the lack of presumption endeared Neil to Evan, made him read his stuff with more kindness and focus than he might otherwise have. "You're a singer-songwriter then?"

"Guitar, harmonica, and my so-so voice. I keep it simple."

"Simple is good. I wish I knew you were playing. We have to leave in a few minutes. But I'll definitely try to catch you one of these Tuesdays. I'd love to hear your stuff."

"That would be very cool. Not to kiss your ass or anything, but your course, besides helping me become a decent poet, also made me a better songwriter. I don't think I'd . . . oh wait, here she is. Felicity, over here."

When a chubby, plain-faced young woman in a slightly ill-fitting peasant's dress and worn sandals comes to Neil's side, Evan pulls his hand across his mouth. Covering the screen of her phone with her palm, Rebecca looks up and smiles.

"Felicity, this is Professor Kamus. Best professor at Northern."

"Hardly," Evan mutters. "Hi, Felicity. This is my wife, Rebecca."

"So nice to meet you, Felicity," Rebecca says.

The young woman nods but avoids their eyes.

"I'll never forget what Dr. Kamus used to say at the end of every class." Neil looks from Rebecca to Felicity, raises a finger and says, "'Go forth and deepen the mystery, folks. Deepen the mystery.' I didn't get it at first, but I think I do now."

"That's a cool thing to say," Felicity murmurs.

"It isn't mine," Evan tells them. "I heard it from Flannery O'Connor. Who I believe got it from Hawthorne."

"Well, I heard it from you," Neil laughs. "So, thanks for passing it on. I try to live it."

Felicity shuffles like a little girl who has to take a pee. "Um, it was nice to meet you guys," she says. "Neil, I have to go outside for a minute."

"Why's that, babe?"

"I just have to do something."

Neil sighs. "I should go tune up. Great seeing you, Professor K. I hope you do come back one of these Tuesdays. I'll buy you a coffee. Nice meeting you, Rebecca."

"Same here. Take care." When he's out of their hearing, she says to Evan, "He's quite a looker, isn't he?"

"You should have seen the way the women in that class swooned over him."

"I don't doubt it."

"To be honest," Evan says, "I would have predicted a little

different type of girlfriend. A little more . . ." He doesn't want to say "attractive."

"What people are drawn to in one another is so unpredictable, though, isn't it? Which I think is a good thing. Keeps life interesting."

"Downright dangerous sometimes."

"All these cryptic remarks, Evan." Rebecca adjusts her necklace. "Anyway, wasn't it endearing, what he said about Felicity being his soul mate? You don't hear that phrase much anymore."

"No. The soul is not in fashion."

"It still is for you, though."

Evan feels a trace of encouragement: she *understands* this about him. "It is for me."

"Well, I agree. And I like the idea of soul mates."

"Everybody deserves one. At *least* one, right?"

"What Neil said about you was sweet. 'Best professor at Northern.' That must be nice to hear."

Evan's fiery tea has lost its heat. "It's been a rough day, Rebecca. So, yeah, hearing anything positive is nice."

"My news isn't positive, then?"

"I'm just adjusting to the new you. Your news is positive, though. It is."

The big black man strides past them toward the makeshift stage.

"Thank you for saying that," Rebecca says, and she sparks back to enthusiasm. "I can't wait to get started. And it's going to work out fine for us in the long run, honey. It'll be crazy busy for a while, but we'll both adjust." She begins to gather her things. "Hey, I'm going to run to the ladies' room, then I have to go."

He knows he shouldn't, but as soon as she's gone Evan lifts Rebecca's phone and presses a few buttons. He scrolls down through two or three texts, to this:

> there's no way you can possibly understand how THRILLED
> I am to have this chance to work with you at last! you won't
> regret it, mister. I promise! Can't wait to start!!!

Mister.

And his response:

we're going to make a great team, luv. already do.

"You know, Ev," Rebecca says, returned—freshly made-up and glossed, "you should stay. Wouldn't Neil love that?"

She touches his shoulder but her fingers feel foreign. "Not in the mood tonight," he mutters. "Next time."

"Okay, suit yourself. I have to go. We have so much to do to get things ready for the study. I don't know where the time is going to come from. It might mean working some nights. I hope that's okay?"

"Nights, huh?"

"Some. What can I say, Evan? I have to do what I have to do. This is just too important."

He touches the spot where, underneath his ribs, a small muscle has knotted and begun to throb. "Yes, do what you have to do." Then, to her skeptical glance, he adds, "You're on a team now."

Dusk paints pink the ruddy streets and old brick buildings of downtown Old Norwood. To keep up with his hustling wife, Evan has to walk more briskly that he feels like. When they come to a small gap between buildings, agitated voices in the ally compel them to glance in. Twenty feet or so into the shadows, Neil's Felicity stands near the thin, stringy-haired guy who'd been blocking the door when he'd arrived at *The Bean & Leaf*. Though his wiry gesticulations look threatening, Felicity stands inches away from him, defiant and firm.

"Yikes," Rebecca says after they've passed. "I don't even want to know."

In front of her white Mazda, which, despite her business, she manages to keep meticulously clean, Rebecca fishes her keys out of her purse. "Okay, honey, I'll see at you home. It might be late-ish if we're going strong. But no later than, say, eleven. Please don't wait up." She touches his elbow. "And thanks for driving over here. And for understanding how important this is to me." Rushing a peck that doesn't quite make contact with his cheek, she drops into the driver's seat and starts the engine. As she pulls away, she waves, but her eyes are fixed on the road.

What can he do but stand on the sidewalk and watch the rose sky decline to gray and wonder if this isn't an image he'll remember years from now: the beginning of the end of a marriage that he, fool that he is, thought only death would extinguish.

Another man would show more trust in his wife. At the very least, he would hope for the best and not worry until he had just cause. The texts are not evidence of infidelity. Nor is her excitement about working with him, nor the fact that she's stayed in touch with him for four years without ever mentioning it.

Down the street, Felicity and the guy in the apron emerge from the ally. Without a word, without touching, they walk off in opposite directions; Felicity toward *The Bean & Leaf*, the guy toward Evan. Watching him approach, Evan spreads his legs a little and hardens his eyes. But the small, rat-like face that passes is wet with tears, and oblivious.

He tells himself to go home.

As Evan drives toward Old Norwood Meadows, he's certain that he's not going to go inside, not going to stride down hallways dotted with octogenarians nodding off in wheelchairs or mumbling to long-dead spouses about what they ought to have for dinner. He won't go peering into every office and conference room until he discovers his wife and Caleb in some breathless, spark-flying state of collaboration. Because, what then? Short of catching them in the act, nothing proves that anything's wrong.

He instructs himself to turn around at the gas station, but keeps going. And again at the bank, and again at Taco Bell.

The large, wooden, green-and-gold sign promises the elderly *Care,*

Camaraderie, and Comfort for Life. His heart calamitous, Evan drives onto the grounds.

In the almost-empty evening parking lot, in front of the sprawling, manicured, single-story edifice, he spots Rebecca's car. Parked to the left of it, very close and slightly askew, is a newer model black Volvo; its vanity plate reads RE-SEARCH. The proximity of the vehicles feels like foreplay, and some fabric in Evan's gut tears. He pulls into the empty space to the right of the Mazda and sits in his own dented little Civic, idling.

Michele's tranquil, resigned voice comes wavering through his brain, instructing him to inhale through the nose, to gently hold in the breath, and, softly and slowly, to exhale through the mouth. Good. Again. And again.

As he grips the door handle, a silver Lexus pulls up in front of the entrance. A middle-aged man in a black suit and gold tie gets out from the driver's side and walks briskly to the passenger side, opens the door, reaches down and says something. A long moment later, an elderly woman, clutching the man's arm with both hands, allows herself to be pulled up from the seat. She's dressed in an elegant black coat and paisley scarf and her silver hair is coifed to perfection. The expression on her face, though, is pure, quivering bewilderment. Bewilderment and rage. "No, Donald," she says. "No." The man places his hands gently on her tiny waist and urges her forward. "It's fine, Mom. It's fine." She stops, again says, "No." She says, "Why, Donald?" but without answering, he nudges her on. Finally, giving up, she teeters toward the doors.

Evan hears himself say, "Go home." You'll only make a fool of yourself here. Go home and work on your old pathetic hockey players. Figure out who the hell they are. Give them lives. Souls. Make at least one of them demented. You don't need Rebecca to tell you what that feels like.

Hurtling along the darkening tunnel of country road, high beams searing into fathoms of woods, Evan knows that when he gets home he'll pace the floors, turn the television on and off, open and close the refrigerator door, text both kids at college to tell them he misses them like crazy and wait for their obligatory "miss you too!"—and hope they mean it. He'll check, again and again, to see if Rebecca has texted. *I love you, Evan. There's no need to worry.* Of course, there won't be any such message; she's too involved, too *thrilled*. Around eleven, probably later—maybe they'll have a drink before they part—she'll come into the house, tired but exhilarated, and wonder why he's still up. He'll wonder how she can possibly not know.

Hugging a narrow curve, low-hanging leaves brushing the car, Evan recalls that he almost killed a deer today. No doubt by now coyotes have finished her off.

Breathe.

Anyway, he's got two of the four old hockey players: one of them was once a highly-regarded researcher, a good-looking guy with a Brit accent and a taste for beautiful women, married or not. One, a poet and teacher of absolutely no distinction. A lifelong naïve sucker. Dementia's got them both now. The poem is called "Sudden Death."

GENERATIONS

JUDGEMENT HOUSE

TODD FULMER

It will go like this: A trumpet blasts and corpses burst out of the grave, skeletons riding dirt geysers up into the sky, dripping flesh, unhinged jawbones spilling forth maggots and singing songs of praise, of worship. Folks ascending out of their vehicles framed by halos of light, floating off into the pale blue yonder, their vacated Civics and Darts crashing into municipal buildings, fire hydrants, and stray vagrants—maybe a baby stroller or two. Terrified flight passengers bust into empty cockpits as their planes drop towards the earth like bombs, every unfortunate thing stuck to the ground below them a potential target. Children leave parents standing panicked in the dust.

"That all?" I say, driving my S-10 along the cracked blacktop, fields of charred-looking tobacco stretching out on either side. It's Halloween, and we're on our way to church for Judgment House.

"That's the gist," says my son. His name is Clyde, like me, but we call him Trey. He doesn't like that too much, but I doubt he'd like "Little Clyde" much better. I know I never did. And calling him by his middle name, Beauregard, would qualify as some form of child abuse. His mother wanted to call him Beau, but that name makes you think of some barefoot hick chewing a straw, or a faithful mutt maybe. Trey's the best I can do for him.

"Your mama's got some imagination," I say, glancing over at Trey sitting Indian-style in the passenger seat.

He's got on a mesh Atlanta Braves ball cap, the kind with an adjustable plastic strip in the back. I gave him the cap on his last birthday even though Trey wouldn't know Chipper Jones if Jones slapped him upside the head. But he likes to keep his head covered. His hair is just like mine–light brown, a thick and curly mess, tangled and knotted like wisteria branches—and he's embarrassed about it just like I was at his age. He takes the cap off, flexes the bill twice, then sits it on his knee.

"Your mama believes in holy ghosts but not the efficacy of a wide tooth comb," I say, taking the cap off his knee and putting it back on his head. "Keep that covered."

"It's real," says Trey with annoyance, adjusting the cap to his liking. "It's all in the Bible. Mama didn't imagine anything."

"The Bible talks about a seven-headed dragon with feet like a bear and a mouth like a lion. They should make a comic book about it. I don't remember anything about folks descending out of cars."

"*A*scending. Not *de-*. And it's in the subtext," he says. Boy's always been sharp as a tack. He could say his ABCs and count to twenty before he could aim his piss, I shit you not. I suppose every father thinks their son's going to be something special. We all want to believe that our batter is of higher quality than the stuff produced by our fathers, but the result is typically the same bland pancake. Though Trey's always been able to pick up on things that others miss. And when I say "others," I don't just mean his sixth-grade peers, but adults, too. That's why it's important that I break him of this thing, so his curiosity isn't stymied by superstition.

"Guess I better open the sun-roof then," I say.

"Way this heap of junk is rusting out, you'll have a sun-roof before long," Trey says. I search for a hint of warmth in his voice—some sign that Trey processes this picking back and forth as just our way of showing love—but I can only detect disgust. I mean, the boy really *hates* me right now. I try to summon words that will close the distance between us—words about acceptance and unconditional love, words about how a man will sometimes dig in his heels when the world turns against him—but I can't get anything out. Because I have to make Trey recognize what he stands to lose, even if I have to lose him myself. What kind of father would I be if I let his soul turn into some ominous black thing haunting over the world?

I've been living at the Budget Inn ($500 a month for long-term guests) ever since Ruth, my wife, found Jesus and joined the flock of Pastor Strickland. She wanted me to find Jesus, too, but He has so far proved elusive.

I always do the same thing when I'm here alone in the evenings or on my days off from working at the furniture plant (the same plant where Pop was a foreman for fifteen years and that will probably soon be relocated to China or some other third-world hell hole): I watch horror movies. I bought a cheap little Sony DVD player that I hooked up to the hotel's twenty-inch flat-screen, and on it I watch one blood-curdling catastrophe after another.

Watching scary flicks was what Trey and I loved to do most together. We preferred watching a psychopath chase horny teenagers around with a chain saw over a game of catch in the yard or a morning of fishing at my father-in-law's pond. Ruth never cared for this particular father-son activity, but she begrudgingly accepted the Saturday afternoon ritual because it was the only time you'd catch my arm draped across my son's shoulders, his head resting in the crook of my armpit. But when Strickland came into the picture, she couldn't tolerate it any longer. Those movies glorify the Devil, she tells me.

When I had Trey to myself one recent Saturday at the Budget Inn, I figured we could sneak in a viewing of *Rosemary's Baby*, a mutual favorite. But he told me it wasn't right for him to watch those kinds of movies anymore. When I assured him that his mother would never find out, he snapped at me that it would be wrong to deceive, and asked how I could suggest he do such a thing. The anger and disappointment in his voice frightened me like Mia Farrow birthing the anti-Christ never had or could. I knew at that moment that I was losing him.

Earlier today, I was watching *Halloween II*—the one where Michael Myers terrorizes Jamie Lee Curtis in a hospital—when the phone on the fiberboard nightstand rang.

It was Ruth calling about my plans for Trey. I wanted to take the boy trick-or-treating, maybe over to the Haunted Corn Maze at Olsen Farms. But Ruth thought that plan sounded too Satanic.

"There's this thing the church does," she said, ending her words with a click of the tongue. She always does that click thing when she's worked up about something. She was anticipating me giving her lip. She was right to be concerned. "Judgment House. It's like a Christian alternative to all the glorification of evil and whatnot. They put on skits acting out scenarios that might get you sent to hell if you're not careful."

"On the Haunted Corn Maze, some dude in a hockey mask tickles your sides from behind," I said. Ruth did not laugh. She found Jesus but lost her sense of humor. I used to always be able to get her going with my jokes, get her laughing in that sweet, high register that made me hard in study hall, but no more. She no longer responds to the same stimuli. Ruth says she's "born again," but to me it doesn't seem like birth so much as usurpation. Jesus has not given her new life; He has taken command of her senses.

Finally, after fuming over my wisecrack for a few long seconds, Ruth clicked her tongue again and said, "If you want to see Trey tonight, you'll take him to the church. *Comprende*?"

Ruth always says *comprende* with just a touch of playfulness, and hearing that in her voice then made my pecker flutter a little, gave me a pang of hope—hope that the old world might somehow be salvaged.

"Okay," I said. "I can do that."

"Pick him up at seven," said Ruth with one final click, hanging up the phone, breaking our connection.

Now, here on the road, the S-10 shakes as the blacktop fractures and collapses into tiny pits, gravel shooting out behind like a bullet hail. The fall sky covers the land like a bright orange sheet, and the tobacco fields give way to a forest of ancient oaks dipping so low into the road that the branches scrape the peeling red roof of the truck.

The forest opens up into a pumpkin patch. Out the passenger-side window, looking past the bill of Trey's cap, I see a man with a straw hat nailed to a cross, black crows perched on the horizontal plank pecking at his eyes. Ever since I moved out of the house I have

waking dreams—visions of men being ripped apart. I know what I
see now is just a scarecrow—it must be—but from this distance I
swear I can see blood and flecks of iris dusting the air, the desperate
flickering of trapped hands. I look over at Trey, his bony legs still
pulled underneath him, who glances out too but shows no indication
that the image means anything to him.

I return my eyes to the road, running the back of my right hand
over my mouth, feeling the dry, harsh grit of two-day-old stubble.

At the far end of the patch is an old cemetery surrounded by a
chipped white fence. My father is buried there. He died of a heart
attack when I was Trey's age. Mom and I noticed him stone dead in
his Barcalounger—his feet up, eyes open, a Pall Mall filter hanging
out of his mouth. Not *found*, but *noticed*.

The three of us were sitting around the television watching *Wheel
of Fortune*, Mom telling Pop that his cigarette's out. He could have
been dead an hour or more, and if not for that spent butt, might have
sat dead another hour or two unnoticed. He was a man uninterested
in speech. I can't even remember what his voice sounded like. What
I do remember is Pop's skin, dried out by sun and smoke, deep leath-
ery grooves suggesting a man of a more advanced age.

I inspect the back of my hands on the steering wheel, their cracking dry skin, knowing that Trey will remember my voice all too well.

The cemetery rests members of Snow Hill Baptist Church, the
church itself emerging over a slope in the blacktop. I've always
wondered how the hell a church around here—a place where even
the cold feels heavy and dry—got a name like "Snow Hill." Probably
just some errant wish.

My parents had been members here and made sure I was in the
pew sitting between them every Sunday, but I quit going once I
moved out on my own. Ruth would take Trey on occasion, but
mainly just for the socializing—the Sunday school gossip and the
cover-dish suppers. But when Strickland took over the congregation
about a year ago, she "caught a fever for the Word," as she once put
it to me. A lot of folks did. Ruth said Strickland wanted worshippers,
not church-goers.

The church is as old as Methuselah, but a fresh coat of paint makes it look as new and white as freshly laundered sheets. This suggestion of newness coupled with the gothic architecture gives me an eerie feeling, like I've taken us through some kind of time warp. I park in dirt grooves that approximate a parking space, looking out my window expecting to see a horse-drawn buggy or even a chariot rather than a four-door sedan.

I walk to the passenger side and open the door for Trey, who hops down and kicks up dust all over my best pair of Levi's without even looking at me.

I absently reach into the front pocket of my orange plaid button-up for a pack of Camels, forgetting again that I quit smoking when Ruth kicked me out. Watching TV alone in the Budget Inn made me think of Pop in his Barcalounger, and I figured it was time to give it up. I don't miss it too much, but my clothes are still cig-haunted; the weight of the pack is still present in my shirt pocket, and the smoke smell never washes out. Even buying new clothes doesn't help.

I pat the pocket twice and watch as Trey ascends the church steps, noticing in the fading light of dusk how his long, flat nose and thin, pale lips twitch in the chill like his mother's.

At the entrance stands Pastor Strickland in a modest black suit and crisp white shirt, his face stretched so tightly you'd think a light flick might cause the skin to snap off. Strickland sticks his bony, blue-veined right hand toward me to shake, and grips my shoulder with the left, the power of his fingers surprising.

"Evening, Clyde," he says, his smile revealing tiny, gapped teeth.

"Preacher Man," I say, "Long time no see," feeling the crushing cold grip of his shake. I call him Preacher Man because I know he doesn't like it. The corners of his mouth twitch in response to the name.

"Decided to rejoin the flock?"

"Not quite. We came for the sugar-free candy and other secular whatnots."

"No candy here. Just the body of Christ and his blood."

"Always tastes like crackers and Welch's to me."

"You lack imagination."

"And you got plenty to spare, I guess."

"Okay, Clyde. Have it your way. Just keep your heart open."

"Sure thing."

Pastor Strickland releases his grip on my shoulder to let me pass through the dimly lit foyer.

Strickland and I go back a ways. We were both in the same Sunday school classes together, both played on the same rusted, net-less basketball hoop in back of the church. I thought he was okay back in those days, but he was always a little off. His mother home-schooled him back when there wasn't much of that going on, and he got stranger and stranger as her lessons started to stick.

One late Sunday afternoon shortly before Pop died, Strickland and I were playing H-O-R-S-E on the creaky old slanting post. I liked to play it loose and crazy, throwing up hook shots with the left hand while standing on one foot, shots from behind the backboard, granny-shots with my eyes closed. But Strickland's approach was more ascetic—a basic jump shot from the free throw line (a piece of packing tape), a bank shot from eight feet out, and a three-pointer from the side. Of course, he always won. But what's odd thinking back was his austere demeanor—he disapproved, without words, of my carefree tactics while taking no pleasure in his success. Even a stupid game of H-O-R-S-E was approached as the Lord's work.

Anyway, this one Sunday, I got on a bit of a roll. Everything was going in. Strickland couldn't match my crazy-ass shooting, and it was clear he resented having to make the effort. With the game in the balance, I banked a granny-shot with my eyes shut. Strickland picked up the ball and stared at it for a moment, then looked at me with his icy blue eyes.

"I ain't gonna shoot it that way," he said.

"Fine. Guess I win then," I said, and did a little victory shuffle.

"You didn't call it. You've got to say you're gonna bank in a gran-ny-shot. But you didn't, so I can shoot it any way I want."

Now, as I know it, this is indeed how the rules of H-O-R-S-E work; you have to call the shot beforehand. But we had never played that way before.

"That's some bull, Strick," I said. "You know we never play it that way."

"I ain't gonna shoot it that way. It's stupid. It's prideful not to shoot it the right way."

"Then you lose, like I said."

He turned to the basket and shot a traditional jumper, textbook form. The ball whistled through the rim, touching no iron. Then, he just walked away without a word.

"Hey, that don't count," I called to him. "You still lose."

But he walked on, and we never played ball together again.

As we got older, Strickland became more and more of an enigma to me. Folks got to calling him Preacher Man, laughing at him in his pressed suits whenever he'd show up in town. As a teenager, I thought it was just his weirdness that bothered everyone, but I think now it was really fear. There's something kind of frightening about a person who views every task, even a game of hoops, as a battle against sin.

Still, I envied his ability to fully commit himself to some greater purpose, even if I thought his chosen purpose was misguided, even dangerous. I've never found anything worthy of that kind of reverence. But now I know I'm going to give that commitment to my son, even if it makes him hate me forever.

I looked around for Trey, who went in the church ahead of me, but I couldn't find him.

After Trey comes out of the bathroom, Pastor Strickland leads a group of about twenty of us into a parlor room with old-fashioned gray curtains and gray carpet. Divots in the carpet suggest that furniture has recently been moved. The overhead lights are out, leaving the room illuminated only by a cheap strobe light.

In the first room, two teenagers agonize over whether or not to have premarital sex. The boy is being pushy, while the girl tries to resist. Fornication goes against God's word, the girl tells us—she actually says the word fornication. But ultimately, the girl gives in and immediately becomes pregnant. I struggle to stifle my laughter, and Trey pinches my arm.

The procession moves on to the next room. In the middle of the room is a gurney, and on the gurney lies a girl wearing a hospital gown, covered in blood below the waist. A doctor and nurse— teenagers both—step into the scene.

"Things didn't go like we planned, Nurse," the doctor says. "We made a mess of it, but the job's done."

"It came out fine, Doctor," says the nurse. "The baby is dead; that's the point."

The doctor and nurse speak to each other in the leaden, practiced tone of inexperienced B-movie actors, yet the inauthenticity somehow adds to the eerie feeling in the room. I put my hand on Trey's shoulder, feel him tense at my touch.

The doctor steps behind the gurney, pulling from underneath a doll resembling a fetus with a pair of scissors lodged in its head.

"Would you like to hold your baby?" the doctor says.

Abortion Girl takes the doll in her hands and begins to scream.

"Why," she wails. "Why did I do this?"

Now the smell of copper fills the room, and I swear the doll twitches.

Pastor Strickland steps into the foreground while the wailing continues.

"This is the ugliness of sin," says Strickland, sticking out his hand towards the gurney. "The price of sin. This is what happens when you tear flesh out of flesh, when you kill something God created and gave a soul. This is how you are left, hollowed out, bloody, and alone."

I grab Trey by the cuff of his shirt and yank him, pulling him out of the room. He says something to me, but I can't hear the words, only Abortion Girl hollering and Strickland incanting.

Outside, I'm getting Trey into the truck and slipping on dirt, unable to think straight. Then I feel a crushing grip on my shoulder.

"Come back in, Clyde," says Strickland. "The show's just starting."

I slap his hand from my shoulder and push my finger into his chest.

"How can you show that kind of ugliness to kids? You're sick."

Suddenly, the severity dissolves from Strickland's face and his shoulders relax, as if some clandestine personality has taken control of his body. With a strange, quiet kindness in his voice, he says, "It's the world that's ugly, Clyde. It's the world that's sick. What you saw in there, that's what sin looks like. Everyone knows about sin, but most can't understand its power until forced to face it head on. What kind of Preacher Man would I be if I didn't teach my flock how to recognize the rottenness all around them?"

He puts his hand on my shoulder again, but this time he applies no grip, just lets his hand rest there.

"You're sick, Clyde. You're sick of spirit. Look what your faith-lessness has brought you to. You're alone in that cheap motel. You don't have your son, your wife; this is what your sin —your pride— has brought you to. Now you've had to face it. That's why you're upset. The Lord is moving inside you. Don't resist."

For a moment I can't move, Strickland's words somehow calming me to near paralysis. Then, I turn my head back toward the church and Abortion Girl is standing on the steps in her bloody gown, smiling at me.

I face back around and Trey is crawling into the truck.

"Don't worry, Trey," says Strickland. "We'll keep working on him."

When he says this, I deck the son of a bitch. A closed fist right to the jaw. He goes to the ground, but doesn't seem all that bothered by the lick, like he's used to this sort of thing. But I'm not used to this sort of thing, and I bust my hand up pretty good. I feel as if I've crushed the bones in my knuckles to dust.

"Let's just go, Dad," Trey says, hanging his head out the passenger side window. "We can just go to Olsen's."

There's a resignation in his voice, and that scares the daylights out of me.

Trey doesn't say much to me in truck. I know I've humiliated him.

I think back to a barbeque Pop took me to a couple of years before he passed; the Collisons'. They had a big barbeque every year on the Fourth, and half the Snow Hill congregation showed up. Frank Collison and Pop were Deacons together. A pig on the spit, bottled RC Colas on ice, kids pulling sand burrs out of their bare feet. That kind of thing.

I had a crush on the youngest Collison daughter, Judy, who was a grade ahead of me. I was trying to impress her with insults and mild physical abuse, the way kids do. I'd say her breath stank, yank her pigtails. Make her run after me and yell mean things back. She'd tell me I had ugly feet, which I do; high arches, and long bony toes.

Anyway, after feasting on a plate of pulled pork and spicy baked beans, I saw Judy blowing dandelions beneath a loblolly pine. The seeds dusted around her face, and it seemed to me that by some strange miracle she existed inside a snow globe. In a fit of longing, I ran towards her, threatening to fart in her general direction.

As I chased her through a gaggle of mixers, closing in, a jerk of the collar stopped my momentum.

"What the hell is wrong with you?" Pop boomed at me. He yanked up on my collar so that his face was just a quarter-inch from mine, and I could smell the mix of mustard and ashes on his breath. "Act like you've got some sense!"

I said before that I couldn't remember the sound of Pop's voice, but in this instance I can remember its feel. It was like some kind of sonic blast that made my skin vibrate, and not in some abstract sense. My flesh was literally moved by the force of his voice. Or, at least, that's how I remember it.

Beyond Pop, Judy had stopped running. She was standing by the spit with her older sister, Dawn. They were giggling at me through their hands, the eyeless sockets of the pig looming just behind, with its mouth beneath the dry snout worked into a grin.

I stared back at Pop with hatred, and I did hate him in that moment. It was the kind of feeling that had a sensation to it, a warm buzz that I can still recall all these years later. The love between father and son, it seems to me, can't be summoned in quite the same way.

Now, here in the truck, Trey has his head resting against the fogged window and I know he's feeling something like that now. Twenty years from now, this is a moment he'll remember with the kind of stark clarity that only hate can conjure.

I'm taking Trey to Olsen Farms like I wanted to from the beginning. Maybe something of the evening can be salvaged.

"Hey, we'll have fun at Olsen's," I say, nudging Trey's knee, forgetting my hand's busted. I wince in agony. I should do something with it—wrap it up or something. It looks like the puffy hand of a 500-pound man. I decide to worry about that later. "You always liked the Haunted Corn Maze, right? Remember Dracula?" I make an evil laugh in a deep tenor, like a Bela Lugosi: "Muhahahahahaha."

"I think I've changed my mind. Can't you just take me home?" Trey says without looking at me.

"Listen, what happened at the church—I couldn't let you watch that. Your mama wouldn't have let you watch something like that a year ago."

"It ain't a year ago," says Trey, tracing a circle on the window with his thumb. "You just need to accept how things are now."

But there's no way I can do that. After a while, the truck stops shaking as the road smooths out, red reflectors illuminating the yellow traffic lines. Just on the outskirts of town, I pull into the parking lot of Olsen Farms. I say "parking lot," but it's really just a rectangular patch of field where Travis Olsen chopped the weeds and cut the grass flat enough for vehicles to park without getting stuck.

At first, Trey won't move to get out of the truck—just keeps his head resting against the glass. I go around and open his door.

"Come on," I say, nudging him with my elbow. "You're not scared of a bunch of rednecks in bedsheets, are you?"

Trey sighs and gets out. "Alright," he says. "Let's get it over with then."

Beyond the parking area, cornstalks rise tall and green. At the far end, Olsen and his wife sit in front of a plastic folding table to collect money—five bucks a person. The old man wears a dark blue dunga-ree coat over denim overalls. His wife stands in a black sweatshirt with a grinning orange pumpkin in the center. She takes our money. We appear to be the only customers.

"Two for you, Clyde?"

"That'll work."

She tears off two tickets and hands them over. It seems to me the tickets are superfluous; they know I've paid, and it'd be a lot of trouble for anyone to sneak in around them. I hold the tickets up to Mr. Olsen and nod to him, arching my eyebrows. He smiles faintly and nods back.

"You'll need this," he says, handing me a flashlight out of a card-board box sitting at his feet. "Make sure you return that."

I place my good hand on Trey's shoulder blade to guide him toward the entrance, and he flinches just a hair.

The entrance is an opening like a large door frame, the stalks neatly cut away with a corn picker. Some farmers hire professionals to cut out elaborate mazes you can get lost in, but Mr. Olsen prefers to do the job himself, and it's nothing too fancy. Nothing that would confuse most people.

For the first minute or so I point the light ahead and we walk, the ground rustling beneath us.

"Who do you think will come at us first?" I say.

"I don't know," Trey says. "Probably Dom Olsen with a burlap sack on his head."

I laugh. "Dom's got the worst case of acne in the annals of time," I say of the Olsens' teenage son. "He'd be scarier if he ditched the sack."

Trey starts to laugh with me. I haven't heard him laugh since I took up at the Budget Inn. Not a real laugh, anyway. When he gets really tickled, his body convulses and his voice rises in pitch until there's barely any sound.

As we round a bend, somebody jumps out of the field and grabs Trey at the sides. It's Dom wearing a hockey mask instead of a sack, and he growls as Trey squeals and runs ahead, laughing. Then Dom turns to me and roars again, his hands in the air with the fingers made crooked like claws.

"Solid work, Dom," I say and turn the flashlight ahead to see where Trey has gone.

We come upon the usual tricks—teenagers wearing white bed sheets or makeup to resemble the dead, all yelling and growling as if the key to fear is a roar of unintelligibility. But as we near the exit of the maze, everything gets quiet except for the sound of night critters. I have my arm around Trey's shoulders. He was relaxed a moment ago as we laughed our way along the path, but now in the silence he begins to tense. I take my arm away.

The light catches the exit and Strickland is standing there with Ruth. I suddenly feel afraid, but not of them. I know they are here to take Trey away from me. I steel myself and walk toward the exit.

"Preacher Man," I say, not yet acknowledging Ruth. "Already concluded your X-rated show? Scared the sin out of enough kids for one night, I guess"

"I'm sorry, Clyde. I really am," he says, and I can tell he means it. He looks at me with a sad look on his face, his tight skin now loosened by pity, then places his hand in the middle of Ruth's back.

"See you Sunday," he tells her, then turns and walks to his truck, an old rusted Ford pickup that idles in front of Ruth's Buick. In the tailgate sits Abortion Girl, still in her bloody gown, still smiling at me. Strickland nods at us as he drives off.

"I guess Strickland called you up and told you I was misbehaving," I say to Ruth. She's wearing a crisp white shirt buttoned to the top and a beige skirt down to her ankles. Not the tight sweater and jeans she would have typically worn before all this happened. "Listen, do you know what they're doing out there? What they're showing kids? I had to get Trey out of there. I mean, did you see that girl?"

"I didn't see any girl, Clyde," she says, and the hairs on my arms stand up. "Pastor came by the house and told me y'all had run off. I followed him out here."

"Glad I can spend some time with my own son without getting

spied on," I say. "You talk about how bad it is letting Trey watch some harmless movies, but then you want him to see that kind of ugliness."

"It wasn't for Trey. It was something you needed to see."

"Me?"

"Yes, you. Trey already understands. He's been saved. We want you to be saved, too."

My neck flushes when I'm angry, and I can feel the blood pumping in my jugular. I start to protest, but then I realize that Trey has not come out of the maze.

"Where's Trey?" I say, looking around frantically. "Did you see him come out?"

"No," says Ruth. "Have you lost him?"

I run back into the corn maze, taking the route in reverse, searching for Trey at every turn and dead end, shouting his name. Soon I come to the entrance and the only sign of him is his hat on the ground, lying still at me feet. Olsen and his wife have left their post and everything is completely dark. I must have dropped the flashlight back at the exit. I wander back through the maze once more, unable to see anything in front of me. With both hands, I grasp at the blackness like a blind man, hoping to feel Trey's tangled curls.

Suddenly, I hear a soft rustle and someone steps out of the field about 20 yards in front of me.

"Trey," I call, but I quickly realize this figure is too tall and thick to be my son. "Who is that? Dom? Have you seen Trey?"

And then I realize the figure is holding something at his side. I slowly step closer and see the white mask. Then the man lifts his object up and yanks at it with the other hand, and the soft chirping of crickets is annihilated by the explosive whirring of a chain saw.

The figure runs toward me, holding the chain saw high in the darkness of the night.

There's no time to speak as the distance closes between us, but as I start to move I think that this is a hell of an improvement over Dom's ass-grabbing.

At first I retreat, stumbling back towards the entrance and my

S-10, but as I start to turn a bend I remember Trey. I can't leave him here.

I pivot back around and Chain Saw Man is closing in on me. I stand bouncing on my toes for an instant, then fake to the right and explode to the left, like I'm trying to lose a defender and drive to the hoop. He bites on the fake and his footing fails on the attempted recovery. I look over my shoulder as I run and on one knee, Chain Saw Man angrily chucks his weapon at me. It propels like a helicopter, but lands well short.

I keep moving.

Soon I can no longer hear the whirring, but I know I'm still being pursued.

A bed sheet with no legs flaps in the chilled air, covers my face and tries to smother me, but I rip it away and keep moving.

A scarecrow sweeps its hand at my collar as I charge past.

I keep moving.

Dracula tries to suck my blood dry, his laugh more terrible than anything Bela Lugosi could ever conjure.

I keep moving.

I'm afraid, but it's not a fear of what might be done to me, but rather of what I'm being prevented from finding.

The maze, which earlier seemed so easily navigable, turns and twists into one dead-end after another. I call for Trey over and over, but he doesn't respond.

Then, suddenly, in the distance I can see a light. I move toward it. Eventually, the single light becomes two, and I realize it's the headlights of Ruth's car.

When I finally make my way through the exit, I have trouble adjusting my eyes to the light. Through squinted slits, I see Trey getting in his mother's car. I shout his name, but he doesn't respond. The car pulls into the road and drives away. I run towards the blacktop and realize that I won't be able to stop them.

Later, I'll go back to my S-10 and drive to the Budget Inn alone and sit on the edge of the bed and open a can of Vienna sausages. I'll stare at the TV, watch Jamie Lee Curtis as she peers out of her broken bedroom window only to find that the terror she thought she'd just vanquished has disappeared back into the black night and will surely come for her again. I'll sit and know that things could be different with Trey if I would just accept how things are, and I'll hate myself for being unwilling to do so.

Standing panicked in the dust, I watch the car go around a bend, and the light vanishes, a trumpet blasting off in the distance.

STEALING HOME

SHARON HASHIMOTO

Jojo lets loose a piercing whistle, rocking back and forth on his perch and flapping his green wings as I kick my two overstuffed suitcases into the living room. My parakeet probably heard the key turn in the lock despite the radio playing to keep him company. Barry Manilow hits every high note of the chorus, wailing ". . . you *caaame* and you *gaaave* without *taaak*ing . . ."

Bags full of last-minute souvenirs drop onto the sofa. My back is aching from the flight and shuttle bus home. Seven days in Peoria, Arizona, for spring training, and I never got a glimpse of any Mariner worth a damn: no Ichiro Suzuki, not even Joe Pineiro. I'm such a sucker.

What sounds good is a hot shower and eight solid hours of sleep in my own bed. The Motel 6 I stayed in had sheets so rough my skin is still itching. My one-week vacation is over. Tomorrow at 6:00 a.m., I'll be driving my bus through downtown traffic.

The house is stuffy with the smell of bird droppings. I open the windows and sliding glass door, turning Manilow off before I get to Jojo. There's something about the living room that feels different, something other than an unhappy green parakeet. Maybe it's because I've been gone so long. What's to miss: the green leather sofa, the coffee table with its watermarks from my beer bottles, the aluminum foil clamped onto the television antenna? As I wiggle my finger through the wires of his cage to offer a head rub, Jojo pecks hard, drawing blood. "Goddamn bird," I yell, spilling his tray and scattering seed onto the already messy rug. Jojo and I are flat-out pissed off at each other.

I rinse my finger under the kitchen faucet, certain I'd left a coffee mug and cereal bowl soaking. The sink shines as if someone had taken a sponge and Dutch cleanser to it.

Jojo continues to scream, his voice rising in a series of insistent squawks. Water drips all over the linoleum floor because I can't find the dishtowel I usually keep on the refrigerator door, so the dust from my tennis shoes leaves muddy skid marks.

When I see a large bottle of no-salt shoyu and five packages of Top Ramen, all lined up next to the toaster, that's when I finally realize Ma's been here cleaning. Tightly wrapping the edge of my T-shirt around the bleeding, I remember that I'd stopped the newspaper and mail. Since Ma kept harping on helping, I'd tried to keep things simple for a seventy-four-year-old lady. All I'd asked her to do was to check my parakeet's food and water—once on Wednesday was good enough. I'm her youngest boy, the one with no wife or girlfriend, the one who drives a bus for the city.

Now that I know she's been here, I coo to Jojo: "What are you trying to tell me? What did that crazy Japanese lady do?"

After all that squawking, Jojo can't wait to get at his clean water. Jojo arches his neck as the liquid dribbles down his throat. Ma has a hard time thinking of a bird as a pet. I can hear her lecture: "Birds should be free to fly, not caged all the time." But what she means is that she wants to brag about something other than Jojo when it comes to me.

Finally, I flop down on the sofa for a few seconds' rest. I'm so tired and my eyes are full of grit. I rub them hard.

When they clear, I study the four walls of the living room. There's a lighter, cleaner rectangle of paint next to the front door, the spot I pass by at least twice a day. My back teeth grind, and my breath explodes through my nose. The only thing I own that gives my house a little bit of class is missing.

It's an old picture, in a 24x20 inch gold frame. A muscular tiger prowls through a black-and-white jungle, its stripes rolling across his shoulders and flanks. It's the tiger picture that my parents had in the living room where I grew up, what Dad gave me when I finalized the loan for my thirty-year mortgage. "Paul, you're grown-up now," Dad had said; "You have a house of your own. A tiger in a house means good fortune. You could use this more than your mother and me. This tiger is now for you, for your future, for good luck."

At first, I check the kitchen and bedroom. Maybe the picture fell down and Ma stacked it up against a wall until I could fix it. But it's a useless search. Nothing could have made this day worse. I feel totally betrayed by more than the Mariners. I can't believe my own mother would steal something out of my home.

*   *   *

Even though I have a key, I ring the doorbell. My brother Frank and I are always telling our mother it doesn't hurt for her to be careful. Just last month, the manager found some homeless guy wandering through the halls on the third floor. Frank made certain that Ma got a two-bedroom apartment with a view of the park here at the Kawabe House, an assisted living place that caters to Japanese-Americans. On the nights she doesn't cook for me, Ma eats in the dining room, joining the other gossipy seniors.

As I wait for the door to open—balancing a bottle of apple jelly in one hand, peach preserves in the other—there's that weird sensation I get of being examined by a single eye through the peep hole, of being studied from the far end of a telescope.

The moment I step into the apartment, my mother asks, "What's wrong with that bird of yours? Squawk, squawk, squawk!"

There's no "Hello," or "How was your trip, Paul?" to start our conversation—no pleasantries. She goes on complaining about Jojo's vocabulary—how I've taught him phrases like "Batter up!" and "My, oh my." Ma's voice is big for such a small woman.

"Parakeet or no," she insists, "he was a green mess of feathers hanging upside down like a bat." Ma taps one finger against the side of her head. "Crazy."

In the ride up in the elevator, I went over my strategy. Though I was lacking actual proof, no one else could possibly have been in my house. If the tiger picture was in her apartment, I could catch my mother red-handed. "What's this?" I could play-act, maybe even be nice enough to let her off the hook a little. "You probably wanted to surprise me by getting this reframed."

More than anything else, what I want is an apology, but Ma's the same silver-haired woman I had dinner with two weeks earlier. Today, she's wearing an oversized Hard Rock sweatshirt with "Las Vegas" in gold block letters.

I hand off my bottles of apple jelly and peach preserves, my way of officially thanking my mother for checking in on Jojo. I know she'll probably "re-gift" them to her friends, but I didn't know what else to get. She has everything she could possibly want.

"That's just what parakeets do. It's normal," I mutter, even though I know my answer is too late. For a moment, I wonder why we never hug or kiss each other's cheek. Ma's always affectionate with Todd and Ronnie, Frank's boys.

Then it occurs to me—my mother must have removed the picture and carried it out in a paper grocery bag. In fact, that's what I should be looking for.

In an attempt to change the subject, I point at the windows and ask, "New curtains?" Of course I'm spying, but I don't want to seem obvious. There are the usual pictures of my older brother, Frank, plus his wife and two sons, on the buffet next to a huge stack of large-print *Reader's Digests*. All the way from Japan, a three-panel screen of long-legged cranes stepping in and out of a lake graces one wall. The framed glossy of my dad sits on its own special shelf with a fresh bouquet of black-eyed daisies, resigned to wearing a suit and tie, when in real life he wore flannel shirts even on the hottest days of summer.

Ma pretends she doesn't hear me. I can tell by the way she glanced at the window before returning to the kitchen. She's more selective in her old age, avoiding questions she thinks are too tiresome to answer. White rice is cooking in a pot on the stove. She's already chopped up her nappa. Tofu, clear noodles, sukiyaki meat—everything is ready; it all just needs to come together. She turns on the electric burner under a beat-up skillet.

As she stands next to the stove, wooden spoon in hand, I'm tempted to tell my mother all about the lousy work days I've had since I've been back from Peoria. There was the SUV that wouldn't let me merge onto the freeway, then the middle-aged lady driver who gave me the finger, or the smart-ass high school kids who piled on at the shopping mall—two of whom conveniently "forgot to pay." It's as if all the hard luck in my day-to-day life has busted through the spot on the wall where that picture hung, like it had been the one rock holding everything back. But I don't say anything about my job or vacation.

Instead I double-check her savings account and pay bills on her dining room table crowded with a paper napkin holder, trivets, and plastic place settings. This is how I know what's going on in her life—how she's donated twenty-five dollars to the Nisei Veterans Sukiyaki Dinner, or that she took a day trip with the Jefferson Community Center to see the Bloedel Reserve on Bainbridge Island. This winter, she's taking a basket-weaving class for seniors.

Ma chatters as she cooks, about how Mr. Yanagihara is losing it, how nobody invites him into their rooms anymore. He just can't be trusted. He thinks everything—mugs, umbrellas, raincoats—are his. Alzheimer's, she says. She stirs the vegetables with a wooden spoon in disgust, shaking her head as she *tsk-tsks* the poor man.

I stop a moment from licking envelopes, trying to follow her round-about logic. There was a time when Ma punched out our last name, Uyeda, on one of those label makers, sticking the bright red strips on the bottom of every material object she decided was important. That way, if someone took it, she'd be able to reclaim it. Of course, whatever the family owned was community property— like when I was five years old, having caught her holding my piggy bank upside down. A butter knife helped guide the coins out of the slot on its back. "We need bread," she told me, the knife jiggling more furiously, "for your school lunches."

As we eat dinner, our chopsticks dangle noodles between mouthfuls of rice. Ma finishes a swallow, then announces: "I took back the tiger to give to Frank."

*   *   *

The seats aren't bad for Opening Day, when hordes of fans swamp Safeco Field. I'm surprised to see the sun shining for the last day of March. Still, I tuck my hands into my armpits. I can't depend on enthusiasm to keep me warm throughout nine innings.

Frank shouts at the boys, Todd and Ronnie: "You guys have had two hotdogs and enough peanuts to stuff an elephant. That's enough. Pay attention to the game." My older brother is shelling out plenty of bucks for this male bonding experience. Frank and I have never gone to movies together, or even had the same friends. Ma must have said something to him about "being an older brother" and "what's good for the family." Other than him having a guilty conscience or wanting to smooth things over between the three of us, I can't imagine a reason for this sudden generosity. It's a good thing Frank is a District Manager for Fidelity Investments.

The four of us Uyeda men sit without speaking until it's the Raiders turn to bat. All around us, fans are chattering. It's a reversal of this loud-quiet that I feel churning inside of me. "You had no right," I had yelled at my mother. My waving hands had knocked over my tea cup. I remember how she had stared at the puddle spreading into the tablecloth, almost flinching in surprise. What had happened to Paul, the pushover?

All these years, I had been making excuses to myself as I spent entire weekends driving her to different shopping malls in search of a "special gift" for the boys' birthdays. How many ugly spinster daughters did I take to the annual church bazaar because I had "nothing better to do"? My voice had been guttural, the words like an avalanche of rocks spilling down a cliff: "You can't take back something you gave away. That picture is mine. I want it back."

Ma had hunched her shoulders as if she'd been struck. But it didn't matter; I was the one who'd been seriously wronged. Still, she managed to turn her chin up to answer: "That would hurt Frank's feelings."

But what I feel doesn't matter, I wanted to say. Somehow, I managed to keep my feet on the floor. I had both hands braced at the edge of the table.

Ma continued on in a whiny tone: "You don't treat it right—all dusty on the wall—all that good tiger luck going down the drain. Besides, Frank's the oldest."

That's when I had pushed back my chair, grabbed up my jacket, and walked out the door without bothering to close it. I haven't spoken to my mother since. Even though the phone rings twelve, thirteen times; I know who it is, so I won't answer.

I crack a few shells, popping the salty handful of peanuts into my mouth. Last year, the Mariners were ranked second in the Western Division, so tickets are expensive. I know when I'm being bribed, but the chance of any promotions other than overtime at Metro is non-existent. I'm a bachelor on a fixed income. I figure I might as well get the most out of the situation. Frank was smart and rich enough to move his wife and kids to Bellevue. Close, Ma would say, to his banking office. *Smart*, her squinty little eyes always seemed to echo behind her wire-framed glasses, each time I had asked her news about my older brother. Ma always made sure I knew how Frank's wife—a nice local girl—invited her to stay on weekends, and that "Grandma" was picked up to attend her grandsons' debates and judo exhibitions.

Together the crowd cheers, the Mariner Moose running in front of the dugout, when Felix Hernandez throws out a pitch against Oakland. I was really looking for Ichiro Suzuki to strut his stuff. Slowly, my nephews start to wiggle in the hard seats, standing up deliberately to stomp the peanut shells under their tennis shoes. Bored with pointing out the fans with blue paint on their faces, Ronnie starts egging his brother on.

"Gimme your hand," Ronnie commands. Across the small palm, he traces a curving line, explaining, "This is a truck on the highway, but it has an oil leak." Ronnie lifts his brother's hand up close to his nose. "Smell it?" I scowl as Ronnie shoves Todd's hand into his face.

I'm lucky that Frank never acted like Ronnie when we were kids—at the very least, Frank was never that blatant. All through high school, teachers would shake their heads at me and complain: *"You're* Frank Uyeda's little brother?" But it was the stuff he and Ma said, how it was "too bad" I never got much time to actually play shortstop for my high school baseball team; it was "really nice" that I even made the team, but I had to remember to keep my grades up. Stuff like that made me feel like a loser.

"Hey, Ron," I smile and give him my middle finger. "You're a real little shit."

Ronnie looks at me and just smiles, a cheesy grin spreading across his round face. Todd shrinks down into his seat, feet kicking back and forth. A younger brother like me, Todd is suddenly quiet, like he knows something is wrong.

"Really adult," Frank says, wrestling my arm down and trying to hide the obscene gesture. But I twist away, shoving both of my hands deep inside my jacket pockets. "How long are you going to give Ma the silent treatment?" Frank starts to lecture. "Jesus, Paul. How long are you going to act like a spoiled little kid who can't get his way?" The batter pops a fly ball into Ichiro's left field. It's an easy out. I keep my eyes on the pitcher's mound, trying to see if there are any signals to the coach.

Frank looks a lot like my mom, especially the eyes that disappear into slits when they smile. The kids do, too. They all have round faces, little button noses, and the straight black hair that tends to look greasy. I'm the one exception in our family who took after my father. At least I'm taller than my older brother. That and the mustache I grew make me different from them. It's always been this way: Frank and Mom sticking up for each other. Dad and me nodding our heads, saying "sure" and "whatever you want."

After the car drive home from Ma's dinner and I cooled down a little, I let Jojo out of his cage. My parakeet minced up my arm to settle on my shoulder. I asked my bird if I was being too hard. The softness of his feathers brushed my chin as he turned around, inching back down to my hand. I stood in front of the missing picture. It's funny how I could see those flowing stripes of the artist's tiger, the huge head turned with the ears lying flat, mouth open. The black lines of the lip make the canines stand out, the tongue lolling, one paw raised to take the next step. The artist had used a gold silk for his canvas, and brush strokes in black ink. Tigers, I learned from the PBS show *Nova* have stripes that go all the way down to the skin.

Frank doesn't really care about baseball at all, so he doesn't see the Oakland player on first base. We're in the bottom of the fifth, and the Mariners should have been more attentive. I'm uneasy about the runner because he's already a good three shuffles off when Felix Hernandez goes to the plate.

Whole rows of fans jump to their feet, myself included, as we boo the steal to second base. My brother is completely clueless.

"What happened?" Frank stutters. Ronnie and Todd jump up and down, trying to see because suddenly they're surrounded by a forest of adult legs.

An older, barrel-round fan tilts back his baseball cap to tell me, "That should never have gone down. Not in the majors."

I nod in agreement, dropping more shells and chewing another handful of peanuts. It's only a second base gain, but this isn't what we fans wanted to see. Good professional athletes shouldn't need this kind of edge, unfair to catchers and infielders. I'm hoping Frank doesn't embarrass me with one of his know-it-all comments, but of course, my brother has to add his two cents.

"But it's legit, right? It's a tactic, a perfectly acceptable game play."

Ronnie watches his father's face, following the discussion between me and the old-timer. "Aren't the Mariners winning?" he asks.

Frank tousles Ronnie's hair until cowlicks are sticking up at all angles. I can tell my brother is trying to impress his sons. "Maybe they'd be in *first place* of this division," Frank winks at his son, "if they used Oakland's strategies."

Everything to Frank is about how he can make himself look good. He's the better son because he has connections and an upper management, high-paying job. He made sure Mom was taken care of after our father died, splurging for a full-out reception for the memorial. Frank's boys will make sure there are plenty more Uyedas in the future.

I stoop down to one knee in front of Ronnie and Todd so I can be eye-level. My index finger scolds the air in front of them. "You two can be just like your Dad," I tell them. "Little chips off the old block."

My big brother raises his hands to shove me off-balance. Suddenly, I'm sitting on my ass, on the cold cement of the bleachers, legs sprawled in the aisle. Frank looks down at me, mouth partly open, a strand of spit sliding down his lower lip.

"All because you can't get what you want," he mutters. A coat sleeve wipes the red face dry. "Paul," he says and pauses. When Frank says my name, there's finality to it, like he's never going to say it again. Then he adds, "There's no way in hell you're ever getting that picture back."

*   *   *

On the way home from Safeco Field, traffic is backed up for miles. Here I am, hands hanging onto the steering wheel the way Jojo's feet cling to the cage bars, trapped behind a semitruck. My Mazda inches forward. Of course I can't see anything in front of me, nothing except Safeway's insignia—a skinny red *S* that looks like a yin-yang sign. For thirty minutes, I read and re-read their slogan: *Ingredients for Life.*

Right now, red is my color. It's in the brake lights of cars stopping and starting. My face in the rear-view mirror is red with frustration. That Safeway *S* seems to twist like a red rope.

What good is it being a nice guy? I'm not about to let a Camaro merge into my lane, just to let some macho punk get home five minutes earlier. Barely three inches separate my bumper from the back of the grocery truck. I shouldn't drive mad, but I am. Actually, I'm not driving at all. I'm wasting gasoline, completely stalled.

"Ingredients for Life," I repeat to myself. For forty-two years, I've bothered too much about what other people might think. It's what my mother trained me to do.

I can't think of any time Ma has said something nice to me. It's always stuff like "You need a haircut." Or "When is the last time you mowed your front yard?" My witty comebacks, those things I should have said, are days too late in the middle of the night. How can I defend myself when she's done such a great job of always making me feel guilty for what I haven't even done yet? Her voice echoes in my head: "Why don't you come visit? Frank does. I'm all by myself, you know."

Putting up with my family deserves compensation. Yin and yang. Tit for tat. If Frank keeps the tiger picture, I should be entitled to something else. There's so much I never even tried to ask for. Because Frank was student body president in high school, he got skiing lessons. Because Frank graduated with honors, the folks bought him a used car.

Logic tells me I've behaved well. Ma doesn't know what a good son I really am; I've had plenty of opportunities to do marijuana and crack. I never hung out with the gangs. My clenched fists say I should act now. Frank didn't even dare me to come and get the tiger picture—he's that sure I'd never even try.

"Ma and Frank," I mumble under my breath. "Frank and Ma." Favoritism sucks. But between the two of them, I'm angrier at my mother. She's the one who started this train wreck.

Against the law, I make a U-turn into the oncoming traffic. Several cars hit their horns, but there's no siren or motorcycle cop on my tail. I head for Ma's apartment. I park three blocks away from the Kawabe House.

The whitewashed stucco building stands out against the sunset. Red paints the entire west side. Most of the twelve stories are dark, but there are a few lights on here and there. It's a little after 6:00 p.m., and many of the tenants eat their prepared dinners on the main floor. Saturdays, the kitchen usually serves seafood—teriyaki salmon being one of Ma's favorites.

Anyone can come through the main entry's automatic doors. Since I'm Japanese, nobody bothers to ask. In the foyer, I nod at the sweater-vested man who could be my father with his thin strands of white carefully combed over his bald spot. But he's turned away, too blind and hard of hearing to really notice. When the elevator arrives at the main floor, a small group of mummified elders crowd out the door. Several speak a half-English, half-Japanese lingo that I don't understand. One woman with unnaturally jet black hair pushes her friend in a wheelchair towards the dining room. I don't recognize any faces, but it feels like any of them could be my parents. That's when I decide to take the stairs.

I'm a little out of breath after coming up the eight flights two steps at a time. But I'm also nervous over what I'm about to do. My plan is to sneak into Ma's rooms and swipe something while she's downstairs eating her dinner. Nobody is in the hallway as I make my way through the building.

The click as the doorknob turns sounds loud to me. It's not even locked. I'm not certain about what I'm going to grab, so I take a few moments to think about it. In the quiet of the kitchen, there are my mother's pills for high blood pressure, a bag of potato chips clipped shut, and a newspaper with pages folded back to a sale—all lined up on the counter. Two mangoes ripen in a bowl, which surprises me; I never knew my mother ate them.

I'm even aware of my tennis shoes brushing the rug, although a part of me is shocked at how easily someone could break and enter. Standing in the middle of the living room, I slowly turn, studying each wall, each possession.

What I take should be worthwhile, and something portable. Nothing like the big-screen television set Ma doesn't know how to program, or the Waterford vase Frank gave her for Christmas. A floor lamp spreads its glow across the sofa with a crocheted afghan draped across the back. Through the curtains, the sunset is still bright against the sky. Gradually, it dawns on me that this is what my mother must see, alone for most days of the year. Frank's touch is there in the Oriental rug and space heater scattered around the room, along with the kid-made artifacts, like Ronnie's clay ashtray from kindergarten. I want something I have a rightful claim to.

Dad's picture catches my eye. Ma must really miss him. His frozen face tells me what I'm looking for. Tucked away in her jewelry box is the gold watch Dad inherited from *his* father—the retirement gift from the Great Northern Railway, from working over forty years in the roundhouse. I remember how its solid weight felt in the palm of my hand, the steady ticking sound as the gears wound down. On the polished back are engraved italics: *Susumu Uyeda.*

Ma doesn't wear necklaces—not the gold chains or even the Mikimoto pearls Dad bought her for their twenty-fifth anniversary. She doesn't like pierced ears, and all the bracelets and rings "just get in her way." Maybe she'll discover the missing watch in about five years; she looks into that lacquered black box so seldom.

With long strides, I head for Ma's bedroom. Just at the doorway, I hear snuffling snores and freeze.

In the dimming light, I can see my mother sprawled out on the queen-size bed. She sleeps only on her half of the mattress, one arm spread across the spot where my father's shoulder would be. There's no movement or sign of her stubbornness, only the gentle rise and fall of her chest. In sleep, her face seems gentled. The darkened age spots on her cheek make me realize she's older. Have I ever seen Ma look so helpless? Is this what she saw when she saw me sleeping as a kid? For a long time, I stand there as the light continues to go—taking in the tilt of her head, the spread of her thinning hair, the cupping fingers. She won't know I'm stealing this moment.

THE KILLING JAR

MARLENE OLIN

At 8:15, five mornings a week, Mara would step out of the coffee shop, gulp some fresh air, and light a cigarette. She'd exhale slowly and watch the plume of smoke curl. The din of dishes and clattering silverware, the smell of hot grease and fried potatoes, would quickly dissipate. Then for fifteen minutes, she'd stand on the sidewalk and wait. It seemed like half of Miami was pushing their way through trying to get somewhere fast.

Like the other servers, she was given two breaks for each shift. For Mara, the breaks seemed endless. She'd looked up and down the street counting every minute, sweating every second. Each day that went by felt like a death sentence reprieve. Hector, the father of her child, the man whom they escaped from, was sure to find her. No matter how many cities she ran to, he always did.

A three-day-old beard. Camouflage pants. An army cap. Hector never served in the military but he liked to look tough. The kind of guy who never hunted but owned a stash of guns. She'd force herself to scan the crowd, sweeping her eyes over each and every face.

It was then that she spotted the peculiar man. He seemed around her age. Late twenties. Early thirties. Clean-cut. Trim. It was his shoulders that caught her attention. They were so broad and square that raindrops sat on them, plump. A side part in his hair and Clark Kent eyeglasses. Any minute she expected him to race towards a phone booth and transform.

8:15. He always wore khaki pants and a light blue oxford cloth shirt. A briefcase was tucked under an armpit, the glass jar in his other hand. Five days a week the same outfit. The same time. He stared at the sidewalk while he walked.

For weeks, Mara watched him. His steps were brisk. His arms cut the air like scythes. Then one morning he abruptly stopped. It was rush hour. Mothers were walking children to school. Suits and sweaters were heading to their air-conditioned offices. A woman with a stroller crashed into the man. A kid on a skateboard crashed into the stroller. A guy holding a cup of coffee crashed into the kid. They fell like dominoes. Still the man with the glass jar wasn't fazed. He kept his hand on the ground, his head lowered. Mara stepped in.

She bent her knees and lowered her face next to his. "Did you drop something?" she asked. She was close enough to see the dark specks in his light green eyes.

"No," he answered. He stood up and smiled. "I found something."

Inside the glass jar was a bug.

"I collect insects," he said.

Look both ways before you cross the street! she always warned her daughter. *Watch out for strangers!* But now she felt like the cartoon character who glances right and glances left only to get clunked on the head with an anvil. Something about the quiet, mild-mannered man made her pulse race and knees weak.

The following day, he walked less briskly in front on the coffee shop. He stared once more at the ground.

"Is collecting insects a hobby?" she asked. "Or is it, like, a job?" She instantly regretted the question. *What a stupid question.*

He tilted his head as if she were speaking a foreign language. "It's my job," he replied.

The rest of her shift was a blur. That night, she listened to the soft snoring of her daughter. Ariel was eight. The apartment had one bedroom and one bed. Mara glanced at the ceiling, thought about the man and his jar, and juggled just the right words in her head. Like time-lapse photography, twenty-four hours flew like a spit in the wind. At exactly 8:15 he showed up once more.

"Are you . . . like an exterminator?" she asked him.

"I'm an entomologist," he told her.

"An entomologist?" she asked. *Stupid question. Stupid, stupid question.*

"I work for the university," the man replied. "I study pests."

She walked back inside the coffee shop and watched him through the plate glass windows. There were customers to wait on and coffee to brew. Still she couldn't get him out of her head. That night in her bed, she examined her ceiling with renewed interest, tracing invisible swirls in the plaster, trying to divine her future the way people read tea leaves in a cup. By the next morning she had a prepared script.

"So what do you eat for breakfast?"

"Oatmeal," he said. He glanced at her face then looked down again at the ground. "I like oatmeal."

The lines she had rehearsed rolled out. "Come inside tomorrow. Ten minutes earlier. You can bring the jar." She talked quickly, afraid he would turn and leave or just keep looking at the ground.

He showed up for oatmeal the next day and the day after that. The following week she invited him home for dinner. "Do you have any preferences?" she asked. She had customers who only ate gluten-free, salt-free, meat-free, dairy-free. The list was endless.

His name was Matthew, he told her. He ate everything.

He knocked on her door with a spray of daisies in one hand and a box of chocolates in the other, again dressed in khakis and an oxford cloth shirt. Ariel had already eaten and was parked on the couch in front of the television. He walked up to her and introduced himself.

"Hi. I'm Matthew."

"Do you like the Teenage Mutant Ninja Turtles?" she asked him.

"I like Leonardo the best," said Matthew.

She appraised him from head to toe. "I prefer Michelangelo," she said. "He's funny."

"He likes pizza," said Matthew.

"Me, too," said Ariel.

She was supposed to watch TV. Instead Ariel disobeyed her mother—*Don't move from that couch! You're going to bed at eight! Eight o'clock sharp!*—and situated herself right next to the tall, neat man. Mommy's new friend was more interesting than Hannah Montana, than the Power Rangers, than any of her cartoons. A purple My Little Pony was clutched in her hand. It scampered across the tablecloth, galloping over forks, knives, spoons.

"Ariel," said Mara, "you're missing your favorite show."

"Neeeeigh," she replied.

Mara offered wine and beer but he refused them both. He ate spaghetti in one long slurp.

"I don't mean to pry but are you in AA?" she asked.

Another stupid question. Mara sat and watched her daughter make small talk with the stranger, this strange man who seemed more comfortable with a bug in his hand and a child by his side. She itched for a glass a wine—even better, a shot of whiskey—anything to calm her down. *Hi Yah!* screamed the TV. Her heart bounced in her chest like a trampoline . . . *Boing! Boing!*

"So you like Ninja Turtles, and My Little Ponies," said Matthew, "and . . . let me guess . . . Strawberry Shortcake?"

Ariel looked down at her pajamas. When she smiled, there was a hole where there should have been a tooth. "Do you want to hold my horse?"

Mara watched the way his hands moved, the long fingers, the mooned nails, and imagined them running up and down her spine. If she splayed herself on the floor like a dead bug, naked with her wrists held high, would he probe her? Would he poke and prod? Would he stick her with his pin? Mara shifted in her seat, her toes *tap-tapping* the floor.

"Would you like a cup of tea, Matt? How 'bout a piece of pie?"

"It's Matthew," he replied. He had put the horse back on the table. Now he was folding paper napkins into intricate triangles and squares. "This is a swan," he said to Ariel. "This is a goose."

Mara wasn't used to kind men. The men she had known . . . her father, her ex-husband . . . drank too much and loved too hard. She had the scars to prove it.

"Can he read me a story, Mama?"

This man was too clean. Too nice. Too orderly. Mara was sure of it. He was probably casing the place, not that she had anything to steal. Maybe he was a pedophile—should she check the computer? There were lists on the computer.

"This is the most delicious meal I've had in a long, long time," he told her. He said *please* and *thank you*. He ate everything she served and asked for more. But when he offered to wash the dishes, Mara drew the line.

Okay, Matthew. If that's really your name. What's the game plan? Do you launder money for the Russian mafia? Do you run numbers for some gang? There must be some catch. Some skeleton in the closet. Some deep dark secret.

The heat from the oven made her flush. Her head began to spin. She was lonely and scared and tired of being tired. She asked him about his job.

He blinked. "I teach in the zoology department and do work for the government. I find fruit flies. Sometimes snails," he said. "People bring me specimens and I identify the pests."

It has been their longest conversation.

"I once had a turtle," said Ariel. "Turtles eat bugs."

"Yes, they do," said Matthew.

Mara felt her eyes water. She handed him a towel. "Maybe you should dry."

Soon, they were spending time at his home. That first night, Mara hired a babysitter. Matthew picked her up at the apartment at exactly seven o'clock.

She knew enough about automobiles to know that his was expensive. And she knew that in Miami, net worth changed from block to block, rising and falling like a heartbeat. Still she never expected that a fifteen minute car ride could change her life. As she watched from the window, the neighborhood outside slowly disappeared. Gone were the concrete boxes, the jalousie windows, the spindly palm trees and neglected lawns. They were entering a whole new world.

They drove past a guardhouse and soon the road widened. A median of lush landscaping spliced the two lanes. On both sides of the street, Mara glanced at the largest homes she had ever seen. Most of them looked like Spanish haciendas with red-tiled roofs and stucco archways. But Matthew's home was different, modern, a jumble of geometric shapes. A large barnlike rectangle sat next to a tall cylinder. Like all the other homes, a gate ringed the property. He punched a code to get in.

"You live alone here?" asked Mara. *Again a stupid question.*

"No," he answered. "I have a cat."

They pulled up the driveway and sat in the car for a few seconds before he opened her door. "You okay?" he asked.

No, she wasn't okay. She was sitting in a hundred thousand dollar car in front of a five million dollar home. Mara deleted every preconceived notion she ever had about the rich and famous. She thought they wore their hair slicked back and slung gold chains around their necks. Matthew's pants didn't quite reach his shoes. His eyeglasses were taped together. He made his way around the hood of the car and opened her door. Then he gently cradled her elbow and ushered her in.

"Do all entomologists live like this?" she asked.

He smiled. "My father worked on Wall Street. And his father before that. Their homes are even bigger."

The living room was like a cathedral. Floor to ceiling windows were at least two stories tall. Beneath her feet, a dark wood floor gleamed.

"It's Brazilian walnut," he told her. "The table's Knoll. The couch Wormley."

Even the furniture had geometric shapes. A chair shaped like an egg. A circular table. The couch, a jigsaw puzzle of cushioned squares. Beyond the windows were a dock and a boat. She could see straight to Key Biscayne. "It's surprisingly quiet," he told her. Tall hedges lined the property. His closest neighbor was an acre away.

He kept his collection inside the round building. He saved that tour for last.

It took a few moments for Mara's eyes to adjust. There were no windows, only a skylight thirty feet high. The walls were covered with his insects, each one pinned and labeled.

"When I was a kid," he told her, "I had an ant farm. You know, the kind where you watch them through the glass. It looked so safe in those tunnels. Everyone had a job. Everyone was busy. That's what it feels like when I'm in here." In the center of the room were his work tables.

He showed her the nets and the receptacles he used for catching insects. He killed no more than necessary, he told her. Only the pests.

They were usually foreigners carried in on a ship or buried in crates of fruit. He held up what looked like a mayonnaise jar with a layer of plaster of Paris on the bottom. "This is my killing jar," he told her. "I put either chlorophyll or acetone on the bottom. It's painless. Sometimes it has to be done."

They ate outside on the patio and let the breeze wash over them. He talked softly, his voice ebbing and flowing with the waves. He was an only child, he told her. His parents lived in Connecticut and believed in boarding schools.

In the distance, they heard people talking. A fish jumped. Water splashed. Mara scanned the bay. Could Hector drive a boat? He could drive anything.

"Do you teach every day?" she asked

"I only teach one class." He tilted his neck from side to side until he heard a crack. "If I'm not in the field, I work at home."

It was Mara's turn to blink. "But every morning at 8:15, I see you in front of the coffee shop."

He laid his hand over hers. "And every morning you're outside. Some days you wear your hair up. Some days it's down. Sometimes your lipstick's pink. Sometimes it red."

At the sink, she washed while he dried. She handed off each plate, each fork, and each knife. They found a rhythm, their feet shifting from side to side, their hips moving in sync. But what Mara liked most was the quiet, the long pauses between sentences, the way no one rushed to fill the empty space. He didn't ask her about her past. He didn't badger her with questions. He simply let her be.

They made love in his bedroom with the curtains drawn, under a nest of blankets. He held her arms over her head with one hand and slowly ran the other down her side. Then he lapped the curves and crevices of her body with his tongue. No longer was her head filled with voices, her mind cluttered with snapshots of her past. For a brief moment, all was erased. She arched her back and quivered.

He never heard the glass break. He slept as soundly as a child, with his knees rolled up to his chest. But Mara heard everything. Right after she heard the crash, she heard the scream.

Naked, she sprinted into his closet and flicked on the light. It was filled with row after row of khaki pants and oxford cloth shirts. Only the shoes changed. Sneakers. Boat shoes. Loafers. She slipped on a shirt and grabbed the closest thing to a weapon she could find. Then, carrying the baseball bat, she tiptoed into the living room. The second scream was like a chainsaw ripping through a tree.

Moonlight cast dull shadows on the couch, the floors, the chairs. A water glass left out on the coffee table was on the floor, shattered. Her jaws locked. The words seeped out through her gritted teeth. "Hector, I know it's you, Hector."

When she heard the third scream, she dropped the bat. A pair of yellow eyes glowed in the darkness. Behind her she heard steps.

"I see you've met Tom," said Matthew. "Tom, Mara. Mara, Tom."

The cat looked at Mara and hissed.

Matthew put his hands on his hips. "So tonight you're a watchdog." He scooped up the cat and ran his hand along his back.

Mara shuddered.

"He's not used to having company," said Matthew. "I think he's a little jealous."

Then he saw the bat. "You planning on killing my cat?"

Mara sat down on the couch. "I have an ex-husband." She struggled to find the words, the right words. Some secrets ought to stay buried. Giving them oxygen could make them come true.

"He wants Ariel. I don't know why. It's not that he ever gave a crap. It's not that he's ever given me one penny. But he's tried to steal her three times. In Omaha. In Toledo. In Atlanta. Wherever I go, he follows. And the worst part is that I never know when he's coming. He drives a truck. Makes long hauls. Sometimes he's out of my life for months and then . . ."

"I won't let him harm you," said Matthew.

Mara gazed at him. His thick hair was tousled. The imprint of his pillow creased his face. Such a shy, sweet man. Except for the glasses perched on his nose, Matthew was naked. He was built like a swimmer. Long and lean. Hector was built like his truck. "You have no idea who we're dealing with," said Mara.

Matthew sat down next to her. Then he cupped her knee with his hand. "Aren't all pests basically the same?"

* * *

Sometimes it smelled nasty. Like nail polish remover and turpentine and the coffee shop's kitchen after it was sprayed for bugs. But there was nothing Ariel liked better than to hang out in the big round room while her mother worked. It made Saturdays even more special.

"The labels," he told her, "always tell you the date and place of the capture. His hands flew like birds. First the forceps then the pins. "We grab the insects once the killing jar has done its work. Then we gently place them right here."

There was a white board on the table. It was spongy. The pins went right in.

"I spear the insect through the thorax." He carefully spread the wings and lowered the legs.

"What happens when the bug is too small?"

"I stick this little flag onto the pin. Then I glue the insect to the flag."

His wrists swooped and dipped. Up down. Up down.

"Can I try?"

Matthew was nice that way. He never treated her like a baby. Her mother always treated her like a baby. He let her use the eyedropper and squeeze the chemicals into the jar. He showed her how to hammer in the pins. Her mother never let her near a toolbox. She and Matthew once spent an entire afternoon building a bird feeder. Of course, she wasn't allowed to use the nail gun. He got to use the nail gun. But he let her hammer them in. *Bam! Pow!* Just like Wreck-It Ralph!

"Mommy thinks Daddy's in Miami," she told him.

His face scrunched like one of his bugs.

"She changed the lock on the apartment."

Sitting on the stool, he scratched his head. "What's your daddy like?"

"One time, he grabbed me outside my school," she told him.

"Then he took me to a house, a very dirty house, where he drank a lot of beer and watched a lot of TV. He watches sports," she told him, "not cartoons."

As soon as Mara walked through the door, Matthew's worried face always disappeared. Instead his nose, his mouth, his eyes shot up like a puppet on a string. Mara always brought food from the diner. Fried chicken for Ariel. Meat loaf for Matthew. Plus a huge scoop of mashed potatoes. They'd eat outside on the patio. She'd kick off her shoes and watch the boats. *How was your day, Ariel? Did you have any homework?* Always watching the boats.

Hector did show up, just not when they expected. Mara had pulled a night shift and hired a babysitter. Of course, she always told the babysitters to be careful, to look through the peephole, to latch the chain. Mrs. Schwartz was like a hundred years old and when Hector pounded on the door she opened it all the way. Smiling. Like it was Christmas and UPS was delivering a package. When he took his gun and walloped her on the head, she folded like a cheap chair.

"Get your stuff," he said. "We're leaving."

He stumbled through the apartment, knocking over lamps and flipping furniture. There was booze on his breath and the smell of something worse on his clothes. Hector was programmed to act tough and mean. So Ariel tried to distract him. Sometimes that worked.

"I'm watching *The Simpsons*. It's really funny."

She didn't want to leave. She couldn't leave. Matthew's voice played like a song. *Scientists follow procedure. You lay out your equipment. You put on your gloves. You cover your nose with the mask.* The plan was hatched in her head. She just needed to take one step at a time.

"We have beer, Daddy." She gave him a hug. "Make yourself at home."

It was like laying out a line of sugar cubes for a cockroach. Hector made himself comfortable and worked his way through one six-pack. Then another. Soon his head was resting on his shoulder, his fingers curled on the couch.

She found the Costco-sized bottle of nail polish remover and put it on the coffee table. Then her mother's cigarette lighter. Finally she fished under the bed for the toolbox. The hammer was almost too heavy to lift. Her father was snoring now, making weird snorting sounds like a pig. When she moved his hand to the side table his eyelids didn't even flutter. She placed the screwdriver on Hector's blue green veins, lifted the hammer as high as she could, and with all her might brought it down.

He opened his eyes and screamed.

"You're pinned," she told him. *Step one.*

She opened the nail polish remover and splashed it on his shirt. *Step two.*

Then she held her mother's Bic in front of his face. *Step three.*

Some insects, Matthew told her, *don't even need the killing jar. The unexpected—a sudden movement, a light shock—does the trick.* Matthew's cell phone number was inked on her palm. It rang once before he answered it. *Step four.*

"I'm coming right over," he said. "Call 911. Don't move. Don't budge. Don't do a thing."

Ariel glanced at her father. Hector was crying like a baby, his nose snotty and red, the ink-black blood from his pinned hand spilling on the couch, his pants, the floor.

"Stay away from me and my mother," she told him. "Or else."

"Or else what?" A corner of his mouth wormed its way up. A spool of drool dripped out the other side.

Ariel appraised the man on the couch like a bug on a microscope slide. "Did you know that a cockroach can live for nine days without his head?"

She took a pack of Mara's cigarettes and placed one between his lips. *Step five.*

WEEDS

TAMMY LYNNE STONER

The sun started setting in a clear sky. I yelled in to Mama. "Okay, I'm off now to see Bo."

Mama sighed and walked over to the broken screen door. "Well, alright." Her black-lined eyes peered up over her leopard-skin spectacles like she knew more than she did. "I suppose it's good you're spending time with him down at the garage, honey. He's lonely."

I shrugged. "Bo doesn't seem lonely to me."

"There's a lot of things in a marriage that aren't what they seem." Here she raised one thin eyebrow. That one eyebrow said she acknowledged, but took no responsibility for, his loneliness. That one eyebrow said that each person must be responsible for themselves. It said that she was the one person—the only person she knew—who understood and accepted responsibility for her own damned life. "I just wish you wouldn't go through the woods to get there."

"Woods!" I laughed. "Mama, that's just a strip of untended land you and Bo are too lazy to weed."

"Weeds don't grow to be forty feet high, PD." She tsked and her drawn-on eyebrows flexed.

"Weeds are everywhere at every height," I said, turning to grab my sneakers before wandering outside.

Weeds, I thought. Some are growing inside my intestines this very moment. Tall, pale weeds wiggling around, thriving off my nutrients. Weeds laughing at me in their darkness, waving back and forth with pulsing ripples as they leech vitamins and minerals from the walls of my intestines.

Weeds take from the Earth. Weeds are cars. Factories. Banks. Governments. Pigs. Trains. Football stadiums. Universities. Mobile homes.

Weeds also grow in the shape of people. People stealing and sucking and sticking—anything to draw a little blood, take a little life.

Mama smiled a smile that told me that, despite anything and everything, I was the light of her life. "Just be careful. Now, git!"

I jumped up, my thin cotton dress swaying in the dead air around my bony, chapped and scabbed legs. *She's fifteen and her legs still look like firewood*, my cousin said last year. The little inbred.

"'Bye!"

She smiled. "'Bye, baby."

About two minutes out, just past the edge where the lawn turns into the "woods," I stopped and bent down to pull out a purple glass pipe from behind my secret rock at the base of the tallest tree. I packed it with some homegrown, working quickly. As I flared it up, the sun sunk down out of the diluted sky, as if it didn't want to see a growing girl stunting herself—undoing whatever good it had blazed all day trying to do.

Jacob called this his homegrown, "worth-the-pain" weed. I coughed, my throat burning. "Dang!"

Hopefully the new stuff I was procuring from him would be a little smoother. I looked up at the moon and pulled the next drag in slower, easing the way this time. After a few hearty tokes—my thumb blistering up from holding the lighter—I tapped out the pipe on the bark of the tall Honey Mesquite, then spent a few minutes following the straggly fingers of the tree toward the sky, watching the way its bark became darker the farther you traveled up from the ground. They say these trees can grow to one hundred and thirty feet. This one's more like a shrub, really, but it was still the biggest in the area, and it did the trick to hide my purple pipe and me.

Mesquite has a taproot that plumbs down over a hundred feet into the earth to get the water it needs here in the heat of Texas. Whatever you need to survive is always there, sometimes you just have to dig deep to get it.

I pressed my nose against the tree's scaly bark and inhaled. Oh, yes, Jacob, this is some nice weed.

"I can give you some of this for free," he'd told me last time, smiling so hard I thought he was going to split open. All he wanted in exchange was to run his dry hands up my shirt. Pull on my nipples a bit, listen to me tell him how I like it.

Silly boy. Truth is, I liked him and I would've let him do that anyways.

I tapped the rest of my pipe into my hand, then dumped it in the dirt. I needed to stop in on Bo so I could make it back to meet Jacob, who worked hard to smell nice for me, all soapy.

By now, the moon lit a bright path for me through the underbrush of Bells' Honeysuckle, proud and sweet in yellows and whites. Bo once told me that honeysuckle is an invasive plant, meaning that it pushes other plants out—meaning that it's a weed. A sweet weed, one that brings back the hummingbirds every damn spring.

With the warm smoke swirling around my insides and my head floating just above my shoulders, I strolled down our property to Hickory Street, where Bo goes every night after dinner to fix up some of the lesser lemons. I like Bo. He and I are similar, both quiet and maybe the types to think about things more than act. He grounded me against the torrents of Mama, and maybe I grounded him too. Yeah, I sure liked Bo.

"Wash your hands before you kiss him hello," I said to myself, remembering that time last month when I'm sure he smelled the pot on me.

*   *   *

I came up on the lot and Bo was doing just what I thought he'd be doing: sipping a cold beer with fingers blackened by auto-residue.

He said, "Thought it might've been a blown cylinder, but it turned out just to be a bad sparkplug."

I nodded, squeezing my eyes nearly shut to make room for a smile that was entirely too wide to be natural.

Bo tapped gently on the hood of the red Falcon. "Come up on over here."

The radio played some loud jug-band music from an AM station. He swung himself up on his workbench with an odd grace. I washed my hands at the sink, using that strong-scented pink soap he always had at the ready. I smiled over at him, the man who had—for all intents and purposes—been my Daddy since just a year or so after I was born. I don't have any memories without him.

"How you doing?" he asked.

"Same since this morning. I saw how much chili sauce you put on your eggs, so I think I should be asking you how *you* are doing."

"Fire below, PD, fire below!" He laughed, coughed, and then laughed again. "Hand me that tire pressure gauge, will ya?"

I walked it over to him.

"Well, I just stopped down to say hi. A quick hello. I'm gonna head back now."

Rather than nodding a goodbye as he usually did, Bo darted across the room and stood in the center of the open garage door. Little streaks of sweat inched across his brow, falling down the sides. He caught some of them with his beer can, trying to compose himself.

"No, I don't think you ought to go now. I'd like us to spend some more time together."

"Bo, we *live* together. We can't get much more time than that without robbing a bank."

"I'd just like to sit and talk with you, girl."

At first I thought he was drinking something with a kick, but that's not really his style. Not that I cared much because Jacob was waiting only a hundred feet away with a big fat bag for me, trying not to mess with his stiffy.

"Can we talk tomorrow?"

"Let me just call your Mama—"

Bo walked over to the beat-up wall phone, swigging his beer like there might be a prize at the bottom. He tossed the can and dialed. He held the phone with one hand and ran his fingers through his hair.

"The line's busy. Tried it twice. How about I walk you home?"

The clock ticked to 7:20 p.m. Ten minutes to get to Jacob—not that he'd take off without giving me plenty of time to be late. Probably sleep there, damn fool boy.

I said, "No, I'm okay."

Bo popped open another beer and leaned back against the Falcon.

"Did I ever tell you how me and your Mama met?"

"No, but I've heard cousin Thomas's version." I glanced to the clock and stood my ground, close to the garage door.

He cleared his throat and rubbed black streaks across his nearly white T-shirt. "Years ago, some boys and me went down to the girls' school hall for their Annual. Thomas was there. Their goal was to stop me from my calling to be a preacher."

"Oh, right, I remember."

"They said, 'If you can make it past a night of dancing with these girls, we won't bother you no more and you can go on to be a preacher.' I said sure, as confident as I once was in my calling."

"So we ambled on down through town to the dance hall on shiny shoes that we'd bought with money made picking quarts of straw-berries that summer. I'd shined those shoes and dressed in my nicest suit with my Sunday white shirt.

"Well, after thirty minutes of standing awkwardly by the refresh-ment table, Thomas pushed me into dancing with a chubby girl named Alice who smiled too much and wore too many ribbons in her hair. It was then that I started thinking that maybe I don't so much want to go *toward* God as I do *away* from girls. I was so reserved, you know."

I smiled. "But you're a good dancer, Bo!"

"No one knew that then. See, for ten years I'd been helping my mother accept the aging process by dancing with her in the living room on Friday nights, so by the time I hit the tender age of sev-enteen, I could lead almost any damn step requested! Only no one knew. I could flip wrists, twirl skirts, dip to the floor, and I even added a few steps I'd come up with myself."

Bo walked over, tossed an empty beer can in a tall metal trashcan, and got another one. I wanted him to finish so badly my feet were twitching.

"Now at the time I didn't know this, but your Mama was the best dancer in the county, *hands down.* And so pretty—that kind of pretty girl who puts pink glitter in her hair. You know what I mean?

"Well, when your Mama saw me mashing potatoes, she made her

way across the floor in the arms of another boy until she was positioned directly next to me. And the next dance, I asked her to partner, and by Jesus, we cleared the floor. The whole damn room nearly went up in flames with the clapping!"

Bo looked out the open door of the garage into the dark night.

"That's a great story—"

"We went out on some dates afterwards, but then for some reason your Mama broke things off—she always said it was because she felt too young to be tied down, but I don't know." He looked up at me. "A decade later, we met up again. You were just a baby. I asked her to marry me, and she said yes. She jumped up and slapped her thighs and said yes, all full of that passion she has. For the wedding, she got her hair done so blonde it looked almost white, like a puffed pastry all dotted with baby's breath."

"I seen the pictures." I said, looking over at the clock as it clicked to 7:30 p.m.

Bo, with his sunburned forehead all wrinkled up, rubbed his stomach. "Okay, I can see you want to go. You head home but don't disturb your Mama. Give her some privacy. A woman needs her privacy now and again. You promise me that?"

"Sure, Bo," I said, wondering briefly why he was acting so peculiar.

Bo, his dark hair messed up, tilted his head toward his beer can, eyeing the contents absently. I hugged him quickly, the way I do, and left him standing there with his free hand tucked into his worn-out belt.

Darkness had taken over most of the area between the garage and our house, so I stayed to walking where the moon fell strongest. Ahead, I saw Jacob—a gangly, stooping shadow between the skinny trees. He smiled and waved, and I forgot all about Bo.

I liked Jacob's height, and the safe feeling I got when he stood beside me. A few times that week he'd even held my hand in the hallway at our high school. I shook him off because I didn't want the attention—and it kept him guessing, you know. But truth is, I *really* liked him. And from the look of the rose he drew for me on my notebook, I think he liked me too.

"Where you been?" he asked as he got closer.

"I had conversational troubles. And now, we got to make this quick since my Mama might be waiting for me."

He leaned against the tree. "This weed's even better than the last."

"Oh yeah?"

He nodded all country-boy. "Yeah, it is. I gave you the same amount but it's better, so it's just like I'm givin' you more."

"Ah-huh," I mumbled, listening to what he was bringing to the table.

"So the price's going up."

I smiled. "Is that so?"

"Just a little," he grinned, hand pulling a pouch from his back pocket. "Wanna smoke first?"

"No, I want to hear what you want from me for this *little, tiny* bag."

"Not too much." He shifted back and forth on his long legs and cleared his throat. "I just want you to hold it in your hands."

"Hold what?" I asked, craning around to see what lights were on in my house.

"My *dick*—you know what. Just hold it."

The outdoor light by the back door clicked off. *Must be later than I thought.* "Sure, okay," I said, "just give it to me. We are on limited time. Mama's shut the lights off."

He dropped the weed in my hand and unzipped his pants until the zipper got stuck. "Dangit."

"Hurry up, Jacob. This is no time to get shy."

"I'm not shy. You know I've been with a few girls before."

"Those weren't *girls*. They were strippers so that doesn't count. Now gimme your dick."

He did, asking me if next time I'd take it in my mouth.

"Sure, if you bring me weed made of *gold*." I moved my hand up and back, feeling the skin give a little for a few minutes. I liked the powerful feeling of controlling this part of him. And, truth told, I could feel myself stirring with some kind of wanting for the thing in my hand. It scared me a little. Then I felt some wetness on the tip of it and I pulled my hand away altogether.

"Hey!" he shouted.

"I held it, now shush!" I yelled as I ran off. "I'm sorry but I gotta go!"

"Dang it, PD!"

"I'm running late!" And I was, but I was also running scared. All that was too much for me to handle right then. All that new desire. "I'll make it up to you!"

I tore past the trees, twigs scraping my legs. My ankles itched but I didn't stop. The moon looked like it was almost sitting on top of my house. The plastic baggie of weed got sweaty in my hand.

I ran into the house, expecting Mama to be standing there, telling me she had shut off the light ten minutes ago. Instead I got a simple note from her: *Be quiet now, I've gone to bed. Good night, baby.*

*   *   *

The next morning, Mama was whistling in our orange-and-brown kitchen. I stepped in and looked around with unconcealed shock—it was *clean*! The newly dusted maple bureau in the corner even had a vase with fresh carnations—all white except two purple ones on the edges. Fresh-cut flowers! Did someone die?

I looked over at Mama and noticed her nails. They were bright red with little white dots on them. Her eyes were lined perfectly, and she had on pantyhose with none of the usual tears dotted with fingernail polish to stop them from spreading.

"What are you thinking about so hard, PD?" Mama asked between humming along with "There's a Tear in My Beer" in the background.

"Weeds," I answered, looking at her.

"You know it doesn't make you an *academic type* to dwell for so long on one topic," she said while she scratched a squishy portion of her left breast that had snuck out from her too-tight bra and her red *Coca-Cola* T-shirt. "Now get the peanut butter out to make your lunch. Bus's coming soon."

*   *   *

Two nights later, Jacob passed me notes in school promising the best bag of weed ever, telling me I better "be ready" for our next meeting. I was. After several hours of thinking about it, getting used to the idea of having these desires and where they might lead, I was ready—willing and ready.

That night, I walked down to see Bo again, in order to give me reason to see Jacob. He looked even more tired than before.

I nodded when I walked into his garage. "Are you feeling Okay?"

"Yeah, I'm Okay." He ran his free hand through his wavy hair and slipped under the Mustang to change the oil.

We talked about a book report I was giving in school on Albert Einstein, who didn't talk until he was three, and about how my feet were outgrowing my shoes again. Then I said it was time for me to be heading home.

Bo rolled out from under the Mustang and stood up faster than a cricket on a bar-b-que. "Stay here a bit more, honey."

"I got to go, Bo, but thanks."

"Come on now." He wiped his hands on a filthy oilcloth. "Besides, your Mama needs some time to herself."

"Why? Is she mad at me?" I felt a sudden panic. Mama wasn't nice when she was mad.

"No."

"She mad at you?"

"Not really."

"What is it?"

"I can't say," he said to the floor.

"Then I'm going." Jacob was waiting.

"No!" He pulled my arm back until my whole body turned to face him.

About five years ago, our dog Putter came home with a rabbit in its mouth. When we finally sprayed him with enough water to drop the poor thing, it was still alive, only it couldn't run since its foot was eaten off. That rabbit had a certain look in its eye, terror maybe—the same look Bo had now.

"You've been acting weird these past few weeks. Every time

I come down here you don't want me to go, but I have to go at
some point!"

"Sit down."

"No—"

"I said *sit down!*"

He'd never yelled at me like that before, so I sat. And there we
waited, me on the fender of a 1973 Plymouth, and him leaning
against the concrete wall trying to gather together the pieces of
something he'd just thrown across the room.

He sighed. "You remember the story of how your mother and I
met?"

"Yes."

"You remember how second cousin Thomas tells it? How he
says that I never did learn to use what God gave me—in the
romantic sense?"

I couldn't help but smile. "Yeah."

"He was right. I knew it, your Mama knew it—everybody knew
it. And nothing's changed over the years. I just never really had the
interest to learn about such matters. First I loved dancing, then cars,
then you. I don't mean to be saying I never loved your Mama. I sure
do, but I love her like I love candied yams. You know how often I
have candied yams?"

"Every Thanksgiving."

"That's right."

I stood up and grabbed a beer from his worktable. He raised his
hand to let me know it was okay. We were talking *sex* here.

"So, now we each give each other—she and I, we let each other
have—PD, you know how much I love you, right?"

Then it clicked. I slugged the whole can of beer. Jacob could wait.

"Lately, while we're down here, she's back there with someone
else." The words dripped from his mouth. "Don't hate your Mama.
This was my idea. She didn't want anything to do with this at first,
but as the years drug on . . ."

Bo got silent.

I tipped back the beer can again. Empty. I stood up.

"I gotta go, Bo."

He didn't stop me.

"Promise me you're not angry."

"I don't know what I am, but I don't think I'm angry," I said, and left—quick.

My mind spun around and around with all the happenings. Jacob. Bo. Mama. Me. I settled on thinking about anything but those things, so I counted my steps as I ran and every time I hit six I'd jump up high, even if there a tree was in the way. I nearly fell twice, but didn't. Then I saw Jacob.

He met me same as always, jittery and smelling like he'd swallowed hot, oily coals that were oozing out his pores. He wanted to touch me down south this time. Maybe poke around inside, he said.

"Jacob, shut the fuck up. I'm having some serious family troubles here and I don't need you literally up in my business."

He bent his lanky body in half when he sat down on the tree stump next to me. He pulled out a joint and lit up.

"What's going on?"

I told him exactly what's going on. What's going on up there where the lights were off and back there where the radio's playing too loud and in here where I felt like beating on that tree stump until my hands bled. I was telling him everything when all the while, a strange thought kept running through my mind: *How could she do this to me?*

Jacob nodded with his shaggy hair and half-closed eyes. "Your Mama? Well, she is kind of a looker. It'd be a shame—"

"Shut up!" I jumped up. "That makes it ten times worse. There must be a line forming outside our door at sundown. Goddamn! Gimme some of that."

We sat there for a few minutes, pulling down his joint.

"Well, I guess if they agreed to it."

"What?"

"I mean, she's got needs, right?"

"God." I stood up and walked away, ignoring him calling after me. *What the fuck is with everybody?*

I channeled my confusion and hurt into anger at Jacob's typical lack of sensitivity. I knew it wasn't fair—that I was maybe blowing it out of proportion—but I had to put all my emotions somewhere.

*   *   *

When I got home, Mama had gone to bed again. I felt sick. Thankfully, I'd palmed Jacob's joint, so when I went to my room, I opened the window with the fan set up and finished it up.

What if she makes *noise?* I thought.

My guts churned again, only slower on account of being so high. I turned on my radio to cover any sounds that might come from Mama's bedroom upstairs—the bedroom she was supposed to share with *Bo*. Now I understood why he'd been spending a couple of nights a week down at the garage.

Wait, I thought, *a couple of nights? How much sex does one middle-aged mother need?*

Suddenly, I came so close to throwing up I had to lean over. Thankfully I had more weed left, so I smoked and smoked until the room spun and I fell asleep.

*   *   *

The next morning, Mama was done up and chipper again. "Eggs, hon?"

What I wanted to say was *Go screw yourself.* Instead, I said: "No, thanks, I'm not hungry."

Mama wore her scarlet red robe that day—*fitting*. Her perfume smelled stale, and she had a mark on her neck that I prayed wasn't a hickey.

"What are you thinking about, PD?" she asked.

"Nothing."

"You know what I've been thinking about?"

Boning? "No, what?"

"You actually got me thinking about it," she said. "Dandelions.

Dandelions are weeds, right? But why do we think so badly of them? They are just fertile flowers with a drive to continue the race. They do what they have to do to live, same as everyone else."

Mama, her hair tucked under a silk bandanna with flowers on it, walked over and cracked some eggs into our banged-up fry pan.

"Moreover," she said, using her smart words, "dandelions refuse to dull themselves down. They're *proud*—with their beautiful yellow flowers. They're *daring*. They let us know they are here and they aren't going to stop being who they are! They aren't going to keep inside boundaries we set. They aren't going to die."

Mama stirred the eggs in the pan with flair. She started to hum again.

I seethed. How *dare* she include herself in my world like this, as some kind of hero. "Those dandelions look like anyone you know?" I asked.

"Oh, I don't know." She looked over at me with her intense eyes. "PD, is there something on your mind?"

I wanted to say it. I wanted to say it, then spit on the floor or throw a mug or do something, but I'd promised Bo.

"Nothing more than usual," I said, lying so hard it burned my throat.

*   *   *

For the next three days, I wandered down to see Bo as usual. We never talked about it again, but he started bringing along extra beers for me. Every night, I passed by my Honey Mesquite tree, but Jacob wasn't there. He hadn't been in school either, so I figured he was sick.

On the third night, I checked under my secret rock and there lay the biggest, fattest bag of homegrown dope I'd seen yet. Bigger than my fist. You could smell it through the bag. He'd even put a pack of papers inside.

A pack of papers, but no note. *What the hell?*

I weighed the baggie in my hand, watching my house for the outside light to click off. That was all I kept doing for a good five minutes: feeling the bag and watching the house.

After the light clicked off, I walked back, taking my time in the cool night air, enjoying my beer-buzz. I listened for locusts and thought about what it must be like to sleep on a cloud.

On my way up the stairs, figuring I'd roll me a nice joint as soon as I got settled in for the night, I heard laughing coming from my Mama's room. I stopped, nauseated again. I recognized the laugh; it was Jacob.

At the top of the stairs, I turned to my left and charged across the dark blue carpet towards Mama's room. I didn't knock. I jerked the doorknob hard twice to the right until I heard the click, which always meant I'd snapped the lock open.

I threw back the door and there was Jacob, standing there in his bright white boxers with his stiffy tenting them out. Mama was smoking on the bed, leaning against the space between the two windows along the wall.

"Shit!" was all I could say. The rest got trapped in the spinning sensation I was trying to control.

Mama turned her head to the side, clearly taken back. From this distance she looked pretty, but I knew if I got any closer I could see the make-up caked in her wrinkles and that waddle of skin under her chin.

"Honey . . ."

I felt Jacob's bag of weed in my pocket, and clenched it in my fist.

"Excuse me, ma'am," Jacob cleared his throat, his hands covering his now-dwindling member.

I looked from him to her. "He's talking to *you*, Mama."

"Can I get my pants over there?" Jacob asked, his shoulders all hunched in.

I glared deep at Mama. "Jacob?"

She nodded and smoked. She turned to Jacob. "Yes, get your pants."

"I've touched *it* too, Mama," I told her.

Jacob sucked in a breath of air.

"Hmmm," Mama replied, cool and collected now. She exhaled a thin line of smoke.

I turned my hot stare to Jacob, who avoided me.

Mama leaned over and threw her cigarette out the window, still lit. She stood up. "He said you guys were just friends."

"Friends?" I shouted.

Jacob shoved his right leg into his black pants. "Were we more?"

"I thought so."

He shrugged. "I never really knew."

"You knew," I said, though I wondered then if maybe I'd played it too coy. "That doesn't matter now. This is my Mama and you knew *that*! You knew she was my Mama and you knew she was . . ."

Mama looked at me. "Was what, baby?"

I didn't take my eyes off Jacob. "You knew she was stepping out on Bo."

Mama wrapped her robe around herself—pale blue tonight—and walked over to her gin and tonic, sitting on her bureau in a Minnie Mouse glass. "PD," she said, "I'm sorry."

I faced her dead-on. "Sorry you got here with Jacob or sorry you can't get with Bo or sorry—"

She walked up close to me, fire rising in her bloodshot eyes. "Stop."

"That what you are, just some lying easy lady of the night?" I couldn't bring myself to say 'whore,' though I thought it.

Mama got red. "You come in here and want to be a part of this world—the world of my bedroom—then *here you are*! So now you listen, PD." She looked right at me. "The man I *want* in my bed is the man who has been your daddy since you could walk. But he's *preoccupied*. He's a *dreamer*. I got you a good father, but I didn't get a good man for myself in the process."

Mama walked past Jacob's shirt, laying on the carpet like a glue leak, then back to me. She put her warm hands on either side of my face. Her fingers smelled like smoke and tea-rose perfume. Her eyes were hot and grey-blue and sad. Her teeth had gaps. She looked beautiful in that fucked-up way that sad women can look.

I whispered, "But *Jacob* . . ."

She dropped her hands. "I didn't realize. You should have told me," she said.

"Maybe you should have asked!"

Mama turned away from me again and walked back over to light another cigarette from the pack on her yellow polka-dotted pillow. Under her robe, the shoulder of her light pink teddy was pulling off. I could see the place where the lace was tearing away from the edge.

"Look, PD," she sighed, "I can't be everything; I can't be a good wife and a good mother and still be the kind of woman I am."

"What about *me*, Mama?"

"This isn't about *you*. That's what I'm saying."

"It should be about me!" I stammered.

Jacob grabbed his shirt from the floor and pulled it over his head. He already had his shoes on. Neither one of us looked at him as he slinked out the open door and creaked down the hallway.

Mama held her cigarette like some woman in an ad. "Not any more, PD. You are a woman now. It's not always about you anymore." She turned her eyes down and her voice got quiet. "I waited until you were a woman. I got you a good daddy and I waited. *Oh*, how I waited! And now, you are not a part of me anymore." Her face went blank and she seemed as far away as the moon, and just as sad. "You stopped being a part of me when you became a teenager. You're a woman now. And so what I do is what I do. Now, be a woman. Be dignified."

"You're telling *me* to be dignified?"

"We all have different definitions of dignity." Here, she straightened up a little. She crossed her arms so the elbow of her smoking arm was resting all Hollywood on her other arm.

I looked at her. The anger in me quieted down a bit.

Mama took in a deep breath then reached out a hand and squeezed my forearm. I could feel her cool nails against my hot skin. She didn't look like she needed my understanding or even my agreement. For the first time—or the first time I noticed—my Mama had an odd confidence about her, standing there with her hair falling out of the chopsticks she was using to keep it together.

Without turning away from me, she said, "Jacob's gone. He's not coming back—at least not for me, and I hope not for you."

I shook my head to agree. I did not need a boy like that.

She smiled. A peaceful look relaxed her face. She dropped her cigarette into her gin and tonic. "It's been a big night."

I half-smiled, regaining my composure. "Yes, it has."

"PD, let's you and me have a late dinner together as real, grown-up women. Let's get to know each other now that we know a bit more about each other."

"All right, Mama," I said, not lying this time, "that sounds good."

*   *   *

We went out for bar-b-que, the kind they cook all night long, taking shifts to stoke the coals. We didn't talk too often, and when we did it was about things that didn't matter much: the heatwave coming in, her joining a bowling league, what Miss Jillian Leigh did to make her tomatoes grow so tall. We talked about my school and I wanted to tell her that I'd recently learned that swans mate for life, but even that felt too close and too soon.

In the long silent patches, I thought about how much Mama had given up for me. She'd been that girl with all the glitter who chose the boy who could dance, though only after she'd had me. She took him on, in part, for me. Maybe, just maybe, *I'd* been the weed—all that dependency on her, sucking the life out of her, though not on purpose but just because that's what kids do sometimes.

Right then it still didn't make everything that had happened okay, but eventually it did. Besides, she is my Mama after all.

REFLECTIONS

INDIA, 1899

N.J. CAMPBELL

The shot echoed over the hard earth and sand in the midday heat.

Lieutenant Jonathan Samuel Saunders lowered his rifle when he felt something hit his eye and he wiped it away. He looked at the discharge in his hand. *Sweat, dirt*—he thought.

He turned to Private Edwards, who was looking through his field binoculars.

"Blood?" whispered Saunders.

Edwards removed the binoculars from his eyes and looked at Saunders's palm.

"Sir?" he asked.

Saunders shook his head. "Nothing."

Ten yards away, a man lay limp and chained to a khejri tree. His body was huddled in a pile on the sand, his torso leaning back on his knees against the tree with his head hanging forward on his chest.

Saunders heard the footsteps of a man approaching them from behind and then the footsteps of another. The four men watched the corpse in silence.

The heat was making the lieutenant dizzy.

"In the heart," Edwards finally said, looking through the binoculars.

Saunders stared at the dead man without wiping the sweat from his brow. The camels moaned in the sun behind them.

*   *   *

"In a month, you'll be on your way back to England. The latest onset cases have been observed at three months. If we had any vaccine, I'd give it to you, but at ten yards the likelihood that you came in contact with the virus is remote, even absurd," the doctor said, looking up from his clipboard. "I don't think you have anything to worry about."

The doctor went back to reviewing his notes.

Saunders sat patiently on the cot.

"You're taking your quinine?"

"Yes."

"No fevers? No dreams?"

"Some."

"Well . . ." He scribbled some notes. "That's to be expected." The doctor stopped writing and looked up again. He squinted at his patient. "And your nerves? How are they?"

"Well enough," Saunders replied, looking at the wall.

"Good," the doctor pronounced. "No cowardice."

*　　　*　　　*

"The incident was eleven days ago?" the captain asked.

"Yes, sir."

"You checked in with the hospital?"

"Yes, sir."

"Exposure?"

"Unlikely, sir. Lt. Harlow had myself and two others chain him to the khejri tree and feed him for several days in observation before the disease took hold."

"Ten yards, you say?"

"Yes, sir."

"So close?"

"To make certain . . ." said Saunders, hesitantly. "To make it . . . as humane as possible, sir."

The captain sneered.

"Mmhmm." The captain turned away from Saunders and looked out the window. The sun was directly over the dry, baked street. "It can't have been pleasant. Rabies is an awful way . . . Not a man's death, really—not at all. Even so, you're the best shot in the company, and there's mercy in that." A Brahman bull walked down the center of the street. "Lt. Andrews informs me that your report says that it was a clean kill and that you burned the body before burial.

Also, that you were friends. I'm sorry about that, but this is India. Sentiment is for home."

Saunders was silent.

Sweat covering his brow, the captain turned back to Saunders and nodded at him. He took a handkerchief from his pocket and wiped his face, and then he took the report from his desk and leafed through it.

"Your report doesn't make clear where exactly this happened. Where was this?" The captain looked up from his notes.

Saunders's eyes drifted and his stare became fixed and lifeless for a moment before he came back to himself. "I'm sorry, sir, we weren't exactly sure where we were. The desert, somewhere outside of Harsawa."

The captain narrowed his eyes at Saunders.

"I see." The captain closed the file in his hands and held it before him. He took a deep breath and slowly exhaled. "This is unusual. This whole situation is unusual. I've learned that you've asked for the address of Lt. Harlow's widow. I will not forbid you to write to her, since you were friends with Lt. Harlow. However, I strongly disagree with doing so. In principal, nothing good could come of it. It could be unkind or it could be . . . distasteful. Whatever it is, it's not a good idea." The captain paused and studied Saunders. A moment passed in silence.

"Dismissed."

*   *   *

Dear Mrs. Harlow,

I am sure the Admiralty has, by now, informed you of your husband's sacrifice. In the most dire of situations, a man's bravery is perceived plainly. It is without pretense or preparation that we face our final mortal circumstance. With this in mind, I have the sad pleasure and position of informing you of your husband's undeniable bravery. He died honorably in Her Majesty's service.

Respectfully,
Lt. J.S. Saunders

*   *   *

Sitting at the servicemen's bar in its dim half-light, Saunders could hear Edwards drunkenly boasting at another table.

"It wasn't much of a shot. I mean, he's the best shot in the company—he never misses—but still, it wasn't much of a shot. I could've made the shot. I could've."

Another man spoke. "What must it have been like to shoot a man like a dog? Brilliant! Thrilling! Good—I bet! I bet it was magnificent!"

Another man spoke. "Shoot your friends for Queen and country!" The whole table laughed.

Saunders pulled on his cigarette. The smoke left his mouth reluctantly, heavy and dry.

His hand shook as he edged his glass towards the bartender. "Another."

*   *   *

In his bed, under the mosquito netting, he heard the sounds of a sitar from the city. As he slipped in and out of consciousness, sweating and shivering, he dreamt of the tree. On fire, from trunk to tip, it burned in the endless heat of a timeless dream sun. It burned forever, brilliant and unforgiving. It stood alone, aflame and indifferent.

Waking to the sounds of the tree's branches collapsing under the flames, he sat up panting in the dawn. Tears pooled in the corners of his eyes, and he waited for his heartbeat to settle before stepping out of bed. He moved to the mirror, leaned over the sink and stared at his reflection.

There were bags under his eyes. His whiskers dripped sweat from his chin. His eyes were bloodshot, pale and gray-blue.

He remembered images from his dream. He moved to the toilet and began vomiting.

The day's heat began filling the room.

*   *   *

The officer's mess was filled with enlisted men on one side and divided by a row of empty tables as Saunders walked into the dining hall.

"What is this?" Saunders asked a lieutenant getting up from his lunch.

"The roof's come down in their mess area." He raised his chin slightly in the direction of the non-commissioned officers. "We eat with the rabble today."

Saunders sat down and an old Indian in a servant's uniform and turban set his lunch before him.

The man's face was oily and round. He had dark eyes and the bags beneath them were heavy and deep. His moustache was waxed.

An officer a few seats from Saunders lit a cigarette. Saunders looked over at him. Several others glanced up from their meals.

"When in Rome," the officer said and waved out his match. He inhaled deeply. "Or, India, rather," he exhaled into the air above their heads and pointed at the other tables. Several tails of smoke rose from the other side of the room.

Another officer put down his utensils and shook his head.

Laughter came from the other side of the room.

"They never get the tea right—ever!" A soldier shouted. "You— Sri Sri Baba Baba—get me a proper cup of tea or I'll sacrifice you to one of your bloodthirsty gods!"

A few men chuckled.

The Indian man smiled stupidly and took the soldier's cup from him.

After lunch, Saunders went to the kitchen. As he entered, he heard mess hands' gossip.

"—laid up with fever."

"Malaria?"

"Probably. Or worse."

When the mess hands saw Saunders, they came to attention. Smoke filled the room. All the English soldiers were smoking. All the Indians were cooking and cleaning.

"At ease," Saunders said, reflexively.

The soldiers' shoulders dropped.

The old Indian man stood to one side of the room drying the clean dishes. His expression was indifferent.

"In the dining hall, there was some confusion about a man's tea. To avoid a misunderstanding, could one of you tell that man over there that the tea he served was fine?" Saunders asked, pointing to the old man.

The soldiers looked at him strangely and then looked where he was pointing. One put a thumb over his shoulder and spoke.

"Who, sir? Hajeet?" the soldier said incredulously, looking back. "Hajeet's English is better than the Queen's . . ."

Saunders stared at the man drying dishes.

*   *   *

Sand blew against the prison at the edge of town. As Saunders left the main office, he saw a soldier leaning against the wall of the building with a piece of paper in his hand.

Saunders turned and stared at the man.

"Name." Saunders ordered.

The man stood to attention.

"Private Ashley Matthew Dunhurst, sir."

"What is this, Private Dunhurst?"

"I was waiting for you, sir," the man said with lowered eyes.

Saunders watched the man.

"I'm sorry, sir. I've just been stationed here, and when I arrived this morning I asked my sergeant if it was true that you were stationed here as well. He asked what business I might have with you, and I told him none. It's just that your shooting is of some note in the army, and I wanted to see if I might persuade you to demonstrate your skills since my duties don't officially begin until tomorrow. He said that you had duties in the prison and that I could find you just north of the city. I didn't want to interrupt, so I've been standing in the sun for some time. I must have started to lean against the wall by accident. It's very hot, sir."

Saunders looked the man over. His uniform was poorly pressed and a little oversized for his build. His face was pale and his eyes looked red. Saunders listened to the sand in the wind hitting the prison's wall.

"I assure you, they're just stories."

"It would mean a great deal to me, sir."

Watching the heaviness and fatigue in Dunhurst's eyes, Saunders nodded. "Very well."

Saunders went back inside and retrieved a rifle.

"What would you have me shoot?" he asked when he had come back out.

Dunhurst held up the small piece of paper in his hand.

Saunders nodded.

They walked in silence to the far side of the prison. As they walked past the barred windows outside the shadow of the building's walls, Saunders wondered where the prisoners were in their cells, what shapes their faces made, how rough their hands were, and if they stared at the sun and the heat all day.

"That tree, sir?" Dunhurst asked, pointing to a tree about eighty-five yards away.

"Alright."

Saunders waited in the heat while Dunhurst tacked the piece of paper to the tree with a pocket knife and walked back to his side.

Dunhurst stepped back and to the right and Saunders took aim. He leveled the rifle at his shoulder and held it lightly in his hands. He breathed slowly and gradually tightened his grip. He watched the breeze in the tree and waited, feeling his heartbeat become slower. His eyes narrowed and he stopped breathing. The report of the rifle echoed over the ground. He lowered the weapon, took a bullet from his belt pouch, and reloaded the chamber. With ease and almost without pause, he lifted the gun and shot a second time. He repeated the process and then held the weapon at his side. A minute hadn't passed between the three shots.

He and Dunhurst walked to the tree in silence. Saunders's face was dripping with sweat. Dunhurst's was becoming red. When they reached the target, two of the three holes were centered in the middle of the paper, one slightly overlapping the other. The third was neither on the sheet nor the tree. Saunders looked over the area and then stared at the two holes.

"Missed one, but . . ." Dunhurst paused, running his fingers over the paper and then underneath, over the bark.

Saunders lowered his eyes. *Was it the first, second, or third shot? The wind . . . an unsteady hand . . .*

"I've never seen anything like it," Dunhurst said in a low voice.

Saunders tried to pick up his thought, but he couldn't remember where it had been going. He continued to wonder which shot he had missed and turned to Dunhurst, half smiling. "Just stories."

"Right . . ."

Saunders felt the sun's heat more heavily now and began to walk back to the prison. He slung the rifle over his shoulder and listened to the paced, dull sound of their boots hitting the earth.

He felt his right hand begin to shake and he pulled his fingers into a fist.

As they reached the prison's entrance, they saw two figures in the distance coming from the city. The figures were running, and as they got closer, it became clear that they were Englishmen in civilian clothes.

"A dog," the first man wheezed, out of breath. He doubled over and placed his left hand on his knee and extended his right hand in the direction of the city. "A rabid dog."

Saunders looked at the man still standing.

"Can you take me there?"

The man nodded, winded but less exhausted than his companion.

"Get kerosene and follow this man's directions," Saunders ordered

Dunhurst while pointing to the man who was now almost kneeling.

"Sir!" Dunhurst shouted and rushed towards the prison's main office.

"Lead," Saunders said and nodded to the man. The man turned and began to run again. Saunders, motionless, looked back at the man who was bent over. The kneeling man looked plainly into Saunders's wild, complete fear. Saunders finally broke the man's gaze and ran after the other man.

They ran through the edge of the city, past shops, carts, and black, shadowed windows. People moved slowly out of their way or not at all, and they weaved through markets and camels and beggars.

They rounded the faded pastels of several buildings and temples more slowly, and Saunders began to hear the sound of their heavy, labored breathing.

"There!" The man said and pointed to a crowd of people.

Reflexively, Saunders loaded his rifle's chamber and raised it to his shoulder in an instant.

"Cāla!" he shouted as he moved forward into the crowd. "Move!"

Several people waved their hands and shouted while moving towards him. "Nahi, nahi, nahi!" They pointed to tables and wood scraps they had used to pen the animal in.

The narrow, enclosed area, bordered by buildings on three sides, was a dead end.

The crowd shouted and hissed at the dog. The dog growled and barked, and Saunders felt his heart beating faster.

"Here!" The man who had brought him shouted over the roar of the crowd. He was pointing to an entrance to one of the buildings.

Saunders moved quickly, pushed open the door, and entered. It was dark except for three dim cooking fires, and it took his eyes a minute to adjust to the low light. There were women huddled over the fires on the dirt floor and half-clothed children staring at him silently, without expression. The room smelled of turmeric and coriander and was silent except for the noise of the crowd outside. He saw a ladder in the corner and climbed quickly to the second floor. None of the women looked up from their pans.

There were two dark shadows on the floor in the corners of the room and two windows without frames. He moved to the window that was closer to the street and raised his rifle. Several people from another building leaned out of their windows to see what was happening, but Saunders could only see some of the people below and nothing of the dog. He climbed down the ladder and took the ladder out of the building without anyone's objection.

The noise of the crowd was louder and the dog was barking without pause. He found a balcony to lean the ladder against and climbed onto it. He raised the ladder to the landing and then climbed to the roof.

The hard clay of the roof burned his hands and he moved quickly to the edge while raising the rifle. The crowd bellowed beneath him and he saw the dog—gray-brown with black eyes and a long body. It was covered in dust, and its ribs heaved with its breath. It ran at the crowd and jumped up against its enclosure, snapping at individual faces. It ran at the walls, scratching and biting at their rough surfaces. It lunged in one direction and then another, shook its head violently and retreated behind an upturned chair in the middle of its makeshift pen.

Saunders was shaking. His heart was racing and his vision became blurred. He wiped the sweat from his face with his palm and then with his sleeve. He watched the chair and squinted. His eyes stung with the bright afternoon sun and the salt from his sweat.

Everything became silent. The muscles in his neck burned with exertion and he felt the blood in his head pounding. His body ached with tension. A rushing sound filled his ears and he started to lose consciousness.

As Saunders's vision clouded over, the dog moved forward. It looked up at him and then was motionless and still on the ground.

He dropped the rifle, exhausted and trembling, and breathed deeply. There were cries of confusion and excitement from below. His vision came back white, then he moved his head and saw that the white was just the pale color of the atmosphere. He found the horizon line and then watched the endless expanse beyond the city where the trees blurred in the heat shimmer between the desert and the sky.

Had it? Had it looked at me?

"Lieutenant," he heard as a whisper as he starred at the shimmer. "Lieutenant," he heard again in the back of his mind.

"Lieutenant, sir!" Dunhurst's voice came shouting from below. Saunders came back to himself, his balance unsteady and his body shaking. He picked up his rifle, moved to the ladder, and climbed slowly down from the building.

Dunhurst stood at the base of the building sweating, with kerosene and matches in his hands. Two other soldiers had parted the crowd, and the stray lay near the middle of the fenced-off area.

Without speaking, Saunders took the kerosene in one hand and the matches in the other and walked through the crowd to the dog.

Mange covered parts of the animal's body, and its head lay cleaved in pieces in a pool of its own blood.

The crowd was silent.

The crisp smell of kerosene came through the air as he dowsed the animal's ribs that shone through its chest, its legs that lay brittle and white, and its feet that showed bruises and gray-purple scars.

The match showed bright in his hand for an instant and then the body and blood were aflame.

As he stepped back from the fire, he saw the crowd watching the pyre in silence. Their faces were fixed and unmoving while the flames beat violently in their cold, knowing eyes. He heard the popping and hissing of burning flesh and smelled the sulfur of burning fur. The fire's heat dried his skin but he felt cold.

What is it? He stared at their faces. *What do they know?*

*   *   *

In the evening after dinner, Saunders walked to the purple building in the old part of the town. As he approached, he saw men standing in front of it.

"Woof-woof-woof!" He heard one of the men shout while the others laughed.

As he came closer and it became clear to the men who he was, they stood straighter and became quieter. Saunders saw that Edwards and Dunhurst were among the men. Edwards's face was red, and he lowered his eyes as Saunders passed. Dunhurst stood nervously as he watched his superior enter the building.

The entryway was half-lit with several lamps and no windows. There was a staircase to one side of the room and a doorway at the other. A painting of an elephant hung on the wall between them. Faint moans and yells came from the second floor. A tall, thin woman in a rose-colored sari came down the stairs followed by a woman in a blue sari and a woman in a yellow sari. The women came to a halt at the bottom of the stairs where their tan, honey-colored bodies blended into the darkness at that side, and Saunders watched the doorway. A small, thin man in a loin cloth came through holding a wooden box. Saunders pointed at the box, and the women bowed in the half darkness and went back up the stairs. The man made a gesture pointing to the doorway and then followed him through. The room was large, and its walls were bare. There were pillows and dim lamps covering the floor. Men sat or laid staring at nothing. The Indian led Saunders to a pillow against a wall and motioned for him to sit. Saunders did as the man gestured and handed him some money. The man counted it and nodded. He set the box on a pillow beside him and withdrew the pipe, filled it with opium, and picked up the nearest lamp. Lifting the cover, he lit the pipe, handed it to Saunders, and walked away. Saunders pulled deeply on the pipe and stared at the flame. He felt light-headed and then he felt a wind pass over his body. His vision blurred.

He could smell the ocean.

*   *   *

He woke before dawn and walked across town to his room. The bright white of the stars had faded to the pale gray of a dawn sky, and then the red and white of the rising sun came over the horizon. The desert air became warm and he started to sweat as he entered his room.

As he pulled his fingers from the door handle, his hand began to shake as he looked out the window.

The street was empty in the cold morning sun.

*   *   *

Dear Clara,

In my dream last night, I was on the boat back to England. There were no other passengers. There was no crew. The light was very sharp. It was very hot. The ocean was a monotony in every direction.

I cannot stop thinking about that monotony. A change is coming over me.

—John

A CLOSER WALK

G. BERNHARD SMITH

Ray Sturtevant was in Orleans Parish prison, awaiting arraignment on felony possession of less than one ounce of cocaine when Hurricane Katrina struck. But there was somewhere else he needed to be. He'd spent that Sunday evening and most of the following day locked down in a cell with three guys he didn't know, listening to the wind howl and watching the water rise. Ray is still haunted by water, the swampy stink of it permeating every dark corner of his psyche, flooding each memory-laden crease of his brain. Muck and grime everywhere—in his throat sometimes when he tries to speak, dripping from his heart when he tries to guess the exact moment that day when his grandmother died, threatening to rise from his lungs as a desperate shriek each time the disaster, now ten years gone, is mentioned.

The pain won't let go, stings like when Grandma Vee used to rub raw onion over his eyes for gettin' out of line. Melvina Sturtevant, age seventy-one. Someone should have come for her, someone besides Jesus. The cops plucked Ray out of prison to identify her bloated body, even let him attend the funeral. Had to keep the casket closed, though.

Hers is not the only death he mourns. Some mornings when he's alone, he cries for New Orleans: The King of Carnival buried beneath muddy black floodwaters, rising like a ghost, awash in grief and bad memories. That's all that's left of his home, or maybe all that's left of Ray—a tired spirit, waking from dreams of a past he can never recapture.

He needs a drink. Coffee won't do. Eleven in the morning and he needs something to dull him into activity. Two soft-boiled eggs and a shot of Grand Marnier—tastes like O.J. anyway, might as well be a part of his breakfast. Ray stows the yolk-stained bowl and dumps the ice from his glass in the sink, grabs his faded alligator-skin sax case and decides it's time to go. He slips out, twists the rusted key in the door's ancient keyhole, spins the deadbolt shut, and then trudges along the second-floor balcony toward the stairwell. The inner courtyard's alive with the scent of blooming ligustrum and ripe green-leaved banana plants. His slave-quarter style apartment house is lined both upstairs and down with more than a dozen single-bedroom efficiency apartments. On his way out through the exit corridor, a flash of red on the inside of his mailbox catches his eye. He stops, opens the lid, removes a folded manila envelope, and reads the address through the transparent wax-paper window.

NOTICE OF DEMOLITION
Raymond J. Sturtevant
532 St. Philip Street, Apt. 207
New Orleans, LA 70116

The city that care forgot (along with every other damn thing) is finally getting around to taking down Grandma Vee's old house. It's still got the spray-painted 'X' on the front door, the number '1' written in the bottom quadrant, meaning one dead body to be found inside. About time the damn government showed up to the scene of the crime. Only took 'em ten years. He opens his sax case, shoves the envelope inside it.

Clouds are building. St. Philip Street smells like rain this morning, like a downspout near the back alley of a bar. He hoofs it over to Bourbon. Maurice, the owner of the Traditions Jazz Bar, lets the house band practice there Mondays and sometimes Tuesdays before open. Ray's always early. Got to make sure his $300-a-week gig doesn't go to some upstart who don't need the money bad as he does. Can't take risks north of age thirty. You only get one second chance.

His pace is slow, methodical, walking with his head on a swivel so he can see what's around him. He steers clear of trouble now, doesn't invite it in for coffee the way he used to. That was a happier time in his life, a time when being close to utter chaos felt like daring life to take a swipe at you. The music was sweeter, the women were wild, and the city felt like it didn't care about tomorrow. Those notes don't bleed from Ray's sax anymore. Today he aches out the sound. The notes wail like bruises from his horn, out onto a lonely alien landscape that won't forgive him.

He ducks off Bourbon through an alleyway and knocks on the back door of the club. The day-manager, Jerome, lets him in.

"How's it hangin', Boy Blue?" Jerome asks.

"Ain't right no white cat callin' me boy," says Ray, shouldering past him, smirking.

"I said Boy Blue, you know?" Jerome calls at his back. "Like 'come blow your horn' Boy Blue?"

"I'm just fuckin' with you." Ray turns and laughs.

"Good, 'cause I don't wanna have to kick your sorry ass."

"That'll be the day."

Jerome's about the closest thing to a friend Ray will allow in his life these days. Two years after his last required parole meeting, and hell if he's ever going back to jail. Easiest solution to the problem: avoid the problem. Don't mess with the man, he don't mess with you.

Only Joe, the upright bass, and Stuart, on drums, are here. Ray doesn't say a word to them as he sets down his case, opens things up, and pieces together the only thing in his life worth piecing together—his horn. The two of them don't say anything to him either. Almost two years playing this gig and Ray can't remember two quieter cats, but they're good musicians, and that's redemption enough. The sudden notion seeps in, maybe there's time to fool around.

"Hey, you guys want to play a little 'Stardust'?" Ray asks.

Joe, a lanky dude with wild Buckwheat hair and droopy eyes, stands up and cradles his bass. "Sure, I know that." He turns to Stuart, a little white kid straight out of NOCCA, the local creative arts high school. "C'mon," says Joe to Stuart, "follow me," and Joe begins laying down an evil meandering bass motive that's like a red carpet rolling toward Ray's feet. Stuart hits the high hat and comes in under the groove like dark magic painted over in purple, green, and gold—white kid can play. Ray blows out the melody. They play "Stardust"—a New Orleans kind of "Stardust"—with hints of second line and sad flavors like French fries in a burned roux.

Ray sinks down into the music, puts out of his mind the fact that no tourists want to hear shit like this. Ain't no high-paying rich folks come to New Orleans to hear some greasy ex-con's version of "Stardust." They got their ears ready for traditional fare, like "Saints Go Marching In," and "Closer Walk with Thee." But, oh, if this place was someplace else, like Chicago, L.A., or New York, no telling what folks would think, hearing this strange, old-style New Orleans blue dissonance laid on top a classic like "Stardust." You can't help but live in the moment when the moment is so sad-sweet.

A few minutes into the tune, Max, the trumpet, shows up and that's it for the good times. He calls himself the band leader, but ain't no one Ray knows ever anointed him so.

"Shit!" Max calls over the sugar-chorus Ray's pounding on, "What the fuck y'all playin'? For Gawd's sake, this ain't no fuckin' strip club." Max is from Chalmette, but that might as well be a thousand miles from here as just east on St. Claude, past the Ninth Ward. Max and his family lost everything in the storm, so the guys all put up with his cracker-ass bullshit. "Lordy, if Maurice could hear y'all he'd fire the lot of us."

Club ain't named "Traditions Jazz Club" for nothing.

Not too long and the rest of the guys begin filtering in—Freddy on piano, Jules the trombone, and finally Skeets on fuckin' banjo of all things. Guy's about fifty-five-going-on-eighty and thinks there's some place for that banjo shit in everything they play. Doesn't matter. Keeps Maurice happy, keeps the tourists duckin' their heads into the place, or walkin' in to order drinks. That keeps the money flowing, and after all, none of 'em can afford to lose this gig.

Max works the band through the repertoire, stopping them every time his white-ass mushy ears think they hear something out of the way, but it's jazz so he generally goes with the flow, allowing everyone to do what they want with their solos. There's enough freedom to have a good time. Ray has an opinion about every stop, about every critical thought Max seems entitled to express, but he never says anything. Grandma Vee used to say, "It's better to be a live dog than a dead lion," and that's all kinds of true. It's in the Bible anyway.

A few minutes before lunch break at 1:30 (the older guys actually rise early enough to take lunch around the traditional hour), a young guy carrying two beat-up old horn cases shows up and starts pounding at the front door of the club. Jerome edges out from behind the bar, opens up, and lets in this tall, dark-skinned kid who looks like he just sailed in on a boat from the Congo. Up to the edge of the stage, he strolls, his big teeth smiling like Christmas.

"Hey, y'all. This is Malik," Max tells everyone. "Maurice called this morning and told me to give him a try-out."

One of the kid's horn cases looks to be the size of a high-register sax, and that's Ray's territory. "Try-out for what?" Ray asks, as loud as he ever talks. "Maurice already got a janitor."

The rest of the band breaks out in hysterical laughter. Max quiets them down.

"Maurice saw this kid play at a wedding this weekend," says Max. "Said he wants him to sit in, see where that gets us."

"'Bout to get me fired is where that gets us," says Ray, and a whole new round of laughter breaks out. The kid just looks down at the floor, the slight crack of a knowing grin on his face, his eyes two red-winged blackbird dots playing in a white field.

"What you got in them cases?" asks Ray.

"Soprano sax . . ." the kid starts.

"Fuckin' Kenny G., huh?" says Ray. More laughter.

Max tells the kid to have a seat near Ray. The kid walks over to a table by the stage, sets down and opens up the smaller of his two cases, pulls out a sweet old clarinet, the black of it rich and dull with a matte finish. Thing must be a hundred years old.

"Where'd you get that, boy?" Ray asks him.

"Name's Malik, Malik Sweet," he tells Ray while walking up the stage stairs. Malik sits down next to Ray and offers him his hand.

By reflex, Ray can't refuse shaking hands with the kid. "Ray Sturtevant."

Malik smiles and keeps on talking. "I told my teacher I was coming by here today. He told me to look you up."

"Who you mean?"

"Dr. Newman. Said he set you in line for this gig. He told me you were one of his best students."

"Shit! Dr. Newman said that, or you just butterin' my bread?"

"Word."

Thank the Lord for Dr. Earnest Newman: Ray's band teacher back at St. Augustine High. Without him, Ray would never have refined his skills as a sight-reader. Ray could always fake along; he had the ear for that. But Dr. Newman made him grind, made him work to *see* a page of music, to channel everything he'd read there into his instrument. He hardly needed that skill anymore, but to pass the audition with Max, Ray had to show he had book chops as well as skills.

"Where'd you get that horn, Malik Sweet?"

"Just call me Sweet."

"Hell, I don't hardly know you." Ray watches as the kid's dark fingers dance atop the clarinet's valves, lightly touching the open holes over the tarnished silver metalwork. It's as if the kid's already playing some secret melody that's alive in his inner being, the black and the white of him a working part of his horn. "Tell me where you got that stick 'a licorice," Ray asks again.

"Found it in a pawn shop down on Magazine."

"What'd you pay?"

"Doesn't matter."

Max cuts in. "C'mon, y'all. Let's get this going. We gonna do 'Closer Walk,' and I want you to throw it to Malik for the melody after the intro, got it?"

Malik's got his horn up and ready.

The direction burns inside of Ray the moment he hears it. Solo melody after the intro's been his ever since he first sat down with the band. Joe, on bass, turns to Ray and stares a steely-eyed line straight at him. Ray smiles, maybe a bit wider than he should. Stuart counts them off.

The tune starts in slow and builds up to when the melody line kicks through. Malik pipes in and it's like a ghost just entered the room. The sweet sound of that clarinet cuts through the wet atmosphere like bait on a fishing hook. Ray doesn't even hear the shit Skeets is trying to do on his damn banjo anymore, just the quiet invitation of that kid and his horn, and a hundred years of solid ebony. For ten minutes or so the group of them live inside the tune in a way they never did with an alto sax on the melody line. Something about a low and slow clarinet that reaches into you, wrings the sad air from your lungs, breaks down the strongest walls. Stuart tops them off when it's done, and there's not a one of them who doesn't know this kid is in the band for as long as he wants to be.

"Hey, hey!" a few of the guys call out after it's over.

"Nice," says Max.

Malik Sweet smiles like a kid that thinks he just farted out something that smells like lilac and honeysuckle. "I heard what you was playin' around me. That was some roastin' ass shit, Ray."

"You blow that like an old corpse," says Ray.

The corners of the kid's lips turn down in a mock scowl. "Why you gotta diss me like that?"

"That's a compliment, boy. You fit right in. Shit, you don't hardly belong in a place like this unless you play like you been dead for fifty years." And that's nothing but true. Thing is, Ray's only been dead for ten.

*   *   *

The narrow corridor leading to the back office is lined left side and right with framed black-and-white photos of the New Orleans legends who've graced the Traditions stage. The place has been around God knows how long. Louis Armstrong, Sidney Bechet, Wynton Marsalis, Al Hirt, Pete Fountain—you name the dude, he's walked this same walk, past the piss-stinking restrooms in the skanky glow of the red-shaded hall lamps, all the way to the back to go get his money.

Ray knocks twice on the seedy black office door.

"Yeah?"

"It's Ray Sturtevant. Gotta talk to you, Maurice."

"Come on in."

Ray walks through the door and into Maurice LeBlanc's wreck of an office. Handbills, magazines, junk mail, and all sorts of Mardi Gras paraphernalia lie strewn over the top of his ancient oak desk and on top of an old gray file cabinet in the corner. A couple of two-tiered in-box trays on each edge of his desktop are filled to capacity with paper, the clutter so thick there can be no way the feeble attempt at organization implied by the boxes has had any actual effect on the owner's habits. Off to the side, forming the clutter heaps into the shape of an *L*, is an extension desk, this one with a nineties-era desktop computer. A still photo of a different buck-naked, bone-thin woman with a huge rack flashes up on the flat-panel screen every five seconds or so—Maurice's screen-saver. You can barely pick out the little round man in the creaky office chair.

Maurice stands about five-foot nothin', weighs in at two bills (at least), goin' on three, with skin white as a bed-sheet, and his jet-black hair combed neat. He wears the same black-lined white suit coat everywhere he goes, and speaks English like he's talking on the phone to the coast—pronounces every letter crisp. You'd think that sort of precision would translate into a man's organizational habits. Ray takes a seat in the rickety wooden folding chair across from Maurice's desk.

"What can I do for you, Ray?" Maurice asks, scowling like a man who doesn't know where his next dollar's coming from, even as it's staring him right in the face.

"Got this notice from the city, says come next Tuesday they gonna tear down my grandma's old house up on Verbina, off Franklin."

"City's finally getting out there, huh?"

"Uh huh. Say, listen, you're a lawyer . . . what happens to everything in there when they demolish a place?"

"What do you mean?"

"I mean like, where does it go?"

"They haul the scrap away at the city's expense, goes into the landfill, I imagine. Then they pay some contractor to take the house down to the foundation."

Ray looks down at his shoes. "And then what?"

"I don't follow."

"I mean, and then what I own? A vacant lot with a slab of concrete on top it?"

"That's about the size of it. Don't know what land back up in there is worth these days, but whatever's left is yours."

"That's what I figured."

Poor his whole life. Ray knew he'd never make it big—no real money blowin' these types of gigs. Still, all he ever wanted was to play music. Crazy thing is, Ray can't remember when he first got the notion he wanted to be a musician. The desire simply grew inside him, a seed planted there by some force beyond reason, an emotion that must've taken root while he sat in Grandma Vee's kitchen, listening to himself play. The place was like a greenhouse full of idea bulbs, and Vee running behind him with an old white watering can and some sunshine. The rest was just magic and the city. That was a long time ago, millions of gallons ago.

That house was where it all started—the headwaters of a mighty river. He wishes it weren't so, but he can still hear whispers when he's in that wreck of a place, a voice that won't let him quit. Soon even that would be gone forever.

"Damn city done left me with nothin' but memories," Ray says.

"Is that what you came in here to talk to me about?"

"Naw." Ray fiddles with the hangnail on his left index finger, trying to figure how to launch into getting this funk off his chest. "That kid . . ."

Maurice brightens. "Yeah! Malik Sweet! How about that name? Like some P.R. firm gave it to him. God! You should have seen him play on Saturday. I was at this wedding up in Mandeville. The couple got him to play one of the violin lines to Vivaldi's 'Four Seasons,' along with a stringed quartet for their processional, and then he rips out a jazzed up version of 'Dixie' for the exit. Man, you should've been there. It was amazing."

"Yeah," says Ray, nonplussed.

"You don't sound that excited."

"No, no. The kid is really good."

"So, what's the problem?"

"Why you gotta do that to me, Maurice?"

"Pardon?"

"Why you gotta hire in someone doin' the same thing as me? I mean, you ain't happy with the way things are workin' out?"

"Whoa, now. You've got it all wrong. I didn't get Max to bring the kid in because I'm unhappy with *you*. It's all about Sweet—the way he plays. We've got a diamond in the rough here, Ray. And you can help me with that." Maurice leans forward and sticks both his elbows up on his desk. The clutter beneath his wide forearms sinks down another half-inch. "You've got to help me bring this kid along, show him the ropes."

"I didn't sign up to be some half-assed wet-nurse, Maurice."

"C'mon, Ray. The kid could be like the next Branford Marsalis or something. Who knows? Do you realize what that could mean for the club?"

"Shit. And what *I'm* gonna do? Max already got the kid steppin' all over my parts. I mean . . ."

"C'mon, wise up. This could mean a lot for you too, Ray. Don't take things so personally. Give the kid the benefit of your experience. Show him what you know. Bring him along."

"For what? So's he can take my place?"

Maurice extends one of his chubby arms and raises his hand in front of him like he's about to preach a sermon. "I think you're missing the big picture here. It's important we nurture young talent. It gives the club a good name, keeps the tourists coming in. C'mon, Ray."

The feel flowing through Ray is that the handwriting's on the wall. The kid's in and he's out, only thing now is waiting for the axe to fall. A week, a month, maybe six, and then what? Doesn't seem fair. Ray's got to admit that even though he's got years more experience, the kid is better than he is. Not so much in ways that another musician would recognize, but to an onlooker, a casual listener, to see the way Malik Sweet plays, the music must seem to dance from that horn like a century's worth of wisdom flowing from the lips of an innocent black cherub.

Ray rubs his hands together, bites his lower lip. "I don't know."

"What am I paying you now, $300? What do you say I slide you another $20 a week? Would that make the sting go away?"

"I didn't come in here to squeeze you for more money, Maurice."

"But you're not going to turn it down, are you?"

Ray rises from the folding chair and turns his shoulders toward the door. "Shit. I guess not." He takes a few steps, but then stops.

"What? I get no 'thank you?'" asks Maurice.

What's on the horizon now is swallowing down more hurt, chompin' down hard on anguish. Ray's gotta be mindful not to let his emotions get the better of him. No use letting pride make his decisions. His heart feels one beat away from deflating like a burning dirigible. The frustration is hard to hold at bay. He still has dark music in him, bad blood he needs a way to get out of himself, now this kid got to come in and plug up his only outlet? Doesn't seem right. But, hell, that's not Maurice's fault, just another damn storm on a summer day.

"Thanks," Ray says, but then, turning back to the little white man who's played him like a sad song, he adds, "You know what? You keep the extra money, Maurice. That ain't what I was talkin' about anyway."

*   *   *

Not many buses running this early in the morning. Ray gets off the Franklin Express a few blocks before Gentilly Boulevard, walks with his sax case in the dark of the morning until he finds his way to Verbena Street. Two blocks down on the left, Vee's old place broods over him like a shipwreck, and even though the neighborhood hasn't lost its familiar charm, the bones of the half-destroyed houses that remain standing emit an ominous, rotting stink. The yards and walks smell like aging insulation and wet pine timber.

This entire neighborhood was once under twelve feet of water, like the ruins of an ancient Mediterranean city, only this isn't some documentary on the History Channel, this is his home, or rather, all that's now left of it. Ray never could make living like some French Quarter rat in a one-bedroom dump feel warm or familiar. He's always felt this God-forsaken house nestled into the near subterranean landscape of southern Louisiana suited him. Fish always return, swim back to the place they were conceived.

The damp morning air whips around him as he strolls up the walk to the dilapidated front door. The front picture window's mostly boarded up, but there's a loose sheet of plywood at the left corner that Ray lifts up so he can slide on through and into the house. The dark doesn't matter. He could find his way to the kitchen of this place with his eyes closed. In fact, he used to do just that when he woke in the middle of the night to steal snacks from the pantry. He steps over a few loose boards and the remnants of an old end-table and couch, but then trips over something he can't identify. From his knees, Ray presses the button for the light on his smart phone and shines the beam around the place. Vermin scatter as he scans through the home's empty landscape. He finds his feet and keeps walking.

The kitchen still smells of rotten tuna fish, even though the refrigerator door's been taken off the hinge, and every other compartment for food has been picked clean. He finds an old red-upholstered kitchen chair, sits and gets comfortable. Ray opens up his sax case, feels the pieces into place and bites down on the reed. He pictures the sun setting over the black water that once covered this place, tries to feel the muddy ooze that filled every crack with despair, the grime that choked the last desperate hope out of his grandma's lungs. Ray tries to imagine her voice saying something like, "It's all right, baby, I forgive you," but it's not really her, just an echo in his heart. No way she could ever forgive him for not being there for her, and it's no use him trying to forgive himself. He closes his eyes, lets the tears come, and then he plays the chorus of an old tune by Randy Newman. He hears the lyrics as he blows softly.

Louisiana, Louisiana,
They're tryin' to wash us away,
They're tryin' to wash us away

Ray stays, sits there and plays a hundred more songs before the
sun rises. When the wrecking crew arrives to do its solemn work, he
won't move.

*   *   *

Ray expects to see his court-appointed attorney, given that the prison
guard is directing him to one of the private visitation rooms, but he's
unprepared for the surprise he finds when they walk him inside. A
dismal list of feelings pump through his heart and then around to his
throbbing head and stiff joints: remorse, sadness and more shame
than relief.

"It's good to see you, Ray," says Dr. Newman. "They treating
you okay?"

"Yes, sir. Good as I have any right to expect." Ray won't make eye
contact with his former teacher.

The guards unlock his cuffs and he sits down at the table across
from the gray-haired old man in the black horn-rimmed glasses. Last
time he saw Dr. Newman was two years ago at Jazz Fest, when he
introduced Ray to Maurice LeBlanc, the owner of Traditions.

Ray peeks up into the man's face. Dr. Newman's smile at seeing
him turns to a squint-eyed, tight-lipped stare. "What the hell were
you thinkin', son? You were doin' so well."

"Don't know. I was just sad, is all."

"They said you wouldn't let the demolition crew do their job. Is
that true?"

"Naw. I let 'em do anything they want. I just wouldn't move out of
that kitchen." Ray sucks in a breath as a means to suppress his urge
to cry out. He stares hot coals into his old teacher's eyes. Nothing
but compassion comes back. He continues. "I told 'em to go 'head

and do what they need to do. I was just gonna sit there, let the whole thing collapse down on top me."

"And what's that supposed to solve?"

"Don't know. I guess I couldn't face seeing it all end—seein' the last place on earth where she lived destroyed. You know? My grandma died in that house, up in the attic tryin' to get away from the water. She's the only one ever loved me. The only one ever saw anything good in me."

"That's not true, Ray."

"Yeah?"

"Ain't nobody who don't love a man give a damn about what's broke inside him. Why you think I got you that job with Maurice, son? What you think brought me here to see you today?"

"Feels wrong to need another man like I do. I don't want to cause you no trouble. You always been good to me, and I could never thank you enough for helpin' me and all. But ain't no one loves you like your mother, and I mean, that's what she was really."

Dr. Newman bows his head slightly and clasps both his hands together in front of his chin. "This isn't a serious charge, Ray. But it's made worse by the fact you're a convicted felon. I talked with the city attorney. They've agreed to release you on bond, and said it's likely if you plead to misdemeanor disturbing the peace, they'll agree. You got to serve parole again, another two years, but then this can all go away. You just got to put things behind you."

"I can't."

"You got to, son"

Ray feels the shriek building in his throat. He chokes back his desire to scream, but he can't help raising his voice. "I can't. I ain't never gonna be able to forget. See, I let her down."

Dr. Newman stands and kicks his chair back with his foot. The sudden noise makes Ray's shoulders shrug up scared.

"All right!" Dr. Newman yells down at him, standing on the other side of the table with his hands on his hips. "So, you fucked up. Ain't the first time, and you're human, so I guaran-damn-tee you it ain't gonna be the last time. But what you gonna do? Throw your whole life away because you can't change the past? Boy, you got gifts the way not many other people walkin' this earth have gifts, and I'll be God-damned if I'm gonna sit and watch you throw 'em away because of guilt."

"I let her down!" Ray yells back. "And there ain't. No. Takin'. That. Back!" He pounds on the table, punctuates each word with a slap of his fist.

"That's right," Dr. Newman says, and then he stops up short. "But that's not what you've got to do to get past this, son."

"Then what?" Ray pleads.

Dr. Newman pulls the chair back up to the table and sits down. He rubs at his wiry gray eyebrows as he speaks. "You ever been to confession? Priest don't tell you to go throw yourself off a bridge 'cause you messed up. He gives you a penance to do, and that's what you gotta do too, Ray. You gotta serve your penance."

*　　*　　*

Ray needs to get moving, needs some extra help. He dashes two more quick shakes of Tabasco over his soft-boiled eggs and then takes too big a sip of his hot coffee. It burns his tongue going down, but that'll likely help wake him. He dips in the spoon and finishes off the last of his breakfast, licking at the yolk left in his bowl. The tang of the hot eggs seeps up his nose. His eyes widen. He slaps his own face, grabs his sax case, and takes off.

The air's lost its humid heaviness, fall setting in. The little white buds and pungent green leaves of the ligustrum are gone, replaced by the wilting brown-and-yellow remnants of summer still clinging to the branches of the bushes in the apartment house courtyard. A cool front's just passed, and Thanksgiving's not far off. It's Tuesday, and that means practice for the band. Ray locks the gate and then heads up St. Philip Street toward Bourbon. Takes him fifteen or twenty minutes to get to Traditions. He knocks at the back door.

"Hey, hey. Ray! Where you at, bro?" says Jerome, his big carefree smile beaming way too early as usual.

"Shit! Don't seem right no white cat callin' me bro. I ain't your brother."

"Fuck you."

Ray slaps him on the shoulder and snickers as he passes by, headed toward the main room stage. There's Joe and Stuart, early as usual, and Malik Sweet, sittin' dangling his legs off the stage, his hands forced into his pockets at a bad angle. He looks cold.

"Why don't you get yourself a hoody or somethin'," Ray tells Sweet. "You don't got the sense God gave a stray dog?"

"Man, why you got to lay into me first thing?" says Sweet, cracking his playful white smile.

"Fuck. Go grab that licorice stick and let's get going."

Sweet slides off the edge of the stage and picks up his clarinet from the stand. He climbs back up the stairs and takes a seat next to Stuart's drum kit. Ray opens his case and pieces together his sax, clips it to the lavaliere around his neck. He climbs the stage stairs, bites at his reed, and then he blows a few lines.

"What we gonna start with today, Ray?" asks Joe, running his fingers through his natural.

Something about the cool air makes this day seem new, but it's not quite enough to run all the demons off Ray's shoulders. He ignores the darkness of memory, ghosts, and shadows. Things could be worse, worlds worse, and that's something to be thankful for. Looking at Sweet, his fingers already dancing over the keys of his horn, inspiration blooms, and it sounds like Vee whispering in his ear.

"Remember that time we played 'Stardust' a few months back?"

Joe just smiles. Stuart picks up his sticks and smiles too, waiting for Ray's cue.

Sweet looks around. "Someone want to tell me what's goin' on?" he asks.

"Pay attention," Ray tells him. "You listen how Joe puts down this grove and then just follow along. Stuart gonna come in and then we gonna show you somethin', and if you ain't careful you just might learn a thing or two."

HOW TO FALL

DIANA DINVERNO

The compartment reeked of stale cigarette smoke and anxiety. Before Bloom hoisted his duffle to the rack above, he removed his tablet and pencil case from the bag. With his government-issued belongings safely stowed overhead, he lowered himself onto the bench and slid toward the window. He needed the light, and when the sky darkened, he would have a place to lean his head. The glass muted last-minute conversations, farewells, and train station announcements; it separated him from the sea of uniforms and their sad-eyed well-wishers. His orders, tucked inside his breast pocket, shuttled him from one camp to another. There was no one on the platform for him.

His mum and his brother, Hank the Shank, were back in Detroit. Tomorrow morning, Bloom would be in Georgia and from there, who knew? He shifted into the corner and opened the tablet; afternoon sun lit the page. His thigh angled across the bench. He reread the unfinished letter to his mum. While he waited for the train's departure, he added a few more lines and signed his name with a flourish deviating from his simple Palmer Method script.

A tall, loose-jointed, private navigated down the aisle. His newly shorn head glinted gold as it swiveled from side to side. He stopped at Bloom's row. "This seat open?"

Bloom looked up and sighed. "I suppose it is." He made room on the bench.

The private pushed his bag over his head and dropped onto the seat, invading Bloom's space. "I'm Dawson."

Bloom shook the extended hand. "Bloom."

"Where you headed? Camp Stewart?"

"Yeah."

Dawson took a swipe at the perspiration on his forehead and pointed to the window. "How about a little fresh air?"

Bloom looked at the Do Not Open sign taped to the sash. "Nope. Must be broken."

Dawson pressed his lips together and spread his hands over the creases of his wool trousers. After a minute went by, he asked, "Where you from?"

"Detroit," Bloom replied. "You?"

"Escanaba."

"Not surprised," Bloom said. "You look like the local boys I met up there in the CCC."

"You've been to Escanaba?" Dawson sounded incredulous.

"Sure. Munising, too." Bloom felt a flush of traveler's pride. Both of the small Michigan towns, situated in the Upper Peninsula, were closer to Duluth, Minnesota, than to Detroit.

"I'd never been to Detroit before I signed up. In fact, I'd never been anyplace downstate."

"What'd you think?"

"About Detroit? Never left Michigan Central, but from the train, the place looked huge."

"It's no Escanaba. That's for sure."

"A real city." Dawson loosened his tie and unfastened the top button of his olive drab shirt.

Bloom concluded he had a couple years on the baby-faced yooper. "You a Finn?"

"*Joo*. My parents came here before I was born, so technically, I'm all American."

"Be careful if they send you to Europe. You look German."

"Okay, Mother."

Bloom nodded. "Sorry." He angled his shoulders toward the window, shook out an envelope from between the pages of the speckled tablet, and placed it on the cardboard cover. He unscrewed his fountain pen and addressed the envelope. Then, he flipped the lid of the pencil case, pulled out a Blackwing, and squeezed his eyes shut, summoning inspiration. Above the envelope, his hand moved in tight circles before he lowered the lead to its surface, creating a string of passenger cars across the bottom.

Dawson peered over. "It's good."

"Thanks."

"No, really."

"Not everyone thinks so. Once, a math teacher caught me drawing in class. She took it and tore it up."

Dawson's eyes widened. "What did you do?"

"Quit."

"Drawing?"

Bloom dipped his chin. "School."

"Really?"

"I was going into the corps, anyway."

"Did you like it?"

"It was alright. I built fire roads through forests, learned to fix engines, and planted lots of trees." Bloom, a city boy, had liked planting trees. Before they shipped him to the Civilian Conservation Corps camp in the UP, he'd never been more than a couple of miles from the brick streets of Corktown. He'd been born there, a stone's throw from Michigan Central Station. "I stayed longer than most," he said. "Mum was happy. They sent her twenty-five bucks a month."

There was no need to explain the reason for his extended tour—his transfer from one camp to another after a group of boys gave him a brutal beating one afternoon as he walked to the bunk house after typing class. When Bloom arrived at the second camp, he abandoned his clerical aspirations and instead earned a mechanic's certificate.

Bloom bent forward, his tongue caught between his front teeth, as he added train details and strokes to suggest movement. After he completed the sketch, he took out his colored pencils.

"My folks didn't want me to enlist." Dawson lowered his voice. "I never manage to hit anything when I hunt with my father."

Bloom arched a brow.

"It never seems like a fair fight." Dawson shrugged. "I think it would be different if the deer had guns and bullets, eh?"

Bloom flashed a faint smile. He wasn't certain if he'd have the stomach to kill a deer, armed or not.

When shadows slid through the car, Bloom put away his pencils and slipped the envelope between the tablet's pages.

Dawson's eyelids fluttered; his head rolled.

Bloom had not enlisted. His friend, Joe Duncan, signed up immediately after Pearl Harbor, and before long had sent Bloom a letter telling him to stay out of it if he could. He took Joe's advice to heart and kept his head down at home. But the letter from the Department of War had come, and that was that.

Now, here he was, on a leg of a journey certain to hurtle him onto a battlefield across the ocean, while his younger brother, Hank, calibrated to be a killing machine, remained in Detroit, likely perched on a barstool somewhere along Trumbull Avenue. Hank should be on this train, not him.

When he was a kid, Hank fell from the roof of their old, grey clapboard and shattered his arm. Everyone deemed his survival a miracle. "Maybe he instinctively knew how to fall," Mr. Flannigan from next door said. The surgeon had repaired and fortified the limb with a sheep's shank, transforming Hank's forearm into weaponry.

Hank learned to swing his arm with precision—splintering the nose of the twelve-year-old bully, Tommy O'Brian, and concussing Johnny Nalley, who'd long been Bloom's antagonist. Neither boy implicated Hank. Tommy said he tumbled down the back stairs of his family's second floor duplex; Johnny claimed he fell off his grandmother's side porch. Falling—it never failed to elicit sympathy—was the alibi of choice when a boy sustained injury but needed to conceal his own unclean hands. By the time he was fourteen, Hank had honed his skills and his reputation. Someone, possibly Tommy O'Brian, called him Hank the Shank, and it had stuck. People from the neighborhood came to him when they needed someone who could be persuasive when street diplomacy failed.

The US government should have snatched Hank up when he appeared at the recruitment office to volunteer his services. Instead, the War Department's doctor, upon completing Hank's physical examination, noted his deformity and limited range of motion, and sent him home with his tail between his legs. Uncle Sam's rejection thoroughly convinced Hank of his disability. He cradled his forearm and began to "borrow" money from Mum's pocketbook, enabling him to wile away smoke-filled afternoons at the Sterling Bar with a steady queue of brown long-necks.

We're both screwed, Bloom thought.

The door at the front of the car slid open and a military police officer entered. He closed the door behind him and moved briskly up the aisle. He looked like all the others of his kind—no nonsense, a flesh-and-blood tank of a man. Bloom glanced over and saw his sleeping seatmate had planted one of his huge feet in the walkway. Bloom gave Dawson a warning nudge, startling him just as the MP approached their row. Dawson's shoe jerked into the air and hit the MP mid-shin. The MP pitched forward and went down hard, twisting toward Dawson before his shoulder slammed onto the floor.

Bloom heard a muffled laugh from behind his row. The MP, his face contorted, looked up at Dawson.

Jesus, thought Bloom.

Dawson, his face slack from slumber, extended his hand toward the MP. "Sorry, sir. An accident."

The MP ignored the hand and slowly climbed to his feet, his eyes narrowed. "Okay, let's go, soldier."

"What?" Dawson said. "It was an accident."

"The fuck it was. On your feet."

"I fell asleep. I didn't know my foot was in the way."

"I said up," the MP said through clenched teeth.

Dawson gave Bloom a bewildered look. Bloom shot a hand across Dawson's chest indicating for him to stay put. "Look, sir, what he said is true. He was asleep. I tried to wake him up so he could get his foot out of the aisle, but—"

The MP shifted his gaze to Bloom. "If you know what's good for you, stay out of it."

Dawson slowly unfolded his long limbs. He stood a full head taller than the MP.

The MP nodded up the aisle. "Let's go." He scowled at Bloom before following Dawson.

Bloom looked out the window, blind to the smear of fading land-scape. He thought about the sneering boys who'd pounced on him when he left the typing classroom. When they'd finished with him and left him bloodied, sprawled in a mud puddle, he remembered thinking: If only Hank had been around.

Bloom sprang from his seat and went up the aisle that divided the compartment filled with drowsing servicemen. He opened the door, stepped onto the platform between the cars, and felt the pulse of humid air. The MP had Dawson by the front of his shirt, pushing him against the rail. The corners of Dawson's mouth turned down-ward, his eyes wild.

Bloom approached. "Hey, stop! He didn't mean any harm."

The MP looked back at him. "Get out of here, soldier."

Bloom stood his ground.

"Out, now," the MP said in a clipped voice that Bloom could just make out over the train's steady thrum of steel against steel.

The MP released his grip on Dawson with one hand and reached toward his service revolver.

Bloom took a step backward and held up his palms. "No. Wait." He caught the look of panic that washed over Dawson's features when the MP grabbed the handle of the gun.

Dawson struggled and broke free of the MP's grasp.

Bloom lunged forward. "Stop!"

The MP raised and pointed the gun's muzzle at Bloom.

With grace and an economy of movement, Dawson bent his knees and wrapped his arms around the startled MP's legs; he lifted him into the air and launched him over the rail into the blur of darkness. The gun clattered to the platform. Dawson's head tilted downward, following the MP's trajectory.

Bloom stepped to Dawson's side and put his hand on his shoulder. "You okay?"

"Yeah."

They stood on the platform for a full minute, silent. "Hope he knew how to fall," Bloom said. With the toe of his shoe, he pushed the gun off the platform. "You stay here. I'll get our bags. We'll need to find other seats."

"They travel in pairs, don't they?"

"Yes, they do."

Bloom left Dawson in the fourth car from where they'd started their journey. He proceeded to a distant car and collapsed onto a vacant seat.

In the middle of the night, he saw an MP walk through the car, his flashlight glancing off the features of sleeping men.

Bloom closed his eyes and had the sensation of falling. He jerked his eyes open, but the feeling lingered. Maybe, he thought, it was the train's rhythm as it cut south, carrying him farther from home.

When the first rays of morning light entered the compartment, Bloom, who had not slept, retrieved the envelope from his tablet and began to draw on its reverse side. He sketched Dawson's open, friendly face, and added the words: A pal on the train. He put the letter into the envelope and sealed it. When Bloom reached Savannah, he deposited it into the station's mailbox before he joined the great tide of soldiers rushing toward the unknown.

THE SEAHORSE

CARO WOODS

We were forever the same height and wore matching fur hats with thick, green, waxy jackets in winter. We climbed the garden fences together, trampling the laurel leaves that had wound themselves through the metal bars. We pretended we were on the run. Just the two of us, bolting through the potato fields that stretched away from the back of the farm. But we had ballet shoes in our pockets. We were running hand in hand toward the empty barn where, every day, the afternoon sun blasted through its barred windows and made stripes all over the floor. We danced and scattered dust between those lines of fading light, while dreaming of audiences and orchestras. We were weary and high with rhythm and hope until darkness forced us home.

*　　*　　*

I am Myra. I had two parents and one twin brother, and now I have none of these. My twin brother was called Robert. My father is not a man I remember and certainly not one my mother talked about, not even about the cheques he sent once a month in the mail; she just cashed those. My mother was a seamstress who specialized in opera and dance and died when Robert and I were ten. But one day, ten years before that, she was at work on a sea green bodice with rose gold seams when a pain in her lower abdomen made her crunch over and creak a noise long and sharp out of her mouth. Contractions started coming once every two minutes at ten seconds each. The bodice fell, my mother wailed, her fellow seamstress sighed, and someone was called on a swivel dial telephone and told to "come right now" with white sheets and a bucket of hot water. That someone was a plump, grey-haired woman who took four thick fingers with every contraction and opened my mother's cervix to the width of a newborn head. Meanwhile my mother held and bruised the hands of a tall and handsome ballet dancer who crouched behind her dressed as a crow in a costume my mother had made.

When the midwife was finished and had moved aside, my mother groaned and cursed "that man" (our father) for an hour. In between contractions, she squeezed out wisdoms on how giving birth was the "real battle" and all men were "cowards." Then she opened her legs and shot us out on the floor of the Dublin Ballet costume department. One after the other, like two hot bowling balls rolling down an alley. Robert and Myra. The subbed-out ballerinas gathered around to look at the red and streaky fluids we'd brought along with us. There was a lot of blood. It spread along the floor and stained their pale blue satin slippers. It was too much blood for one woman to lose and look after two children alone, especially in a city with the world as it was. Seeing this, the tall and handsome ballet dancer stepped more completely into the light and into our lives. He removed his papier-mâché beak and black feather eye mask with a flourish as he explained to our mother the plan. He would swaddle us up like two small bound feet and send the three of us straight to the coastal town of Dalkey, where we would be taken care of by his mother. It would be a pleasure for her, he said; she lived alone, and he hadn't been able to give her a grandchild. It would be in gratitude of all the fantastic and comfortable costumes, too, because after all, he said, beaming, "A comfortable dancer is a happy dancer and a happy dancer always dances their best."

Our Dalkey home was a perfectly square flint stone cottage—two stories high and one room deep—that looked out onto the ocean. The back garden was sliced in half by a thick rope for a washing line, and the front was hemmed in by a low white wall, which Robert and I would eventually walk along, in single file, forwards and backwards, while practicing second position with our arms winged out to right and left. The front door was olive green; the knocker was a brass lion's head and long out of use. We had few visitors. Apart from us, the two most important things my mother had brought with her from town were a mauve Romeo and Juliet tutu worn by a Capulet dancer

in the *corps de ballet* and a record player on which she boomed Satie
and Debussy and her most favorite of all, Igor Stravinsky. She had
an A3 poster of Igor in her bedroom. She quietly told us over supper
one time that what she really wanted out of life was another life;
one in which she was part of the Ballet Russes of Paris, at the height
of its interdisciplinary collaborations with commission scores from
Debussy and Strauss and costumes designed by Pablo Picasso and
Leon Bakst. One in which she and Igor were married and had two
boy children called Sviatolsav and Sergei.

The tall and handsome ballet dancer's mother was a thickset
Scandinavian woman who lived next door. When we first arrived in
Dalkey, she brought my mother warm fluids in a blue glazed bowl
held in two hands: boiled goat milk with Swedish cocoa and spices
or thin chicken soup with crushed pearl barley and too much ginger.
She was a religious person who smacked us if we swore and invo-
cated before she ate. She made us clear our plates at every meal and
sometimes we could hear her praying at night, exotic foreign sounds
unfurling over and over out of her window and into the wind. In
summer, she washed her back-of-knee-long black and silver hair,
sat in the sun, and ran a wide-toothed comb made of whalebone
through it until it was dry. On a loom, she once wove us a small
prayer rug with a miniature Alhambra at the center. We placed it
where a doormat would be and used it to wipe our feet. In games of
hide-and-seek, we pretended it was a magic carpet. It wouldn't take
us far away, but we could stand and disappear there. Eventually, the
Scandinavian woman taught us how to make black cinnamon tea
with single cream and jaggery stirred straight into the pot for our
mother. We did this often and drank the leftovers cold before bed.

Our mother's health was a tide that went in and out. She was
always too hot or too cold. Months of her being bed bound with hot
water bottles and hats were broken apart by an odd day or two when
she would wander into the garden, barefoot, pulling at grass with her
toes, and scattering it lightly in a different place, or she might take a
rusty deck chair into the rain and sit out on the front lawn, wearing
a bright yellow mackintosh, sipping fresh mint tea from a thermos.

Most days though, she sat in a winged gingham armchair by an open window and propped her feet up on a bright green Moroccan Pouf with embroidered silver stars. Her record player sat on the side table. It was a constant accompaniment to her humming and swirling her head above her neck in a sweet, slow sort of movement.

On bad days, she would haphazardly cut articles from newspapers about bombs and death tolls and stick them to the fridge with matching watermelon-shaped magnets. Then she would take them down almost right away and fold each article neatly on top of each other in a Mexican cigar box she slid carefully under her bed. On good days, she knitted blankets and scarves or crocheted hats and socks. We would try and sell them when the knitting convention came to town. This rarely went well but it didn't matter; we got by with what our father sent us by cheque in the post. Neither of us knew what our father did or where he lived precisely. Our mother said he was always on the move and we would never track him down. It was, she said, "An impossibility." But the envelopes were often stamped with a London postmark.

In summer, Robert and I would spend long days at the beach, always in hearing shot of our mother's classical records. She said we would be okay if we stayed within the stretch of that sound and that she didn't need to be able to see us to know we were safe. We usually sought out rock pools along the shore. We squatted on either side of the water and waited, quietly. Every time I quickly counted and shouted "one-two-three" before we shot forward to pinion unsuspecting crabs with two bamboo poles we had sharpened with steak knives. We peed and swam in the ocean and collected shells in our pockets to take home to our mother. She laid them out on her lap, shook her dress side to side, and flicked the cracked or broken ones out of the window and on to the lawn, like a little dry dusting of hail. Any shell that was whole and pearly and shining she kept in a jar on the mantel. Over the years, we filled five large jars and lined them along in a row on the bathroom shelf.

One day, we found a dried and perfect seahorse hidden within the grains of sand. When we came home that afternoon, our mother laid our shells on her lap, shook them right and left; she selected the seahorse, raised it to the light, and smiled. She jumped up, tipping everything else to the rug, and—following her into the kitchen—we found her ransacking the drawers for sticky tape. She methodically trapped the tiny seahorse inside a clear square of tape and, at the corner, threaded it through with black cotton; she looped it around her neck, tied a knot to secure it, and went to bed. The next day, in a herculean twist of strength, we three took the Dart to town. We followed the coast from Glenageary to Sandymount before turning away from the sea at Grand Canal Dock and curving inland all the way to O'Connell Street. Mother sat in the middle of us holding one wrist each while staring at a poster for Swan Lake performed by Dublin Ballet on the train. She tapped her shoes on the floor of the bus and mumble-sang Tchaikovsy's "Dance of the Black Swan" under her breath. On either side of her, we ate banana sandwiches with one hand and wriggled ourselves free from crumbs.

In the city, she dragged us down O'Connell Street, flew us over the Ha'Penny Bridge to the other side of the River Liffey, through to Temple Bar Tattoo Parlor. We didn't ask any questions, at seven years old, about where we were going or what we were doing. For all her illness and silence and song, we trusted our mother. In the parlor, she pulled free her seahorse pendant, slammed it on the counter, signed three sheets of paper and, one after the other, the inside of our left wrists were marked forever with the outline of a seahorse. The blood rose up to fill in the lines and bubbled into tiny red beads. The tattoo artist patted our bleeding wrists dry and taped medical wadding to our arms.

On the way home, we had to balance out our blood sugar levels. Mother was particularly weak that day, her breathing was quick and short; her face, though shiny with sweat, was suddenly too pale. We went to the station café and bought sweet tea and a whole jar of blueberry jam. I asked for three spoons and we ate so much our mouths went blue. Robert forced mother to eat more than each of us; he stroked her red hair and told her it would be okay. He had looked up seahorses in his Encyclopedia Britannica the night before: "They have exoskeletons," he said. "Their whole body is armor; they must be indestructible." Then he grabbed my and my mother's wrists and held them skyward: "We must be indestructible!" It wasn't until our wounds had healed that we knew our tattoos had been done in a shimmering white ink, like a corrected mistake on the skin.

But even before our bandages had come off, the Swan Lake poster had worked its magic on our mother and catalyzed a whole new dimension to our small lives. She ordered a beginner ballet book in the mail; it had a pictorial array of positions with simple explanations she could read aloud or point at. From her armchair by the window, she would pick a position at random and shout it, short and sharp, and Robert and I would race to make the shape. More often than not, we arranged ourselves in exactly the same time. We lay on our backs with our legs in the air at ninety degrees to our bodies, and wrote the alphabet out with our feet. We wrote the alphabet backwards. We wrote Robert and Myra. We wrote whatever other words she told us to write. We strengthened our ankles and deepened our arches. We picked up coins with our toes and put them in a marmalade jar. We pointed and flexed, we chanted a mantra in unison: "good toes naughty toes good toes naughty toes." We sped it up and slowed it down. Our mother conducted our movements for weeks and then she sent us out to class.

On Wednesdays and Fridays and weekends, the Scandinavian woman took us to and from ballet school, buckled in the back seat of her beat-up navy blue Saab. It smelt like chicken and spidery houseplants that hadn't been watered. When condensation steamed up the windows, Robert drew our names out backwards on the glass with a plus sign instead of an "and" in between the words; we looked like a confused equation. In the basement of the local church, we were the oldest in a class of beginners because we were late starters. But we loved it. The gentleness and rhythm and grace extended into our lives. The way we moved in class informed everything that we did. We corrected our posture while we waited at bus stops. In shopping lines, we found our centre: we imagined thick shining ropes of light shooting up from the core of the earth into our bodies and through the tops of our heads out into the sky. We were more careful and gentle and strong as we held hands on sidewalks or locked our bicycles to lampposts. We learned what discipline was. We were never late for anything and always did our homework. Robert had a tougher time keeping his words between the lines and didn't understand capital letters. We practiced tendus under our desks. Dance enabled us to be more in tune with other people and each other, and we became even more deeply entwined in partner work in the centre of the room. In the back of the Scandinavian woman's Saab on the way home from class, we played rock-paper-scissors without caring who won, while she played us cassettes of Johan Helmich Roman, who she called the Swedish Handel. When she told us once that, when the time was right, we would travel to Sweden ourselves, we didn't know what she meant.

I do not remember when our mother died, which day of the year, or exactly how. There had never been a doctor to tell us what was wrong; only, at the end, a small, skinny, balding pastor who pressed her eyes closed and covered her head with a sheet. I do remember the poorly attended funeral and how there were no fresh flowers. Robert and I were ten and wore mismatched charcoal grey suits. We wandered down the aisle together like pageboys for a different type of marriage where no one left the church in love. A man we had never seen played the organ, and it was out of tune. The Scandinavian woman stood alone in the first pew on the right hand side. On the left hand side was the plump, grey-haired woman who told us how we were born and the tall and handsome ballet dancer who had never visited his mother but warmly joined us at the wake. Over thick-sliced ham and salted tomato sandwiches, he told us the story of our being sent to the seaside. He spilled milky coffee into his saucer and slurped it while he told us how it was only now that the tutus our mother had made for the company were wearing out and looking sad. He bit into a slice of wholemeal Irish soda bread spread with fresh yellowy butter and told us how it was only recently that the dusty brown silks had been oxidized to orange. Then he opened his briefcase and gave us a thick leather-bound book filled with black-and-white photos of ballerinas and ballet dancers and scraps of fabric and patches of color. He called it our mother's Bible and told us to take it with us wherever we went, and then he looked at his mother and smiled.

It wasn't long before we packed our lives into boxes and sold them on the street outside our house. We lined up all except one jar of shells along the low wall and gave them away for free. On that night of emptiness and change, Robert held me close while I cried; no one had ever held me like that: silently, in the dark, giving me everything while saying nothing. The next day, I cleaned and locked all the windows while Robert carefully kept aside special items which would now always be reminders of our past: mother's record player and Stravinsky records, the A3 poster of Igor in her bedroom, the ballet Bible we had just been given. We wrapped the mauve tutu from the back row of her cupboard around the best jar of shells and taped the parcel together in black tissue paper. We bought three one-way tickets to Sweden. We travelled by boat and bus and train, with the Scandinavian woman between us. Robert and I spotted jellyfish in the water as we leaned overboard to look. Halfway between Ireland and Sweden, Robert pulled the last jar of shells from his backpack; he unscrewed the lid and scattered the shells while saying "ashes to ashes, dust to dust." I put one hand in his pocket and watched the shells spiraling into the wind and come to rest on the water. I tried not to think of my mother. When we arrived, we were amazed at the rolling green land of Sweden, at the clarity of the sky and the redness of the dirt.

At first, we lived in a high-ceilinged flat in Stockholm that looked straight into the arched windows of the building on the other side of the courtyard, like each of our rooms were a museum exhibit. We felt watched all the time. We struggled at an international school with our soft Dalkey accents. But I came to love science lessons, especially biology and its revelations of how the human body worked and how these could be related to dance. Ballet was a constant force in our lives, and we went to as many classes as we could, all over the city. I progressed to pointe and smacked my shoes into shape on the street. We remembered our mother while sitting on the front stoop as Robert helped me sew reams of elastic and ribbon into the seams of my shoes.

We adjusted to the new language, the foreign smells and the peculiarly dissimilar sky. Then the soldiers came. They wore black boots and a grey uniform; they had thick Kevlar vests and rarely took off their helmets. They roamed the streets methodically, always carrying guns and gently whistling songs from their homeland—occasionally, mockingly, the Swedish national anthem. Two uniformed men could terrify a room of twenty people and soon people were no longer allowed to gather in groups of larger than six. School was out. Ballet classes were cancelled. Adults continued to go to work but more frequently called in sick. Everyone was afraid. Soldiers sometimes pounded down our doors as if they were looking for someone and pointed guns at random people. The first time they came into our apartment, they pushed the Scandinavian woman against the wall and tried to terrorize us with threats. She shouted at them in fractured English, repeating over and over:

"We are nothing. We are no one. Leave the children be."

The second time the soldiers came, we had been out skimming stones on the canal and, when we got back, the Scandinavian woman was waiting outside the apartment. Our mother's record player was on the stoop, collapsed on its side with a few records in a cloth bag with strong handles. She wouldn't let us go upstairs. She said the soldiers had come again and now we had to leave. We couldn't bring anything else. It would be sent later. She had organized everything. Her cousin had a potato farm in the countryside; we just had to get there. We told the soldier on patrol we were going to the cinema. He was young and didn't seem to know the bus routes so we got on one heading in the wrong direction from where we told him we were going. We travelled all night, and I worried a hole in my cardigan because I couldn't sleep on the bus. I wanted my mother. I wanted to breathe in the Irish Sea. I wanted to dance outside in the street with Stravinsky spinning himself hoarse on her record player. I wanted to jump into Robert's arms and for him to spin me around his body until I slid to the ground. I wanted him to lift me up. I did not want a war.

Yet there was a small comfort to be found in the countryside and in routine. It allowed an escape from the constant anxiety of knowing the country you live in is not at peace with the country of someone else just like you. On the farm, we existed inside a self-enforced and life-saving rigidity. We rose at six a.m. and ate rye bread without spreads. We pickled quail eggs that took us forever to peel. We ate them for lunch with herring rolls and sauerkraut. We mucked out sheds and brushed down horses. We laughed more loudly and less awkwardly than the farm workers who did not know our language. Robert cleaned farm machinery and repaired tarpaulins and nets because he was the stronger one of the two. I sharpened knives and shined the silverware. We were home-schooled by an elderly history professor from the village who spoke English and knew a spattering of other subjects. I struggled with history and Robert enjoyed math. We distracted our minds with equations and facts. We employed our bodies with labor. We made ourselves useful.

We cooled down from our day on the farm by warming up and flexing our muscles in the empty barn at the farthest reach of the potato field. We kept our mother's record player in the corner and played Stravinsky on repeat. We leapt and pranced. We stretched our muscles and curved our limbs. Our mother had often told us how Stravinsky had composed each piece of music in contrast to the war through which he lived—as though we would find solace in knowing other people found peace in his sound. But it was tricky to dance to and Robert found it hard to keep count. Unless I was keeping track loudly "one two three, one two three," he would lose his step and fall out of our rhythm. We wore ourselves out every evening. We broke ourselves free.

When, one day, seven men in uniform ambled into the barn, Robert continued to dance and dance and dance, spinning and leaping and twisting for a different type of audience. The lieutenant and his six men were aged between their late teens and early thirties. I kept count more quietly under my breath "one two three, one two three."

Robert couldn't have heard me but he did not drop out of the dance: one two three, one two three. He kept perfect time. The lieutenant was a strong looking, fine-boned, boy with thick blonde hair swept to one side and dark eyebrows. He had very blue eyes. The soldiers watched every move their lieutenant made while he watched every move my brother made. Stravinsky played on and on while Robert danced and I thought of my mother and the ocean and how far we were from Ireland, and then, the young man with blonde hair and blue eyes pulled out a gun, and the six other soldiers followed suit. The young man counted "one two three," and with one bullet at a time they wiped out my whole world.

*   *   *

It did not matter then that the lieutenant struck a match slowly along the sole of his boot, lit his cigarette, and on his way out of the barn turned, looked at the men, looked at me, and told them:

"You have some time."

It did not matter that the six men gathered round me and pushed the youngest one forward. He had greasy hair and a spattering of acne on his jawline. He began to take my clothes off slowly, fumbling apologetically with the buttons on my dress. He pressed me onto the floor of the barn and cried while the five men watched in silence: the men that had killed my brother. It didn't matter that when the young boy was finished, another man came forward, and another, and another until the circle of men had been broken by each of them one by one. They had shot my brother nine times. It took two bullets to shatter the base of Robert's spine, one struck his left hip, one had blown the back of his head off after ripping a hole in his face, another pulled free his right ear, one pierced his left lung, two broke into his stomach, and one tore apart his right knee cap. I had felt every bullet. I was already gone. When the lieutenant returned, he reached down and pulled me up. He swung my dress carefully around my shoulders. He smelled of smoke and exhaustion. He had good manners. He held my hand for a moment, twisted my palm to the sky, and pressed his thumb lightly against the white outline of a seahorse on my wrist. He seemed to be seeking some sort of pulse, some sort of connection, something to make us human again. He leaned in and told me quietly that he liked Stravinsky too and that I must stop shaking now.

*   *   *

I can see Robert pirouetting for the first time in the basement of Dalkey Church. I can hear him telling our mother how he had learned: sauté, releve, retire, and how he pronounced all the French words wrong. I picture us walking back and forth along the wall outside our house, keeping our balance with our arms stretched between our mother and the ocean. I lean into the past and listen for when he told me after our mother's funeral, when we had sold all of our furniture and were trying to sleep on the floor of our empty house, that we would always have each other. I remember how he had pulled off the bandage of his tattoo too early and picked at the scabs so often that his seahorse was a different shape from ours; ours were perfect: two Fibonacci spirals side by side and held together in the armor of an exoskeleton. But I had always felt that mine wasn't right if it wasn't misshapen and wrong and the same as my brother's. The seahorse on Robert's wrist had always looked fragile, ever so slightly kinked in certain places, the outline frayed like a dress rehearsal.

TWO AND A HALF ARGUMENTS FOR THE EXISTENCE OF SOMETHING LIKE GOD

GINA WOHLSDORF

Ready?

It's night. A quiet neighborhood. Not a city, not the country, houses all around, hopscotch grids. The hopscotch grids are blurring—because it's raining; it's coming down in sheets.

Everybody put their cars in garages in case of hail. There's only one car on the street. That one car is a police car.

There hasn't been a murder or a kidnapping or anything like that. And no, *nothing* isn't going to happen here. There's not a heartbroken academic wandering the block because his woman cheated, or a mid-mid-life-crisis housewife drinking cognac in a dark window as she contemplates cheating, or even a kid in a race car bed listening to his parents fight about—no really, guess—how one of them cheated. Fuck that.

"Soon as it stops," says the policeman.

The girl in the backseat smiles.

"Soon as it stops, young lady—I mean it."

The girl is wearing a police issue rain slicker. Under that, she's not wearing anything else. The slicker's polyurethane suckers to her thighs. She thinks it's like living in a rubber chrysalis. She should feel ashamed and afraid and worried to be sitting in the back of a police car, but she's not particularly good at feeling what she's supposed to be feeling at any given moment. She feels the polyurethane on her thighs, and she likes it, so she notes it—like the whole point of liking things is to take notes.

"Best case scenario," says the policeman. "Best case scenario: you catch pneumonia."

She says, "It's eighty degrees, dude."

"My cousin died of pneumonia," the policeman says. "My little cousin Trudy, when I was eight. She caught it in summer, matter of fact." The policeman squirms, and his vinyl seat reports every shift with a squashed chirp, like flatulence. "Plus there're sex fiends. You think of that? Course not. Kid like you grows up in a place like this— kid like you never has to deal with any mess." He gestures out the windshield at the storm. "Mess just washes away for a kid like you. So, you're at a—what do you call 'em?—you're at a sleepover with your girlfriends? It's summer of—what, your junior year? You're sleeping over and you've had the pillow fights and you're bored. You say, 'Hey, it's midnight. Midnight and it's raining. Hey, let's go streaking, guys.'" He picks his nose absently. He catches himself, stops, and blushes. He's used to being in this car all alone. He's used to talking to himself while patrolling in this car all alone, all night.

In the backseat, the girl smiles.

"You dumb kids." He sits straighter, straight as he can, trying to seem official. He's wearing a gun; why doesn't he feel official? "Soon as it stops, I'm going right up that walk. See what your parents say. See how they like their little girl naked in the back of a cop car at 1:00 a.m." He points over his shoulder, but he doesn't look at her. He's scared of her, so he's trying to scare her. "See if I don't, honey."

It's eighty degrees outside, but the police car is much cooler than that. The AC is on. He's glad he gave the girl a coat. Because he guessed the girl's age exactly—junior year, sixteen—and that age is many girls' fullest flower. The policeman is a good man and is married and was driving in the driving rain and saw the girl—deep tawny-tan flashing like the flesh of a thoroughbred mare, bare feet to bare calves to bare thighs to bare, black, bushy, beautiful flower to bare, bouncing B-cup breasts to, maybe, a face, to goddamn it, bitch—and put the flashers on and drove after her and swerved around her. Got out, gave chase, caught, tried not to touch too much, and wrapped her in the slicker. Said, "Where's your house?" Said it 'til she answered. Drove her here.

So that catches you up, which is nice. But the policeman is lying about his cousin. Trudy died of cholera, not pneumonia. Her parents, the policeman's aunt and uncle, were missionaries in Paraguay. Also, the policeman, in warning the girl about sex fiends, is intimating he's seen terrible things as a cop—things that the girl can't begin to imagine—but he hasn't. He's only been a cop for two years. He used to run a grilled sub sandwich franchise. He's seen some terrible grill burns. He shifts in his vinyl seat to hide actual flatulence and patrols at night because he snores and his wife prefers to sleep alone.

It's a great arrangement: he works all night, gets home, they have sex while the sun's coming up, they shower together, shoot the shit, he makes her breakfast while she puts on her face, they eat together, she goes to work as an RN, he sleeps, she gets home and wakes him when she's done making dinner, they eat together, shoot the shit, watch some TV, he kisses her goodnight and goes to work. Their friends all assume this working nights crap must be killing their marriage, but it's not. Working nights brought their marriage back from the dead. The policeman's incredibly grateful for this, because he's thirty-nine and feels way too old to start over. When his sub franchise folded, his wife asked for a divorce. He pleaded, "Gimme six months," and he got this job. Now they're good again, better than ever. So the policeman's faking his misfortunes. People do this all the time. Writers do it more than most people.

The last thing the policeman said—remember—was: "See if I don't, honey." As in, he would, once the rain let up, walk to the front door of the girl's house and knock to tell her parents he'd found her running naked by the river.

The girl in the back, smiling, says: "This isn't my house."

The gist of what the policeman says is, "What? What do you mean this isn't your house?" and he says it about a hundred different ways, with as many different inflections, for probably five minutes.

This is frustrating, because you want the girl to do something besides smile and be a wise-ass. But she doesn't need to do anything else, and the reason why is both totally shocking and completely predictable—use 'surprising yet inevitable' if you want—the girl is me.

Forgive me for interrupting. Only cool male writers wearing beards and bandanas are allowed to do this, and I'm a woman of minimal accessories. Additionally, I like Peter Cetera's eighties power ballad "Glory of Love" way too much; it was the romantic theme song played over the credits of *Karate Kid Part II*, starring Ralph Macchio and Noriyuki "Pat" Morita, so there's no possibility whatsoever that I am anyone's definition of cool. And I also, at six-teen, used to sneak out of my house during rainstorms and run naked around Bismarck, North Dakota. But I never got caught, so this is still fiction. Meaning, I guess, I have to do something—the girl in the back of the police car has to do something.

The girl—as the policeman rants about the meaning of this not being her house—yawns. She wriggles out of her polyurethane sleeves. She spreads the folds of the coat to either side of her like shiny black wings. She sits in the slicker's outline like it's a polyure-thane cape. Like she is a poor man's super-heroine, only nude. She's doing this simply to provoke the policeman, because although she prizes moral courage above all else, she can be—it must be said—a real bitch. The policeman's rant cuts off. He is awash in horror and offense; they quash any would-be arousal.

He barks, "Put that back on!"

The girl laughs.

"Put that coat back on this instant, young lady. I'm serious!" The policeman stares fiercely out at the rain—rain that looks like clear curtains of water. On the sidewalk is a sick swirl of pink and blue and yellow puddles from a hopscotch grid. He pictures girls with pigtails singing to each other as they bounce from square to square, their minds riveted on where their feet land. It isn't too late for him and his wife to have kids. She's been mentioning it lately, but the policeman's worried they'll have a girl. Then what?

He looks in his rearview and sobs, "What's wrong with you, girl?"

The girl stops laughing. She's not sure what's wrong with her. She pushes things. She wants things she's not supposed to want—not mansions, not a Lexus, not like that. Like, it was raining outside so hard it made her bedroom window a porthole in a submerged submarine. She couldn't sleep—she gets cold too easily. She wishes there was a nice warm man in bed beside her she could snuggle close to. But she was raised to believe it'd be like a knight in shining armor from long, long ago: that was sacred, and everything else was dirty. She's failed to answer the policeman's question for many seconds, and the quiet in the car has become threatening, mainly due to the staccato rain on the roof. The rain's staccato now, not a roar. It'll stop soon. Then what?

Then they should each make their arguments for the existence of Something like God. The only problem is, I've read that arc a billion goddamn times. I hate minor grace note endings. I hate how they're required now, how somebody's supposed to close a door or make a cup of tea and that's your resolution. How I have to hide profundity in mundanity so as not to appear epiphanic. Screw you, Charles Baxter, because the girl is free but she's alone and that's a blessing as well as a curse—the justice of a cruel god. The policeman is enslaved but he is loved and that's both blessing and curse, too. I think that if humanity really is doomed, it's because we're too chickenshit to say these truths out loud. We can't even say them in stories because we don't know where we go from sucking down forty-some years of po-mo literary Kool-Aid, learning that to make an impact you need to not care. "Here's what you do, up-and-coming author: know your exact dick measurements and how far you can piss with it, that's all." It's a competition of indifference, it's the Tour de Sarcasm, it's the Olympics of Irony, so I think the brave thing is to throw the race, take a fall, tap out. Give up on cool. It won't keep you warm at night.

But I won't pretend I knew all this when I was sixteen, sneaking out at midnight to run naked in the rain, feeling the thunder tickle up my clit like a finger rattling a maraca, watching the lightning right after, the lightning lighting the sky on fire right above me, boiling out from there, webbing out, and the river swollen and my body swollen and the rivers running down my skin darkened in long days of sun, sun, sun. If I'd have known then the price I'd pay, I'd still have run—I believe that, I believe it still—and I even still believe we're gonna live together, knowing forever that we did it all for the glory of love.

The policeman startles. He was falling asleep, staring at the hop-scotch grid. It's gone now. Even the subtlest attempt at a shape has washed away. He gets out of the car. The rain is an aggressive sprinkle; he's not immediately soaked. The storm is migrating, like the geese will do in a few more months when it's autumn again. As he's walking around the car, he thinks about autumn, how it's his favorite season up here because it's over almost as soon as it starts.

The girl flinches when he opens her door.

"Go on home," the policeman says, his wet sleeve flapping toward all the directions she might head. "Go home and get some sleep, all right?"

She stays sort of curled, getting out. She thinks of saying, "Thanks," but takes off instead. There's lightning still in the east, so she runs toward it. Head tilted at the clouds, she forgets her shyness around a corner and goes full-out for home. But this is home. She carries her home with her, and it's so lonely to do that, so unfair—like a sinkhole, sometimes, where her soul ought to be. And then, other times, she'll fall madly in love with people in worlds that look a lot like this one but are brighter, dimmer, better, or worse. And there's the sensation that her heart is a firework, one of those they save for the finale. And it's rising as if it sees its fate in the face of a star. It's ascending, it could climb and climb forever——but her heart makes such vivid colors when it breaks and splashes all over the night sky. She's sorry, she's so very sorry for this blatant egomania, but she cannot afford to be ashamed.

The policeman watches her run. He watches until she turns the corner, then he goes around the police car's front. He stops in the headlights, the rain like rugged diamonds in their glare, and he raises his arms to the sky. Thinks, as he does, that he'd give anything to be bold. He imagines a daughter's tiny hand on his big shoulder. It makes him happy. He is, in myriad ways, a very bold man. He gets in the car. Starts it and steers it around.

You're wondering about the "and a Half" from the title. It's across the washed-out hopscotch grid, over the wet, scrubby lawn, and up two stories of Midwest Dull architecture.

An old lady comes to the window when the police car's lights bathe her bedroom. She sees the car is turning, the rain is lessening. Since she's awake, she won't get any more sleep tonight. She walks toward the hand-knit slippers she keeps by the closet.

The old lady is not the "and a Half," either. The "and a Half" is the black widow spider she almost steps on when crossing her bedroom. It's a spider at peak deadliness. It watches her walk toward it—watches with a hundred eyes. The old lady's heel misses the spider by inches, and she walks on. She slips her feet into the slippers. Closes the bedroom door and ventures toward tea.

While the black widow dances to a vent in the floor and crawls to a crawlspace that's like another half-story under the house's other two. The spider isn't glad, isn't sad. It didn't want to kill and it didn't want to die but it's a dumb animal with a hundred eyes so it's only really good for one thing.

I only streaked once, on a dare, at a sleepover.

BIOGRAPHICAL NOTES

N.J. Campbell lives and writes in the rural Midwest. He was the winner of the 2015 Little Tokyo Short Story Contest. His debut novel, *Found Audio*, is forthcoming from Two Dollar Radio.

Diana Dinverno, author of essays and features for a variety of Michigan newspapers and magazines, is the recipient of awards from Detroit Working Writers (fiction and poetry), Rochester Writers (memoir), and the Poetry Society of Michigan. Her work appears in *The MacGuffin and Peninsula Poets*. She has completed a work of historical fiction set in Renaissance Florence, and is currently working on her second novel. To learn more, visit **dianadinverno.com**.

Nicole Idar is from Kuala Lumpur, Malaysia. A finalist for the *Bellingham Review*'s 2015 Tobias Wolff Fiction award, her stories have appeared in journals like the *New Ohio Review, Rattapallax*, and *World Literature Today*. She teaches writing at George Washington University and is a recipient of fellowships from the Library of Congress, the D.C. Commission on the Arts and Humanities, and the Virginia Center for the Creative Arts.

Annabelle Larsen received her MFA from Columbia University School of the Arts, where she was a Joseph F. McCrindle Fellow. She is a recipient of the Elizabeth George Foundation writing grant. A finalist for the Third Coast 2013 Jaimy Gordon Prize in Fiction, her stories have appeared in *Post Road Magazine*, *12th Street Journal*, and *Opium Magazine*. Annabelle is currently at work on a novel.

Steve Fayer's documentary scripts for PBS have been recognized with a national Emmy, a WGA award, and a Special Jury prize at Sundance. He has received five prizes for short fiction and has recently completed two short story collections: *The Diver's Game*—about street life in Brooklyn's Holy Cross parish—and *The*

Settlement—about a scandal haunting black and white families in a Catskill village. He is also co-author of *Voices of Freedom*, a history of the civil rights movement (Bantam, 1990), a *New York Times* "Notable book of the Year." In 2014, almost 25 years after publication, *USA Today* listed it as one of "10 Great Books on Civil Rights." His latest project, *The Politeful Harpooneer,* is a memoir about the ill-starred schooner, *C'est la Vie*, built in Denmark by an American dreamer (and con man) who spun a web of lies about U.S. government backing for a round the world marine biological expedition. After the owner abandoned ship, Fayer was one of six who resolved to take *C'est la Vie* across the Atlantic in the tail-end of hurricane season 1966.

Todd Fulmer was a finalist for the Frank Howard Mosher Short Fiction Prize. He has served as an editorial assistant with *Waccamaw,* and is currently an MFA in Fiction candidate at UNC Greensboro.

Sharon Hashimoto teaches at a community college in Washington. Her poems and stories have appeared or are forthcoming in *North American Review*, *Crab Orchard Review*, *Tampa Review*, *Blue Lyra Review*, *Kettle Blue Review*, *Shenandoah*, and others. Her book of poems, *The Crane Wife*, was co-winner of the Nicholas Roerich Prize and published in 2003 by Story Line Press. Her collection of short stories, *Almost Best*, was a finalist for the Prairie Schooner Book Prize in Fiction. She is currently at work on a novel.

Jill Kalz lives and writes in New Ulm, Minnesota. She has published poetry in *The Nebraska Review*, the *Ohio Review*, *Cream City Review*, and other magazines. Her short story "Last Call" was a runner-up for Minnesota Monthly's Tamarack Award. A 2008 Minnesota Book Award finalist and winner of the Readers' Choice Award for her picture book *Farmer Cap,* Jill is also the author of more than 70 children's books. She holds an MFA from Minnesota State University, Mankato, and works as a children's book editor.

Charles Kowalski writes from Mount Desert Island, Maine and Kanagawa, Japan. His novel, *Mind Virus*, won the Rocky Mountain Fiction Writers' Colorado Gold Award and was a finalist for the Adventure Writers' Competition and the Killer Nashville Claymore Award.

Robert McGuill is a four-time Pushcart Prize nominee whose stories have appeared in *Narrative*, the *Southwest Review*, the *South Carolina Review,* and other publications. His fiction has been short-listed for awards by *Glimmer Train* and *The New Guard*. His short story collection, *The Outskirts of Nowhere*, was a semi-finalist in the 2014 Leapfrog Press Fiction Contest.

A child of Palestinian immigrants, **Sahar Mustafah** is drawn to stories of "others"—Arab Americans deemed disparate from the larger racial society. Her work has most recently appeared in *The Bellevue Literary Review Story*, *Great Lakes Review*, *Flyleaf Journal* and *Chicago Literati*. She was named one of "25 Writers to Watch" by Chicago's *Guild Literary Complex* and was their selected artist for "Voices of Protest," a collaboration co-sponsored by the MacArthur Foundation. She's co-founder and fiction editor of *Bird's Thumb*. You can visit her at www.saharmustafah.com.

Marlene Olin's short stories have been featured or are forthcoming in over seventy publications. She is the winner of the 2015 Rick DeMarinis Short Fiction Award as well as a Best of the Net nominee. Born in Brooklyn and raised in Miami, Marlene attended the University of Michigan. She recently completed her first novel.

Steven Ostrowski is a fiction writer, poet, and songwriter. His work has been widely published in anthologies, literary magazines, and journals. He's published three chapbooks. For fifteen years, he's been a teacher at Central Connecticut State University.

Charlotte Schenken is a writer who was born in New Orleans, lives in Omaha.

G. Bernhard Smith earned his MFA in Creative Writing from Hamline University in St. Paul in 2012. His short story, "The Bluebird Hotel," is a finalist for this year's Slippery Elm Prose Prize, and his short, "The Immortal Mrs. Trubridge," won runner up honors in the Chicago Tribune's Nelson Algren Short Story Contest last year. A native of New Orleans, he is a former musician and software engineer. He lives and writes in Burnsville, Minnesota with his wife of 27 years, Jill. They have two daughters.

Rosanna Staffa is an Italian born playwright and author. She holds a PhD in Modern Foreign Languages from Statale University in Milan, Italy and an MFA in Fiction from Spalding University. Her short stories have been published by or are forthcoming from a variety of literary journals including The *Baltimore Review* and *Story # 6*. Her plays have been staged in Tokyo, New York, Los Angeles, Seattle, and Minneapolis. She has been awarded fellowships by the McKnight and Jerome Foundation, and an AT/T On Stage Grant. Her plays are published by Smith & Krauss and Heinemann. The Innocence of Ghosts is included in the Lincoln Center Theatre on Film Library. She is an Affiliated member of The Playwrights' Center in Minneapolis.

Andrew Stancek grew up in Bratislava and saw tanks rolling through its streets. He currently dreams and entertains Muses in southwestern Ontario. His work has appeared in *Tin House* online, *Journal of Compressed Creative Arts*, *Vestal Press*, *Every Day Fiction*, *fwriction*, *Pure Slush* and *Camroc Press Review*, among others. He's been a winner in the *Flash Fiction Chronicles* and *Gemini Magazine* contests and been nominated for The Pushcart Prize.

Tammy Lynne Stoner doesn't love you the way you are; she thinks you can always be better. Hopefully that is the kind of love you are looking for.

Gina Wohlsdorf's debut novel, *Security*, was selected as an Amazon Top Pick of June, as well as a Best Book of 2016 So Far. It is currently available everywhere books are sold.

Caro Woods was educated at Trinity College Dublin and Goldsmiths University of London where her portfolio was shortlisted for the Pat Kavanagh Award for an outstanding piece of fiction. She now lives in Boston.

Melissa Scholes Young's work has appeared in the *Atlantic*, *Washington Post*, *Narrative*, *Ploughshares*, *Poets & Writers*, and other literary journals. Her stories have been nominated for four Pushcart Prizes. She earned her MFA at Southern Illinois University-Carbondale where she was an Assistant Editor for *Crab Orchard Review*. She's currently a Contributing Editor for *Fiction Writers Review*. She teaches at American University in Washington, D.C. and is a Bread Loaf Bakeless Camargo Fellow. Her novel was a finalist for the James Jones First Novel Fellowship and will be published in July 2017.

ABOUT NEW RIVERS PRESS

New Rivers Press emerged from a drafty Massachusetts barn in winter 1968. Intent on publishing work by new and emerging poets, founder C. W. "Bill" Truesdale labored for weeks over an old Chandler & Price letterpress to publish three hundred fifty copies of Margaret Randall's collection, So Many Rooms Has a House But One Roof.

Nearly four hundred titles later, New Rivers, a non-profit and now teaching press based since 2001 at Minnesota State University Moorhead, has remained true to Bill's goal of publishing the best new literature—poetry and prose—from new, emerging, and established writers.

New Rivers Press authors range in age from twenty to eighty-nine. They include a silversmith, a carpenter, a geneticist, a monk, a tree-trimmer, and a rock musician. They hail from cities such as Christchurch, Honolulu, New Orleans, New York City, Northfield (Minnesota), and Prague.

Charles Baxter, one of the first authors with New Rivers, calls the press "the hidden backbone of the American literary tradition." Continuing this tradition, in 1981 New Rivers began to sponsor the Minnesota Voices Project (now called Many Voices Project) competition. It is one of the oldest literary competitions in the United States, bringing recognition and attention to emerging writers. Other New Rivers publications include the American Fiction Series, the American Poetry Series, New Rivers Abroad, and the Electronic Book Series.

Please visit our website
newriverspress.com for more information.